Nowhere

Other Books By Cissy Hassell

A Knight This Way Cometh
The Same Love Twice
Thorns

Nowhere

Cissy Hassell

NOWHERE

Cover Art and Interior Design by Cissy Hassell

Published April 2005

Rose♥Heart

www.roseheartbooks.com

ISBN:0-9767634-0-0

Printed in the United States of America

To those who never lost faith.
Thanks for believing in me.

PROLOGUE

ℵ

She didn't know what she was doing in his house. She just wanted to be inside it again. Take in his scent and remember. Running her fingertips across his shirt that was flung over the back of a chair brought an ache to her heart.

She'd had it all, she thought.

It had been the best of times. Period. The best that life had to offer.

Love. Happiness. Joy.

A joy that filled her very soul, brimming over and making her whole again.

And life.

The life that dreams are made of. She'd had it all in her grasp. Her second chance, so different this time around.

And yet...

She'd lost it all in the blink of an eye.

She'd let it slip away like fine-grained sand swirling through the small opening in an hourglass because she was too much of a coward to allow herself to trust.

She knew deep in her heart and soul that given the option, she would jump at the chance to do it all over again. Just for the sheer joy of being.

The happiness she'd felt in the safe haven of his arms was heaven itself. She'd walk the same path a million times if need be, even knowing that in the end she'd lose her heart.

She started as she heard the squeak of hinges, held her breath as she watched the knob turn. She had no-where to go, caught like a thief in his house.

Caleb halted his entrance into the room when he spied Harleigh standing there. His heart sank deep into his soul. He didn't like that trapped-animal look that crossed her features.

He dropped his hand from the knob, closing the door behind him with a light push. "What are you doing here, Harleigh?"

Right now, what she wanted to do was bring him close to her and touch him. The compulsion to do just that had her taking a step forward before she could stop her feet from moving. She longed to run her fingertips along his jaw line. Longed to kiss his closed eyelids, to feel the texture of all that dark hair, so thick and full it made her fingers tingle.

But she couldn't tell him that.

He raised an eyebrow when she didn't answer.

"I just wanted to see you, that's all."

There was still residual anger in those pearl gray eyes, she noticed. But at least his tone of voice wasn't so hard it would crack a block of ice.

She knew it would be futile to begin any kind of explanation of her past. If she couldn't explain it to her-self, how could she explain it to anyone else?

"Is that all?"

"All?" What more could there be? she wondered. Wasn't being here enough?

"So you didn't enter my house without invitation for any other reason?" He heard the accusation in his voice and wanted to give himself a swift kick in the backside. Hadn't he been on the lookout for her anyway?

His condemnation hit and sliced, cut deeper. Bruised by his direct insult, she breathed deep, drew herself up and put on a brave front, hard as it was. It was going to take everything she had to get over this obstacle in her path.

"I wanted to clear the air a bit ... you know, try to explain some things to you."

This was what he wanted, wasn't it? What he'd carried on like a crazed lunatic about? And now that Harleigh was here, ready to bare all, suddenly he wasn't so sure he wanted to know about her past. About her life with Stewart Pennington III.

"Maybe we better sit down for this." He trembled inside and his knees had suddenly grown so weak, he doubted he could make it much further than the sofa.

Reluctantly, Harleigh took the chair opposite where he was sitting. As hesitant as she felt, she wanted to look him square in the eye and tell him what he wanted to know.

"I'm not sure where to start, what exactly it is you want to know about my past. I've already told you bits and pieces."

"The shoulder, Harleigh. Tell me about the back of your shoulder."

God, give me strength, she prayed. She closed her eyes against the avalanche of nausea that racked her body and the pain that hurt her in places she thought long dead. She licked her dry lips.

"Stewart was ..." Her voice cracked as she started to talk. She cleared her throat, felt tears burning the back of her eyes. Tears, that even now clogged her breath but she gathered her strength and went on.

Caleb sat back and waited, chewing on a thumbnail while Harleigh composed herself and related the horrifying details of her abusive past. He saw her struggle, wanted to stop her, say to hell with it, that it didn't matter anymore. But his need to know overrode that objection.

Now, hearing of the humiliation and degradation she'd been subjected to, made him forget he was a doctor. For the first time in his medical career, he wanted to take a life, not save one. Wanting to kill Stewart Pennington tugged on his sense of honor with sharp talons, his need for justice, his desire to make things right.

It took all his strength to stay seated and listen to a story so horrific it made his blood run cold.

Chapter One

ℵ

Harleigh stared woefully at the black lettering on the stark white paper lying on the cloth-covered table. For a moment the words blurred and ran together. Nausea rolled over her like the churning waters over Niagara Falls, settling like a dead weight in the pit of her stomach. She placed a hand across her middle to rub away the upheaval and tried to hold back the bile that was burning its way upward in her throat.

This is the first day of the rest of your life, she chanted silently. Pick up the pen and start writing. That's the next step. That's all you have to do.

Just pick up the damn pen!

Dear God, whatever had possessed her to take this action?

Fists. That's what.

Hard-knuckled fists that kept coming and pounding away at her. Brutal fists. Never giving relief till she thankfully slipped into a welcome oblivion and could not feel another devastating blow.

"Are you all right?" The waitress asked, setting a steaming cup of herbal tea in front of her.

Harleigh jumped at the interruption, startled by the sudden intrusion. Then the aroma of peppermint filled the air and she settled. "I'm fine," she managed. "Just a little tired from too many hours on the road."

"My name is Sophy. Here, drink this." She pushed the cup closer. "It's the cure for what ails you or so Ma Forrester says. Besides, you look a little on the pale side."

"Thanks," Harleigh stated politely. "It *has* been a very long day."

Sophy glanced down at the paper Harleigh fiddled with. She dipped her head toward it. "That won't bite, you know. It's only a job application."

"Yeah."

But it's a whole new life for me. The words rang like pealing bells in a church tower through her mind.

"You can't go wrong working for the Forrester's. They're wonderful down home people. We seem to have more than our share of those kind in this neck of the woods."

"Sounds like my kind of place."

Just what I need, she added silently. People who care. It seemed like an eternity since she'd known those kind. And she needed that. And, someplace I can lose myself, she amended. Someplace to hide.

"Well, if you need anything," Sophy said, turning to go behind the counter. "Just give a yell."

Harleigh curved her mouth in a semblance of a smile at the local lingo. She glanced out the window and scanned what she could see of the little town of Nowhere. A little Podunk town if she ever saw one. But it was *her* choice. Underneath the cracked, dusty sidewalks and down home locals, there was a welcome hominess to the place. A welcomeness that she'd been looking for. That she needed. And she knew it the minute the bus pulled into town. She hoped that welcome feeling included her.

Heaven knew, she needed to feel welcome somewhere. She was just plain tired. Tired of the running. Of the constant looking over her shoulder. At jumping at every little sound and movement like a scared little rabbit. She wanted a normal life. To feel normal again. Just to *be* normal again.

Yes, she was afraid of her own shadow, she admitted and she had every right to be. But she had endured. And now this ... this town. This town called Nowhere would be her saving grace.

Nowhere was the end of the road for her, though. Come what may. The longing to put down roots had become overpowering of late. And a home of her own. She wanted one with every breath she took. Badly.

A little yellow house. One with a white picket fence and white shutters. A fence running the entire perimeter, a front porch swing where she could busy herself watching the world go by. And flowers. Lots and lots of them. Every kind, shape and color. Daises and Black-Eyed Susans. Lilies and Bearded Irises. Jasmine and Lilacs. And Roses. A whole yard full of them. She didn't care if she even had a blade of grass. She wanted flowers.

Oh, but that was just a dream. A dream that kept her going. That kept her putting one foot in front of the other. A dream that was all but lost save for the last brutal beating she'd taken that was her wake-up call.

Get out or die!

So she had. She'd fought and she'd run. Hard and fast. And every single moment since then had been filled with such excruciating terror that in her more lucid moments she prayed for death. Just wanted to lay down and die. Save for the dream. Save for that little yellow house with that white picket fence that beckoned like a beacon on a cold dark night. It glowed with warmth. And offered promises.

Sometimes, when she let her mind wander and let her heart hope, she would close her eyes tight and let the dream fill her soul.

And sometimes, she'd take a deep breath and the scent of all those flowers would invade her being and cleanse that part of her that needed to be cleansed, that part that had been beaten down…and let it heal a small part of her soul. She imagined herself in the midst of a field of wildflowers, running and laughing and feeling free.

Free.

Oh, what a wonderful word. A word that even now seemed out of reach.

But she was closer than ever before. Closer than she could of hoped to ever be. Even the fear, her constant companion, had lessened. Even more so since she stepped off the afternoon bus and right into the Nowhere Café.

New beginnings.

This was it.

If she could just put her name on this application.

But, she couldn't. She couldn't put down her real name. He'd find her in a heartbeat if he were able, if he were still alive. So, now what? She couldn't lie. She had to tell the truth.

But …

She picked up the pen and filled out the required information. She stopped abruptly. She would have to attest that the information was true.

Well, it was. Sort of. It just wasn't the whole truth.

Was the omission of the truth still a lie?

Her heart sank. Yes. It was.

Then she stiffened her spine. Determination gushed within her like Old Faithful shooting high into the sky and she scrawled the name on the dark black line. She preferred jail to a living nightmare any day.

Before she allowed herself to change her mind, Harleigh rose and quickly stepped to the counter, carrying the untouched cup of tea with her and laid the application down.

"All done?" Sophy asked brightly.

"Yes. Would you know how long it will be before a decision is made?" Harleigh hesitated then rushed the words out before she lost her nerve. "I really need this job. I'm new in town and I really need to find one as quick as possible."

Sophy smiled, her eyes sparkling with amusement. Oh boy. Ma Forrester's going to love this little chick. One more wounded soul to take under her wing.

"Do you have a place to stay yet?"

"No," Harleigh admitted. "I stepped off the bus, saw your help wanted sign and came right in. I didn't even look around. Do you know an inexpensive place I could rent?"

Harleigh didn't want to tell Sophy how little money she had. She was bordering on desperation but was too embarrassed to let a stranger know how destitute she was. She'd said enough as it was.

Sophy saw the hopelessness Harleigh couldn't hide. And something else that could only be described as misery in the shadows of her eyes. Something in her own heart ached with recognition. She, too, knew what it felt like to be without hope. But she'd healed. She'd learned to live again. And, she gave all the credit to Nowhere.

"You've come to the right place," Sophy assured her. "Knowing Ma Forrester, she'll help you find a room."

"That's fine but ..." Harleigh wavered. She couldn't tell this total stranger how very troubled she was, even if the woman had a smile on her face that could light up the night sky like a full moon. Did she outwardly seem as desperate and frantic as she felt inside? The desperation clawed its way madly to the surface with talons of sharp-edged steel. What did it matter? She was desperate!

"But what?" Sophy went on. "You know, you never did tell me your name."

Harleigh opened her mouth to state the name she'd put down on the application but the lie wouldn't come through her lips. It was as if Stewart had his hands around her throat, cutting off the air into her lungs. If only she could take a deep breath.

And suddenly, she was thrown back into that nightmare that always lurked in the shadows of her mind. The horror of it all welled up and hit her in the stomach like a jackhammer.

And her world went black.

א

Nausea churned in her stomach like a roiling sea in a water-tossed storm. Harleigh slowly skimmed the edge of consciousness, felt the leaden weight of it in her entire body. From a far away place, she heard the murmur of voices.

A warm masculine hand touched her throat and hysteria spewed hot and heavy from the core of her being.

Stewart? But how? She'd covered all her tracks. Painstakingly so. Not knowing whether the blow she gave him on the head when his back was turned killed him or not, she didn't care. She'd given him one swift kick in the ribs when he hit the floor just for good measure and because she felt he deserved it after all he'd put her through. Then ran like the hounds of hell were after her.

The hand moved around her throat and instantly she flung her arms across her face to protect herself from the blows she knew were coming. Despair shot through her and she whimpered like a wounded animal.

"Please," she begged. "Don't hurt me again."

He always liked it when she begged. Stewart felt powerful and in charge when she broke down. Oft times as not though, the beatings were prolonged as if her pleas fueled the fire of his overblown ego. And, sometimes too, he would apologize half-heartedly afterward and ask her why she always provoked him. As if his propensity for violence was her fault. As if she was just asking to be punished, to be pummeled until she bled.

She never knew what would set him off. So she'd learned to be a mouse and never say or do anything that would make him turn on her. Everything she did and said was precise and mechanical as a well-oiled machine. Failure was not an option. But even then, he'd find something to fault her for.

She'd rearranged the furniture one day and felt so good about it, she'd added homey little touches to a room that was never used, a room that was dull and dreary. She'd sewn new curtains from a set of sheets that had been a wedding gift. She thought he'd be pleased with the way they'd turned out. How much more the room seemed to come alive.

She hadn't spent any money so she figured he'd be happy about that. She didn't understand his reasoning about money, he was rolling in it and never wanted to spend a penny.

Instead he was livid with rage, his face purple, the veins standing so far out in his neck she thought they'd burst. And somewhere deep inside her, she hoped they would.

He'd hurt her so badly that time, he'd had to take her to the emergency room. All the while telling her she didn't have his permission to do anything with his house. She didn't understand why when he never allowed her to use the sheets on the beds in the first place. They'd been in the wrappers, still unused, for nearly two years. She thought she was putting the gift to good use.

The excuse he gave the emergency room was that she'd tripped starting down a flight of stairs. The doctor and nurse both knew he was lying. They knew the signs of abuse. But she'd agreed with Stewart and their hands were tied. She refused to press charges.

When the assaults became more brutal, Harleigh finally admitted she had to do something to save herself. She forced herself to check into the Spousal Abuse Program for Battered Women. Of course, Stewart demanded her return but with their help, she'd remained unyielding and had refused. She'd gotten a divorce in exchange that she not press charges against him. Even though he'd agreed, he bided his time and came after her to start it all over again.

She thought the law would protect her when she'd placed him on peace bond. But he'd find subtle ways to get to her that she couldn't prove. Then he assaulted her that last and final time, tying her spread-eagled to the bed and brutally raping her as an added punishment, telling her it was just a warning. If she went to the authorities, next time he would kill her. And there *would* be a next time, he promised.

He'd cut her bindings, then turned his back to pick up his shirt where he'd thrown it in his fit of rage and she bashed him over the head with the brass lamp that sat on the end table. His knees buckled and he went down in an undignified flop. Blood spurted from the gash in his scalp. At first, she was afraid that she killed him but saw the pulse beating in his throat. Then her own pent-up rage boiled over and she kicked him. Why should she care?

She hurriedly washed, dressed and threw a few things in a duffel bag. Near the door, she turned back and stood over him for a moment. Then kicked him again just for good measure with all the strength her body would give her. It felt good. Damn good.

Then she ran. And ran. And ran.

And now. It was all for nothing. Now he'd caught up with her and it was going to start all over again. Now he was going to fulfill his death promise. Hysteria rose fast and painful in her throat.

Hands clamped around her wrists as she fought and

then went limp, knew it was useless to struggle. But somewhere deep inside, she'd lost the desire to care what he did to her anymore. Let him kill her and be done with it!

The turmoil she felt floated around her and struggle she did. She kicked out and connected with a body. She tried again and the hands tightened around her wrists. A muscular thigh held down her thrashing legs and she braced for the impact. Knew it was just a matter of time until Stewart beat her again.

Through the terror of having Stewart finding her, confusion settled in and diverted her attention from it. And another emotion that she couldn't identify and made her aware of other things. Like the hands holding her, they weren't the bruising kind. She was certain of it. She was held in a firm grip but not a painful one.

"Settle down, miss. I'm not going to hurt you."

She opened her eyes, blinked rapidly and stared into the most beautiful face she'd ever seen. His eyes were pearl gray and mischief-filled. Unruly locks of sandy colored hair fell across his forehead in a roguish manner. But it was the devil smile on his lips that took her breath away. She was so dumfounded she could only stare. Then slowly, degree by nth degree, as a gentle tide comes in and caresses each grain of sand, her body felt the warmth of his. She became all too aware of the power of the thigh that lay across hers. For the first time ever, she was aware of every intimate detail of a man. No one had ever affected her this way. And that frightened her just as much as Stewart finding her.

Just at that instant the sun seemed to shift its stream of light through the slats of the wooden blinds and danced dust motes in the beam between them.

There was something almost magical about the moment.

Then Harleigh looked around at Sophy's anxious face and remembered where she was. Remembered that she was on the run and there was no such thing as magic. Especially where a man was concerned.

Her eyes narrowed and darkened. Never again.

"Get your hands off me, mister!" Harleigh demanded, intent on putting as much distance between the two of them as possible. She was mortified by what these people must be thinking. What a show she must have put on for them. She was still the pathetic person Stewart professed her to be. There was no getting passed it. These people must be laughing behind their teeth at her display.

Oh, she remembered well the degradation she'd been subjected to when he'd made that claim. Even now, she trembled from the memory. The few days she spent locked in the clothes closet, if nothing else, taught her to be obedient as a well-trained Doberman. That's when she'd spun into the depths of her own private hell and came to rest in the safe haven of an abyss where she'd watch the glow through the mist in her eyes.

"Please," she pleaded softly, her newfound bravado short-lived and fading away. "Please let me go now."

Caleb Forrester released his firm grip on Harleigh's wrists, held up his hands, and she scurried backward until she hit the wall. He studied her pale face and searched the depths of her sky blue eyes. What he found unsettled him, twisting his heart and ripping his insides at the things she unsuccessfully tried to hide.

A tortured soul and wounded heart. It was there in

the sag of her shoulders, in the way her gaze fell away from his. An untold horror that went so deep it fractured the very core of her being. He held out his hand, just as much to soothe as to try to help her to her feet. And saw her flinch.

Harleigh ignored the outstretched hand, not wanting to come into contact with the man, or any of the male species for that matter, and hauled herself unceremoniously to her feet.

Sophy stepped forward. "Are you all right, honey? You sure gave us a scare. It's a good thing Doc Forrester here stepped through the door and caught you as you were going down. I thought for sure you were going to hit your head on the edge of the counter."

Harleigh focused her attention on the man standing there with his hands on his hips, a look of concern on his handsome face. But she'd learned one thing from her past. Evil lurked everywhere. It hid behind the handsomest of faces. Stewart was living proof of that. She'd be damned if she'd subject herself to that again.

She glanced around the interior of the café, refusing to meet his gaze head on as if that would allow him access into her mind. And no one got there anymore. No one! She gathered the corner of her blanket-world around her so no one could gain entrance into her past and see the horrifying things that had happened to her. And what she'd done to escape it.

Then for some reason she didn't understand, she had to look again. The pull was too strong. She wanted to look through the window to the soul of the owner of those gentle hands. Seemed like it'd been forever since she'd known such a gentle touch.

She set her apprehension aside and raised her eyes

to meet his, her insides as turbulent as a raging storm. Unconsciously, Harleigh ran her tongue over her dry lips and his gaze lowered to her mouth following every movement of her darting pink tongue then back again. The expression she encountered in his features and in his pearl-gray eyes frightened her as much, or more than anything Stewart had ever done. Here was a man who could possess her body and soul. Just the sensations she felt from the palm of his hand on the column of her throat attested to that.

Look away, she told herself. Look away!

She had to. Knew that she should. But like steel shavings attracted to a magnet, she was locked to his gaze. And it was not the aftermath of a trauma that played her body like a well-tuned violin. Or left her trembling like a leaf in the wind. It was this Doc Forrester.

Harleigh tried to swallow down the rising panic so she could make rational conversation, but was having a hard time getting past the boulder-sized lump blocking her way. Somehow she managed with great effort to get through the weight of it and vowed never to let this man see the depth of the disquiet he made her feel. Nor the reason for it. The awareness of him literally robbed her of all her breath.

She steeled herself. Harleigh would never allow a man to get close to her again. For whatever reason. She'd never leave herself open to that kind of torture. To become another cringing coward. Or even worse, make a fool of herself with unrealistic hopes and dreams. Or be seen for what she was and bear the brunt of his laughter. Even now, Stewart's laughter at her expense echoed loud and clear in her mind.

And this man.

This ... Doc Forrester ... could break her more thoroughly than Stewart ever could. She knew it with every shuddering breath she took.

Sophy looked from Harleigh to Caleb and back again, feeling like a ping-pong ball going back and forth over a table. Neither seemed aware of her existence. They were mesmerized with each other, caught up in their own little world. As if the only communication wasn't the spoken word but eyes filled with emotions that were more eloquent than any words could ever be. Sophy expected that at any moment something would catch fire from all the electricity they generated. She felt it and the hair rose on her arms. Powerful stuff, she decided. And neither one even bothered to notice such a phenomenon.

Well, now, Sophy thought, a little indignant at being so totally ignored. It seemed an eternity had passed and she decided it was time they came up for air. They couldn't stand around the rest of the day just staring at each other, could they?

She picked up the application where Harleigh laid it and read the name. How cute, she thought. She reached out and clamped down on Caleb's forearm to get his attention. When he continued to ignore her with his intent perusal of Harleigh's features as if she weren't there, Sophy shook his arm.

And for Caleb, the world had indeed fallen away. The only thing that existed for him was the tortured soul that stood so exquisitely before him. The tortured soul that he wanted to take into his arms and heal. To take away the pain life had dealt her. To make the rest of her life have meaning.

He blinked in confusion then fixed his stare at the hand on his forearm. There must be something wrong with my hearing, he decided. He could see Sophy's lips moving but couldn't hear the words coming out of her mouth. Then slowly, as if coming out of a deep sleep, he became aware of his surroundings and the woman who stood before him and wondered what the hell just happened.

Harleigh didn't know how much time had passed. Possibly an eternity? If not for the interruption by Sophy, she would still be hypnotized, held spellbound by the charismatic presence and intensity of pearl-gray eyes. Transported to the far side of a mystical world where only she and this enigmatic stranger existed.

Even though he hadn't laid a hand on her, her skin felt flushed, as if caressed by a lover's touch. As her heartbeat slowed and her erratic breathing returned to normal, Harleigh realized that a perfect stranger had held her enthralled. With only a look. It would be too easy for her to become his pawn. To do with as he wished.

What was wrong with her? She knew the dangers! How could she have let this happen?

Harleigh backed away as panic set in. She ordered herself to take deep breaths while she slowly removed herself from such close proximity to this stranger.

"Uh, thanks Sophy, for everything," Harleigh stated nervously, slowly backing toward the door. "I'll be back later after I've found accommodations and maybe by then you'll have an answer for me about the job."

"Wait. Wait. You don't have to go anywhere, honey," Sophy told her, satisfaction making her face glow. "The man you need to see about hiring on here is standing before you! Harleigh Bleu meet Caleb Forrester."

Forrester! Of course! Why hadn't she made the connection? What was wrong with her brain?

Harleigh's heart sank to the soles of her feet. Instantly, a negative thought ran through her head as she studied the handsome man who stood before her with a devastating smile on his lips. What would she have to do to keep this job? she wondered. She reminded herself that not all men were like Stewart. But she also reminded herself that Evil lived in the most unlikely of places. Hiding behind handsome faces and hearts with no soul.

Caleb held out his hand. Tentatively and with great trepidation, Harleigh placed her small hand in his. The handshake they shared was warm. A tingle glided a slow dance up her arm. It was comfort, and strength all rolled into one package. She gazed uncertainly at the man who held her future in a handshake. Then, as if the hand she held was rift with some deadly disease, she jerked hers away.

"Nice to meet you, Miss Harleigh Bleu. You're hired. When can you start?"

Harleigh's eyes widened in surprise. It couldn't be this easy! Elation ripped through her and she ordered herself not to jump for joy. Then the ever-lurking suspicion set in and she found herself unwilling to accept it had been so simple.

"Just like that?"

"Just like that!"

"Aren't you even going to go over my application? Check out my references? Interview me?" Harleigh asked then wished she'd kept her mouth shut. What was she objecting to? Wasn't this what she wanted? A place where no questions were asked? Obscurity?

Caleb grinned. And it was wicked. A good wicked, Harleigh decided as white even teeth sparkled.

"Are you an axe murderer?"

"No."

"Bank robber?"

"No."

"Nasty to children, dogs and the elderly, not necessarily in that order?"

"Of course not!"

"Are you wicked? Full of sinfulness, immorality and depravity?"

"Certainly not!"

Harleigh knew her face was flushed from the indignation she felt. Her temper, an emotion so rarely there, simmered just beneath the surface. This had to be the most exasperating man she'd ever met.

"Are you a witch then? Recently flown in to wreak havoc on our little town and turn our unsuspecting citizens into toads?"

"Mr. Forrester!" Harleigh exclaimed, her eyes flashing with restrained anger, which illuminated her features.

Caleb thought he'd never seen anything like it. He grinned again. Wickedly. It devastated Harleigh. She felt the fireworks start deep and explode outward.

"Interview over. You're hired."

Harleigh felt foolish. The man had been joking with her and she took it seriously. Or maybe this was just his way of reeling her in for the kill. Somehow she doubted it but she had to be careful. She'd learned to be very cautious the hard way.

"Thank you, Mr. Forrester. I'm sorry to seem so difficult," she offered apologetically. "I've been traveling what seems like forever and I'm really tired."

"Are you too tired to start tomorrow?"

"No, tomorrow will be fine."

CHAPTER TWO

ℵ

Caleb Forrester enjoyed life. Especially in the small town he swore he'd never return to. But return he did when big cities and rat races wore him thin. He'd learned to roll with the punches. To bide his time. And read people.

He could read Miss Harleigh Bleu loud and clear. And she was in trouble, more trouble than she could handle.

She fascinated him. He didn't really need another waitress. That old Help Wanted sign had been in the window for two years. He'd never gotten around to taking it down and everybody knew it. Everybody except strangers.

Why Sophy hadn't told Harleigh right off, he didn't know but he was glad she didn't. She, Sophy, had been the last person hired. She'd replaced his sister when Phoebe swore to one and all she'd fallen in love, swept off her feet by that shyster lawyer of hers. That's when he'd come home to talk her out of it and realized he belonged in this nothing town. It was Sophy who needed help then. She'd walked in the door during a heated argument he was having with Phoebe with a hangdog expression on her face like she'd just lost her best friend.

Sophy must've seen something inside Harleigh just like he did and knew she needed help. Sophy had that sense of things about her.

There was just something about little Harleigh Bleu that aroused his curiosity—among other things. And he meant to find out all he could. He'd seen what lay beneath the surface that she tried so desperately to hide. And he felt a desperate need to protect her crawl under his skin and into his heart.

She had a bruised soul. An almost childlike purity. But also, a wealth of temerity hidden there that she was just now finding and learning how to use. He wanted to watch it evolve. Maybe even help her develop that courageous spirit that dwelled within just waiting for the right moment to show its bold colors.

Caleb seated himself at the counter as Sophy sat a steaming cup of black coffee in front of him. He spooned in sugar and stirred. He patted the seat next to him. "Sit. Take a load off. Want a cup of coffee or something?"

For the first time since she'd fled the maniacal life with Stewart, Harleigh let herself relax. The man was just being nice. After all, what could happen there? There was a sense of safety about the place and it was a good feeling to have. But just for a moment. Just for a moment, she decided, she would pretend everything was just fine and there was no one lurking in the shadows waiting to bring her down. She'd pretend, then her guard would go back up in full force.

Caleb noticed the indecision then the visible loosening of the rigid restraint that bound Harleigh in its grip. Somehow he would make her smile, he decided. A real smile. A smile that would curve her mouth and bring light to her eyes.

And laugh. He'd make her laugh, too. A loud belly laugh. One that brought tears to her eyes. He'd make her carefree and happy. He wanted to replace her troubled soul with delight. To erase the sadness that lived in her haunted eyes and fill her with joy.

Abruptly Caleb squelched his wayward thoughts. What was he thinking? She was a stranger. He didn't even know this waif-like creature who wouldn't weigh a hundred pounds soaking wet.

Oh, but he would come to know Miz Harleigh, Caleb vowed. Yes indeed, he would.

Harleigh sat down on a red-covered stool three places away from Caleb, ever cautious of getting close to the male of the species. This man was to be her boss after all and she really did need to show proper respect and courtesy or he would fire her before she even started to work.

And like so many times in her twenty-seven years of life, she stood at the edge of an abyss as if waiting for a connection to the other side. As if somehow part of her lived there, standing there, watching, waiting, anticipating the time when they would come together. But she couldn't see it for all the mist that lay between.

During her teenage years, she'd become obsessed with these feelings and had analyzed them, trying to reason out some logical explanation for them. It was then she discovered she was adopted and was convinced the rift somehow represented a link to the remnants of her past. She firmly believed that part of her was missing, that one day the aperture would close and once she got to that other side and found what waited for her, she would be whole.

Over the past few years, when she stood there and looked across through the swirling mist, there seemed to be a soft glow of some kind that hovered then faded. In her worst moments, the pull was stronger. And comforting.

To this, was where she'd escape when Stewart's madness was too much for her to stay in the world of reality.

"Miz Harleigh?"

Jolted out of her thoughts, Harleigh nearly upset the cup of tea Sophy had poured her. She caught it just in time, mortified by her clumsiness. She knew she turned a dozen shades of red from embarrassment, her face was so hot. And, her heart thrummed madly in her chest from the effort to not let it show.

"Sorry, Sophy. Mr. Forrester, I'm not usually this clumsy. Fatigue, I guess. Did you want to ask me something?"

"Just wanted to let you know that even though we open with the chickens, you don't have to be here till eight or so. Mama handles the early morning bunch. No one pleases that crowd of country yahoos like Mama's coffee and hot cakes. Great woman, my Mama." He picked up his cup and blew on the dark liquid to cool it before taking a sip. "Ah, that's good. Goes down smooth."

"Eight is fine. I'll be here whatever hours you want me to work."

"We're probably a little more laid back in these parts than what you're used to. Even though we get up early, we like to have our coffee on the porch, watch the sun rise to meet the morning and welcome in a new day."

"That sounds like an excellent idea, Mr. Forrester," Harleigh told him, thinking he painted a breathtaking picture. She savored that memory and filed it away. She could use mornings like that herself.

The little yellow house with the white shutters and white picket fence surfaced and she longed for it. Saw the first rays of the morning sun kiss the horizon like a long lost lover come home. Saw the world enthralled in velvet shades of mauve and purple. Harleigh imagined herself on the porch of that house, coffee steaming up in her face and breathing in a new day. A joyous new day. Where happiness abounded and never ended.

"We don't stand on formality around here either so call me Caleb."

"Caleb, it is then," Harleigh replied, then something Sophy had said occurred to her. "Why do they call you Doc?"

"He's our homespun doctor in these parts," Sophy said, joining the conversation. "Our own famous Dr. Caleb Forrester."

Harleigh frowned and felt herself withdraw. It wouldn't do to know someone famous. "Famous for what?"

"I'm only famous for being the 'small town boy makes good'. In these parts that's a big thing."

"But you came back," Sophy reminded him.

"Yeah, I did. Just an ole country boy at heart."

"He had it all, Harleigh. Big practice. Big house. Living in the fast lane."

"And hating every minute of it," Caleb supplied in explanation. "This is home."

Harleigh envied him that. A place to call home.

And the ability to help people. To treat illnesses and save lives. She surveyed the neat-as-a-pin café where she would be carving out a life. Everything was clean and perfect. At least perfect in her eyes.

She reminded herself not to become so complacent in these surrounding that she became careless. She realized she was on the verge of that and forced herself to pull back again, tightening the grip on her resolve. She had to maintain a constant awareness to always be on her guard. To never let down her defenses. To trust no one.

"Why don't you come back to the hole-in-the wall I call an office with me and fill out the tax forms," Caleb was saying as he picked up his coffee and tucking her application under his arm. "Follow me, then I'll take you over to Ma's and find you a place to stay."

Harleigh looked over at Sophy as Caleb walked away as if asking her if it was safe to follow. She didn't want to ever put herself in a position where she was alone with a man even if that man was to be her employer and seemed nice enough. But she knew from experience that looks were indeed deceiving and what dwelled within was the devil himself.

Sophy sensed the unasked question. "It'll be just fine, honey. Caleb is one of the dearest, sweetest men you'll ever find. I'm surprised that some woman hasn't grabbed him up by now. And it's not for lack of them trying, if you know what I mean. He has to beat them off with a stick. None of it fazes him, though. Says he'd rather wait for the right woman than make do with the wrong one. So you're safe with him. Go on back and get those papers taken care of so you can get tucked in for your first day of work tomorrow."

Harleigh nodded her thanks and slid off the stool. She had no choice now but to follow her source of anxiety through a small storage room, down a dimly lit hallway to the hole-in-the-wall office Caleb described. Checking her surroundings, making mental notes, she looked for a means of escape if need be, just in case he had more on his mind than filling out tax forms. She knew it was probably wrong of her to think along those lines since he was giving her a job. A break that she so desperately needed without checking her out. But she wasn't putting her new life in anyone's hands but her own.

The space Caleb occupied as an office was small and confining. Just big enough for one person if that one person were normal-size but Harleigh noted as Caleb went through the doorway how broad his shoulders were. If they were any wider they would brush against the sides of the door. He made Stewart seem so insignificant.

She glanced around the inside of the room. The office held an old beat-up desk that even though loaded with various stacks of papers was surprisingly neat. Bills, invoices, inventory list and menus each tagged the contents and stored in trays. Just enough space was left for a computer, which looked like the latest piece of equipment on the market. A shelf had been added for a fax-printer-scanner all rolled into one. A CD player sat beside it along with a stack of CD's.

He pushed a button and something country played, one of those beer-drinking songs you'd most likely hear in a smoky juke joint.

Harleigh felt smothered by the cramped space, as if something had sucked all the air out of the room. The door leading outside the back now seemed much farther away than she was comfortable with and she was ready to bolt at a moment's notice, praying the door wouldn't be locked.

As Caleb took a seat, she lingered in the doorway, panic clogging her throat, its long tentacles wrapping around her insides and squeezing her till she thought she would burst. She had to get out. To breathe. Just as she was ready to run, Caleb looked up, saw the hunted look on her face, knew instinctively what she was about to do, bolt like a skittish mare and granted her a reprieve.

"Why don't we go back out to the café where there's more elbow room on the counter or a table so you'll be more comfortable while you're filling this out? Then I'll take you over to Ma's place and get you settled in."

"What do you mean 'settled in'?"

"Hey, don't be so prickly," Caleb told her. "My Mama also runs a day-stay house for want of a better word, down the road apiece. It's not a motel. More like a bed and breakfast house. She just rents out rooms. Cooks the guests a Sunday dinner."

"Oh." Harleigh felt foolish but still wary.

"It's a perfectly respectable establishment if that's what's worrying your mind so much. My Mama is an enterprising woman. Has her fingers in all sorts of things, that one. A heart of gold as big as Lake Okeechobee. If ever there was a woman destined to walk through the Pearly Gates of Heaven it would be her."

"You sound like you're very proud of her." Harleigh sighed, her anxiety slowly abating. Pride overflowed the timbre of Caleb's voice as he spoke of his mother, love pouring out of those pearly eyes of his. Wouldn't it be a wonderful thing to have someone rain praise down on her that way?

"Couldn't be more proud. She raised me and my sister on nothing. Back in those days, the little woman was supposed to get married again and let a man take care of her. But not my Mama. She did it all on her own."

"You don't have a father?"

"My daddy died when I was eight, killed in a freak lightning storm. Got hit by it and killed instantly. To this day, Mama still grieves for him."

Harleigh heard the sadness in his voice and her heart couldn't help itself. Something touched her deep inside and she reached out and stroked the back of his hand. She ignored the rush of sensation she felt and didn't jerk away from the contact like her mind screamed at her to do.

"I'm sorry." Harleigh said then slid her hand away. The warm fluttering of her pulse still remained.

"Yeah, it's the only regret of my life. He was a good man." Caleb collected the appropriate papers and handed them to Harleigh, aware of her closeness and the lingering touch of her silken fingers on his skin. "Come on, let's go out front."

Harleigh followed Caleb out, took a seat and filled out the tax forms he gave her. When done, she handed them back to him.

He glanced down at them. "I did pronounce your name right, didn't I?"

"Yes. It's just like the color blue but spelled differently."

"It suits you." Caleb handed the forms over to Sophy. "Take care of this for me, will you? I'm going to run Harleigh over to Ma's place and see what we can do about getting her all tucked in." He looked around the café, noting the old beat-up bag beneath a chair. "Where's your luggage?"

Shame washed over Harleigh like water over a waterfall. How could she tell him the contents of that bag represented all that was left of her life? That all she owned in the world lay within? She tried to say something bright and witty but her brain went on overload, blanking out any excuse she could come up with.

Caleb notice the distress cross her features and saved her. "Traveling light, huh?"

Ever grateful for any straw to grasp, Harleigh pounced on it like a hawk on its prey. "Yeah, no use dragging stuff all over when you're just looking."

"Come on, then."

Caleb grabbed the bag from under the chair, couldn't believe how light it was and headed for the door. Harleigh followed, watching his every move, just in case. He held himself erect, tall and proud, carrying his frame with an ease and grace that belied his size and strength. She felt his strength and power in his handshake even now. She shuddered to think of the pain all that strength and power could inflict.

Then remembering her manners turned back to Sophy as she reached the door.

"See you tomorrow and thanks for everything."

"Any time. You get some rest and I'll see you tomorrow."

Caleb opened the door to his Ford Ranger crew cab and with the sweep of his hand motioned Harleigh in. She just stood there motionless. The opening of the door a giant maw just waiting to gobble her up. She swung wide terrified eyes and clashed with Caleb's own scrutiny.

He couldn't stop his desire to comfort her. He reached out to cup her cheek in the palm of his hand then hesitated, not knowing what her reaction would be. Harleigh froze in place then felt the comforting warmth of a remembered touch. She knew she shouldn't allow it but just for this moment in time she needed it. That this stranger should dare to lay a hand on her should frighten her, maybe even anger her but none of the usual responses came into play. Even though her mind told her to move away, she took pleasure in the way the warmth seeped into her skin and gave long overdue comfort to her damaged soul. Yes, she savored the warmth of his touch and knew she shouldn't. Knew she should loathe it.

Slowly, Harleigh moved her eyes away from his, backed away from his touch, realizing too late what she'd allowed. She tried not to show his effect on her. How she trembled. Ached. Wanting things she couldn't have.

Caleb dared to touch her again. She couldn't hold back the tiny gasp of pleasure that ran through her as his fingertips traced the outline of her cheekbone from her earlobe to the center of her chin, then lingered, caressed and moved up to feather along her lower lip.

"I won't hurt you, Harleigh," he murmured, closing the space between them, his breath caressing the path his fingertips had taken. "No matter who's hurt you in the past or whatever's happened to you, know this, I will never hurt you."

As Caleb spoke the words, he wondered if he was

out of his mind. He didn't even know this woman and she probably thought he lived on the backside of Nutsville, USA. Who did he think he was saying these things to? Yet, even as he asked himself that question, he realized he meant every one of them.

Harleigh stared at the pulse beating at his throat. Felt his fingertips upon her lips. Heard his words. Felt the warmth spread within her.

"Look at me, Harleigh."

She raised wary eyes to his.

"Trust me enough to get you to my Mama's. Okay? You can even ride in the back if you want."

Harleigh saw the teasing light in his eyes, turned without saying a word and slid across the seat. He shut the door behind her, walked around to the driver's side, set her bag in the bed of the truck and opened his door.

Instantly the air was sucked out of the cab as he slid behind the wheel and closed the door behind him. Caleb noted her reaction, saw her face pale and leaned across her.

She gasped for air, gripping the door handle until her knuckles turned white and gave a soft mournful cry.

"It's okay, Harleigh. Don't be so jumpy," he stated, rolling down the window. "This way you won't feel so confined."

Even as he heard himself saying those words, he wondered what had been done to Harleigh to induce such a violent reaction to a man. As a medical doctor, he knew she'd been abused. The signs were there like a giant banner flapping in the breeze. What no one would know or even guess, was how bad.

He turned the key in the ignition, put the truck in gear and pulled out onto the highway. He tightened his grip on the steering wheel as thoughts of what kind of torture had been inflicted on the pretty young woman who sat beside him, terrified down to her toes. He calculated every kind of torture he'd ever heard of that he would personally inflict upon the bastard if he ever met up with him. The intimate details of that act reverberated through his brain. He vowed he'd find out who and that man would be punished severely. Whatever it took.

He'd start off with his best friend, the county sheriff, Grady Sackett, who was a throwback from back in the day when a man was the staunchest defender of a woman's honor. Then move on to his brother-in-law, the ever-resourceful attorney, Gentry Beckett, who knew everybody in the world it seemed. Between the three of them, they should be able to find out something about that pervert.

Harleigh finally allowed herself to breathe, somewhat dizzy from taking such shallow breaths. Releasing the door handle from her rigid hold, she tried to relax and enjoy the countryside. The breeze coming in the window calmed her.

Out of the corner of her eye, she secretly watched Caleb. Then she turned toward him, pretending to scan the wooded areas along the highway. For all the attention he paid her, she decided, he might as well be riding alone. He was in his own little world, brows drawn down over thunderous gray eyes. The storm brewing there should have frightened Harleigh so badly that under normal circumstances she would have wrenched open the truck door and jumped out of the moving vehicle.

But the only reaction she had surprised her.

Curiosity. A compelling interest into what caused

the gathering storm. What was he thinking? What was so infuriating that had his brows furrowing like a couple of wooly worms marching over his eyes? And the gathering storm brewing so dangerously could have tossed the very waters of the sea into a massive tidal wave.

Harleigh had to admit the man intrigued her. As much as one could these days. And she had to watch that. She forced herself to step back from the situation. She wasn't about to allow herself to take an interest in anyone. Male *or* female. She was on her own. Finally. As precarious as that may be. And, she meant to keep it that way.

Caleb hit his blinker to make a right turn. Harleigh was astonished at what lay ahead of her. She'd seen tourist housing before. Even ones more elaborate but none quite like this one. This one was in a class by itself. And bigger than life.

The Victorian-style house sat serenely at the end of a short driveway lined with a variety of colorful roses. The atmosphere the inn secreted was of a time gone by, easily transporting a lone individual to a more surreal tranquil time of life.

A veranda hugged the front of the glistening white house with loving banisters bracing a scalloped-edged overhang. The roof was gabled over the steps then angled down over the remainder of the structure that was enclosed by a posted banister.

The house itself was multi-windowed. The second floor hosted a partially enclosed alcove for each room that allowed privacy. A castle-like turret nestled against the left side of the house as if holding it in a loving embrace.

Enchanting. That's the first word that popped into Harleigh's mind. There was an air of enchantment about the place that beckoned her to enter and explore the mystery inside.

The Rose House.

The intricate lettering on the sign painted the name with a calligraphic flair.

"Well, this is it," Caleb told her as he shut off the engine.

"This is the most magnificent place I've ever seen," Harleigh breathed in response. "There is only one other that surpasses this."

"And what is that?"

"My dream."

"Your dream?"

"Yes. My dream. There's a house that I ..." Harleigh stopped abruptly, suddenly aware of what she was revealing. Her overwhelming response to the Rose House distracted her from her path. She had to get her priorities back in order. That meant keeping her big mouth shut.

"Harleigh?"

"Yes?"

"You were saying?"

"What?"

"You were talking about a dream and a house."

"Oh. It was nothing." She shrugged as if to say it was of no importance.

But Caleb had seen the light come into her eyes and open up her face. He saw the magic and wanted to see it again. And he would, he promised. He would put that light there again and bring back the magic. If only she would let him in.

A tough time lay ahead. But he'd had tougher times. He'd have to scale that wall to see what was on the other side.

First things first, though. He'd deal with Harleigh and her phobias later. For now, it was time to take Harleigh to meet his Mama if she was home.

"Come on. Let's go meet the mistress of the Rose House. I can assure you, you'll like it here."

Harleigh placed her foot on the first step and felt the rush of welcome surround her. It was like stepping into another time. It was coming home and being welcomed by warm and loving arms. With each step she took the warmth seeped inside and touched her soul. As she stepped upon the porch, she glanced to her right. Wicker tables and chairs sat at different angles across the veranda. White in color, designed with roses painted in the back, each table wore colored antique vases with a fresh rose to match the color. Pots of various plants sat haphazardly along the banisters and between sat ladder-backed rocking chairs waiting to be filled with warm bodies.

Caleb opened the bevel-glassed door, etched with an intricate rose design and ushered Harleigh inside. She was too absorbed in her surroundings to notice his hand on her back guiding her along.

She took a tentative step into the foyer and viewed the inside with awe. The charm and elegance of the two-story foyer gave way to a great room that continued the homey welcome she had felt upon taking that first step. It was as if the place were wrapped in a mystical charm of its own.

Harleigh left Caleb behind as she became engrossed in the wonder of the Rose House. Her gaze traveled over the Victorian furnishings and lighted on a see-through fireplace looking into an elegant parlor.

"Look at this. It's *so* beautiful," she whispered stroking the marble mantel and bending to look through it to the parlor on the other side.

"Yes, it is. I've never seen anything more beautiful," Caleb replied. But he wasn't thinking of the old Victorian house. He was thinking of Harleigh and what a picture she made. The magical quality in her features had replaced the fear that lived in her face and filled her eyes. He figured he better move along before he did something stupid to spook her. Like taking her in his arms and seeing how her mouth fit against his.

"Come on," he stated huskily. "There's more to see but if you're tired, I can find Mama and see what she has available. She only has eight rooms and I'm not sure what's open. But then, Mama has a knack for choosing the right room to fit the person. She's never turned anyone away."

"No, please," Harleigh insisted. "Show me the rest."

She had to see this house. There was something here that called to her, that settled within her and gave her peace.

For the moment, anyway. And that was a blessing.

Moments were all she had.

Even though awareness of her predicament was returning, this amazing house was the most wonderful thing that she'd ever run across, Harleigh decided. Even wandering through the music room with its baby grand seated by the bay window, she realized she was alone with a man and had no fear of him. Not that gut-clenching dread that strangled, trying to squeeze the life out of her. She was wary, yes. And, that scared her more than if Stewart were breathing down her neck.

"Let's check out the registration book and see what's open. Maybe, I can guess where Mama would put you," Caleb told her. "She's probably at her sewing circle or she'd be here by now."

She followed Caleb to the registration desk and breathed in the scent of the house. Even that was familiar. There was nothing she could go by to describe the incredible carefree feeling it all gave her, she decided. She stood there taking it all in while he searched for a room. The scents, the atmosphere, the textures. It was a bit overwhelming but she loved it.

Still, all in all, she felt secure there. Wrapped in the warmth of the old house. It was as if it knew her and was giving her sanctuary. Here, in this house and this town, she would be somebody else.

She wanted to get to know people. She wanted to shed her skin and take up a new life and that's what she intended. She wanted to smile at people and not hide anymore.

It was all wishful thinking, she knew. But the thoughts were pleasant and gave her hope.

The first thing she'd do when the sun kissed the horizon would be to go out on her own private balcony. Just think … hers! Then she'd welcome the new day with a cup of steaming coffee in her hands. She would breathe deep, let go of her fear and sip her coffee in celebration.

She couldn't wait to get to the café either. To start the first day of her life on the job. What would that be like? she wondered. She envisioned keeping waiting cups filled, calling out food orders and ringing up tickets. All mundane things to most people. But to Harleigh, it was a new sense of freedom and she would hold it tight and cherish every delightful moment of it.

She'd be eternally in the Forrester's debt for all they'd done for her already and not even a day had passed yet. That was a miracle in itself.

She'd make a go of it here. In this little town of Nowhere. She'd dig in deep and she'd hide, she promised, and stay forever. Here in this place, this safe haven she'd found. A sanctuary for all lost souls passing through. A safe haven for the weary to rest and seek peace and heaven knew, she was weary. She hoped and prayed that it would protect her and keep her secrets safe.

"Well, it looks like there's no room at the inn," Caleb told her.

Harleigh drew in a sharp breath and her stomach hit rock bottom with a swift plummet as the heaviness of what Caleb was saying sunk in.

"No-no room," she sputtered. "There's no room for me here?"

An unexpected rush of tears burned her eyes as her sudden expectations shot into a rapid descent with no where else to go. She had her heart set on this wonderful old house.

That's what I get for wanting this, she thought miserably as disappointment jabbed at her heart. What I get for wanting what I can't have.

Caleb took one look at Harleigh's face, saw the misery lining her features and the tears she was trying to push back and knew he had to think of something. He wouldn't be able to stand it if one of those glistening tears slid down her cheek.

"You know what, I think the turret room can be made available. I'm sleeping in there now, but I'll move my stuff out and back into my place. I'm having it painted and was rooming here until it's finished."

She started to say no, that she couldn't take his room away but he was already out the door.

אֲ

Harleigh stepped out onto the balcony. *Her* balcony, she thought, her very own. And, just in time. The morning sun peeked through the bank of clouds waiting for its arrival to spread its orange glow through its mists. She listened in happy silence to the trilling of the morning birds as she took a seat in the white wicker rocker, sipped her steaming coffee, ready for the new day to get under way.

She wasn't sure why she looked to her left, some inner instinct, she supposed. But when she did turn her head in that direction, she choked on the coffee she was trying to swallow and gasped for breath.

In the distance, bathed in the glow of the early morning sun, sat a little yellow house with a white picket fence. A wave of dizziness passed over her and she sat back down again until it passed and closed her eyes. Afraid to open them again, she sat quietly, afraid to move, trying to catch her breath, calm her nerves and slow her galloping heart.

She had to see it. Had to make sure it was real, not a hallucination. Had to make sure she hadn't wanted it so badly that she'd willed it into existence. Once she opened her eyes, would it fade away, like the misty dew on the morning glory? This illusion … that she was sure she'd created in her mind?

She cracked an eye just a notch, so if it had disappeared and everything was back to normal, she wouldn't be so disappointed. She held her breath and released it slowly. The house of her dreams shimmered in the early morning light as if it was going to fade from view back into the misty forest from whence it came. Then, like a miracle, the golden rays of the sun made it stronger and it settled into the meadow, settled into her heart.

It was indeed a solid structure, made of wood and nails and stone. It was not a figment of her imagination. A smile curved her mouth and she hugged that knowledge to her chest and savored it like sweet dark chocolate melting on her tongue.

The first step would be to find out all she could about that house, who owned it and how could she get into it. Her goal was to own it one day. There, she told herself, the first decision of my new life. The next, she decided, would be to buy something just for herself. Something inexpensive, naturally. She remembered an antique store near the café and would visit and explore. That very afternoon. In fact, right after work, she promised.

Ah, work. She certainly liked the sound of that. And, speaking of work, she reminded herself, she must get ready. Caleb would be her transportation until she could make other arrangements. She prayed she could ride with him and not be afraid. She'd be cautious, of course, but never again would she be afraid.

Cloaked in her new sense of freedom, Harleigh headed for the shower. She undressed and stepped into the stinging spray, relishing the hot water streaming over her body.

Hot water. Another mundane thing that she considered a luxury. Something that she was deprived of. But now, it was one she could enjoy. She found herself humming as she washed her hair. Another thing she seldom did. There hadn't been happy moments these past years. But she was bound and determined to rectify that mistake.

She must remember to thank Ma Forrester for all the personal accessories that came with the room. The only thing Harleigh had brought with her was a toothbrush and what few cosmetics she'd allowed herself. She left everything else behind except a change of clothes. She wanted nothing from her old life to mar the new one that she planned. And, the new one was taking great shape right before her eyes.

Harleigh dressed with care in the borrowed white uniform, giving herself a critical once-over in the mirror before she turned to go. She glanced around the room that was her very own, a surge of happiness flowing outward. She deserved this, she told herself. At the last minute, she decided she had to see the object of her dreams again before leaving for the day.

She smiled as she glanced over at her dream house, a happy glow streamlining her face. Her entire body accelerated into high gear at the thought of entering that dream and making it her own. She'd put her mark on everything and no one would enter that door with the intention of telling her what to do. She would blanket herself with flowers on the outside of this safe haven and it would be a virtual jungle on the inside. She would set a dieffenbachia near the front door or maybe near the window in the living room. There would be an array of different plants. There would be a zebra plant here and a philodendron there. And, definitely a rubber tree plant to remind her what an ant could do.

Oh yes, and she would have window boxes put in and they would be overflowing with all sorts of beautiful plants with petals and blossoms hanging everywhere. There would be a rocking chair out on that wonderful front porch right along with that front porch swing. A ladder-back where she would sit every single morning and welcome the day. No more would she bow to someone else's wishes.

Then her face slowly lost the glow and the smile on her lips froze as the front door opened and Caleb Forrester stepped out on the front porch. The sight of him standing in the rays of the early morning sun stole her breath away.

And with it, all her dreams shattered.

CHAPTER THREE

ℵ

A man stood between her and the dream that had kept her going for months. That familiar helpless feeling invaded her and the remembered darkness began to close her vision. The fear and terror that had momentarily taken a back seat to all else was back.

No, she would *not* allow anyone to slide her back into that deep dark hole. It took all the inner strength she had to fight the burn that prickled her eyes. She wouldn't resort to tears and feeling sorry for herself again. Ever. She wouldn't live on pity, wouldn't wear those faces again. Those faces that evil commanded her to wear at the snap of his fingers. When she smiled, it would be a real smile. When she laughed, it would be because she found something funny. And when she loved, well, she didn't want to go down that path for a long time. That path was still too painful to travel.

Even though Caleb was a man, all that stood between her and her dream, he was not Stewart. She may not trust him, would never put her trust in another living soul, but instinct told her he was different.

One thing was for sure, she wouldn't start off the morning of her new life by being afraid. She would remain cautious, keep them all at arms length but still find a way to embed herself into this community that had chosen her. She belonged here and refused to give it up without a fight. She'd come too far for that. She would find a way.

Harleigh squared her shoulders, standing tall and proud, opened the door to her room and stepped out. Inhaling deeply, she proceeded down the stairway. She didn't want to think of being afraid. She was going to climb into that truck with Caleb, she told herself with determination, and think of good things today.

This, the first day of her life.

Caleb met Harleigh coming out the front door as he bounded up the front steps. For a moment a thread of fear leaped into her eyes then slowly dissipated into a guarded expression on her features as she realized he was no immediate danger to her.

"So, Harleigh," Caleb began, wanting to break the ice on a cheerful note, "are you ready to take on the Nowhere Café?"

There was a teasing light in his eyes, Harleigh noted, and for the life of her, she couldn't think of anything appropriate to say. She wished she could enjoy the kind of friendly banter that people engaged in. One day, she swore, one day she would be just an everyday person who could smile and joke, laugh and tease.

But not yet. She wasn't ready. She would take it one step at a time. Never mind, that for most people it would be a teensy weensy step. For her it would be a giant leap into the unknown.

But for today, she would take that first step and smile. And, when she did, Caleb thought his heart would explode from the affect of that mouth curving upward had on him. He'd skip over the wariness in her eyes. For today, he promised.

"Yes, I'm ready to begin," Harleigh told him lightly. "I'm ready for Nowhere."

Still, when Harleigh climbed into the cab of Caleb's truck with nothing but empty space between them, it was all she could do to keep herself from throwing open the doors and jumping right back out again. Instead, she held the door handle in a death grip, small comfort that it was. She still had trouble catching her breath and beating down the fear that laced her insides.

Caleb saw the white-knuckled hold on his door handle and looked away, wondering what had happened that had her cringing in terror, what had happened that was so bad that wound her up tight as a spring. Call Grady first chance you get, he ordered himself. Get that ball rolling and see what's hurting her so badly.

Caleb made small talk on the ten-minute ride to the café, trying to lighten the mood, trying to make Harleigh feel more at ease in his presence. He fell way short of that mark, so far it wasn't working and he told himself he was just making the strain between them worse. Then, he pulled into a parking space in front of the diner and before he could shut off the engine, do the gentlemanly thing, and open her door for her, Harleigh was out of it like a shot.

Her nerves clattered as she pulled open the café door and stepped inside and her stomach did somersaults with trepidation. The place was filled with the morning crowd, most stopping in for a cup of Ma's coffee to sustain them as they began their workday.

Sophy waved a hello from her spot behind the red-top counter. "Over here, Harleigh, come on and get an apron and I'll start you off right here."

Breathless now, Harleigh scurried behind the counter where Sophy stood with flowered apron in hand. Grabbing the coverup from Sophy, she tied it around her waist. Caleb observed the eagerness she displayed from his perch on the stool at the opposite end where she stood with Sophy, listening with rapt attention to the instructions she was given.

Harleigh heard all the words Sophy said but it was a constant struggle not to run from the place screaming like a banshee. Then she told herself to get a grip, this was the chance she was waiting for.

"Another thing, we never leave the coffee pot just sitting on the burner with old coffee in it. Gets Ma's goat. She hates coffee that taste like it was brewed last week. That's one of her pet peeves and one of the things she's famous for in these parts. The coffee's her own blend. Most of the people that sit at the counter are easy, just in to have that cup of morning coffee, maybe a donut or Danish. Once the morning crowd goes, you can get acquainted with the way things are set up."

"I'll work really hard, Sophy," Harleigh managed to say.

"I know you will, hon. It's easy working here. The hometown folks are friendly. Once in a while we get a stranger or two but none we can't handle." Sophy watched Harleigh's face turn pale as alabaster at the mention of strangers and told herself she'd make sure she'd take care of any that entered the door. "It'll be all right, so don't worry. We'll take care of you."

Even though she didn't feel at all relieved of the apprehension sprinting up and down her spine, Harleigh took that first step again that she promised herself she would and smiled. "Okay then, where shall I start?"

"How about starting with that handsome customer at the far end of the counter? He likes his coffee black."

Harleigh glanced up to see who the handsome customer was that Sophy referred to and nearly choked when she met Caleb's gaze. She stared right into the smiling eyes of Caleb Forrester and had to suppress a surprising rise of heat. She turned quickly, grabbed a cup and poured coffee into it, placing it before him before she barely drew a breath.

Before long, though, she'd forgotten all the fears that had consumed her. The Nowhere Café was a jumping little community hot spot and she had no time to dwell on anything else but concentrate on the job at hand. She'd lost count of the cups of coffee she poured or slices of toast she'd popped in to the toaster. Everyone seemed to smile and say howdy and before long, she was doing the same thing. And, it gave her a warm feeling to be included in those welcomes.

Caleb hung around longer than necessary, knowing he had no appointments until later in the day. And as soon as he stepped foot out of the café, not only was he going to call Grady but Gentry as well, enlist his aid since he owed him one big-time and he, Caleb, was going to collect. Gentry owed him for talking his Mama out of putting buckshot in his backside like she threatened to for carrying her only daughter off into the sin-laden city. He'd run over, beat down the local sheriff's door, and see what he could get Grady to do as soon as he was absolutely certain that Harleigh was going to be okay on her own.

He watched as Harleigh slowly lost her fear and confidence slowly trickled in. He liked the way she smiled, way too much in his estimation, especially when the Johnson brothers, owners of the local garage welcomed her and made her feel at home with their constant banter. Even old Mr. Jenkins, with a toothless grin, put a light in her eyes when he regaled his tales about his pot-bellied pigs.

Right then, Harleigh Bleu looked like any average working girl should. It was only when asked where she was from and what she was doing in this old country town did she start to withdraw and shut down. Caleb saw it and hated it but knew he could do nothing at the moment to bring back the light. He stayed in earshot, just in case.

"You gonna be stayin' in these parts long?"

Harleigh struggled to keep the smile on her face. She didn't need or want these kinds of questions. She didn't like being questioned, period. She picked up a cloth and wiped at the already clean counter to give her hands something to do while her stomach did flip-flops. Her nerves were edgy but she decided the new Harleigh would answer and not turn inward. She had to try.

"As long as I can."

"Jes' wondrin. How 'bout transportation? Got any?"

Harleigh kept the smile on her face, noting that the local folks eliminated all unnecessary words from their conversation. "Not yet. Today's my first day and I think I need to get paid before I start buying things."

"Mebbe, I can help you out in that department. I'm Butch Cassidy. I own the car dealership up the road apiece."

"Butch Cassidy? You've got to be kidding. Is that your real name?"

"Yeah, my mama's got a sense of humor. Loved Butch and Sundance, she did. Now, how's about you have the doc here run you over to my place after work and take your pick of the used cars on the lot?"

"You're joking, right?"

"Jokin'? Don't rightly think so. Sellin' cars is my business."

"Why would you help me? A complete stranger?"

"It's how it's done in these parts. Besides, you won't be a stranger for long if you stay around here. Nowhere takes care of its own and if Ma and the doc are willing to take a chance on you, then I'm willing to do the same."

Harleigh noticed Butch lost his good ole' boy accent when he was serious. She really wanted to take him up on his offer but then she didn't want to be obligated to anyone. She already was to the Forrester family and that was enough.

"That's really nice of you, Mr. Cassidy – ,"

"Whoa there, little lady. My name's Butch."

"Okay … Butch, then." Harleigh took a moment to study his face. He wasn't much older than she was despite the way he talked. Crinkly lines were beginning to show at the corners of his eyes and around his mouth. Laugh lines. A good indication that he laughed a lot. He was handsome enough, she supposed. But, keeping him a stranger was something she wanted to do right now.

"Anyway," she continued, "I can't accept your generous offer. Not until I have money of my own to repay you."

"Hey, now, don't let a little thing like that stop you. I'll float you a loan, set you up with payments. Make life a little easier."

He looked harmless enough, Harleigh decided. Friendly. But she knew looks were deceiving. And, she'd been deceived one time too many. The bruises she'd carried on her body and in her soul attested to that.

"We'll see but I can't make you any promises."

"Good 'nuf. How 'bout givin' me a cup of Ma's coffee in a big ole' to-go cup."

Harleigh poured the steaming coffee into a Styrofoam cup, popping on a lid like she'd been doing it for years. Even that little bit of nothing was an accomplishment for her. She silently patted herself on the back.

"Think about it," he told Harleigh as he handed her a five, "and keep the change."

She smiled a goodbye, really liking his face, not minding at all the scar running from his hairline, making a jagged dash down along the line of his jaw. She felt especially pleased with herself that she'd been able to hold a coherent conversation with a stranger. And, most of all, had done it without feeling any fear. Whether her confidence was boosted by the fact she had a crowd around her or not, she didn't care. She'd done it and it felt good.

Caleb decided he'd better get himself off to work before Miz Lackey, his self-appointed guardian, called out the cavalry. She'd be heating up the phone lines, calling Grady then his mother. He reminded himself that he needed to see Grady anyway, as he pushed on the door on his way out, and have him do some checking on Harleigh.

And, he was right. Just as he inserted the key into the car door, Grady pulled into the parking space next to his.

Grady stepped out of his patrol car, his grin wide. "You're late, Doc. Miz Lackey's in a tizzy, chompin' at the bit 'cause she can't find you."

Caleb grinned good-naturedly. "I didn't know I was missing."

"You know how your guard dog is. Ma's next on her list, you know."

"Yeah, I know."

"Don't know why you keep that old battle axe on at your place."

"Aw, Grady, she's not so bad. All bluff. Just a little lonely, that's all. Quit running down my employees."

"And, speaking of employees, hear you got a new one."

"Yeah, news gets around fast, don't it?"

"Small town. What else they got to do?"

"I guess."

"Another bird with a broken wing, I suppose."

"Yeah. I think this one has a lot more broken than a wing so take it slow and easy and don't go spooking her when you go inside."

"You make me sound like I'm gonna go in there and brow beat her, pounce on the poor defenseless girl with my nightstick the minute I open the door." Then Grady noticed the serious look in Caleb's eyes and quit teasing. "I'll just get me a cup of Ma's coffee and be on my way. How's that?"

"Can't hope for more than that. I owe you one."

"And, I'll make you pay," Grady told him with a smile.

Caleb slid into his car then remembered he wanted Grady to do some checking up for him. He opened his door a notch and peeked through the opening. "Uh, Grady?"

Grady dropped his hand from the door and turned back. "What is it, Caleb?"

"How 'bout me owin' you another one?"

Grady placed his hands on his hips and eyed Caleb. Everybody called this his cop stance. He frowned, pulling those wooly brows down until they met in the middle. "I don't suppose it'd be about that new employee of yours, now would it?"

"Maybe."

Grady grunted. "Uh, huh. What is it you want to know?"

"Not sure. She's wounded deep, and scarred bad, and I want to find out why and, more importantly, who."

Grady straightened and stepped forward. "This isn't gonna be another one of your crusades, is it?"

Caleb bristled. Grady knew him too well. "Crusade or not, the young lady is terrified of something that goes soul deep and I intend to find out who put it there."

"You're not thinking about taking the law into your own hands, as they say, are you, Doc?"

"I want to find out what made her this way."

"And, one way or another, you'll find out, I suppose," Grady drawled.

"One way or another, Grady."

Then Grady laughed, a rumbling that started deep then roared out of his chest. "Oh, Doc, if you could just see your face. Not even here a day and that girl's already got you wrapped!"

א

It was evident when he opened the door. Grady sauntered up to the counter and waited, saw her eyes go wide and the fear that jumped into them on his approach. She didn't want to wait on him, he realized, didn't want to be anywhere near him. She even went to the far end of the counter to avoid him. But, Sophy ended her temporary flight.

"The sheriff takes his black, Harleigh, with just a tad of sugar. Lord knows, that man's sweet enough without needing any outside help in that department. Hello again, you sweet man," Sophy directed her comment to the sheriff, with a wink and a big come-on smile, then turned back to Harleigh. "Might as well throw in one of Ma's sweet rolls, too, cause he's such a nice customer. No charge, either, for our local law enforcement."

There was no way around it. Reluctantly, Harleigh picked up a cup, willing her hands not to shake. Still, she could feel the sheriff watching her every move. Somehow, she managed to get the coffee into the cup and a lid on the top without spilling the contents. The biggest feat of all would be turning around and facing this man who could very well want to question her.

She didn't know what was with Sophy all of a sudden. She acted like the man was a God or something, the way she was flirting and looking him over with eyes hot as coals, like he was the man she'd waited for all her life. If she liked him so much, why didn't she wait on him? Harleigh thought resentfully, then batted the resentment away. It was her job anyway. She'd been assigned to the counter.

She tried to keep her voice light, and hope the trembling that wanted to take over her whole body didn't show. She handed him the bag, avoiding contact with his hands. "Here you go, Sheriff. Black, a little sweet and a sweet roll. Just like you want."

Grady noticed all this, rolling the toothpick he always had in his mouth from one side to the other. "Thank you much. Name's Grady Sackett. And, you?"

Dear God, what could she tell him that he wouldn't want to race back to his office and start punching the keys on his keyboard, trying to pump official records for information about her? Finally, she opted for the truth. Well, as much as anyone else here knew, anyway.

"Nice to meet you, Sheriff. I'm Harleigh Bleu."

"How d'ya' like our little burg?"

"It's really nice here. Everyone so far has made me feel welcome."

Her words hung in the air and Grady could see what Caleb was talking about when Harleigh finally met his gaze. He saw her flinch, saw the resignation sag her shoulders, the soul-deep suffering she'd endured. It made him want to lighten her load, too.

Yeah, he could see where Caleb was gonna be brought down by this one. He was glad he'd be around to watch him fall. And, that made him a happy man. He'd been waiting a long time to see that happen.

"Add my welcome to your list, Miz Harleigh," he drawled in his best, lazy welcome, southern drawl. "This is a good town and we take care of our own here. If you need anything, help of any kind, we're all here to help you out." Knowing he'd said more than he intended, Grady tipped his hat. "Have a nice one today. And, you, Sophy, I'll take care of you later."

"I'll make sure of it, Sheriff," Sophy answered with a knowing smile, and something more in the way her hungry gaze followed him out the door that gave Harleigh cause to wonder.

Grady slid under the wheel of his cruiser, picked up the mike and made his request. "Phyllis, request a background on Harleigh Bleu. Jot this down. Particulars. Female, age twenty-five to thirty, weight one to one-twenty. Eyes, blue. Hair light blond. 5'6". Make it ASAP."

Apprehensive, Harleigh watched Grady step through the door and return to his car. She froze as he picked up his mike and talked into it. Maybe he was just checking in, she tried to assure herself. And not until he pulled out of the parking lot, did relief flood her body and she breathed steadily again.

The incident didn't remain with her long. Before she knew it, the lunch crowd had descended, then it was open-faced roast beef sandwiches and pots and pots of hot steaming coffee, burgers and fries and sodas. Or as the locals called it, pop. And so many slices of apple pie, she lost count. She was too busy to even think. Even though she still covered the counter area, there was a steady stream of customers. Everyone and his brother must've decided to come to town today, she thought. So much for trying for obscurity.

Then, the afternoon wound down and Sophy was telling her what a great job she'd done and how lucky they were that she was there when the door opened and the most beautiful woman she'd ever seen walked through it. She looked like a beauty queen. Massive amounts of golden hair flowed down her back, bouncing at her hips. Her face held the perfect classic look that all photographers clamored for. Flawless skin, deep green eyes and a smile that would knock the socks off any man.

Then the smile went away, slowly sliding off her face and Harleigh wondered what happened. The woman in question glided to the counter as if she floated on air and looked her straight in the eyes. Didn't say or do anything, just stared at her as if she were assessing her character. Then, like the sun coming over the horizon to welcome the day, the smile was back.

"So ... you're Harleigh, huh?"

Harleigh couldn't tell if it was a loaded question or not. There was nothing in the tone of that silken voice suggesting it was or wasn't. Her voice was pleasant, warm and cultured. And, the accent surely didn't fit here. She definitely was not one of the natives.

But, what could she say to this beautiful creature? Harleigh never thought too much about appearances but this woman would make anyone fade by comparison. What did she want with a plain Jane like her?

"Yes, I'm Harleigh," she finally managed to say.

"You met my husband earlier, I believe. Butch Cassidy?"

Butch Cassidy? She couldn't make the connection between this classy looking lady and the man with the scar. "Yes, ma'am. He came in for coffee this morning. Nice man."

"So, you like Butch, do you?"

"Uh, I can't really say. I don't know him."

"I'm Delilah. I'm here to make you a proposition."

Harleigh was taken back for a moment, wondering why on earth another man's wife would come looking for her, wondering what exactly she meant by proposition. Then something slimy crawled along the surface of her skin and she cringed. Where would Delilah get an impression like that anyway? Had Butch Cassidy read more into their conversation than there was?

She cringed as the evil she'd known surfaced, looking for a place to re-establish itself. She fought it down as she scanned her brain trying to come up with a reason for Butch's wife to be tracking her down. It couldn't be bad … Delilah was smiling. Still, she knew first hand that smiles were very deceiving.

"I know, I know. You're racking your brain trying to figure out what I want with you. But this is a joint effort on our part to welcome you to our community and let you know that we care about you and here, in this place, you will find what you need, what you seek."

What was this woman after? What did she want from her? Harleigh couldn't put her trust in anyone. Not now. Not ever. "I'm not sure what you mean, Ms. Cassidy. I appreciate your concern and offering to help me but I'm fine. Really."

"That's what I thought when I came here, too. I was on the run like you."

"But, I'm not –"

"Maybe not. I was running from myself." Delilah had seen what Butch had seen and Butch was never wrong. "Now, you, I'd say you were running from *someone.*"

Fear swept through Harleigh so swiftly she gripped the edge of the counter to keep from dropping to the floor, the force of it was so strong. What was wrong with these people that they could see through her so easily? Was she that transparent or did these people have a second sense about such things?

Delilah saw the panic stream its way through Harleigh's eyes, the surrender in the slope of her shoulders and the recognition of defeat that encompassed her soul. Harleigh needed help and needed it bad.

"The people here are the genuine article, Harleigh. I know right about now you think we're all a bunch of lunatics that need to mind our own business." Delilah laughed, remembering her own resentment at what she considered undue interference in her life. Especially Butch. He wouldn't let her alone to wallow in her own self-pity. The man wouldn't take no for an answer. "One of these days, I'll have to tell you about me and Butch ... and his sister, Sundance."

Delilah saw Harleigh's anxiety ease as she knew it would. There was even a faint smile tugging at the corner of her mouth. "Yeah, Butch told me his mother had a sense of humor."

"She would've made a great flower child from the seventies. She's a wonderful lady. You'll meet her soon, I'm sure, Sundance, too. I'm sure you've met Grady Sackett, our sheriff."

Alarm sprinted through Harleigh at the mention of the sheriff. Were all these people connected? No one was going to get close enough to find out a damn thing about her past, she was unwavering in that respect, especially the sheriff. She had to close herself off from everyone, even this friendly creature. If she were to survive, she had to do it on her own. Alone. She couldn't afford to let her guard down and let anyone, *anyone*, inside.

She couldn't afford to let anyone know anything about her past either. She knew all about betrayal, knew all about the two faces of man. One looked at you with concern on their features, offering friendship, the other came with a turn of their head and there would be their true face. The face of evil.

Harleigh chose her words carefully. Even though she knew she couldn't give herself away, she also knew that in order to live here she'd have to allow a certain amount of invasion into her privacy.

No one knew her so she was certain she could invent a life that suited her, one that was believable, of course, and they could think what they wanted. She didn't owe an explanation to anyone. She was way passed the point where she would answer to another living soul or allow anyone to bend her to their will again.

"Ms. Cassidy, — "

"Delilah."

"Delilah, I really appreciate all this town has done for me already. Heaven knows, they didn't have to do a thing for a stranger. It's a bit overwhelming to say the least. I've never felt more welcome anywhere than I do here and I will always remember that. But, right now, all I want to do is get settled and fit in. I don't have much room for anything else in my life at the moment."

Delilah smiled her sunshine smile and backed off. One thing at a time, she told herself. She'd been there, done that and thrown away the T-shirt. She'd thought these were a bunch of nosy busybodies herself when she first came to town so she knew where Harleigh was coming from.

"At least, take these. Don't worry about arrangements, that's the least of our worries at the moment, isn't it?" Delilah held out her hand, keys dangling from her fingers. "Go on, take them. Courtesy of the town of Nowhere and Cassidy Motors."

Harleigh stared at the keys with rounded eyes. She wanted so much to reach out and clasp them in her hands but she didn't dare. The price was too high. Instead, she looked into the expectant face of Delilah Cassidy, saw an eagerness in the depths of her eyes that gave her hope. But still, she couldn't be obligated to anyone. She already was to a certain extent and that's as far as she'd let it go.

"I'm sorry, Delilah. I can't accept this."

"Don't get the wrong idea, Harleigh. Even though, we're trying to help you, it doesn't come without a price."

And here it comes, thought Harleigh. Here comes the clincher. This is what they really want. She cringed at the images that swam before her eyes.

"Look, Delilah, I really don't want to seem rude. But, I don't want to be involved in what you're suggesting."

Delilah took one look at Harleigh's face and doubled over with laughter. Soon tears were rolling down her cheeks and she had to take a seat before she ended up on the café floor. Harleigh looked on in horror as it dawned on her that she and Delilah weren't at all talking about the same subject.

"I can't believe you thought I wanted you to be part of that kind of thing," Delilah sputtered between bouts of laughter. "Once you get to know me, and you *will* get to know me, you'll see that I don't share my Butch with any woman."

Okay, Harleigh decided, she'd change tactics. Somewhere in her past life, before Stewart had beaten her down, she'd been a fairly intelligent person. She wouldn't embarrass herself further by her bumbling attempts at conversation. She'd converse with Delilah and make sense.

Feeling more at ease now, Harleigh smiled. It was the strangest thing. This place called Nowhere. With each passing moment and each person she spoke with, she was finding her way. She was going to make it here. This place was going to be home. She could remain anonymous, stay in the background of this busy little burg and still live here. She wanted that more than anything. So, the best place to start would be now, with this woman.

"Well, Delilah, I can see I misunderstood the whole thing. And, believe me, I do appreciate your offer of the car. It means more to me than you'll ever know to take such a risk like that on someone you don't know."

"Think nothing of it, Harleigh. Please say you'll take it. It will mean just as much to me as it will to you. Once, not too long ago, I was in your shoes and it was my darling Butch that stepped in and made me see reason. Saved the day, so to speak. Since then, it's been my purpose in life to help as many women as possible that crosses my path. Look upon me as the local Welcome Wagon."

Before Harleigh could speak another word, Delilah saw the distress zip across her face and turned to see what had produced such a change. Over her shoulder, she caught a glimpse of the police cruiser pulling into the parking space directly in front of the café door.

She wondered what Harleigh had to fear from the police, what she was running from and who or what she was hiding from. And, what she, Delilah, could do to keep her that way. Hidden.

Yes, she'd been in those shoes and she knew how hard it was to keep yourself blended in with the crowd and hope no one noticed you. Knew how desperation ruled your life. If there were anything she could do, she'd find a way.

"Harleigh, you have nothing to fear from Grady," Delilah assured her. "He's a good and decent cop. Besides, he's not here for you."

Harleigh finally caught her breath and the agitation began to subside. She decided the best way to handle the situation was head on. "I met him this morning. Of course, I have nothing to fear from the sheriff. Why should I? I've only been here a day." She paused and eyed the length of him as he pulled his long form from the car and walked like a predator to the door. He looked dangerous to her. But weren't law officers supposed to appear that way?

Delilah placed her fingertips on the back of Harleigh's hand, stopping the constant wiping of the same spot that Harleigh was determined to clean. "Grady's here for Sophy."

"Sophy? Why? What did Sophy do?"

"He's probably going to haul her off and make her do something indecent."

Harleigh's eyes rounded and a thread of anxiety raced across her skin. Dear God, what had she stepped into? This placed seemed so peaceful, and now? She felt like an animal caught in a trap. She could feel the teethed jaws around her throat.

She swallowed the fear that had lodged itself in deep and said, "But I thought you said the sheriff was a good and decent man."

"Oh, he is. Grady is one of the best. But, he's also a husband who wants his wife home at the end of the day."

"Wife? I thought you said you were Butch's wife."

"I am. That big, tall hunk that's opening the door belongs to Sophy."

"Sophy?"

Delilah saw the tension racking her body and decided to stop teasing. "Relax, Harleigh, take a deep breath, loosen up and take it slow. Grady is Sophy's husband. He's here to take her home."

Harleigh saw the amusement on Delilah's features and realized that she'd been teasing her. She tried for a smile and hoped it didn't look as shaky as she felt. Inside, her stomach was fluttering and her nerves had taken flight. This was not the way she wanted to be. She wanted to be able to tease and be teased.

"Howdy, ladies."

"Hey there, Grady, how goes it?" Delilah answered, hoping to put Harleigh at ease. "You here for Sophy?"

"Yeah. I need my woman home." Grady grinned, tipping his hat at Harleigh and drawled. "How's your first day in Nowhere, Miz Harleigh?"

Harleigh's nerves stabilized and settled. They were both trying to put her at ease, she realized. It was up to her to accept their homespun hospitality. She reminded herself to follow Delilah's suggestion and lighten up and take it slow.

She could at least give him a truthful, honest answer. Besides, the sheriff was married to Sophy and Sophy was the greatest. He had a nice smile, too. "It's been fantastic! I love working here."

"You'll find that it don't get much better than this. Most people think of small towns as nothing more than a bunch of hicks or a bunch of illiterates running around. Take my word for it, you ain't never gonna find another town like this one." Grady smiled that smile she liked then his eyes took on a softness sliced with an unrestrained hunger as Sophy swung open the kitchen door. "There's the woman I'm after."

Sophy brightened, glanced over at the two women at the counter and winked. "If this man is bothering you, let me know, I have an in at the sheriff's department."

"Come on, woman, take me home, feed me and I'm yours."

"Ha! You're mine, anyway, mister, and don't you ever forget it."

"You guys are a trip," Delilah told them as they headed for the door. "See ya' later."

They waved goodbye as they exited the building. Grady opened Sophy's door and gave her a long kiss before he shut it behind her. Harleigh kept her eyes on him and didn't take a deep breath until he pulled away.

Caleb pulled in just as the cruiser pulled out. They exchanged greetings by waving a hand in the air. He sat for a minute taking stock in the passage of the day.

One thing he knew for certain, he wanted to find out more about Harleigh. She'd crossed his mind all day in regular intervals and he already knew she'd come here alone. Had been for some time if he her actions of yesterday were any indication. And had been through a lot.

No, he decided. That wasn't right. She'd been

through hell. It was up to him and the friends she'd make here to keep her safe from whatever trouble she left behind. One thing he'd found in his thirty-two years of life, was that no matter what, trouble had a way of finding you.

Caleb put a welcome smile on his face and entered the café. Harleigh watched each step he took. He brought out the curious side of her. And more than that, she admitted, he made her edgy.

In another time and place, if she didn't have all the baggage of her past to carry around weighing her down like a pair of concrete boots, she may have allowed herself to be a little more than a passing interest. This turned up her mouth in a smile. A real one.

"Evening, Miz Harleigh. Hey, Miz Dee, what brings you down here at this hour?"

"Hey, Doc. Butch and I are just trying to roll out the red carpet for your new employee." She held out her hand. "Here, we'll work out the details later."

Caleb stretched out his palm and Delilah dropped the keys into it. "What's this?"

"This is our way of saying thanks and my way of giving back what everyone gave me. Don't let her say no. See ya'."

With that said, Delilah immediately headed for the door before another word could be exchanged. "Well, I guess that means you're the proud owner of whatever vehicle Miz Dee decided on."

"Doc, I appreciate everything you and the other folks here in Nowhere are trying to do but I can't allow something like this."

"Why not? You need help, don't you?"

A thread of hot resentment drifted through her but

she realized that this was the way things were done here. She should appreciate the fact that they were willing to go to these lengths to help a virtual stranger. Not many people would.

But, she didn't want to get this close to anyone. Didn't want to feel obligated. She'd made it this far on her own but she was tired right down to the bone.

Could she? Could she really let her guard down and allow someone to pass through the gates she surrounded herself with? No, maybe not let her guard down, nor through the gate but she could meet them there. And see what happened.

Caleb saw her hesitation, saw her trying to decide what to do, which way to go. "Come on, Miz Harleigh, go ahead. None of us can really say no to Miz Dee." Knowing she wouldn't accept the touch of his hand, he laid the keys on the counter. "Take them. For tonight, at least. Sleep on it then if you feel the same way tomorrow, we can return the keys. If not, we can go down to Cassidy's and see which car those keys fit. Look at it this way, if you have your own ride, you won't have to put up with me."

Harleigh kept her eyes turned away. She didn't want Caleb to see how close to the truth he was. It wasn't a matter of putting up with him. It was a matter of wanting to walk this path alone. Her preference.

"You're right, Doc. It's the least I could do."

"Right. Is everything checked out?"

"Yes, Sophy counted out the drawer, gave me a rundown on what we had to do to close up for the night and briefly clued me in on side work. She did most of it, though, said I'd done a good job and was glad I was here," she told him, relishing the satisfaction it brought her.

Caleb locked the door as he ushered Harleigh out. She took another look around her. She'd been in this wonderful old place for only one day but now she was part of it. It'd taken her in, surrounded her, blending her in with its wonderful atmosphere and it made her heart swell that she could actually be included and participate in something this lovely.

This place, this town of Nowhere, was hers. She breathed in the evening air, felt a sense of well being that hadn't been felt in months and knew that this was where her life was going to change. That here, her new life would begin.

CHAPTER FOUR
N

Harleigh opened one eye when she realized it was morning and if she didn't hurry the sun would greet the day without her. She was eager to be up and about and doing in this second day of her new life. Excited now, she rushed out of bed, ran water for the two-cupper coffee pot to heat while she took a quick shower. She didn't want to miss not one bit of the welcome waiting for her outside her door.

Refreshed from her shower, she toweled off, threw on a robe that was in the closet and threw open the door to her balcony. She smiled as the sun made its first peek over the horizon. She strode forward to the railing and breathed in deeply.

Suddenly she felt a warm breeze surround her. Glancing over at the maple trees at the end of the house, she noticed not a leaf stirred. Confused now, she turned to glance over at the little yellow house with the white picket fence. The trees that stood guard there were motionless as well.

Still, the air stirred and blew gently around her. Then as if plucked straight off the balcony, she could swear someone or something moved her. And zoom. She was at the edge of the abyss. The mist swirled up and around her. The edges of her reality dimmed and she was looking through that mist to the other side. Closer than she'd ever done before. The chasm was nearly closed and if she tried real hard, she could've jumped across to the other side. She was almost tempted to do just that but waited in anticipation instead.

Here it is, she thought as she stood at the edge of the void. All those times she'd stood waiting for a connection to the other side and here it was. That part of her that she'd always thought lived there had come visiting her without the terror that always brought her to stand to watch and wait. She felt the anticipation of that time and welcomed it. The mist that lay between her and the golden glow began a slow swirl upward.

To be sure of where she was at, though, she glanced down at her hands. White knuckled fingers were tightly wrapped around the railing. She was here, but she wasn't. Then, the warm glow from across the abyss enveloped her as the air continued to shift and stir more rapidly.

The faint light in the swirling mist became stronger. As she glanced up, shapes moved, outlined in the shadows. Then a figure stepped forward. A figure that Harleigh recognized.

No, Harleigh thought, firmly rejecting the idea of what she saw. Yet, there she was looking back at her own image. A mirror image of herself. It was, but then again, it wasn't. Something wasn't quite right about the image that was staring back at her. It was a similar likeness but different somehow. But she recognized it all the same.

From somewhere inside the mist, another shadow

formed and emerged. He was a handsome man, Harleigh thought, in a strange kind of way. In his hand, he held a small piece of equipment that he punched at constantly. His mouth moved as if speaking but Harleigh couldn't understand what he said. He turned toward the other figure, the image of herself, as that figure raised her hand, reaching out towards Harleigh.

Harleigh blinked and just like that, it all disappeared, just as if someone had flicked off a light switch. She sat down hard on the edge of the wicker chair. What had just happened? What had she just seen? None of the explanations that came to mind were viable ones. Small tremors ran through her as she tried making sense of the situation.

There hadn't been one thread of fear born of the incident, then or now, she noticed.

The sun was over the horizon now. Somehow, she'd missed its coming. She tested the temperature of her coffee and found it cold. That in itself was an indication that something had gone on and she wasn't sure she liked that at all. How long had she stood there, waiting, watching, hoping? How much time had passed then? What had held her enthralled in its clutches?

The air was no longer stirring, the morning, as if the incident had never been.

What did it all mean?

More than a little confused now, Harleigh picked up what remained of her cold coffee. Once inside, she took note of the time, realizing she had very little time of her morning left before Caleb came knocking. She walked to the bathroom, dumped her coffee and rinsed the cup, setting it on the counter upside down to dry on a washcloth.

Thankful her hair was easy to fix, she pulled it back and wrapped it in a scrunchie. Next, she applied a little makeup. Satisfied with herself in the mirror, she pulled on the uniform that Sophy had loaned her, put on her only pair of scruffy shoes, vowing that would be the first thing she would buy herself with her first paycheck … providing she had any money left over after paying back all the obligations she'd incurred over the last two days.

Even so, that would be first on her list. That's what she'd do in her spare time, make a list and prioritize. She reveled in the freedom that simple task gave her. High on that list, would be how to go about acquiring that little yellow house across the way. For right now, she'd have to be content with the view from her balcony.

Hurrying, Harleigh raced towards the door, not wanting Caleb to knock and she not be ready. Somehow, that would be too much of an invasion of her newfound privacy. A luxury that she'd not had in years. And time to call her own.

She stepped out on the veranda, discovering she'd beaten Caleb to the front of the house. She forced herself to relax and waited, her mind wandering. Wouldn't it be wonderful if she didn't have to wait on anyone? That she could come and go as she pleased?

Mmm. Another item for her list.

Harleigh took a moment to study her surroundings before Caleb arrived. Everything was green, it seemed. Every leaf on the trees, blades of grass on the lawn. Even the roses were blooming in riotous color, their leaves a deep shade of green. So many different varieties and shades.

Then Caleb strolled around the veranda unaware that she was sitting at the far end at a table. She found that she liked the way he held himself with confidence and self-assurance. Then something he did, the turn of his head maybe, setting his face in profile, flung her back into the past.

Stewart had his hand on the small of her back, nudging her forward. She could tell by the way he touched her that he was angry. She cringed, not wanting to get into the car that waited for them in front of the theater.

He must've felt her reluctance. He took her by the hand and assured her no one could see what he was doing, then proceeded to bend her fingers backwards until she grimaced from the pain he caused her. He opened the door for her as they approached the car, every bit the gentleman to observers. But Harleigh knew what awaited her on the inside. Fear crawled down her spine as she slid onto the seat, making room for him. Even though she scooted to the far side of the car giving him ample room, he slid right next to her and placed his arm around her shoulders.

This was one of the things he liked to do best, inflicting pain upon her in public where he could so easily be caught and daring her to cry out or ask for help when others were present. He enjoyed the fact that he could do this with a smile upon his lips and no one would be the wiser. The one time she did cry out, he made sure she regretted it once they were behind closed doors and knew she best not do it again.

She endured the pain, endured the constant tugging on the hair at the nape of her neck. He yanked sharply, just enough to bring tears to her eyes. And when she would try to wipe them away, he dug his nails into the tender flesh of her upper thigh. He liked to see the tears roll down her face when they were alone. He'd told her that on many occasions, said it turned him on, then he'd fling her on the floor, bed, whatever, it didn't matter, then continuously assault her until he got it out of his system.

On that occasion, before she could take an even breath, they were home. This time she hoped he'd just lock her in the closet as he was wont to do when he was more than a little bored with her. She preferred the darkness to his presence. Even there, though, she wasn't safe. He'd left her there for a full twenty-four hours once and when her bladder could no longer hold against its natural function, it expelled itself and soiled her clothes and the floor. That time he'd beaten her with his leather belt. Even then, she was thankful for that mercy. He hadn't seen fit to use the buckle against her flesh.

When she'd scoured out the closet to suit him, do-ing so in her soiled clothing he hadn't allowed her to change into something clean and dry, he'd shoved her in a cold shower, clothes and all, and left her until he said she could come out.

Naturally, this was more than she could hope for as the tears on her cheeks had him ready when they reached the front door. There was no escape, except into the mist and wait for the glow to warm her and the mist to swirl on the other side.

Then later in their marriage he'd had … problems. Erectile dysfunction was a condition that drove him far-ther into the pits of hell and he dragged her down with him. Those appalling things she couldn't allow to surface.

"Harleigh? Harleigh?"

Caleb's touch was warm against her cold flesh. He took note of it ... and the terror that filled her eyes when she glanced up at him. She cringed from his touch, drawing herself back tightly against the chair for protection. He knew what or who she was seeing and it made his flesh crawl.

"Harleigh? Honey, it's me. Caleb. Don't be frightened, I won't hurt you. Harleigh, do you hear me?" As a doctor, he recognized the symptoms as he stood helplessly by until she could compose herself. He knew what the next step would be and he wanted to relieve her of any embarrassment and humiliation that may be waiting in the wings once she was coherent.

Jerking spasmodically against the terror that was clawing her gut, she drew in deep breaths to ease the anxiety that was choking the air out of her lungs. She looked around her in confusion, then realizing that it was Caleb standing over her and not Stewart, she wanted to break down and weep with relief. Not wanting to appear as foolish as she felt, she tried for a smile, a sorry one at best, she was sure but tried nevertheless. She recognized gallantry when she saw it and went weak with the knowledge that he was trying to spare her any indignities.

"Good morning, Caleb. I must've fallen back asleep," she offered in way of explanation as the lie rolled off her tongue. She was getting damn good at this, she thought. Pretty soon, she'd be able to lie with the best of them. Of course, she had the best teacher. But she didn't want to think of him now. She didn't want the thought of him to dirty up this time and place in her new life. She'd do anything to keep him at bay.

Here in this place, this wonderful old town of Nowhere, she'd slither into the cracks, would become just another face, so familiar that no one would give her a second thought. And when, if that time ever came, when asked if anyone here knew her, they would quickly say no. She'd be one of them.

She knew all this was wishful thinking but right now wishful thinking was all she had, was all she'd allow herself to have. Suddenly, realizing Caleb waited, she felt the warmth spread across her cheeks and bowed her head to hide it away.

Caleb allowed her this, ignoring the faint blush that colored her features. He smiled and turned away. "We best get going," he teased. "Seeing as how your boss is a tyrant, he'd have my head if I didn't get you to work on time."

She followed behind Caleb as he walked away and loped down the stairs. She even liked that about him, she thought. Then reminded herself, not to like too much about this man. That kind of thinking was dangerous and she didn't need any more danger than what she already had.

He opened the truck door, and helped her into the cab, noticing that this time she didn't pull back or flinch from his touch. He was grateful for that, grateful for any progress, no matter how trivial.

Caleb didn't try any small talk this morning. He turned on the radio to a country station and hummed along with George Strait. He kept tabs on Harleigh out of the corner of his eye.

Secretly, she did the same. She noticed how easily he smiled, how comfortable he was in his own skin.

Once upon a time, eons ago it seemed, she was like that and hoped she would be that way again soon. If she could just learn that not everyone was out to get her, that would allay some of her fear. But it was so hard to let go of those old friends.

A quick glance his way gave her a surprised bolt from out of the blue when he smiled back at her. It was so unexpected, she wasn't sure how to react. She'd experienced something since first meeting the man but nothing like this. The attraction to him was sudden. Hot and skin absorbing. Pleasant. Even so, she told herself, it wasn't anything she could consider and explore. Yet telling herself didn't stop the jingling of sensation skipping along the surface of her skin.

She did her best to ignore it and eventually it ebbed into the background until it became enmeshed in the incident of the early morning. It was that which now invaded her thoughts. She still couldn't fathom what had happened. She knew she was standing on her private balcony but that was the only thing she was certain of.

Who were those people she saw in the mist? Who was that woman who looked so much like her? Was she reaching out across the span of glimmering darkness, reaching for her?

These questions stayed on her mind throughout the day as she met more of Nowhere's colorful residents. She began to enjoy her new role and laughed and joked with the locals. She remembered laughter, this kind of laughter, from long ago. Before Stewart. Now, Wilbur Nexley regaled the performance of his foxhounds.

"Yes, ma'am, best in the county, probably the whole state if'n you ask me. You should hear 'em, Miz

Harleigh."

"The poor foxes," Harleigh empathized with the unfortunate animals. "Do you really kill them?"

"Kill 'em? Have you lost a noodle or two, Miz Harleigh? God forbid, you don't hurt the creatures."

Confused, Harleigh looked at Wilbur as if he were the one who had lost a few noodles. "What do you do with them, then?"

"Don't do nothing with them, Miz Harleigh. You go fox huntin' just to hear your hounds howl. Most wonderful sound, it is."

"The howling of your hounds is wonderful?"

"Music to my ears, listening to 'em. I can tell which one is leading and which ones are lagging. 'Specially if ya' have a full moon. Can't get better than that."

And so it went. They all had a tale to tell. And she found, if she just stopped a moment and listened, well, that's all they wanted. Nothing more. Just talk. And this, she reveled in. This was the way it should be, she thought, so glad that she'd stepped off that bus.

She was surprised how quickly the day passed. She realized it when Caleb walked in the door. Her stomach fluttered and jumped as he walked up to the counter. It was best to ignore it, she commanded. This was an attraction that she didn't need.

"Hey, Miz Harleigh."

"Hey, Mr. Caleb," she returned.

"How's your day been?"

"Wonderful. Absolutely wonderful. I've never met more caring people. It's amazing! I love it here in this town. It's the best place I've ever been. Love working here, too."

Harleigh stopped her wayward mouth when she realized the words were tumbling out in a mad rush. She tried not to blush but could feel it crossing her cheeks. There was something about this man, this Caleb Forrester that unnerved her. She didn't want to go down that path. He was something she didn't need. She wanted to get her life together and start living without any hindrances or obstacles in the road she was trying to travel alone.

And, if she paid attention to Caleb, he would be a big one that would get in the way of what she wanted to do.

"So, Miz Harleigh, what d'ya think about running by Cassidy's and take a look at the car that key fits into?"

Harleigh had forgotten all about the token of friendship they'd offered. She knew she should say no but she really needed to have transportation of her own. Besides that, she couldn't figure out a way to tell Delilah thanks but no thanks.

"No one else can either."

"What?" Had she said that out loud? He couldn't really read her thoughts, could he?

"Tell Miz Delilah no. That's what you were dwelling on so hard, wasn't it?"

"Yes, but — "

"No, I'm not psychic. We've all been there. Delilah has a way about her that makes you want to bend over backward to please her."

"Yeah, I guess you're right."

"So, how about it?"

Before Harleigh knew what happened she was the proud owner of her very own car. Turned out it had been Delilah's and she'd been looking for a good home for it forever, she said. And, Harleigh was the best candidate she'd come across yet.

It was baby blue in color and drove like a dream. The best thing of all was that it was a convertible. The first thing she did was put the top down and race down the highway leaving Caleb behind.

Eat my dust, she thought. She was high on this accomplishment, drunk on the excitement of the moment. The euphoria she felt was something she wanted to remember. Always. Remember and savor.

She drove herself to work and back. She hadn't come down to earth yet, still floating on a cloud. And before she knew it the rest of the week was gone and Sunday was waiting.

Sundays were for going to church according to Ma Forrester so she closed down on God's day. But Harleigh had bowed out of going to church. Tomorrow would be her very first Sunday here and a day that she wanted to spend alone, going and doing and just being.

But right now it was a Saturday sundown. The evening quiet. A glass of tea in her hand, she was content to watch the sun slide down the horizon in an orange ball. Her thoughts took her back over the first week of her new beginnings and she toasted herself on the way things had gone. Sure, she was wary, her guard still up, her self-imposed emotional exile in place, but she could feel the confidence growing, the self-assurance coming boldly to the forefront. This added an additional edge to her happiness.

Happiness. Who'd ever thought she'd ever find it. Here.

But she had, she, and it would continue. She'd do

everything in her power to keep it that way. Tumbling thoughts of plans she wanted to put into action swirled inside her as her eyes closed, contentment a warm blanket around her.

Something warm tickled her arm. Slowly opening her eyes, she stared at the furry gray ball sitting on the arm of the chaise lounge where she'd fallen asleep and slept the whole night through. The cat was bigger than any feline she'd ever seen. The whiskers on its face were long and each time the feline moved, the ends would stroke along her skin.

"Hello, cat. How are you this lovely morning?"

The cat purred in answer, its pink tongue came out to cleanse the fur on its right leg.

"I agree."

This was the morning of all mornings. The one she'd been waiting for. The sun was streaming warm on her face and right at this moment in time, all was right. She wanted to savor it, remember it, know that for at least one moment of her new life she'd been happy. This was the way it was supposed to be and she prayed that there'd be more to come from this place she was glad to've found.

And, glad that Nowhere had claimed her for its own.

נ

So, here she was, the whole day ahead of her. What could she do to make this day special? She emptied the remaining tea down the sink and rinsed out the glass. She'd take it down to the kitchen, along with the cup sharing the towel, to give a good wash.

Stepping into the hot shower, she shampooed her hair, lathered up her body, shaved her legs, rinsed and was ready to go out to meet the day. Anxious now, she dressed, throwing on her only pair of faded jeans, an old tee that she'd been able to grab on her way out the door those long months ago and her ratty old sneakers. It didn't matter, this day she didn't care what anyone thought about her state of dress. She was going to enjoy today to the fullest.

She jumped into her car, thinking she'd have to come up with a name for it. She marveled that this was her very own and thanked the powers that be for belching her up like chunks from a volcano and plopping her down in this town ... and for meeting up with Delilah Cassidy.

They'd worked out the terms of payment. Delilah had waived the normal contract, refusing to put Harleigh on the regular timed payments to a financial institution, instead opting to allow Harleigh to pay her twice a month. Delilah was more than reasonable, going way beyond the normal business relationship in order to give her a break, Harleigh thought, to give her a new start and for this she was grateful.

She hoped there'd come a time when she could repay her. And everyone else for that matter. These people were taking her under their wing and doing their level best to help her. She'd keep track of everything they did and little by little she'd return the favor in kind.

She drove into town, cruised up and down each street, made mental notes of all the businesses and picked a few she could browse through today. When she spied a nursery, she remembered wanting a rubber tree plant for that little yellow house across the way if she found a way inside to claim it for herself. Today though, she'd settle for a small one for her living quarters at the moment. Who knew, sometime in the future this same plant and she would be living across the way together.

Once inside, she wandered down aisles and through doorways to where the hanging plants were. Then finally she found what she was looking for. She selected the rubber tree plant that appealed to her the most and crossed the area to check out. As she walked, a lone zebra plant sat on a ledge. She didn't like the idea that it was alone, so she picked it up and brought it along. Now she'd have two companions to nurture.

All the way back to the Rose House, Harleigh kept up a constant chatter, talking to the plants as if they were people. Oh, she knew she was being silly but it felt so good to be that way. Hell, just to *be*, she thought, then immediately admonished herself for cursing like she did. She smiled though. Even those hastily spewed words felt good.

Harleigh turned into the driveway leading down to the Rose House. There were no cars in the parking lot which was just as well. She really meant to go down to the Sunday dinner Ma Forrester served up to her guests but she decided to continue with her one step at a time method. It was the best way to go. There would be time to meet them, to get acquainted. First, she wanted to get acquainted with the new Harleigh Bleu.

And that began with her new companions. She held one in each hand, murmuring to them each step of the way up the staircase. Once in her room, she looked around but found no place that appealed to her.

Ah, of course. The balcony. That was the only place for them. They could all three sit and watch the sun play peek-a-boo through the morning clouds.

She placed one at each end near the railing then stepped back for a better view. She drew in a deep breath, closed her eyes and smiled.

Caleb stepped onto the front porch. The sight of Harleigh, her head thrown back, a true smile etching across her lips, stole the next breath he was about to take. He'd never seen anyone more beautiful. And, he was sure, if she knew she had an audience, if she knew he was watching, she'd freeze and revert to the Harleigh he first met.

He stepped back into the shadows so he could observe undetected. This was the Harleigh he knew waited underneath. The Harleigh he wanted to get to know.

Harleigh looked out over the area, too absorbed in the day to even notice the shadow of Caleb's form elongated along the porch. Something caught her eye then, off to the left and she noticed a well-worn path leading into the trees.

The day was young yet. Today was a day for exploring and she was dressed for it. Before she allowed herself to change her mind, she was out the door into the welcoming day and striding down the path as if it were her own private lane.

Ten minutes into her walk, Harleigh came across a hewn-out log. She sat, taking a moment to study her surroundings and take pleasure in being alone.

The light in this area was lighter, she noticed. The atmosphere, surreal. Almost as if it were enchanted.

Not of this world. She felt ... something. Couldn't describe it. Could only feel it.

She wasn't afraid. It was a pleasant acceptance. Warm. Embracing. Almost loving.

Off to her right, a colorful array of wild flowers caught her attention. She hurried to the thickest spot and picked a few different varieties to take back to her room.

On her way back through the whimsical setting, she laid the flowers on the hewn-out log. She wanted to remain here but knew she couldn't so she turned in a full circle and took in every inch of the place, committing each and every tree, leaf, stick and bush to memory.

On impulse, she took a few of the daisies and wound them into a crown and placed them on her head. A happy laugh built inside her and erupted through her lips, adding a tinkling echo to the edge of enchanted forest as she pulled one more daisy from the pile and between her fingers.

She took another full circle, gathered her flowers and with a light heart, headed back toward home.

Home. Wow. She hadn't had one in such a long time, the word was almost foreign to her ears. But home it is. And, then the little yellow house with the white picket fence came into view.

Home for now, she added.

Caleb didn't let Harleigh see him. He wasn't hiding. Exactly. He just wanted to watch her. She'd become an obsession with him. Well, almost.

She was an interesting case, he told himself. But he knew he was lying. A big fat one at that. He wanted to know about Harleigh and his medical profession didn't have a damn thing to do with it.

He slipped inside the gazebo that sat a few feet from the back of the house. He could see her as she stepped from the shadows of the trees into the sunlight. A crown of daisies decorated her head and that only added to her appearance. Only made his heart beat harder. Only made his breath come faster.

And what he heard sent both into hyperspeed.

"The house will be mine," she whispered as she pulled off a petal and let the wind carry it away. "The house will not be mine." She pulled another petal away from the yellow center and let it float away.

When she was down to the last petal, she smiled and pulled. "The house will be mine!"

She stretched her arms wide, raised her face to the sky, closed her eyes as the warmth of the sun washed over her and turned three times. She'd read somewhere that if you found a place like this, if you turned three times with your face skyward, good luck would find you.

Oh, she knew it was silly, but now she could be silly. Could be as silly as she wanted.

Something, a movement maybe, made her aware that she was no longer alone. He saw the happiness erase itself from her features, a creeping wariness move at a snail's pace into her eyes.

Caleb hated that it was he that made her lose that small amount of pleasure she'd found. He tried to remain as still as possible. But when he saw the pleasure written so clearly in happy etchings on her face, his body moved itself out of the shadows without Caleb realizing he'd taken a step.

Harleigh's heartbeat slowed when she realized that

it was Caleb inside the gazebo. Habit had her prepared to run. There was no one around but the two of them but she didn't feel the gut-wrenching terror in Caleb's presence that she felt in Stewart's. Some of the tension that had wrapped its tendrils around her throat, eased and she could breathe again.

She shouldn't even make that comparison, she chided. Caleb was a whole different person from Stewart.

"Hey, Miz Harleigh," Caleb greeted. "How'd 'ya like our little piece of heaven back there?"

"It was wonderful."

Having a conversation with Harleigh was like pulling teeth with a pair of tweezers, Caleb decided. He searched his mind for things to say but since he'd never been one for long conversations himself, he was hard-pressed for a subject.

"You want to sit with me awhile? The gazebo's a really nice place to kick back."

"Yes, well ...," she hesitated, wanting to walk on.

"Well, what, Harleigh?"

"I've got to get these flowers into water before they wilt. Aren't they lovely?"

"Yeah, lovely."

"So, I'll see you later."

Harleigh thought she'd made her escape. She stepped quickly to get back inside the sanctuary of her room.

"Hey, wait up. I can finally give you that tour of the Rose House I promised you."

In two strides he was by her side. Now what could she do? How could she get rid of him? She didn't want to be rude and she would be if she turned him down.

But one more try wouldn't hurt, she decided.

"It really isn't necessary, Caleb," she told him, trying to keep the stiffness that was riding her spine out of her voice. "It's just a house."

"Well, that's one way to look at it, I guess."

"What do you mean by that?"

"The Rose House carries a lot of mystery within its walls.

"Mystery? You mean history, don't you?" Harleigh offered.

Caleb kept walking by her side, that slow walking that everyone seemed to do in these parts. A slow kind of wandering, no-hurry stride that sometimes wore her thin. She was always in high gear, had to get things done before…

Then she remembered. She could do that no-hurry kind of walking, too. She belonged here as sure as if she were born on this piece of earth. And, she could damn well do what she pleased … now.

"Well," Caleb drawled, as slow and easy as his walk. She slowed, matching her stride to his as he continued. "It's kind of both, you see and then some. A bit of scandal and such. Word down through the generations said that this house was originally built for the Faire Sabra. There was a big mystery of where it came from. Kind of just appeared as did Quentin Demascus. Seems as if he just popped in one day, stayed awhile and just like that he was gone again."

Caleb sank his long frame down onto the back steps, patting it when he settled in. "Here. Take a seat. I'll tell you everything you ever wanted to know about the occupants of the Rose House."

Intrigued now, despite herself, Harleigh sat by

Caleb, careful not to allow any part of his body to touch hers, or even allow her clothes to come in contact with him. Non-threatening he may be, but this was as close as she wanted to get.

"Maybe the townspeople just weren't paying attention to what was going on."

"May be, may be. But there was a man in the town that desired the Faire Sabra and she wouldn't give him the time of day. So — "

"So, he made it hard on her to survive and took exception to the fact that a total stranger won her over," Harleigh added, not proud of the tinge of bitterness she allowed to enter the tone of her voice. But there it was anyway. It couldn't be helped after all she'd been through.

"That's about the gist of it. Then, when she became pregnant, that added more fuel to the fire. Living in sin and all, they called her every vile name in the book and naturally, Quentin tried to protect her. They tried to hang him and it seemed he disappeared before their very eyes. Scared some of the good folk of this territory away. Said he was the devil incarnate.

"It wasn't long, though, before they became convinced that she was possessed and wanted to ride her out of town on a rail. Then suddenly, James Barouche himself disappeared and things slowly died down. There was really no one else that kept the townsfolk stirred up into a frenzy the way he did and the Faire Sabra was left finally alone to raise her daughter, Ladye Faire. She inherited the Rose House but that's another story altogether."

"But what happened to Faire Sabra? That can't be the end of it."

Caleb shifted positions, careful not to stray into Harleigh's space. Knew he was as close as he was going to get. For the moment, anyway. He wasn't going to push it.

He could tell she was fascinated by the story. He wanted to keep her that way so he could spend time with her. He didn't care what the reason.

"Well, it seemed that some residents of this fair city claimed, well, swore that every blue moon they saw Quentin appear. Said he would stay awhile like before then go away again. No one ever really knew for sure. No one was brave enough to check it out. They were convinced this was all the work of the devil. Especially, since Faire Sabra disappeared from the Rose House one day as well."

"How? Does anyone know?"

"There's lots of speculation about that. Some say foul play. Some say the devil got his due. No one will ever know. There were no witnesses to her disappearance."

"What about the daughter? Ladye Faire?"

"Well, things were a little strange there, too. Seems the man in her life just appeared the way her father did. But they pretty much left her alone. At first, anyway."

"What do you mean? Did something bad happen?"

"No one can say for sure. At first, rumor was that she was a harlot just like her mother. What did you expect? It runs in the blood. That sort of thing. He came and went in the same space of time that Quentin did, staying around awhile, getting her started in the Rose House. Then he was gone again. Seemed two things happened during all those comings and goings of his. Roses appeared right along with him. It was like magic.

A new bush would just be there. Then, when he went away, he left her pregnant.

"Then a year later, it happened again. When it happened a third time, people really began to talk, seeing as how each time he came back and was gone again, there was another child left behind."

"What about Ladye Faire? Why did she keep taking him back if he was a no-gooder."

"Well, see, that's the thing. The Ladye Faire loved her man. But she never told anyone anything about him. She'd just smile at anyone who asked and be on her way."

"Surely the local historical society would have something on it, wouldn't they?"

"You'd think, wouldn't you?"

"You mean they don't?"

"Nothing. Not record one. Other than his name on the birth records."

"So, what happened to her?"

"Heck, even that's just a rumor, too, not a proven fact. Always the same time, every blue moon. Like clockwork. Someone kept track of all the mysterious happenings, writing it all down in a journal. Tried publishing but they had no takers except the local paper put it as a weekly short story. It only added more speculation to the mix.

"The Ladye Faire wasn't too concerned that he kept coming and going and leaving her pregnant, it seems. She was perfectly happy with the living gifts he left behind. He returned to her, that's all that mattered. But there were no more children, just the three girls, Liberty, Justice and Harmony. Seems the girls were equally as besotted with their father as their mother was. Many a hair-pulling, free-for-all erupted in this town due to the things said about their Daddy. And those three girls, they were having none of it. A little rowdy. A little wild. Then one day, after the girls were grown, the man came and took the Ladye Faire away. At least, that's the way the local legend goes. And she was all too willing to go with him. Occasionally, it's said, the two of them would return to visit the girls always on a blue moon. Kept a low profile.

"Ladye Faire and Maximillian would come and go to the day, stay the same length of time. But no one seemed to know from where or knew anything about him. The girls and the Ladye Faire were tight-lipped when it came to giving the locals an account of him."

"As if they were guarding some big secret."

If anyone knew about secrets, it was Harleigh. And, she was a master at keeping them. Knew all about being tight-lipped. She was a master at that, too. She knew all too well what lengths she would go to, to protect her own secrets. In this sense, she related to Faire Sabra and Ladye Faire in a way few people could even imagine. Hers may not be the same as theirs, but the reasons for keeping them safe were. She wished there were a way she could find out more about the past inhabitants of the Rose House. The more she heard, the more she wanted to know.

"So, what you're saying is that no one knows any more about the Lady Faire and her family than they did a hundred years ago."

"Well, you see, that's another thing." Caleb shifted his position, making sure it appeared as if his knee grazed the fabric of Harleigh's jeans. Even so, Harleigh felt the jolt of electricity arc up her leg and zap her with the power of his presence.

That's as far as he would take the intimacy today. What he wanted to do was pull her into the circle of his arms and plant a warm kiss on her mouth to see if it was as kissable as it looked.

She shifted her body but the electrical energy still played a tune along the surface of her skin. She even felt her breath hitch, a breathlessness she was trying to get under control. She knew all too well what all of that meant.

The awareness of his magnetism brought a denial to her lips but she buttoned them together and tried to concentrate on what he was saying. She didn't want to admit, or even acknowledge how attracted she was to this man. And heaven knew, she didn't want, or need, *that* kind of trouble.

She would have to remain on alert at all times, she silently told herself and her heart as the heat began to subside from her body.

"Both Faire Sabra and Ladye Faire left journals. The Devreaux girls all swore to that. But none have ever been found. The girls sold the house once they all married and moved away, it passing through a number of families. Then it stood vacant for a number of years. Vandalized as the years went by before it was sold to a politician from a big city. Tallahassee, I think. But his wife didn't like it here so he put it up for sale. Before Mama bought the Rose House, most said they thought it was haunted. Saw shadows and heard things."

"Was the destruction bad?"

"Not really. Broken windows. Loose boards and places pried apart where people thought the journals would be. Back then things were different. By the time

Mama took over the Rose House and made it into a tourist home, the atmosphere of the town had changed. The residence became more close knit. Gathered themselves into a big family, embracing the knowledge that the town could be a better place to live if they took care of their own. And it's been that way ever since I've lived here."

The soft hum of a car engine made Harleigh realize she was so totally absorbed by the story Caleb was telling her that she'd been sitting alone by him for quite awhile. Thankful now for an excuse to extricate herself from his presence, she rose.

"Sounds like someone may be here."

Caleb rose as well, noting the quick withdrawal back inside herself and the wariness creep back into her features. He hated it. He wanted the Harleigh back that had been sitting by him, totally relaxed and at peace. But what could he do?

He wished Grady would hurry up with the information he wanted. Part of him hoped he found what he was looking for and the other part wasn't sure he really wanted to know. Either way, he'd at least know what had caused Harleigh to be so jumpy with every little thing that happened.

"It's probably Mama getting home from church. She's going to have my hide for not going."

Caleb reached out as Harleigh turned to go up the back steps, placing his hand above her elbow to steady her as she went. She gasped as her body welcomed the warm pleasure that seeped its way up her arm and throughout the rest of her body. Her mind, though, was another matter.

She knew she shouldn't be feeling anything. Didn't

want to feel a damn thing for anyone if you got right down to it. What was it about this man, anyway? He'd gotten under her skin in a hurry. And, if his latest touch was any indication, he was slowly working his way into her life and she couldn't have that. She had to get back in control again. Fast.

How had that happened? She didn't have time for this. She wanted to get her new life started without a hitch and she was finding a broad-chested, six foot-two obstacle stretched across her path as if he thought he belonged there.

She followed the fingers of the hand wrapped around her upper arm, up the muscular brown arm attached to it, on up to the smile that thumped her heart as if it were going to make a giant leap from her chest. It was on the tip of her tongue to tell him to back off and take his hand off her person but something in his eyes stopped her and damn it all, there was a smile curving its way along her mouth in answer to his. There wasn't a damn thing she could do about it. But blush.

It crawled its way up the smoothness of her neck and settled into her hairline. Just the way the warmth had done and settled into the core of her. She wanted to protest, to insist that he not touch her but she just couldn't summon the inclination to do so.

This time, she'd let it pass, she decided and went on.

"Mama's probably gonna want to stuff us with some concoction she's whipped up. She was up and at 'em pretty early, stirring this and measuring that. Sunday's her best day."

"I never learned to cook much," Harleigh confessed. "There wasn't much point, we ate out a lot."

Caleb wanted to ask who the "we" in "we" were but didn't want to spoil the moment or ruin the start of a relationship if this was what it was, so he pushed open the door instead.

"Nothing beats a home-cooked meal. Especially Mama's."

"I always wanted to be a chef. I always thought cooking was a fascinating subject. I never had the opportunity, though."

Caleb heard the whimsical note in her voice but tried not to let it show that he noticed. He'd put a bug in his Mama's ear. He was sure she'd take Harleigh under her wing and teach her everything she ever wanted to know about cooking.

CҺAPCER FIVE

ℵ

Caleb sat at one end of the oval table watching his mother as he had all his life. It just seemed a natural thing to do. In this kitchen, things had been discussed, argued over and in this kitchen his mother had baked up the most delicious things and the main ingredient had been love.

Harleigh had deliberately positioned herself at the opposite end of the table away from Caleb, closer to the doorway, he reasoned, so she could bolt like a startled animal if it came down to it.

She'd already had enough of his male presence out on the back porch. Although that had been a pleasant interlude, she wanted no more of it. There was an awareness that flowed between them that she found very hard to ignore. It took all the willpower she could summon, and then some, for her to do so. It was almost as if something in the house pulled them together as one.

She sat watching Caleb as covertly as she could. Watched his hands circle the glass of tea his mother sat before him. The way he held it was almost like a gentle caress and was giving her one of the biggest goose bump moments of her life. Then she realized Mrs. Forrester was speaking to her. Now she was doing it again. Blushing. Seemed like that's all she'd been capable of doing since she came to town.

"Would you like a glass of ice cold tea, Harleigh?"

"That would be great."

"Are you hungry? I can fix you a snack to tide you over until dinner."

"No, Mrs. Forrester. The tea will be fine."

"You call me Kate. Mrs. Forrester was my mother-in-law." She turned back to the counter to continue doing what came naturally. Baking.

Kate Forrester learned in the days and years long past to be observant. Doing so had enabled her to study people and anticipate which way the wind blew so to speak. She was doing just that with the two occupants in the room. And her heart was happy.

She longed for her son to settle himself down with the woman his heart and soul desired and have a family. She knew in her heart that he secretly longed for it, too. Knew that he sought for it while away in the big city. Knew it would make him complete. But he'd never been able to find what he was looking for and wouldn't settle for anything less.

Now, watching the interaction, or lack thereof, between Caleb and Harleigh gave her hope. They were both trying very hard not to notice each other, or let on that there was any pull of the soul between them. Heavens above, anyone with a little gray matter could feel it if they walked in the room. It was thick and hung heavy in the air. Almost as if it were meant to be. And maybe it was.

Things just seemed to happen in this house without explanation. She knew that first hand. There had been no reason for her to end up in this place but something drew her and she followed it.

There'd been a lot going on in this house and its surroundings when she finally came upon it. She'd been told all the horror stories, that it was haunted and all the goings on with the first owners. But she'd ignored all the rumors, gossip and tales they had to tell. She wanted this old house and it wanted her.

Her buying the Rose House was the answer to her prayer. Just as if it were meant to be as well. She'd raised two wonderful kids in this house and never encountered a thing.

Well, that wasn't quite true. She'd heard a few things ... saw a few things. But she never told a soul. She didn't want anything started up again about this wonderful place. She would keep its secrets.

"Has my son given you the grand tour of the Rose House?"

Harleigh squirmed a little in her chair, realizing her thoughts had become so focused on the man at the other end of the table, that everything else had literally vanished. Again, she warned herself to be more careful and keep a fair distance from this man and the feelings she shouldn't be having.

"He told me some of the history of it."

"Oh, did he now?" Kate looked at her first-born with a knowing question in her eyes. She knew he would rather have his fingernails pulled off than discuss anything about this house of theirs. She added another tick mark in her mind in the hooray-for-Caleb column. "Told you all about the two Faire's, did he?"

"Yes, and I found it quite interesting. He also mentioned that your woods in the back were enchanted."

Kate looked over at Caleb and raised her eyebrows. Caleb bent his head at the look she gave him, feeling like he was caught stealing a couple of warm cookies straight out of the oven. He wasn't embarrassed, just a little uncomfortable that he'd been caught.

"Some people call them haunted but I think of them as enchanted. They seem to have a magical quality about them. Did he tell you about the hewed-out log?"

"Actually, I saw that myself. I took a walk down that way and came upon it. I found it to be a charming place."

Kate was a little taken back by her statement. This was interesting. Most people thought it an eerie, otherworldly kind of place that they'd rather not ever see again.

"So, you liked it, did you?"

"Very much."

"I can see that you found our meadow of wildflowers."

Harleigh frowned for a moment then remembered the crown of flowers circling her head. She reached up and removed them, feeling a little foolish and immature that she had done something so juvenile.

"Oh, by all means, leave them on. It fits you. Makes you look a little like a fairy princess. Don't you think so, Caleb?"

"Huh?"

Kate gave a throaty laugh. He had that little-boy-caught expression on his face again and she loved it. This had all the makings of a love connection. She hoped.

"I said, don't you think our Harleigh looks like a

fairy princess with her crown of flowers on her head?"

"Yes, she looks exactly like that." Caleb knew he needed to extract himself from the presence of these two women in order to recoup his emotions. He was getting too many ideas about Harleigh, nor did he miss the little innuendo his mother had thrown into the conversation. Our Harleigh, indeed.

He could see wheels turning in that lovely head of hers already. Knowing his mom, she would try everything short of casting a love spell to get them together but right now, he just wanted to go off and think. To get things straight in his mind. Which wasn't going to be an easy task. Harleigh had gotten under his skin, too soon, too fast and he had to sort it all out before he did something really stupid.

Kate looked them both over and decided to give it a nudge. "Since you haven't showed Harleigh the upper rooms, why don't you do that now? Show her where the girls' rooms were and what we've done with the reconstruction of the place."

"Okay," Caleb agreed reluctantly, knowing if he tried to put it off, she'd find another way to get them alone. Might as well get it over with so he could get back to his own safe haven. "Harleigh, if you will allow me to escort you around, I will give you the best tour ever."

"That's my boy," Kate said, with a twinkle in her eye.

Harleigh had no choice. She certainly couldn't insult her hostess or upset her in any way, not after everything she was doing for her. She could do this, she decided, it was just a tour after all and Kate would be downstairs.

She rose, tension strapping her body in an iron grip but she moved forward. Even managed a smile. She followed the hand that Caleb had so grandly swept through the air like he was an English butler.

"See you kids later," Kate called after them, crossing her fingers that her ploy would work … or at least add more fuel to the fire. She hummed to herself as she turned back to making her famous Rose House cake for the remaining guests.

Harleigh could do nothing but watch the denim-clad backside of Caleb as she followed him up the carpeted stairs. Several times she ordered herself to look away but it was almost impossible, it being right there in front of her face and all.

Think of something else, she told herself sternly. But what in the world would that be?

She nearly collided into Caleb when he stopped abruptly at the top landing. He paused, frowned at her and turned down a hallway that she'd never been down. This was the rest of the guesthouse, she supposed.

"Here we are," he said, stopping in front of a pale pink door with the name Liberty scrolled across it. "As you can see by the name, this was Liberty's room."

He opened the door and stepped in. Harleigh didn't want to follow but did, making sure the door was left open wide in case this was a trick to get her alone in a room where she couldn't protect herself. She knew she shouldn't be thinking along those lines but from the experiences she had with Stewart, that's when he would strike. He was big on doing things to her in public, daring her to misbehave. Then when he got her behind closed doors and she protested, there was hell to pay.

She was having none of that ever again. And she

would start with one Caleb Forrester.

"This really isn't necessary, Caleb. I know you're just doing this to placate your mom. There must be a million other things you want to do besides usher me around."

Caleb took one look at her, realizing her problem. "Well, why don't I do this? I'll go open the doors of Justice and Harmony's room, you can peek inside and when Mama asks you, you can say you've seen them. Okay?"

"I really don't mean to put you off this way," Harleigh said, feeling extremely guilty about the situation. Still, she didn't like the fact that he could read her so well.

"I understand, Harleigh. I do. Go ahead now and look around. I'll go open the other two doors and meet you at the end of the hall. There's a small balcony there that overlooks our enchanted woods. I think you'll like that, too."

Harleigh nodded as Caleb walked out the door, leaving her alone to explore the room on her own. The room was lovely, decorated in soft hues and tones of lavender. It was smaller than the room she was presently occupying and had none of the amenities that she found in hers.

She looked over the furnishings with approval, though. It still held the appeal and nostalgia of an age gone by. She would almost bet this was the original layout that Liberty Devreaux dwelled in during her growing up years. Here there was comfort and belonging. It was in the air. It surrounded Harleigh and made her smile.

It made her want to check out the rooms of the

other two sisters. She turned, half-expecting Caleb to be there but she was alone. That surprised her a little. But she should have known he'd be true to his word.

Closing the door behind her, she walked to the next open door. Harmony. Now she began to wonder about the girl's names. What prompted the Ladye Faire to give them such names? Was there a reason behind each one?

Harmony's room was much the same. Furnished in an era gone by. But this one was decorated with extra throw pillows and done up in a pale peach color, more feminine than Liberty's.

Harleigh hurried on to the door that had Justice scrolled across it. She swung it open expecting much of the same in the way of interior design. What she got was something of a shock. The girl that had occupied this room was nothing short of a tomboy. Not that there was nothing feminine within these walls for there were. Right along with a western gun belt holding a six-shooter inside hanging on the bedpost. Chaps lay across a ladder back chair with a cowboy hat on the top.

No faint of heart, this gal, she thought. She was a gun-toting babe. No taking nothing from anyone kind of gal. Harleigh wished Justice were here to give her pointers. She needed all the help she could get.

Quietly, she closed the door behind her. Her first inclination was to scurry like a mouse back to her own room and hide there. But the time had come for her to stop those kinds of things and meet the world head on. Even if that involved being alone with Caleb.

She had full intentions of opening the door to the landing at the end of the hall where he waited. She swallowed her inhibitions and placed her hand on the knob. But she stopped short of turning it. Yes, she should go through that door to where Caleb waited on the other side. Hadn't she just told herself to meet the world head-on?

No matter how hard she tried she knew inside that she just wasn't ready yet. There was no way she could force herself to do it. No reason to subject herself to things she was slowly learning how to handle. She'd already let her guard down too much where this man was concerned. Her hand dropped from the doorknob and she intended to make a fast getaway.

But Caleb raised his head at the moment she was turning away and their eyes met through the glass window. Before she could retreat, he tugged the door open and offered his hand.

She stepped out and found that he was right. The view of their self-proclaimed enchanted forest was breath taking from this view.

Caleb watched in fascination at the animation spreading across Harleigh's face. Her gaze was fixed intently on the expanse of trees across the way. There was light in her eyes and happiness on her features. And, God help him, he did what he knew he shouldn't do.

He curled his hand around the back of her neck and brought his lips to her before she could protest. He felt her body stiffen and deepened the kiss. He wanted to do more but knew he already stepped across the line. Reluctantly, he released her, saw the shock on her face. Knew he should apologize, but why? He certainly wasn't the least bit sorry.

He stepped away, found there was nothing he could say. Somehow he needed to make her world right. Wanted to take whatever happened to Harleigh and bury it deep in those enchanted woods along with whoever it was that had so injured this woman.

Before he could allow himself to do anything more, he knew the wisest choice was to make a quick exit. He turned to walk away but couldn't leave it like that. As he reached out to grasp the doorknob, he turned back.

"That was good, Harleigh, good and sweet."

א

Harleigh stood where he left her, still reeling from the taste of Caleb on her lips. It was not quite what she expected. From earlier experience from his touch, she expected it to be one wild ride. But, this, this sweet, slow meltdown of her senses was far from that.

The touch of his lips was gentle, a velvet whisper … warm like summer sunshine on a breezy day. Comforting like a well-worn pair of jeans on her body.

There'd been no time for her to react, to push herself away, to tell him no. There'd been no repulsive reflex that kicked in that made her want to gag when his tongue skimmed her lower lip. There'd only been the softness of his kiss sinking into her … a warm sensation spilling over her like warm rain on a summer evening.

His release of her was of the same gentle nature. He smiled, caressed the nape of her neck, eyes warm with affection.

She knew it was best to extract herself from the feelings so she concentrated on the view by turning her attention back to the path she'd walked earlier. She closed her eyes and breathed in deep trying to eject the taste and feel of Caleb from her body and felt the pull of the forest as it reached out to her.

She was beginning to believe the Forrester's claim that the forest was enchanted was right. She'd felt the magical quality it radiated when she stood in the center of the small glade.

And, still felt it, even now.

A soft breeze began to stir around her. She knew what she'd find when she opened her eyes and inched her lashes open to see if she was correct in that assumption. The magical glow was there inside the tree line where she had stood and the tug and pull was strong.

It was almost frightening in a way but she knew that what was there, what urged her to come to it, held no threat.

Then the curling mist began and swirled upward, revealing the couple she'd seen before. Her image smiled. The forest vanished within the mist, the space it occupied giving off a brighter glow. The mist moved, swirling from the forest floor and spread upward like a fast moving tornado.

Harleigh looked down at her hands. The skin on her arms took on the same translucent glow. She raised them to get a closer look, turning them forward and back. She noticed as she did that the air shimmered and pulsated.

She tested it by slowly extending her hand outward. The air wavered. It reminded her of the scenes in a sci-fi movie where the players walked through a gated wheel into other worlds.

In its midst, a clearer image of herself stood, recognition on her face. The man beside her pushed at his ear then lowered his hand to the device he held. He turned in several directions with the device held out in front of him as if trying to locate something, then pointed.

As the glow faded, the mist thinned and the air stilled, the object of the man's attention was the hewn-out log that sat in the clearing. Then as if it had never been, it began to fade away.

Harleigh blinked rapidly and it was gone. Now she was starting to question what she saw. Was her sanity what was at stake here? How could she begin to explain it and sound like she had not lost her mind? Had that really happened? Now that she had time to think about it, she wasn't so sure.

There was no evidence that anything out of the ordinary had taken place. Was all that her imagination then? Had the tales Caleb had been spinning stirred her active imagination into something more than it was?

א

Caleb called into his answering service to check for messages. It would be just like Bettlyn Dooley to go into labor today. Seems like all seven were born on Sunday. Why should number eight be different?

He raised an eyebrow at the message left by his sister, Phoebe. Something about good news and bad news and which did he want first. What the hell was his loving sister up to now?

In a way he was glad she was interrupting his too quiet life. When Phoebe appeared, trouble followed very close behind. What kind of fix had she gotten herself into that she doesn't want that shyster lawyer husband of hers to know about? he wondered.

Maybe if Phoebe paid him a visit, it would keep his mind off his preoccupation with Harleigh. If anyone could do it, it would be his self-assured sister. Harleigh took up more of his thoughts than he would dare admit to anyone, let alone himself.

More than once in his life, he wished he were more like his sister. She always seemed to know what she wanted and went after it. She was tenacious ... resilient, with a personality much like Delilah's. It was very hard to tell her no.

And, Phoebe. Heaven help him if he told her no and meant it. He'd rather incur the wrath of the devil than a dressing down from that woman's razor-edged tongue.

He loved her dearly.

He punched her number up on his cell and hit dial.

"Make it fast, brother, I'm in the middle of something with that hunk of a husband of mine."

"Hey baby sister, quit chewing on the shyster's ear and tell me what you wanted."

"Mmm."

"Phoebe?"

"Mmm."

"The picture I'm getting here is not one I really need. Talk to me and quit with the heavy breathing."

"Damn it Caleb, can't you tell I'm busy at the moment!"

"Evidently your good news, bad news was something of a joke, huh?"

"Hell, no, it wasn't a joke. Wait a minute." Caleb

heard smacking of the lips and chuckled. "Don't move from that position, sweetcakes. This'll only take a minute."

More smacking and heavy breathing sounded in Caleb's ear. "Phoebe?"

"Okay, Caleb, listen up."

"I'm listening."

"First the good news. Are you anywhere near Mom?"

"Not right at the moment. I'm standing on my front porch." He almost added, looking at the most beautiful woman in the world but he held his tongue. Phoebe would come on like a drill sergeant trying to get to the bottom of it.

"Good! I think I'm pregnant, Callie."

Caleb took note of her pet name for him, a telltale sign that she was excited. He was glad for her, too. He knew how much she wanted a baby but couldn't let a chance to throw a dart at Gentry Beckett go by.

"Heaven help us. That's all we need … another Gentry running around the countryside all dressed up in Armani suits."

"Caleb Forrester, if I could get my hands on you, I'd give you a nugget for slandering the most brilliant attorney in the lower forty-eight … maybe even the world."

"Hah! In your dreams, baby sister."

"Only one thing, though."

"And, what is that, pray tell?"

"Don't tell Mom."

"Why ever not?"

It was then that Caleb took note of the underlying edginess lacing her voice. He pushed the familiar banter aside to assimilate what she wasn't saying.

He knew Phoebe and Gentry had been trying for a couple of years to start a family without any luck. She'd had a few false alarms, even a couple of pregnancies only to lose the child in the first trimester. Another disappointment was the underlying cause for the request. Not only for the two of them but for his mother, too.

"I didn't want to even breathe with a flicker of hope this time. I'm already into my fifth month, Callie. My fifth month! I've never been this far before."

"Baby, that's wonderful."

"That's why I don't want to tell Mom yet. You know how much she wants a grandchild to run the hallways of the Rose House."

"Okay. I won't say a word," Caleb promised. "So, what's the bad news?"

"I'm gonna be in your face in a couple of weeks, big brother!"

"Oh, great, you mean I'm going to have to put up with your ugly face every time I open my eyes?"

"Not only that dearest brother of mine, but Gentry's coming, too."

Caleb's groan was deep and audible. "Tell me it ain't so! Anything but having to look at that pretty boy of yours."

"Aren't you the lucky one?" Phoebe grew serious now as she needed to give the reason for the impending visit. "All kidding aside, Caleb, Gentry and I want to tell Mama ourselves. You know how long she's been praying for this and how many times I've let her down."

"Come on, Phebs, you know that none of that was

your fault. It just wasn't the right time, that's all."

He could hear the tears in her voice and wished he were there so he could soothe them away like he used to. But, then, he knew that Gentry loved his little sister and Caleb had relinquished that duty to him when she had given him her heart.

"That may be and that's one reason why I haven't said anything till now. The OB thinks I have an excellent chance now to make it full term since I made it through the first trimester and well in to the second."

Phoebe's heart hurt from the loss of the miscarriages, the babies that were never to be that she wanted so much. That Gentry wanted. The times that the disappointment overpowered her sense of purpose.

She was scared. Scared through and through but could not, *would* not, breathe a word of it to anyone. There was this underlying fear that if she voiced the trepidation she felt, it would come to pass. And, heaven knew, she didn't think she could survive another devastating loss.

She shook it all away in favor of positive thinking. And, faith. She had to have faith. That and hope that she would come through this pregnancy with the end result being a bouncing baby boy, or girl. She didn't care which. She just wanted to hold that warm, cuddly bundle in her arms and give it all the love that was bursting to come out.

Caleb couldn't help it. He could hear her fear churning and wanted to give her something to take her mind off her inner turmoil. He knew it would peak her interest and her thoughts would be focused on him.

"By the way, there's someone I want you to meet …" The pager on Caleb's belt erupted with a Dixie jingle, loud and insistent. "Phebs, I hate to interrupt this little chat of ours but I'm getting a med buzz. Call me later, 'kay?"

"Wait, is it a girl? You want me to meet a girl?"

"You could say that. I just want to see what you think."

"Mmm. Must be serious if you want me to take a look at her. Got your heart throbbing, huh?"

"Phebs, I got to go."

"Okay, okay. Don't forget, Callie. Mum on my news until I get there. Promise?"

"You got it. See you in a few. Say hello to your pretty boy toy for me."

Caleb heard her shriek then a gleeful chuckle as he punched the end button on his cell. He held up his pager, pushed for the number to be displayed and frowned. The Wilson's. Hmm. Wonder what's going on there?

He punched in the number, listened to the rings and waited.

"Hello, Doc, is that you?"

"Yeah, Sally Ann, what's up?"

"Ah, Doc, it's my Johnny," she told him, a little panic entering into the tone of her voice.

Caleb knew that Johnny was the middle child, a five year old with a sense of grand adventure about him. He wanted to go and do. Just watching him on the move made Caleb tired.

And, he was also the child that Sally Ann was so afraid of losing. There had been so many complications during the pregnancy and in the early months of his life that were frightening.

But you couldn't tell it now. The boy only had one

speed. Warp speed and it was turbo charged.

"What's the problem with Johnny?"

"You know there's no keeping him down, Doc," Sally told him, in a vain attempt to explain the situation.

"And?" Caleb prompted.

"He decided he wanted to climb the sycamore tree out in the back field. He was about halfway up and fell."

Caleb envisioned the daredevil scamp scrambling up a tree like a monkey. Then the doctor in him kicked in. "Can you tell if anything's broken?"

"There's something wrong with his shoulder, Doc. It looks like it's fallen." The tears were there now along with a touch of hysteria in her voice.

"Fallen? Sally Ann, calm down and tell me what you see."

"But that's what I see. It looks so strange. Oh God, Doc, what am I gonna do?"

"Don't move him and I'll be right there."

א

Harleigh watched Caleb as he vaulted off his porch and ran to his truck. Then was back out again in a flash, taking the steps in one leap and through the front door. Just as quickly he returned carrying a black bag. His medical bag, she supposed, wondering where he was off to with such an intent look on his face.

A medical emergency, probably. Must be nice, having someone need you like that.

Harleigh turned away, slipped back into the hallway and meant to go on to her room. Instead, she decided to return to the kitchen and seek the company of Ma Forrester.

She was there, as if she were waiting for her. That gave Harleigh pause to wonder.

She shrugged that eerie feeling away. "Mind if I sit with you awhile, Kate?"

"Not at all. You sit right down and make yourself at home. How'd ya like the view?"

"Oh that was wonderful."

"But, you're frowning," Kate observed.

"Well, you can't beat the view but, uh ..."

"But?"

"Things seemed to happen to me." Harleigh realized how silly that sounded, wondered if Kate thought she was crazy. "Now it sounds so absurd."

Kate pulled out a chair and took a seat. "Why don't we talk about it? I want you to feel at home, to like it here."

"Oh, I do like it here. This is the most amazing place, this Rose House of yours. I've never felt such a welcome as when I stepped upon the veranda and Caleb escorted me through the door."

"That's good to know." Kate scooted her chair close in to the table, settling in for a girl-to-girl chat. It'd been a while since she'd a heart-to-heart with anyone and she was so looking forward to this. "Now, tell me what bothers you about the Rose House."

"I can't say anything really bothers me, Kate, it's just ...," Harleigh paused. What would this woman that she liked so much think if she told her what she'd seen, what she felt or the way the house seemed to wrap around her and draw her close in a warm embrace.

"Just what?" Kate prompted.

"You'd think I was losing my mind."

"Let me be the judge of that, Harleigh. It may not be as strange as you think."

"I don't know, Kate, there've been a lot of strange happenings in the past then since I came here these happenings of mine have escalated."

Kate sensed Harleigh's reluctance to reveal herself. Then decided to make it easy for her. "I know what you mean. The same thing happened to me."

"You're just saying that to make me feel better, aren't you?"

"In a way, I guess."

"It isn't necessary."

"I know it isn't but that doesn't take away the fact that I want you to be comfortable here. I sense that you're hiding, that you're running. I can tell you first hand that you'll be protected here."

Harleigh froze. How could she be so transparent that everyone would know her deepest secrets? If that were the case, then she would have to hit the ground running and keep on going in order to stay hidden. Right now, all she wanted to do was stay here, dig in and become a part of whatever pulled at her. She loved this place but she'd have to leave soon if she was this easy to read, no matter how many times she swore this was the end of the line, end of her running. This had given her breathing room, at least. A stab of regret sliced through her. Now it was back to being scared of her own shadow and looking back as she ran.

It was a never-ending phase of her life. The running.

Keep on running? How long was she going to have

to be on the run? Forever? Wasn't there ever going to be a time when she could just live and love like a normal person?

Normal? For her, normal was forever going to be looking over her shoulder, watching and waiting in fear every single second of every day. And that knowledge hurt.

She'd had a taste of freedom, had a taste of normal, had a taste of what could be. She would relish that, would savor those memories, would always remember what could have been.

"Harleigh? Do you hear me?"

Harleigh realized that she'd been so deep in misery that Kate had been talking to her and she hadn't heard a word. She also realized it was time to prepare, make plans and hit the road.

"Yes, Kate I hear you. Look, I, uh, I hate to cut our talk short but there are things I need to be doing so I'll talk to you later."

Kate allowed her the space to get as far as the doorway. She said softly, "You don't have to run, Harleigh. No one here will hurt you. Please, come back and sit a spell with me."

Harleigh didn't want to turn back, didn't want to give Kate the chance to know how much she wanted to do just that. Didn't want her to see how scared she was. Yet, she owed this wonderful lady, at least a little of her time before she turned tail and ran.

She turned to face Kate and choked off a gasp. She couldn't tell where Kate ended and the shimmer began. It was as if they were one. She started to speak but the fascination of what she saw kept her silent.

Kate lifted a hand toward her and beckoned.

"Come back and sit down. Let's talk."

Harleigh was more than reluctant to move, to do anything. She was held spellbound. Yet, at the same time, she felt a flood of gentle warmth surround her.

"We will keep you safe and hide your secrets."

She heard the words, heard the silvery tinkle of a voice but Kate's mouth had not moved. The shimmer danced and slipped from view. Kate moved then and patted the spot near Harleigh's empty tea glass.

"What did you say?"

Harleigh heard herself ask the question but the voice that went with it was slightly breathless. She took a few tentative steps forward, back inside the doorway. She wanted to hear those words again, wanted to make sure she heard right and wanted to ask what she meant. Even how Kate knew so much about her when she hadn't uttered not one syllable to a single soul in this town.

"I said sit down and let's talk."

Harleigh blinked away her bewilderment, not sure now what she'd heard. Was there something wrong with her hearing then? Right now things appeared so ... normal.

Then remembering her new purpose in life, to cast off the old shell of Harleigh and become the new, she pulled out the chair she previously sat in and eased down into the seat like she was about to sit on something that would break.

"Kate," she began, wondering what she was going to say. Was she going to appear just a little shy of this side of crazy? To keep her nervous fingers busy, she picked up a saltshaker and twirled it between her fingers. "A few moments ago ... just now ... I mean ..."

"What is it, child?"

"You're going to think I'm crazy," Harleigh offered.

"I told you there isn't a thing that you could tell me that would make me believe that of you, Harleigh. My eyesight is still as good as it ever was, twenty-twenty vision and you're a good grounded girl. Give it a chance, honey. Things will work out for you. We'll all pitch in and help you with whatever you need."

"Thanks, I appreciate that you want to help me but some things you have to do on your own."

"That's true. I've certainly been there. Still, a shoulder to lean on, an extra pair of helping hands, an ear just to listen, those things will get you through whatever hardships and problems you endure or suffer."

"You may be right," Harleigh agreed, giving her that but still unwilling to unload the kind of baggage she carried.

"Now, what was it you wanted to ask me?"

Harleigh smiled. She really liked this woman. "Well, a few minutes ago when I turned back to you, there was this ... light, I guess. Yes, a shimmering light that I saw around you, maybe near you. See, I told you it was crazy," Harleigh told her, embarrassed now as it indeed sounded a tad over the top to her own ears.

"Oh, I don't know about that. Nothing in or around the Rose House surprises me. Besides, there probably was an aura here."

"What? Do you mean I actually saw that?" Harleigh's laugh was just short of a croak.

"It's the house. I'm sure Caleb touched on the history of this wonderful old place."

"Yes, he did but I thought he was just pulling my leg." Harleigh felt her face burn at the reference to her anatomy. The image of his hands wrapped around her ankles flitted through her brain. She was surprised by what she felt. It certainly wasn't fear. She pushed it away, refusing to try to dissect that emotion.

"Knowing my son, he was trying to impress you with the local folklore and legends. He thinks he has bragging rights since this will all be his some day."

"It's a lot to brag about in my opinion, this is such a great place. I'm really enjoying spending time here."

"Then, you won't leave? Any time, soon anyway?"

Harleigh couldn't figure a way out of giving her an answer as that plan was already spinning around in her head like wool on a spinning wheel so she skirted around it with another question. Kate recognized it for what it was but never mentioned it. It was enough that the girl was comfortable enough to be sitting with her and talking.

"What did you mean earlier when you said you would keep me safe and hide my secrets?"

"Earlier? When?"

"Remember earlier when I was telling you about the shimmering light?"

"Yeah, I remember."

"Well, at the same time the light was shimmering, you were saying that you would keep me safe and hide my secrets. I could hear the words but it was like you weren't saying them. What I mean is I could hear but I couldn't see your mouth moving. You were just sitting there smiling at me."

"It's the house, Harleigh. This house is special. Now, I'm the one who should say this sounds a little crazy, if it was anyone else I'd keep my mouth zipped but I can see you're special, too."

"That sounds a little ..."

"Crazy?"

Kate lifted her glass of tea to her lips and sipped, waiting for Harleigh's response. There was a hint of a knowing smile on her lips. She knew it sounded crazy, *was* crazy but there was something about this house. It chose its occupants very carefully. But do you explain something like that to non-believers? Thankfully, the majority of the residents of Nowhere were.

Of course, there were a few cynics, skeptics and doubting Thomases. But those wouldn't have believed, if it jumped up and bit them on the backside.

Harleigh could think of no response, wasn't sure there was one. Then it occurred to her that she was actually engaged in conversation, albeit wobbly as it was, she was still sitting here talking like a normal person. Still, what could she say now?

If she said it was just on the short side of lunacy, would Kate resent her? Dare she say what she truly felt? Anytime she'd tried that before she was struck down with such staggering force, she was surprised she recovered.

Yes, she remembered, she had recovered but there had been a price to pay. She'd picked up all the broken pieces and precariously super-glued them back together. She doubted she would ever be able to accomplish that feat again.

Kate reached out to Harleigh, placing her hand atop hers when she noticed the hesitancy, the slight agitation and frustration at trying to come up with a simple answer.

"It's okay, Harleigh. It is crazy. One day, I'd like to tell you about myself and how this house chose me. And, I want you to know that I'm here if you need someone to shoulder your burden with. All of us are."

Then like magic, the light shimmered again. There was no sound. Nothing.

All else receded as if it were nonexistent. At that moment, to Harleigh, it was.

And, like before, she was surrounded in a gentle warmth and with the warmth, the shimmer wavered and vanished.

Well, Harleigh contemplated, a deep frown burrowing across her features, that certainly gave her a lot of food for thought.

א

Time seemed to stand still in Nowhere. She knew it was passing by but peace and harmony ruled the day. Not to say nothing ever happened here. There were the occasional overturned garbage cans and dented mailboxes. Teenage mischief according to the sheriff. Nothing to be concerned about. He was a member of that elite tribe, once upon a time, he was fond of saying while he switched that ever-present toothpick from one side of his mouth to the other.

Harleigh was getting used to the citizens of this little burg. She found herself looking forward to each day at the café, looked forward to the presence of the colorful local folk as they frequented this wonderful place she found. No, chose her.

According to Kate, everything happens for a reason. And she was beginning to believe it. If it had been her fate to endure the hell Stewart had put her through to get to Nowhere, then it was worth every punch, every bruise, every drop of spilled blood.

Every time she allowed those thoughts to surface, the panic twisted her stomach and tightened her chest. She awarded herself by a silent pat on the back that she'd locked them up and they hadn't been able to escape to overwhelm her of late.

She'd even stopped stiffening and flinching with alarm every time the café opened and a stranger walked through the door. She'd always have her guard up, she knew that, but she also knew she didn't have to always be suspicious of every person she met.

Just as these thoughts were running through her mind, her skin began to crawl with fear. She stopped wiping down the counter long enough to glance out the window and her heart screeched to a stop a full minute before it started beating again. She could hear the surge of blood in her ears, feel the erratic pounding in her chest, feel her lungs seize the last bit of air. She felt the resistance against it and struggled to drag a deep breath inside.

It was all she could do to keep herself upright. The panicked seized her by the throat and the last thing she remembered was Stewart walking through the door with Grady by his side.

Chapter Six

ℵ

"Deep breath, Harleigh," Caleb said. "Take a deep breath." He tapped her on the cheek lightly to try to bring her to the surface.

From a long way away, Harleigh heard the words. Confusion held her hostage then the wheels of her brain began a slow turn to the surface. Her stomach began the remembered churn.

"Please, Caleb, don't let him near me. Don't let him hurt me."

"It's okay, honey. You're safe. Nothing can hurt you here."

"Promise me, Caleb, promise me."

He could see the frenetic hysteria building in the way her body was wired with tension, could see the blinding terror that seized her, catapulting her beyond the capacity to sort through and understand what was happening.

Panic surrounded her like a dust storm and rode her high on the back of a wild stallion. All she wanted to do was get off the back of this raging monster and catch her breath.

Caleb took her vitals again and his own settled back into their normal rhythm when he found they were stabilizing. He'd been scared nearly out of his own skin when Grady had opened the door to his clinic and just stood there with Harleigh in his arms, a stricken look of what-do-I-do-now on his face.

Immediately, Caleb had taken her from his arms into his own and even that little gesture seemed so right. That she should be there.

Now he watched as Harleigh struggled to surface from whatever nightmare had its tentacles wrapped tight around her. He knew better than to touch her at this point. He'd learned that from her last excursion into darkness. Instead, he stood by and helplessly watched her break the surface, watched the paleness recede from her face, and the shudders rack her body and subside.

Finally, Harleigh was able to open her eyes, was able to only because Caleb had reassured her that she was out of harm's way.

"Where is he?"

"Where's who?"

"Stewart! Where is he? Is he still with Grady?"

"Stewart who, Harleigh? I don't know who you mean."

Harleigh felt the panic rise like a flash flood through her soul. She knew if she didn't stop, if she didn't get herself under control she'd have a full-fledged panic attack and there'd be no stopping the disgrace she'd bring upon her head. Talons of steel were already banding about her chest, tightening, squeezing, crushing. Slowly, the panic was winning, knew it was wrong before the words ever spilled out of her mouth.

"Why are you lying to me? Are you all in this together?" she accused, knowing how false the words rang in her ears.

"Harleigh, stop for a minute and take deep breaths. It'll help clear your head," Caleb told her, her words stabbing at him painfully hurting him more than they should. He knew she wasn't yet fully coherent, knew she was still caught in the throes of delusion. Still, the pain was there and he did his best to push it aside. "Then I want you to think about what you just said."

She did, think about it that is, and shamed rolled over her like water running off a duck's back. She couldn't look him in the eye for the accusations she'd just flung his way. How would she ever be able to look at him again after that senseless act?

Knowing how she was feeling, he turned away, pulled a cup from the water tank and filled it with water. He palmed a couple of Tylenol and held out his hand.

"Here, take these." He held out the paper cup as she picked the two tablets out of his hand. "It's just Tylenol. I'm sure you have the beginnings of a pounder hammering at you."

"Thanks." What else could she say to relieve the tension she was feeling? Was Stewart right then? Was everything she did stupid? "I think you may be right."

"Harleigh?"

She heard the unasked questions. Truth. Knew it was time for truth. She owed him that. "Stewart is my ex-husband. Where is he?"

"I don't believe I've had the pleasure or displeasure of meeting your ex-husband."

"But you must have. He was there with Grady. I—I saw him." She blinked back the confusion, popped the pills in her mouth, taking a deep swallow of the water and handed the cup back to Caleb.

"I'm not sure who you saw. I wasn't there. Grady will be swinging by with Sophy in a few minutes, we'll ask him. In the meantime, if you want to talk about it, I'll be glad to listen."

Harleigh looked at him then, the sordid details of the last few years on the very edge of spewing out. But she couldn't tell him, couldn't tell him the dark secrets. Could never let anyone know the extent of the humiliation she'd suffered, the damage to her soul. Yet she owed him something. From day one, he and this town had seen after her.

"There's not a whole lot I can tell you at this point and time. I have secrets, Caleb," she confided. "Dark ugly secrets."

"Everyone has a skeleton or two in their closet, honey. There's always one thing in everyone's past that they wouldn't want spread around."

She heard no criticism when he spoke, no superficial concern for her well-being or self-righteousness superiority. Just a simple explanation of circumstances. Because of it, Harleigh wanted to offer an explanation of her own. She opened her mouth but the opening of the outer door had her closing it again.

"Hey, good-looking, you in here?"

Harleigh felt the silk of that voice slide across her skin and the immediate smile that lit up Caleb's face told the story. She shouldn't feel so bereft, she told herself when he turned away.

He'd only taken two steps when the door was thrown open and a petite brunette flung herself at Caleb with such force it knocked his tall frame backwards. And for a reason that Harleigh didn't want to rational-ize into a sensible action, her heart dipped in her chest.

"Whoa, baby cakes, you're about to crack my ribs."

Baby cakes. A sweet endearment. No doubt now, who this lovely creature was. Harleigh's heart took another dip and skittered. The pleasure etched on Caleb's features as he held the young woman in his heart was a testament to his feelings.

She wanted to edge herself around these two individuals doing a happy dance in the center of the room and disappear out the door. Quietly. Unobtrusively.

Dropping down off the examining table, she held on to the edge as the room swirled then righted itself. She waited a moment then proceeded across the floor, hoping to remain nothing more than a moving shadow.

"Callie, I think your patient is escaping."

This statement jerked Caleb's head upright and put a sharpness in the tone of his voice. "Harleigh, where do you think you're skulking off to?"

The razor-sharp harshness scratched at her skin with a brutality she'd never experienced with an ex-husband who had beaten her senseless. But she wasn't given time to wonder at it. Her natural instinct for survival kicked in, had her shuffling backward until her back hit the hard surface of the wall. Had her flinging her hands up to protect herself from the brutality that would be forthcoming before she could stop the action.

"Caleb! What have you done to this poor creature that has her cringing in your presence! Have you lost your mind? The woman is totally terrified of you!"

"Phoebe, let it lie. You don't know what it's about."

"Damn it, Caleb, you're supposed to be a doctor.

What kind of medicine are you practicing here? Scaring the patients to death?"

"Damn it, Phebs, would you shut the hell up!"

When she opened her eyes and lowered her arms, Harleigh was sure she'd find her supporter cowering in terror from the dangerous anger in Caleb's voice. Instead she watched in detached fascination as a brunette-topped whirling dervish bore down on her, eyes flashing with determination.

"I'm taking her to Mom, *Dr.* Forrester."

Caleb knew there would be no talking to Phoebe when she was like this, no explaining what had transpired, what Harleigh herself had been through.

Dutifully, he closed the clinic, all the while muttering under his breath what a hardheaded, stubborn brat his sister was and followed behind her while she maneuvered the shiny black Jag out of his parking lot, vaguely wondering where that spiffy-dressed brother-in-law of his was when he needed him. He was the only man on the face of the earth who could handle Phoebe when she was in a snit.

"You don't have to do this," Harleigh was saying, all the time wondering who this person was that had deliberately snatched her away from right under Caleb's nose.

The most astounding thing of that whole action was that Caleb hadn't done a thing to stop her.

"Yes, I do. Sometimes Caleb doesn't have brain one in his head when it comes to women and what they need."

"But …"

"No, buts, Miss. Caleb is a great doctor, don't get me wrong and I love him dearly. If you were suffering from an injury, bleeding profusely, had a broken arm that needed setting, or a hundred other medical reasons he could fix, he's the best you can find. But when it comes to inner healing, he hurts right along with you."

"Oh."

"Just oh? Mmm. Not too talkative are you?"

Harleigh didn't have a clue how to answer. The whole thing was just a bit bizarre. They were headed in the right direction to the Rose House, though, she noted, at least she wasn't being abducted.

"Doesn't matter," Phoebe told her. She took one look at the sheer bafflement on her passenger's face and vaguely wondered if this was Caleb's latest bird with a broken wing. She decided to push. "Yeah, Caleb has a hard-head, always wondered how such a bleeding heart became a doctor."

"But, Caleb doesn't have all the facts. No one does."

"Well, now's a good a time as any to tell someone the facts. Hi, I'm Phoebe, Caleb's sister. And you?"

Well, that answered that, Harleigh thought, as a warm pleasing rhythm echoed in the area of her heart. "Harleigh Bleu."

"Nice to meet you, Harleigh. What's up?"

"Up?"

"What gives with you and my brother?" Phoebe asked briskly.

"I'm not sure what you mean," Harleigh answered her, still trying to make sense of the conversation. She was finding it hard to think, hard to keep up.

"Sure you do. You got a thing for Caleb?" she teased. She glanced over at Harleigh to gauge her reaction to that question. It was not what she expected, certainly not something you get from ribbing someone for fun.

Harleigh went totally still. Her breath froze right along with her heartbeat. She was on a downhill slide to total shut down and didn't know how to stop it. Panic attacks were one thing, but this, this full-blown escape inside herself was something new, something she never experienced before. And it frightened her just as much as the abuse she'd received from Stewart's hands.

Phoebe reached out a hand to touch her, took note of the blank expression on Harleigh's face, and pulled over to the side of the road. "Harleigh? Are you okay? You're awfully pale."

Phoebe placed her hands over Harleigh's. They were ice-cold. She took one in her hand, rubbed vigorously, then did the same with the other.

Harleigh blinked, stared down at the hands rubbing over hers, and jerked them back as if she'd been burned. Awareness of the situation startled her then shame washed over her in waves. She grabbed for the door handle but missed and felt the tears build and burn behind her eyes.

"Harleigh, it's okay. I was only joking. Sometimes my big mouth runs away with itself and crazy things comes out of it. Caleb's always saying so."

Phoebe felt the pain alter and twist in her heart as she held on to Harleigh. She couldn't understand what she'd done to warrant this type of reaction. It was only a joke, she assured herself. A joke it may have been but whatever it was, she, Phoebe, was at fault. She and only she was to blame.

She'd get to the bottom of it. Down to the dirty bottom.

Phoebe kept her eye on Harleigh as she pulled her cell phone from her purse and flipped it open. She punched in Delilah's number and waited.

"Come on, come on, be there, be there," she said into the ringing phone.

She heard the click and knew it was the answering machine.

"You have reached the Cassidy residence. Please leave a message and we'll return your call as soon as possible."

"Damn it, Delilah. I need to talk to you now!"

"Hey, Phebs! Calm down. What's got you going into overload?"

"Come over to Mom's ASAP."

Sundance looked down at the phone in her hand, a phone that had just had a disturbed frantic woman on the other end and frowned. She turned to her sister-in-law with mild stupefaction on her face.

"Hey, Dee," she called out to Delilah. Butch had just come home and they were playing with the twins in the middle of the living room floor. She could hear the squeak of the squeeze toys, the laughter of the parents and the giggles of babies, a happy family. It sounded good to her ears. "Hey, Dee, you had a frantic call from Phoebe. Wants you to go over to Ma's ASAP, she said."

Sundance replaced the receiver in the cradle and walked to the doorway, took pleasure in watching the scramble of bodies before she interrupted again. She surveyed what she always thought of as family enter-tainment. Butch had Lilah down on her back blowing kisses on her tummy, while Delilah was lying on her back body lifting Chandler in the air.

"I hate to interrupt this little family gathering, guys, but I think there is a family crisis over at Ma Forrester's."

"What makes you say that, Sunny?" Delilah asked as she lowered her twin and turned toward Sundance.

"Something in Phoebe's voice. There's not much that frazzles our Phoebe but something has. Wants you to get over there on the double. I'll go with you if you want. Sounds like an emergency."

"Give me a sec." She rose, planted kisses on both kids, planted a more lingering one on Butch's lips. "I'll change and be right back."

א

Harleigh glanced over at Phoebe and tried to smile. She realized too late that she'd overreacted and hadn't a clue as to how to rectify the situation. She felt like such an idiot. She wished she had more social skills but those had been lost somewhere along the line. She'd lost those along with her dignity and self-esteem.

Somewhere deep inside, she drew on an inner strength that had been building since she had stepped off that bus and landed in this town. She felt it swell from within and it seemed like she could feel it surge and soar upward, outward into the rest of her body.

"I'm really sorry," Harleigh began, knowing an apology wasn't enough to make up for her behavior.

Phoebe pulled the car back on the road and headed home. "There's nothing to be sorry for except scaring ten years off my life."

Harleigh held back a groan and crossed her hands

in her lap. She tried not to fidget, tried not to worry her fingers, tried to ignore the embarrassment that still clung to her cheeks and clogged her throat with unwanted tears.

"I don't know what to say, Phoebe. I'm not good at this sort of thing."

"What sort of thing?"

"You know … this."

"Well, no, I don't know what this is."

Harleigh sighed deep and long. How could she explain to Caleb's sister what a failure she was? She covered her face with her hands, took another deep breath with the thought that this situation shouldn't be so hard to explain.

Maybe for normal people but for her it was like trying to grind stone with a toothpick. Impossible. No, not impossible, she told herself as she straightened, pulled her hands away. Wasn't that what this new path she was on all about? So she could be a normal, every day person?

She was going to be this normal, everyday person that she'd step into the shoes of, if it killed her.

"I don't know what happened, Phoebe," she confessed. "I guess I just stopped thinking. It's not something that has ever happened to me before. Not like that, anyway."

"One thing you're going to learn about this town is that these people care about you in a way that you won't find anywhere else. Besides, what you need is a support group."

"A support group? For what?"

"This is only my opinion, of course, but from the looks of things you could use a friend."

"I'm making friends here, Phoebe. Everyone has been great, especially your mom and brother. I couldn't have asked for more."

"No, Harleigh. You need friends. Girl pals. Ones that will stand beside you, hold you up, hold you together through any crisis. And believe me, we all have them."

"I've never had anyone that close," she admitted.

"Everyone needs a pal. Ones that will laugh with you, sometimes laugh at you. Ones that will cry with you, gossip with you, just be silly with."

Harleigh longed for what Phoebe made sound so simple. But she knew she couldn't take the chance of being close to anyone. Couldn't allow anyone within her circle no matter how much she wanted it. She'd given up on that a long time ago. With the way things stood now, it was too dangerous to get involved in any kind of relationship.

"That's a nice thought, Phoebe, it really is. But I've always been a loner."

"Yeah, but sometimes even a loner needs a shoulder, you know? It's all about needing. What's the harm in needing?"

Everything, Harleigh thought to herself. Everything.

ℵ

Instead of stopping at the Rose House when she pulled the Jag into the driveway, Phoebe followed the drive around the house and stopped in front of Harleigh's dream.

"Come on, let's go raid Caleb's fridge. The troops will be here soon."

What did she mean? The troops? Who could she be talking about?

Then Harleigh remembered vaguely that Phoebe had put through a call to Delilah when she had gone ballistic on her. Okay, she could be with Delilah. She knew her, trusted her as much as she allowed herself to trust anyone.

She didn't ask, didn't want to open herself up to anything else. She'd already said and done enough on the crazy scale for one night.

Riding in the car with the ever inquisitive Phoebe had drained all her reserves. The girl chattered like a flock of birds and wouldn't stop questioning and pushing and trying to involve herself with Harleigh's troubles.

And with the kind of troubles she had, Harleigh didn't wish them on anyone. She tried to hold Phoebe at arm's length. But trying to hold Phoebe back was trying to hold back a raging bull.

"Are you coming, Harleigh?"

The look in Phoebe's eyes had Harleigh reaching for the door handle, getting out of the car and following her up the front steps and onto the porch without even thinking to say no.

The house was exactly like she'd envisioned. But even more as Phoebe opened the door and she, Harleigh, entered on her heels like an over-excited puppy.

She was inside! Inside what had been a dream, the adhesive that held her together in the bad times. Her hope, her light in the darkest of moments. She wasn't prepared for the elation she felt, the lifting of her spirits. It was the most wonderful of all the feelings she'd ever experienced.

"This is … extraordinary!" She breathed the words, feeling so breathless from it all.

"Yeah, it is kinda nice. Caleb loves this place. Says it says welcome every time he steps in the door."

Harleigh understood. She was feeling much the same way. But this she would keep to herself. Would keep it, remember it when she needed to and cherish.

"Come into the kitchen and let's see what big brother has to eat and drink." She yanked open the fridge, grumbled to herself and shut it again. "Who does the shopping around here? Doesn't even have any cold beer in there or pizza to nibble on. Creep!"

Harleigh watched in silence as Phoebe filled a tea-pot with water, placed it on the ceramic top of the stove and turned the unit on. While waiting for the water to boil, she went through the cupboards in search of tea, cups and all the fixings.

Harleigh took this time when Phoebe was absorbed with the hunt to step back and take a look at this young woman who had literally kidnapped her. Her looks were as deceptive as Stewart's, she realized. Phoebe's pixie-cute looks exuded a sweet innocence that she, Harleigh, knew to be way off the mark.

She was strong inside, this sister of Caleb's. And fearless, Harleigh added. She had to be to just up and inform Caleb of what she was doing, practically daring him to voice an objection.

Oh, to be able to have enough confidence and in-testinal fortitude to speak your mind. To just say what you thought and not give a flying flip what anyone thought.

"So, Harleigh. What's with you and Caleb?"

The screeching of tires and the sound of gravel flying ended any further conversation and Harleigh was glad for it. There was no way she could have explained what was between her and Caleb Forrester. How could she explain it to anyone else when she couldn't explain it to herself? She only knew that whatever it was, she couldn't allow it to develop.

If she did and in the event that Stewart ever found out about it, he may strike out at Caleb … or any of the people who'd helped her along the way. And this she couldn't allow.

Before Phoebe could get the door, Delilah, Sophy and someone Harleigh had never seen before literally burst through the door.

"What's the emergency? Is your mother all right? What can we do to help?"

Harleigh couldn't tell who said what but the girls had pushed their way into the living room and were backing Phoebe into the kitchen.

"Oh, hi, Harleigh, how goes it?" Delilah greeted and commented all in one breath.

"Who's hurt?" Sophy wanted to know.

"Tell us what's going on."

While the girls conversed in a style all their own, talking over and around each other in a blast of questions and comments, Harleigh tried to keep up. It was one of the hardest conversations she'd ever tried to follow. Just when she thought she was getting everything sorted out, all four young women turned in unison and stared at her.

It made her feel like she had something all over her face at the curious way they were looking her over.

Then the friendly exchange of banter finally clicked and she realized they'd been talking about her.

They all walked forward, each pulling out a chair and sat as if it had all been choreographed. Crossing their arms in front of them on the tabletop, they sat expectantly as if they were going to share a long long talk. She wanted no part of that. It was time to leave.

The teakettle whistled. "Tea, everyone?"

"Yeah, that will be great," the girls chorused in unity.

"I need to be getting home." Harleigh slipped wayward strands of hair back behind her ear and started to rise.

"Please, stay with us. Let's talk and see what we can do to help you."

Harleigh looked from one hopeful face to another. What a blessing it would be to unload all her problems … but she knew the kind of baggage she carried would have to stay locked inside her own heart.

Nonetheless, they'd taken her by surprise with their sincerity and their offerings to lend a hand. Then it occurred to her that she still had no idea who the third person was that had walked through the door.

"Who's your friend, Phoebe?"

"My friend? Who do you mean? We were talking about you. I want to be your friend."

"We all want to be your friend, Harleigh."

"We want to help."

"I don't even know you people," Harleigh insisted, finally scooting her chair backward and getting to her feet.

"Then give us a chance," Phoebe told her as she placed the teapot, sugar and cream on a tray and carried it to the table. "Give us a chance to be your friends, Harleigh."

Hesitantly, Harleigh reseated herself, took the cup of herbal tea Phoebe handed her and stared down into it as if looking for a direction to go. "I don't know you guys, Phoebe. You don't know me. There's nothing I can tell you that I need help with. Nothing that you could help me with in any case."

"Yes … you do know us," Delilah told her. "You know this town, the people … us. You know we care about you. Know that we would move heaven and earth to help you."

"You're one of us now," Sophy put in. "We can help you no matter how bad you think it us. Everyone needs a helping hand now and then."

"I know you've never laid eyes on me before, Harleigh. I'm Sunny, Butch's sister. He and I are fraternal twins."

Baffled, Harleigh just stared at Sunny. That was the last person she would've expected her to be. Yeah, she could see it now. It was the eyes. They were the same and that strange quirk at the corner of the mouth. The same. She wondered then what had happened to Butch's handsome face to have scarred it the way it was.

Harleigh heard the crunch of tires on gravel, cars stop, doors slam and footsteps on the porch. Her heart shot up into her throat as the front door opened. She heard several male voices come from the direction of the living room, longed to make a run out the back door and into the forest where she knew safety waited.

She gripped the edges of the chair to keep herself seated, knowing that beyond the confines of the kitchen, Stewart was waiting for her.

Caleb entered the kitchen with a scowl on his face. His gaze landed first on his sister, which Phoebe's reaction, Harleigh noted, was to stick out her tongue at him. He gave her a lopsided grin then slid his eyes over to Harleigh.

She felt the heat lick at her belly and wanted to groan out loud at the pleasure that small gesture gave her. Realizing what the possible repercussions of that could be, she literally washed that out of her mind, refusing to deal with it at this time. Or ever, for that matter, she adjusted her thinking. She didn't need that now or anytime in the future.

She didn't dare let her eyes slide to the left. There was a body standing next to Caleb that she was sure would turn out to be Stewart. Instead, Harleigh glanced to her right where Grady stood.

He stepped up behind Sophy and laid his hands on her shoulders. He bent down and kissed the top of her head then gave Harleigh a fleeting look.

"Hey, Miz Harleigh. Feeling better?"

"Yes."

She realized her answer was stiff but that's how she felt. Stiff and rigid all the way down to the bone. Muscles frozen solid, knew that if she moved they would break and splinter into shards of ice.

"I hope Gentry and I didn't scare you. He's an ugly sort."

"Hey, that's my man you're badmouthing. Besides, you're just jealous that you're not as handsome and sexy as he is."

"You wish." Grady told Phoebe with a grin on his face.

Harleigh watched the friendly exchange between the sheriff and Caleb's sister. She wished they would all go away. She wanted to slip away to her room, shut the door and not come out for a long time.

"Harleigh, I'd like you to meet my husband, Gentry."

She heard Phoebe speak, heard the word, husband and vaguely wondered if somehow Stewart had found a way into the lives of these people to get at her. Somehow ... no she wouldn't let herself think along those lines.

She tamped down the fear that was starting to rise from the pit of her stomach. She didn't want to meet this man but what choice did she have?

Finally having no other recourse, she raised her eyes to the man who was going to splatter her to hell and back, the first chance he got.

Shock was the least she was prepared for. The man before her was the most glamorous man she'd ever seen. There was no other way to put it.

This couldn't be the same man that was with Grady earlier, she knew it couldn't be. He was so different than the man she had seen.

Maybe she hallucinated. Seeing things that weren't there. Seeing people who weren't there. Seeing Stewart.

She assessed Phoebe's husband, comparing him with her ex. He was dressed much the same that Stewart dressed, like a GQ man, he liked to say. The facial features were close but this man, this Gentry, his face contained all the power and intensity that Stewart lacked. And his eyes a startling color of quicksilver and they held a light deep within.

Without a doubt, those eyes could be cold, would

freeze like an Arctic wind, if he were crossed or if someone stood in the way of what he desired. She knew that somehow, could feel that. Like the woman he loved. Phoebe. But the way his fingertips absently caressed the ends of her hair, his touch was gentle.

"Nice to meet you, Gentry."

She heard her voice falter. Knew the others had heard it, too. Thankfully, no one uttered a word about the odd inflection in her voice.

"What's going on here anyway?" Caleb asked. "Is this one of those old biddy tea parties?"

"Maybe," Delilah informed the men slyly.

"And, since it is," Sunny put in, "you guys aren't invited."

"Yeah," Phoebe added, "so get out. Go find guy things to do."

"Wait just a minute," Caleb insisted, throwing up his hands and punching himself in the chest with his fingers, "this is my house."

Phoebe gave him a warning glare, then Harleigh could almost see the communication pass between them. Unspoken but understood.

"Okay, then," Caleb turned his head toward Grady, "Glad we got that straight. I guess we need to go do guy things, guys."

Grady and Gentry followed Caleb's lead and fell in behind him. Caleb returned a moment later, stuck his head in the door and gave Harleigh the once over.

"You all right, Harleigh?" he asked, skimmed her face for any telltale signs of trauma and smiled.

For the first time since she entered the house, Harleigh smiled, too. A genuine smile. She felt it from within, felt it curve her mouth upward. Felt it enter her eyes. She couldn't help it, couldn't hide it and for some reason, didn't want to hide it.

It was that boyish grin that lifted the corners of his mouth, uncovering the serrated edges of his teeth then literally floated upward into his pearl gray eyes that did it. That little boy grin of his that had her heart slapping her ribs sideways. That silly-assed grin that slid over her skin like satin, tingling and skipping its way all the way down to the ends of her toes. Even curled them up a bit, too. That was why she had a silly-assed grin of her own on her lips.

"Yes, Caleb, I'm fine now," she answered softly. "Thanks."

He patted the doorframe, returned her smile and was off again to do guy things with the boys.

The four girls saw the smiles, the warmth, the beginnings of a sizzle in the trade offs of unspoken body signals. Eyebrows raised, knowing glances exchanged, and fingers tapped against lips as though in silent agreement to say, *Mmm, what was that?*

"Thank goodness, they're gone," Sunny commented to cover their assessment of the situation. Of course, she doubted Harleigh would even have noticed. She was too attuned to Caleb. "I'm sure glad you three are the one with the men and not me. I don't need that kind of aggravation."

"Jealous, sis?" Delilah needled.

"Of what? You and that silly, macho man you're married to? Hardly," she scoffed.

"Now, girls," Sophy scolded good-naturedly, "Let's behave ourselves in front of our guest."

The girls shrugged and laughed.

"Sunny here, is looking for love in all the wrong

places," Delilah teased.

"Who says?"

"What do you do for a living, Sunny?"

"I'm an forensic pathologist."

"Exactly." Delilah slapped the table as if that one word made her point.

"What's that supposed to mean?"

"It means, dear heart, that you like playing with dead things."

"Girls, girls, didn't Sophy say to behave yourselves in front of Harleigh? She'll think we're all a bunch of nutcases." Phoebe swung her eyes Harleigh's way. Harleigh hadn't uttered one word since Caleb left with that lovesick grin on his face.

Harleigh had been mesmerized by the display going on between Delilah and Sunny, sisters at heart. Never in her wildest dreams would she ever have thought she would be sitting here in her dream house, listening to two young women tossing words back and forth and enjoying it.

Now all four pairs of eyes were on Harleigh. Four pairs, waiting expectantly.

"No," Harleigh confessed, "I don't think you're a bunch of nutcases." She laughed. It felt good. Felt good to be able to do something so simple. "A little strange, maybe."

"We're that," Phoebe agreed.

"I guess I've never had the pleasure of being in company like yours. Each of you is so … different. Yet …"

"Finish it, Harleigh," prompted Sophy. "Tell us exactly what you think, what you feel."

"When I look at you, you're all the same. Sincere.

Caring. And strong. You're all so strong on the inside."

"Is that what you need, then? Strength?" Phoebe's voice was quiet yet at the same time there was a pull to it that made Harleigh want to answer, wanted to give her whatever she sought.

"Yes. I want to be strong. I want to be able to do what you did, Phoebe."

Phoebe frowned, searching her mind for what she, Harleigh, was talking about. She hadn't a clue what her point of reference was.

"What exactly did I do? I just met you, I haven't had time to do anything. Yet," she grinned impishly. "There isn't anything I can think of that I did to warrant you thinking I was strong. Tell me."

"Back at the clinic, you just up and walked me out of there, daring Caleb to stop you. How were you able to do that? That took strength to stand up to him like that, even though, you didn't need to. He hadn't done anything wrong."

"Shoot, Caleb's my brother. He wouldn't hurt me, or anyone else for that matter. He's about as dangerous as a wet paper bag. He blusters around, making you think he's this big bully but that's all hot air. Is that what happened to you? Did someone hurt you?"

"You can trust us with your secrets, Harleigh," Delilah added, taking a sip of her tea. "You can tell us anything." She paused. "Or not."

"As much or as little as you want," added Sophy. "Whatever it is, we can help."

"Yes," urged Sunny, "even if it is just to listen."

Harleigh looked from one set of eyes to the next, making a complete circle of the faces before her. She took a deep breath and took a giant leap forward.

"I tried to kill my ex-husband."

CHAPTER SEVEN

ℵ

It wasn't quite what they expected but, hey, who were they to pass judgment, Phoebe thought.

Sometimes you had to do what you had to do.

Harleigh watched and waited.

The four girls sat in stony silence. No recriminations, no judgments, no shock. Just acceptance of a secret to be told.

And, no questions, comments or psychoanalytic babble. Just an unnerving quiet.

Harleigh reached for her cup of tea and drank. She didn't particularly want it but she was too nervous to just sit there. She alluded to one of the biggest secrets of her life and they just sat there as if she'd just told them she'd just gone shopping.

Her nerves were stretching like a prisoner on a torture rack. "Well, aren't you going to say anything?"

In unison, they raised their cups to sip, and replaced the delicate china into its matching saucer.

"Did he deserve it?" Delilah asked softly.

Startled, Harleigh jumped. "Deserve it?"

"Yes, did he deserve to be killed?" Phoebe knew without asking the question that he had.

"I — I wouldn't have done it otherwise."

Sophy twirled her cup in the saucer, it making a soft grinding sound as the bottom slid around and around in the small plate. "Then, that's all that matters. Tell us what happened. We'll listen."

She wanted to. It was on the tip of her tongue to blurt out the whole sordid story but she bit down and wouldn't let the words take flight like they wanted to. How could she when the reason behind it was the darkest of all?

The humiliation of how it came to be still dragged her down. Even now. How much less would they think of her once she told them all the dirty details?

She pushed the urge away, knew she had to keep her secrets deep within herself. She wanted to, God only knew, how bad she wanted ... needed to lean on someone. Needed to unload the horrendous burden she carried around with her.

This was no place, nor were these the people, she wanted to drag down into the bowels of that rank pit with her. They were too good to concern themselves with something that despicable.

She decided to be as honest as she could without divulging any of the truth.

"It's a long story. One I'm sure would bore you to tears. It's just your average spousal conflict, things got out of hand and I bashed him over the head and left him for dead. Simple."

Phoebe picked up her cup, sipped and stared over the rim directly into Harleigh's eyes. "Not so simple, if you were being abused."

"There's nothing that I can tell you," she murmured. "Nothing that you would understand."

It was there. Phoebe could see the suffering she'd

endured. It was there in the sadness, in the pain she tried so hard to hide, to put behind her. "I think, though, that to make you feel better about yourself, about the whole situation, to get it all out in the open, maybe you should tell us more."

She was like a steamroller, Harleigh decided, staring back at Phoebe, wondering why she wouldn't let it go. These girls wouldn't be so curious if they knew the truth, knew the most vile things she'd endured, had allowed to take place and wished a thousand times over for death to take her.

Sophy saw the hesitation, knew the gnawing in-the-gut feeling of wanting to confide in someone but pride wouldn't permit it.

Phoebe stretched out her palm and entwined her fingers around Harleigh's. "We're only here because we care about you. We're not here to judge. If you're not ready, we understand. We'll be here when and if you need us to be."

She squeezed her hand, pushed back her chair. "Girls?"

The other three rose, took their cups to the sink, rinsed and placed them in the drainer.

"We won't push," Delilah told her. "When you're ready."

They began to file out the door. Harleigh couldn't bear it. They'd all treated her with respect. Treated her as an equal and had asked nothing of her, except to share the burdens of her past. Wasn't that what she'd always wanted? To share? To be normal? To be like others?

Couldn't she do that now? Begin that life that she'd so desperately wanted that she killed for it?

"Wait, don't go." Harleigh gnawed on her lip, nerves jangling, throat burning with some of the old fear that if she voiced it, it would come back and drag her down again.

"If you're sure?" Sunny saw the fear she couldn't hide, the fear she was choking back. And her heart went out to her. Whatever she'd been through must have been brutal if the terror of it lived on the surface, she thought.

"Only if you're sure you want to hear it. It's not pretty."

They retrieved their cups, sat down again, poured more tea and waited. Saw Harleigh gather herself and agonized with her as she fought to find the words. Watched helplessly as the tormented soul surfaced.

They laid their hands, palms up, on the table, reached out and entwined their fingers together. To her right, Phoebe sat with her hand outstretched. Seated by Phoebe was Sunny, then Sophy and then came Delilah whose hand beckoned to Harleigh to complete the circle.

Hesitantly, Harleigh met the waiting fingers with her own and immediately felt the strength surge from one to the other, giving her parts of them. Their hopes, wishes and dreams. All to be shared, one with the other. And now, now she was part of this.

This town had welcomed her, claimed her and now, she knew she could share some of her secrets. Those that weren't the most vile and hate-filled.

She could share them without fear. Without recriminations. Without judgment.

"I don't really know where to start."

"Wherever it's easiest," Sunny suggested.

"There is no easy to any of it," she confessed.

"Well, why don't you start before all the bad stuff happened?" Sophy sympathized with her plight but there was nothing she could do to help her over that first hurdle.

"Once upon a time I think I was happy. The past few years seems like I've been wandering around in a fog. Seems like I've been to hell and back a dozen times."

The hands that held Harleigh's squeezed hers, giving her confidence, strength and the courage to continue. She held on as if that contact were a lifeline and her own depended on it for survival.

"I first met Stewart at an art gallery. I was standing in front of this painting trying to figure out what the significance of it was. Turns out, he was the artist they were giving the showing for. I should have known from the painting what kind of person he was but I was flattered that someone of that importance would notice me, let alone talk to me and take the time to interpret the meaning of the painting.

"The painting itself was beautiful in its way but had a dark side to it. There was a tree in the foreground, a tree with dead branches. There was a trickle of a stream by the tree. It didn't look like water, though. More like a rivulet of mercury. The night was pitch black with a stark silver moon hanging in the sky. The moon was full, perfectly rounded, shaded in places like in photos, yet there was something menacing about it. "

She closed her eyes and sat in silence, remembering. Then with a deep sigh, she continued on while all around her, there was quiet encouragement.

"He was very bright, Stewart was, very intelligent

and very moody. I'd never met anyone like him before and he fascinated me. In the beginning, he did. We began dating, he was charming, attentive, adoring. And I liked it. I was a little shocked when he asked me to marry him. I didn't think he was the type to marry. That's shows my stupidity."

"Don't put yourself down. You weren't stupid," Sophy commented. "Just overpowered by all the attention."

"It's hard to describe, really, how he made me feel. He was so incredibly gifted. A good artist. I'd never known anyone who had such a flair about them. He commanded attention just by entering a room. And people flocked to be in his presence."

"Understandable," Sunny commented. "A true intellect."

"He made me feel special. Like there was no one else like me in the world. Like I was his world. We saw each other for about a year, I guess. I attended all his showings. He would fly me wherever he was. We would attend the showing together, the celebration afterward and he would always surprise me with some small gift afterward. Flowers. Music boxes. And figurines. Windup figurines, that spun around with music," she whispered and shivered, as if something crawled across her skin.

"It wasn't until then that I discovered he was a very rich man. He wanted a pre-nup signed, which I did, I didn't want his money. He came from old money and it was his way of assuring it would stay his. His parents had died a year before and he was the legal heir to millions of hotel chains and gambling casinos. When we were married, he took care of all the arrangements, said he wanted the biggest and best for me. It was his gift. To me, it was an empty occasion. Over a thousand invitations, and as many attendees came out to see and be seen. I didn't even get to select my own bridesmaid."

"Oh, dear heavens, Harleigh, I think I attended your wedding, if you're who I think you are," Delilah stated. "You had short curly hair then I think."

"Yes, my hair was short then."

"You were married on one of their gambling boats, weren't you?"

"Yes. Once we walked down the aisle, everything changed, though. He was dark and brooding when were alone. His artistic personality, he said. Anyway, he wanted me to wear my hair this way, he wanted me to wear these kinds of clothes, in this color. Again, I was flattered. I thought I was improving myself for him. I didn't realize he was molding me into what he wanted. Into how he wanted me to be. Into what and how he wanted other people to see. Once the reception was over, and guests gone there was only us. Our wedding night was a joke. That's when it all started, I suppose."

"You don't have to tell us anymore if you don't want to," Sophy told her, not sure she wanted to hear more.

"No, I want to. Actually, I think I need to face this, get some of it out where I can really see it and deal with it."

Phoebe squeezed her hand. "That's our girl."

"We were out a lot, attending parties, social gatherings, seeing and being seen. In public, outwardly he was always attentive, affectionate, even loving. Little did anyone know, that when he was dancing me around the dance floor with a smile on his face, he was hurting me."

"He abused you in public?"

"Not enough that anyone would notice. He'd slide his fingers inside the sleeve of my gown like he was caressing my skin. Only I could see the evil on his face. He would begin by pinching me severely. The first time I protested that he was hurting me, he stopped then the moment we got home he slapped me across the mouth, dragged me to the bedroom by my hair, ripped of my gown and took me like an animal."

"Oh, dear God."

"No, it's all right, Sunny, really. That more or less started a pattern to our life together. He had brought me a dancing figurine earlier that first night. Then I started noticing that every time he brought me one, the evil in him came out and would grow with each incident. He even started winding them up and playing them while he punished me for whatever slight I'd done against him. As time passed, he would cause me great pain in public just to see my reaction, and dare me to flinch or even allow tears to show."

"What an asshole!"

"He liked doing things while out in the public eye, doing little things that they couldn't see. He thought it was a challenge to come up with new ways he could inflict pain without any one being the wiser. He would bend my fingers backwards and dare me to cry out when he held my hand. He would be talking to some-one, smiling as if everything were okay, all the while doing what he did best."

Abruptly, Harleigh stopped talking, memories swirling upward from where she thought she'd laid them to rest. She knew she needed to continue. To tell parts that could be told, get it out.

"Once, he bent them so far backward, he snapped one of my fingers. Sometimes, to others it looked like he was caressing the nape of my neck while all the time he was twining my hair around his fingertips and pulling slow and hard. He liked dancing, too. Liked it best I think because he could have his hands on me and dig his fingernails into my arm or my side where they lay. A lot of times, when we were sitting at a table, he would slide his hand up my thigh to touch me there and if I objected he would dig his nails into my upper thigh or go ahead and jab me wherever he could."

"What a sick man."

"I learned his anger by his touch. If it was more than a nudge, I knew what was going to be waiting for me at home. Any reluctance on my part only made it worse. He would make sure I was punished for my own good for being a disobedient wife. If I did object, he would be on me the minute we got into the limousine. He'd put the glass partition up so the driver couldn't see what he was doing. He would hurt me, then tell me I could cry then because no one could see and he liked the way the tears rolled down my face and off my chin. He said it was such a turn on. Those times, the minute I was inside the door he would grab me and do whatever, most times, we'd barely get in the door and he wouldn't stop until he got the evil out of his system. Always said it was my fault for turning him into a sex-crazed maniac."

Harleigh sniffed back the tears that were burning her eyes and clogging her throat. She wouldn't cry now, she told herself. That part of her life was over.

Still, when Delilah rose to bring her a tissue, she was grateful. She wiped her eyes and nose, took a deep breath and took in the compassionate smiles that surrounded her. She placed her hands back where they were and began again.

"There's not much more I can tell you. I remember one time, we'd been to the theater and he'd been especially brutal to me. I hoped that he'd just lock me in the closet, and leave me like he would do when he thought I needed to be corrected. He'd leave me in that darkness for hours on end, sometimes a day or more. No food, no way to go to the bathroom. If I did that, it meant a beating with a belt or the buckle. He wouldn't allow me to change my soiled clothing. I had to clean the closet out to his satisfaction then once that was done he would push me under a cold shower, clothes and all and leave me there.

"I finally got up the courage to leave him when he nearly killed me. Even went as far as getting a divorce. I thought it was all over but he'd find ways to get around the law. I guess I left him for dead because I knew that if I didn't get away from him and save myself, the next time he'd kill me."

"That night, he came to my apartment, let himself in and waited. Then when I came home, he attacked me, tied me spread eagled to the bed and just watched me. I couldn't close my legs. He would tell me in crude words how ugly my body parts were but still he'd get up, pinch and jab, just to hear me cry out. He'd laugh. Then, he took the dancing figurines, wound them all up and raped me while they played. Afterwards, he told me that if I went to the police he'd kill me. That it was my punishment for thinking I could divorce him and get away with it. While he was dressing, he untied a leg, then an arm, then I was free. He sat on the edge of the bed, putting on his shirt, telling me all the time that this was all my fault, that I shouldn't have divorced him. I reached out, grabbed the brass lamp off the end table and hit him with it."

"Good for you."

"Yes, good for you," Sunny agreed. "It was a long time coming."

"Too damn long, if you ask me." Delilah voiced her opinion.

"I'm glad you killed him," Phoebe told her. "He deserves to be dead."

"That's just it. He isn't dead."

"What?" they all said at once.

"What d'ya mean he's not dead?"

Harleigh took note of the shock registering on their faces, noted the absolute stillness and wanted to lighten the mood. It had become way too serious.

"I didn't say I killed him, I said I tried to kill him. Guess that's the last thing you expected, huh?"

"Yeah, well … I guess you could say that." Phoebe cleared her throat, gulped her tea and tried to calm herself.

"Wait a minute. Wait just a minute, here," Delilah ordered, her voice catching on nerves that were beginning to thrum.

"Exactly," Sunny exclaimed.

"We've got to do something," insisted Sophy. "We've got to make plans."

"Plans for what, girls? What're you guys thinking? Why do you never say anything but yet you know what is not being said?"

Harleigh sat by, watched, waited. Slowly, each one stopped speaking, turned their attention back to her, then they all laughed.

"How do you feel, Harleigh?" Phoebe placed her elbows on the table with the raised cup held in her hands and sipped. The wheels were turning in her head all the while.

"Actually, I feel quite good. Soul-cleansing."

"That's a good word for it."

Phoebe looked at the faces around her, looked into their eyes, deep into their eyes for answers to her unspoken questions. They all nodded as a unit.

"So, what do we do first?" Sunny asked.

"Well, we've got two of the best people at our disposal," Phoebe said with a smile as the wheels went right on turning.

"And, I just bet you're talking about that man of yours who just happens to be a super attorney as one of them."

Harleigh watched the smile curve Sunny's mouth upward as she teased Phoebe. These girls confused her with each moment that passed. Wondered if she would ever be able to tease and be teased like this. Wondered if she would ever be able to keep up.

"And, why not? He's remarkably intelligent, incredibly handsome, and hot as a red hot chili pepper in the court room."

"And, the other?" Delilah asked.

"Grady, of course," put in Sophy. "Best law enforcement officer in the state of Florida."

"And, don't forget Caleb," added Sunny. "He knows everybody. He could call in favors from Atlanta."

"Wait. Wait." Harleigh threw up her hands as tension stirred her stomach. She was beginning to understand a little of how they worked things out together. And what they were getting at scared her down to the bone. "There's no need. I'd never put anyone at risk."

"Think nothing of it. We're not at risk, you are."

"And, when one of our own is at risk, it's up to us to step up to the plate and hit it out of the ballpark."

"Meaning?" Harleigh wished she hadn't asked. She wasn't sure she wanted to hear the answer.

"We're going to devise a plan, enlist the help of our darling spouses and nothing or no one will get close enough to hurt you."

Phoebe reached over, laid her hand atop Harleigh's and squeezed assuringly. Never had she dreamed that what Harleigh had been through had been so brutally hideous and repulsive. How she, Harleigh, had been able to come through the horrific and gruesome treatment at the hands of a deranged madman and still remain sane was beyond her imagination. She was sure there was a lot more to the story than Harleigh was admitting. Much more that she couldn't bring herself to repeat, a lot more horrific and gruesome details The man didn't deserve to draw another breath as far as Phoebe was concerned.

It was more than Harleigh could stand. She couldn't allow Stewart's evil to spill over into this community. This town that handpicked her, called to her. Couldn't allow Stewart to hurt any of these people that were so willing to go out of their way to help her in every way.

"I can't let you do this. I'll just pack and be on my way again. It's no big deal. I'm used to running, I just thought …"

"No," Phoebe told her with a stubborn set to her jaw, the same one Harleigh had seen when Phoebe took her by the arm and led her out of Caleb's clinic. This wasn't going to be easy, she thought. No way was it going to be easy to talk her out of plotting and planning.

"It's time he was stopped, Harleigh. What if he hurts someone else the way he hurt you?"

Harleigh's forehead scored a frown as she dragged her brows down. That was one thing she hadn't even thought of. Would Stewart have given up the chase? Gone to another woman and treated her as despicable as he had her?

It sickened her as she considered the possibilities of him doing just that. Could she allow it? Allow someone else to endure the torture, the mind-numbing repugnance of what she had had to endure?

It was on the tip of her tongue to refuse their offer, inform them that under no circumstances were they to get involved with her and the personal baggage she carried around but the room started to blur, faces receded, the air stirred.

She felt the strands of hair that she couldn't keep tucked behind her ear, move, as if carried away from her face on a gentle breeze. And along with the breeze came the warmth that always surrounded her when the world went away.

But this time, this time she was within breathing distance of herself. Curiously, she stretched out her hand. The closer she came to her image, the more she glowed. She pulled her hand back, spread her fingers, turned them back and forth in wonderment.

Palm down, she stretched her fingertips up and out-ward, reached out across the short span of space, and it was gone. Blinked out as if someone had hit the off switch and turned the light out.

"Geez, Harleigh, where have you been?"

"Been?" She was still sitting at the table, still in the kitchen, still surrounded by a group of young women who were more than willing to go out of their way to lend a hand. Yet, she knew something had happened. What that something was, she hadn't a clue.

They were staring at her as if she had grown an-other head.

She couldn't help it. She had to ask. "What are you staring at me like that for?"

There was no way to come up with a lucid expla-nation for what she'd just seen. Sophy tried to rational-ize the fact that Harleigh had shimmered and glowed and wavered right in front of her eyes. But she'd be damned if she were going to let one word of *that* slip passed her lips. She was going to keep that little bit of info right behind her teeth where it was going to stay. They'd have to pull her fingernails off before she'd give that up.

Delilah was of the same mind. Her mouth opened and closed and opened and closed. Again. Then gave a final snap. She was literally at a loss for words. Look-ing around her, she realized the others were in a state of shock, too. It was all right there … right there, up front for anyone to see on their faces. But she, Delilah, was going to keep her mouth zipped.

For once, Phoebe's motor mouth crashed and burned. She was as quiet as she'd ever been since the day she took the world by storm. Her brain was on overload, couldn't comprehend what her eyes had seen. And she wasn't telling either.

"What the hell was that?" Sunny demanded, her voice pitched high and squeaky. "Did you guys see that? Wasn't that awesome? Are you some kind of psychic?"

Sunny's acceptance of what had transpired finally loosened their tongues.

Phoebe's motor hitched into overdrive. "I don't think I've ever seen anything so unbelievable. Can you do that anytime you want? How do you do that? Can you teach me? I'd love to do that?"

"Yes! Yes, how do you do that?" Sophy's interest was spiking high. She'd never encountered anyone who could go transparent and radiate their own light.

"I'm not sure I want to know anything, girls. That was just a little too bizarre for words." Delilah finally got her breath back. She wasn't ready to fully admit what she'd seen, wasn't ready to believe in anything supernatural or whatever the hell it was.

Now it was Harleigh's turn to stare.

"What did you see? Exactly," she finally got up the nerve to ask. Had they seen the shimmer of light? Had the air stirred around them?

"I'm not sure I want to even put it into words," Phoebe told her.

Delilah had no qualms in that quarter. "I know I don't."

"Well, I know what I saw," Sunny insisted with a stubborn set to her chin. "I saw you glow, Harleigh. Glow. There was this shimmer of light around you and your hair was blowing back like someone had turned a fan on you."

"Did you see the image of me, then? Did you see the other people in the room, too?" Harleigh was nearly breathless with excitement, hoping that maybe they'd seen that other being, that other side of her.

The girls exchanged glances ... and frowns ... and curiosity. They shook their heads. In disbelief. In bafflement. In abject astonishment.

"No." It was Delilah who finally spoke, giving in to her inquisitive nature, and looked around at her friends. "But you guys saw something, didn't you? The same way I did. And, you, Harleigh, you saw something, too, I know you did. There was this awed expression on your face."

"Yes." She admitted. "It seemed like everything faded away, then the air seemed to swirl and envelope me with a warmth that was soothing, peaceful. I looked at my hands and there was this light that seemed to be coming from the inside of me. When I looked up, it was like looking at myself in a mirror. I reached out to touch it and it disappeared. And, I had this deep sad feeling."

"You faded, too, Harleigh," Sophy explained. "You were a shimmer of light. I could see through you, like you were an ethereal waiflike being or something. How can you explain that?"

Harleigh couldn't help it. The girls looked so befuddled. So perplexed. So she did exactly what she felt like doing and laughed ... and kept laughing until tears slid down her cheeks and bounced off her chin. Laughed until she had to hold her stomach, it hurt from laughing so hard.

"If you only knew what you looked like," she sputtered. "Talk about seeing a ghost!"

"I don't think it's quite that funny, Harleigh," insisted Sophy.

"I fail to see the humor in it myself. Damn, Harleigh," Delilah swore. "You sure put a new take on the word shine."

"Yeah, Harleigh, you weren't the one getting the bejesus scared out of you with a supernatural visitation."

Harleigh sniffled back another giggle, smothered the urge to laugh out loud again, and gave her new-found friends a watery smile. Friends, she thought. She had friends! Something she had wished for, for so long. Something that she'd stood on the outside looking in. Something she coveted, craved, longed for. Something she thought she'd never have.

And now, they were here.

She looked around at the faces that she was coming to know. Then, they, too, began to laugh, the sound flowed out on a merry flight, took to the air and spilled outside where the men were still standing.

Caleb immediately knew which one was Harleigh's, vaguely wondered how those girls had put the joy he heard into her laugh. That deep-down carefree laugh that he wanted for her. That was his intention, he'd have to ask his little sister about how they achieved that. He needed all the help he could get.

He tipped his head back, looked up at the fading light then glanced over at Grady and Gentry who were sizing him up with a knowing gleam lighting up their eyes.

"What?"

Grady elbowed Gentry in the ribs. "What, the man says. What's your opinion, counselor?"

"Well," Gentry drawled in his best Southern accent. "In my professional opinion, the verdict could only be guilty."

Caleb frowned. "Guilty of what?"

He didn't have to ask. He knew these two like he knew his own hand.

"That lovely young lady in your house there, been here what, nigh on to two, three weeks, maybe?"

"So?"

"So, look at you."

"What about me? There's nothing wrong with my looks."

"Maybe."

Gentry watched the by-play between the sheriff and his brother-in-law. He'd seen the spark of longing in Caleb's eyes when they were inside in the presence of that young woman and wondered about it even then. He hadn't thought anymore about it since the object of his desire was first and foremost on his mind. When he was around Phoebe no other woman existed for long.

But this, this held a new appeal for Gentry. He'd long wanted to play get-back with his brother-in-law. The Doc had sure given him enough hell about Phoebe. Of course, he could understand it in a way. He, Gentry, was city-born and bred, didn't know a thing about the country and country-folk. He lived and breathed the big city. The law.

Well, he did, until he'd gotten lost on the back roads of a hick town called Nowhere and walked into the Nowhere Café to ask where the hell he was and tripped over his tongue. And he hadn't been the same since.

There was no way he could describe Phoebe.

Fresh, he decided. Clean.

So different from all the made-up, perfume-laden, jewelry-weighted, empty-headed women that hung around on his arm in Atlanta.

Phoebe was a vision to behold with that pixie face and here-I-am-take-me-bod. He'd never stopped wanting her.

And now, now it was his time to give back to Caleb. Of course, his would be a gentle ribbing and not the I'll-kick-your-ass-if-you-hurt-my-sister attitude that the man laid on him at their first meeting.

Gentry tilted his head down, disturbed the gravel with the toe of his shoe and hid his grin. "Well, Caleb, the way I see it, you're hormonal."

"You're shittin' me, right?"

"Doc. Such language," admonished Grady. "I may have to take you down to the big house for such a public display."

"Go to hell, Grady."

Grady glanced over at Gentry, winked, then turned back to Caleb. "The list is gettin' longer, Doc. Public nuisance, verbal assault of a law enforcement officer. What d'ya' think, counselor? Ya' think the charge'll stick?"

"No doubt about it, Sheriff. Unless, of course, I defend him in a court of law."

Caleb eyed the both of them with angry sparks swirling the pearl gray eyes into a storm. "Both you idiots can go to hell."

He stomped off toward the Rose House, knew they were just needling him, but he didn't need that kind of needling. Especially when he didn't know where he stood with Harleigh.

Caleb had never been in a position where he'd felt this way, had never cared for a woman the way he cared for Harleigh. She was unique, pulling at him the way she did, diving into the deepest regions of his heart and sparking an ember to life that he never thought existed.

The guffaws followed him up the stairs and he knew the originators of those deep sounds wouldn't be far behind. He also knew he'd have to put up with the two of them for the rest of the evening. So he might as well prepare himself for it and their incessant teasing. He knew they wouldn't let it alone. So, he took a deep breath and waited.

א

"There are plans to be made, girls."

She didn't know where to start, but Phoebe knew they had to start forming some kind of protective barrier around Harleigh so if and when the day came, they could take a stand. Then, there was this other thing, this glowing thing they had to find out about.

She, Phoebe, had grown up in this house for the better part of her life. She knew the story, heard the rumors and all the ghostly stories, had even seen a few unexplainable things a time or two. But she'd never seen anything like what happened with Harleigh.

She wasn't frightened, wasn't alarmed or even panicked. Knew there was nothing to make her go screaming from the room in holy terror. But … there was something here, something that needed investigated. Who knew, maybe Harleigh was the catalyst to all the speculation about the Rose House. About the Faire Sabra and her Quentin. How it all started.

As far back as she could remember, Phoebe had been intrigued by all the stories surrounding the Rose House. She'd listened to all the folklore told by the locals, read the books from the library, walked through the forest glen where it was said to be haunted, even searched for the famous lost journals of the Devreaux sisters. But had found nothing, had felt nothing or had nothing bathe her in a surreal wash of shimmering light.

"And, then this other mystery," she added. "Right?"

They'd all heard the rumors. But nowadays, the citizens of Nowhere thought of it as their own legend. It was an accepted part of the colorful past of their town.

Even so, it left many to wonder just what happened to the occupants of the Rose House and the journals.

And these girls were no exception.

They'd have to talk it out, work out a solution for both situations and enlist aid where it was suitable.

"I think you're right, Phoebe," Sophy agreed. "Let's tackle the ex issue first. I can get Grady to check his sources. I'll need name, age, description."

Phoebe started gathering up the empty teacups, turned and placed them in the sink. "What about you, Dee? Think Butch can help us in any way?"

Delilah chewed on her lower lip in concentration. "I can't think of anything legal Butch can do but I still have contacts that I can call. They can be discreet."

"And, I'll have Caleb call his buddies in Atlanta."

Harleigh could sit here and let them convince her that she would be safe, that they could keep Stewart away. But they didn't know him, didn't know what they were up against, didn't know the evil that rode his back like a demon from hell.

She couldn't take the chance that he would hurt one of her friends. She had to stop them, had to put a stop to what they were planning. The fear that she'd expected to rise up through all this and slap her with a panic attack had tried but her strength of mind to rid herself of it and Stewart pushed it back.

Speaking of her ordeal, sharing some of the load off her shoulders had freed her from the chains that had held her down. Freed her from the weight she carried with her every waking moment that made her fight for every wink of sleep she got.

For the first time in a long time, she had something else to occupy her mind besides looking over her shoulder and running for her life. That in itself gave her strength. Strength that she'd been looking for, strength she needed to do what should have been done a long time past.

"Look," she finally spoke up. "I appreciate your willingness to go to these lengths to help me. But, it's time that I did something about my ex-husband my-self."

"But we can help." Phoebe turned back to face everyone. "All of us will find an avenue of resources at our disposal. Whether it's our husbands, friends or this town."

"I know and you'll never know how good that makes me feel. But, it's time I took a stand. Stewart robbed me of everything. My self-esteem, my dignity, my hopes and dreams for the future. It's time I took it back."

Delilah knew all about stolen hopes and dreams.

She'd lost a few of hers along the way. Butch had helped her reclaim them. "You'll never find another place or finer people than here in Nowhere. And I, for one, agree with you."

"You agree with me?"

"Yes, I do. Nowhere is a great place to make your stand. Not only will you have the four of us, but you'll have our significant others."

"I don't have one of those," Sunny put in.

"One day, one will ride in on his white horse and you'll never know what hit you."

"That'll be the day."

"Just wait, sister-in-law, your time's a comin', honey," Delilah taunted, "and you're gonna get smacked but good. Now, where was I?"

"Making a stand, I think."

"Yeah. Not only will you have us and our guys, except for Sunny Delite here, but you will have the town of Nowhere to watch your back. From day one, Butch has always told me that Nowhere is a sanctuary for lost souls."

"It will keep you safe and hide your secrets." Harleigh repeated what she'd heard when she'd turned to Kate. The light was there , too. Maybe that in itself was a sign.

"What did you say?" Phoebe had a deep frown tugging at her brow.

"You wouldn't believe me if I told you."

"Try me."

"Okay, but don't laugh and call me crazy."

"Gotcha. We all do. Don't we girls?"

They all nodded in agreement.

"I was talking with your mom the other day,

Phoebe. I was trying to leave … get out … run when the subject was something I didn't want to discuss. We were in the kitchen, I turned to leave, got as far as the doorway when she asked me to stay. There was something about the way she asked that made me turn back. Around her, behind her, beside her, I don't know which, she was encased in this halo of light."

"Like the one we saw today?" inquired Phoebe.

"Yes."

"That's eerie."

Goose bump moments, thought Delilah, looking around as four pairs of hands ran up and down forearms to smooth away the shivers that had puckered their skin and made their hair stand on end.

"Anyway, that's what she said. No, I take that back, it's not what she said. It's what the house said."

"Excuse me?" Sunny questioned. "The house *talked*? You've *got* to be kidding."

"No joke. When I asked Kate about it, that was her comment. Said it was the house, something about it was special and it had chosen me."

"Wow."

"I know it's weird, sounds weird just saying it. There's something else I must confess since I'm baring my soul," Harleigh told them, her gaze lighting on each one's features for a moment, assessing the reactions to their conversation so far.

Delilah laid her well-manicured hand across her forehead and moaned. "More? There's more? I don't think my psyche can take it."

Harleigh glanced over at Delilah with misgiving settling like rocks in her stomach. Maybe she was unloading too much. "Sorry. I guess I've given you guys enough food for thought, enough of the finer points of my life to absorb for the time being." She rose as if to leave. "Lots of crap for one person, huh?"

"Where're ya' going, Harleigh?"

"I'm going to go to my room, clear my head and work out the details of what I'm going to do."

"Five heads are better than one, don't you think?" Sophy asked, still trying to get her mind wrapped around what she'd seen and what she'd been told. It was a struggle.

"I know but my troubles are my own, besides, Delilah's psyche can't take it."

Delilah took her hand off her forehead, stood, planting her hands on the table and leaned forward. "I'm not the delicate flower that Butch tries to make me out to be, Harleigh. I'm from New York, for heaven's sake. This is a sisterhood, we'll deal with whatever comes our way. Agreed?"

"Agreed," they all chimed in ... except Harleigh.

"Harleigh, got a problem with that?"

There was a frown on Phoebe's forehead. It faded, turned to a smile and the girls held their right hand up in the air.

"High five, girls. Harleigh?"

Tentatively, she raised her hand, prepared to smack her palm against theirs.

"To the sisterhood," Phoebe exclaimed.

Slapping palms, female giggles and friendship filled the kitchen, zoomed its way inside Harleigh to fill an empty spot in her heart and she felt as if she'd found her way home.

CHAPTER EIGHT

א

The moon was raising its sliver of a new moon stage into the evening sky when the newly formed sisterhood stepped out onto the front porch to cross to the main house. From this viewpoint, Harleigh took note of the silvery image the structure projected in the moonlight. The Rose House extended its welcome in the cool of the evening just as much as it did in the light of day. She knew at the midnight hour, the welcome would be the same.

As they walked, she listened to the chatter of the young women she called friends. She knew that eventually they would come up with a plan and put it into action with or without her permission. She'd have to talk them out of it. Somehow. For their own protection.

She wondered how she could get around them, how to convince them to give up the quest. Stewart would chew them up and spit them out without blinking his eyes. How could she protect them against that?

The only path left to her was to be on her way out of this place she wanted so much to call home.

She'd have to have a plan of her own. Would first have to get it clear in her mind how to slip out of town quietly and unobtrusively as possible.

For the first time since she'd smacked Stewart up-side the head with that brass lamp and ran for her life, did she have to run for reasons other than herself. Somehow that made it that much more personal. That much more worthwhile.

The guys turned as the five women entered by way of the back door, looked them over and knew something was in the works. There was a killer glint in their eyes that bore witness to their suspicions.

"Ladies." Gentry dipped his head in their direction.

"What ya' drinking?" Phoebe leaned next to her husband, took the glass out of his hand and breathed in. "Yuk. I should have known. Scotch."

Sophy walked over to Grady, gave him a lingering kiss and pressed close. "I'll take a coke, Grady, if that's what you're drinking."

He kissed her back, picked up his glass from where it sat on the counter, offered it to her and drawled, "Anything for you, my little southern honey."

Harleigh glanced at the two couples, reminded herself not to envy them overmuch, just enjoy the way love was meant to be while she was with them. Later, when she was gone, she would remember her friends, their relationship and they way they loved.

Making memories, she thought. Right now, in this moment, would be a memory she would cherish forever.

It was all she could hope for. All she would have.

"You guys hungry? Where's Ma? She go up to bed already?"

"She's over at Molly's. It's Wednesday. Her turn to host the quilting circle."

"In that case," Grady rubbed his hands together in

anticipation, "Let's raid her fridge and see what lip-smacking, mouth-watering, to-die-for treats we can find."

"Wait. Mom was baking up a German Chocolate cake earlier," Caleb enlightened them. "She makes a killer cake. Yum-mee."

"Gentleman," Gentry informed the assembled group, "Stealing is unlawful, however, since it's Ma's super scrumptious cake, I'll look the other way and imbibe of that sweetness myself. Especially since our esteemed sheriff is the instigator."

Soon the cake was found, cut and enjoyed. Harleigh marveled at the camaraderie between this group of people she was fortunate to call friends. It seemed just an ordinary thing but to her it held a special sound, a special meaning.

This was an event she never thought she'd be part of. Here she was eating cake, laughing, enjoying the moment and not once since Phoebe had snatched her from Caleb had she been driven by fear. It seemed to be taking a back seat to what she was feeling and doing now. And that in itself was a blessing.

It'd been a long time, it seemed, to have gotten her to this moment. A long road she had traveled to get to this point in her life.

Normal, she thought. She was beginning to feel normal again.

She almost wanted to jump up and shout Hallelujah for the sheer joy of it.

For tonight, though, she'd shelve that emotion and just enjoy what they were giving her, try to give her friendship in return. Limited as that may be.

And Caleb. What to do about him?

Harleigh knew his eyes strayed more than once in her direction. She could feel his gaze wander over her. Feel it touch and caress her from across the room where he stood, listening, chatting, laughing.

More than once, she'd sneak a peek his way. Just checking, she told herself.

When their eyes met, she shored up her body and heart for the impact that would come. His visual caress slithered soft and warm along the surface of her skin. If it hadn't been for the fact that he stood across the room from her, if she closed her eyes, she would swear it was his fingertips that played along the sensitive parts of her body.

It was sensual. Exotic. Special.

Another memory in the making.

She moved toward him without even realizing she did it. Her feet moved and she was just there.

"Harleigh. Enjoy the cake?"

"Yes." Harleigh set her crumb-laden plate in the sink, giving herself a mental reminder to clean it up afterward. "Listen, I want to apologize to you, and Gentry, too for what happened this afternoon."

"No explanation is necessary. Chalk it up to stress."

"Thanks."

"No need for that. You're part of us now, you know."

"It's a good feeling."

"What?"

"Being part of things. Being accepted."

He brushed her arm as he reached around her, placing his own plate in the sink. That brief encounter rushed a quicksilver blast of hot sensation to places she thought long dead.

"You'll find that here."

"Nowhere is a good place to be."

"Nowhere is a sanctuary for lost souls, Harleigh. Take Sophy over there. She was hiding when she came here. Was in the witness protection program until the perp found her and nearly killed her. She ran, decided to go undercover herself, found Nowhere, met Grady and the rest is history."

"That's how Sophy met Grady, then?"

"Yeah, there'd been an APB put out on her, for her own protection, of course. She stepped into Nowhere, was apprehended by Grady then all hell broke loose when they came for her. The idiots in their haste to bring Sophy in and put her in a safe house, led them right to her. If it hadn't been for Grady, she'd probably be dead."

"That's not a good thought."

"No, it isn't. But she gave him a run for his money."

"How so?"

"Well, she didn't care for his manhandling ways, if you can believe that of Grady. She told him in no un-certain terms what he could do with himself and where he could go."

Harleigh looked over at the chummy couple, their arms around each other, and could tell they cared for each other. Body language. It was all there.

"Then, how did they get together?"

"Grady's silver tongue and his southern charm, so Sophy says, broke her down." Caleb laughed, remem-bering.

She nodded toward Delilah. "What about Delilah

and Butch? They just seem an unlikely pair."

"A pair of what?"

"Exactly." She nodded, glad he understood what she meant.

"Ever hear of Lilah?"

"Lilah?"

"Yes, Lilah. She was a model. New York. Mostly did what she refers to as spare parts. Did some runway stuff. Didn't like it."

"What's spare parts?"

"Hands. Feet. Face. Hair. Body parts, that kind of thing, rather than full body shots."

"Yes, I do remember the *Lilah* at my wedding. Everyone was in a buzz about such a glamorous celebrity being in their midst. However did she get here?"

Harleigh stopped, drew in a deep breath, realizing she'd been standing close, having an intelligent conversation, realized again how normal it was. Should she take it farther? She waited for Caleb to answer her question about Delilah before going through with what she had in mind. She might as well, she decided, it was all she had. Memories. These memories she was making this night would have to be enough to sustain her when she was alone. When she was alone ... lonely.

She'd think of Caleb. And remember. And be warm.

She turned her attention back to Caleb and the memory she wanted to make.

"You mean you know Delilah?" He filed that bit of information away to take up with her later. Information he could give to Grady and Gentry.

"Not really. I know about her. I didn't get to meet her that day. Saw her from a distance, though. What happened to her?"

"Seems she was being stalked, decided to take some time off and wound up here. The stalker followed."

"I hate to interrupt the two of you and your delightful conversation," Sophy teased, tugging on Grady's arm, "but I'm taking this tall dark handsome man home so he can relax before he gets a midnight call from Miz Janine about Wilbur and his hound dogs."

"Right behind ya', guys," Delilah chimed in. "Gotta go see about my babies."

"I gotta go, pack and be gone from this Podunk town," Sunny told them with a smirk on her lips.

"Hey, don't put down our little town, Sunny!"

Phoebe stepped forward. "I'll walk you out to the car." She turned toward Gentry and held out her hand.

Harleigh watched in silence as he took it, pressed the back to his lips and tucked her into his side.

"So, it's just you and me now, Harleigh."

Why wait, she decided. She'd put off living long enough.

"Let's sit on the back porch and you can tell me about what happened with Delilah."

Caleb masked his surprise and followed her dutifully out the back door. He decided he'd let her lead this dance and see where it took them.

Once they settled on the steps, he continued with his story.

"Butch. That's what happened."

"Butch?" She was confused. Weren't they talking about Delilah?

"Yeah, the scar on his face. That's how he got it. Walked into a switchblade."

"How awful!"

"Mmm. That switchblade was meant for Delilah. If he'd been another minute later, it would be her that wore that scar."

"Is that why she married him, then? She felt sorry for him?"

"Sorry for him? Hell, no. She worships the ground he walks on. It was Delilah that did the pursuing. But, personally, I think they both chased the other until they got tired of running. I know Gentry did."

"Gentry?"

"Lost his way, found this little burg and that was all she wrote."

"What do you mean by that?"

"He met Phoebe. Need I say more?"

Harleigh laughed then. It all made sense. "No. I guess you don't. Some things defy explanation."

"That's Phebs, all right. She's one of a kind." He lifted a hand and pointed to the velvet-lined, diamond-studded sky. "Hey, look at that moon, would you?"

Harleigh looked upward, frowned. What was he talking about now? There was just a sliver hanging in the sky.

"There isn't much of one tonight."

"But it's still a beautiful sight. The moon in any form is a painting waiting to happen."

She gave a shudder, remembering the painting of Stewart's. The one she'd grown an aversion to. The comparison was too close to the evil that taunted her still.

She knew she shouldn't be having a reaction like this. Knew the moon itself had nothing to do with Stewart and the corruption of his mind.

It was now or never, she decided. The first step was always the hardest.

"Listen ... before on the veranda ... when you kissed me ... I wanted you to know, I thought it was sweet, too."

"Yeah?"

She ran her thumbnail over the fabric of her jeans. "Yes, I did. And, good. Good, too. I didn't want you to think I didn't...I also didn't want you to get the wrong idea."

"And, what idea was that?"

"That I was easy. That I allow that sort of thing. I don't."

He scratched his chin, heard the scrape of nail on whiskers. He'd shaved early that morning and now he was sure he was sporting a five-o'clock shadow. "I never thought that for a minute, Harleigh. You're a beautiful woman and I'm attracted to you. I think you're attracted to me, too. Aren't you?"

How should she answer that? She opted for the truth.

"Yes, I'm attracted to you, Caleb. More than I want to be."

"I'd like to explore that arena. I think it would prove to be enjoyable for both of us."

"As much as I want to, I can't. I have nothing to offer you."

"I don't want anything but you."

"I can't take that kind of chance ... make a commitment. If this was another time and place, maybe. I can't bring anyone else into my problems."

He laughed. "If I'm any judge of human nature, I'd say those four women that walked out the door are already knee-deep in it."

"I really can't allow them to get involved, Caleb. They don't know what they're up against."

"Then, why don't you tell me what they're up against?"

Frustrated that she wasn't getting through to these hardheaded people, she inhaled and blew her breath out again. This lunacy wasn't why she came out here. All she'd wanted was to maybe, if she got up enough nerve, kiss him one more time. To feel his mouth on hers once more while she had the chance. "You guys are a glutton for punishment, aren't you?"

The glance she threw him was harried and intense. He smiled and raised his brows. "I try."

"You're as obstinate as your sister and her friends."

"Your friends, too, Harleigh."

"I know and I don't want them hurt."

"We'll keep everyone safe. Trust us. Trust me."

She wrapped her arms around her waist. As much to protect herself from her own recollections of what had transpired in her past, as much to ward off the horrors that could happen to her friends at Stewart's hands.

"I can't afford to trust, Caleb."

"Give them a chance, Harleigh. Give me a chance."

He reached out, placed his hand on her shoulder and massaged. The way she was feeling right at this moment, she wasn't sure what she should do. Knew she should shake it off. Knew the dangers of letting someone, *a man*, get this close. Then he removed it himself. She wasn't sure if she felt relief or regret.

She cleared her throat. Let it pass. "It's in my

thoughts."

"Then follow through. You won't regret it."

"I can't talk about things I want to forget, Caleb."

"I understand."

She breathed deep and gave a ragged sigh. "No, you don't understand. Not about this. Only another in my position would understand."

"What, Harleigh? Understand that you've been abused? Humiliated? Degraded?" he questioned intently. "How far off the mark am I?"

With surprising agility, she jumped up, nearly falling forward across Caleb in her haste to remove herself from the line of conversation that was taking place. He caught her, steadying her, keeping her upright without any effort on his part, as if she were a child he sat back on her feet.

He straightened, drew her close enough for a direct look. The pearly gray of his eyes swirled before he released her. "Hit a nerve, did I?"

"Let me go, Caleb. You don't have the right to touch me." She could feel her anger grow. That was another surprise. She was astonished that she wasn't cringing from his touch. What she was feeling, however, was something that at the moment she didn't want to examine too closely.

"Maybe not now, but, remember this, Harleigh, the day will come when you want my touch. When you hunger for it, hunger to have my hands on you."

Harleigh opened her mouth to form a reply but the words never came. She had every intention to push him away. Or, to push herself away from him. She didn't know which. Whatever it was never happened. Instead, she just stood inches away, her body welcoming the heat. Welcomed the round of pleasure that skimmed and sizzled over and through her.

She reminded herself one last time that it was in her best interest to drop her hand from his chest where she placed it, intending to push him away. Instead, she felt the acceleration of his heartbeat. An acceleration that was keeping pace with her own. This wasn't why she was here, she told herself. She needed to get away, away from this new danger. More dangerous to her heart than anything Stewart had ever handed out.

And that hunger that he'd warned her about just moments ago sank its teeth into her and rendered her breathless, trembling, weak in the knees. And the desire. A desire so hot and fluid it raced over her with lightning speed. That's when she curled her hands around the cloth of his shirt and held on fast.

The desire took shape, circled through, around, went deep. It was only natural that she press herself into him. Only natural that she return his kiss when he dipped, tasted, tested, took and gave. And, she gave in return.

Caleb relished her mouth, dipped inside for one sweet taste, lingered and reluctantly let her go. There was so much more he wanted to sample. So much more he wanted, period.

Without thinking, she lifted a hand and sketched the contours of his jawline and made another memory. The roughness of the stubble on his face. The shape. The strength.

His hand came up, encircled her wrist, wrapping it with gentle fingers then pressed his mouth against her palm. It was warm. Good. Another memory to file away, she thought.

"This is a good thing, Harleigh, this thing between us. We're good together, you and I. Like peanut butter and jelly. Good and sweet."

He smiled down at her, let his fingertips glide across her chin, allowed himself to follow the softness of her skin down the column of her throat. Then just for himself, he kissed her once again, a feather-light kiss that left promises of good and sweet things to come.

א

There was a lull in business, giving Harleigh time to breath. Time to catch up on side work. Wrap silverware. Check levels of condiments.

Even so, she hurried through it all, smiling, re-membering, loving it. There was a saying, she reminded herself, thinking maybe, just maybe in her case it rang true. There is always a chance that wishing will make it so, it went. She certainly had wished and hoped that she would have the life she was living now.

Still, it would be to her advantage to stay on her toes. She'd noticed of late that she'd become lax, far too relaxed in this atmosphere to let her guard down. Granted, she was surrounded by people who genuinely cared about her, who would go to any lengths necessary to protect her. But deep in her heart, she knew she needed to get back in that groove and prepare for any occurrence.

She needed to go on with her plan about getting out of Nowhere, too, giving up all she'd accomplished being Harleigh Bleu, giving up all she ever wanted.

It was for the best.

She had to protect her friends.

"So, how goes it with you and Caleb?" Sophy roused her out of her thoughts, a knowing smile sliding across her lips, raised her eyebrows, even wiggled them at her. "Hmm?"

"What do you mean, Sophy?" The denial was in her throat. One thing she was finding out about these girls who had taken her under their wing was they would not be put off. Their antenna was always up, always attuned to each other in eye-opening clarity. "There's nothing going on between me and Caleb."

"Hmm," she murmured.

It irritated Harleigh that she could be read so easily. "What is that supposed to mean?"

"Just hmm. Wondering."

"Wondering what?"

"Far be it from me to say so but, uh, unless you've forgotten this little tidbit, I was here when the two of you first met. There was so much electricity in this room you could have lit up the whole town for a week."

Harleigh felt the heat race across her cheeks. Knew that she could do nothing about it. Knew Sophy saw it. So she did the only thing she could. She giggled.

"I suppose the whole town is jabbering on about it."

"In a place like Nowhere, where we take care of our own? Yes."

Harleigh made a note in the back of her mind to be more discreet where Caleb was concerned. All this talk made her want to hide from prying eyes, shut the door behind her and hide away. Not in fear or shame. But to keep her emotions, her apparently transparent reactions to herself.

She needed to keep in the forefront of her awareness, the war with Stewart, that it could never be won
in traditional ways. Evil dwelled deep in his heart and
soul. He'd stop at nothing to get at her. She'd won a
battle here, a skirmish there. But if he ever found out
that she cared about Caleb, he'd do more than cause
him injuries. He'd kill him, of that she was sure.

Just as sure as she took her next breath.

"I hope it's not going to be run though a rumor mill
and gossiped about. I don't need gossip."

"Well, I can't say it's gossip exactly. More like
taking a bet on when Caleb falls."

"Taking bets?" The hair on her arms rose. Another
goose-bump moment. She wasn't sure whether to be
pleased, angry or just annoyed. "They're taking bets?"

"Yeah." Sophy took a swipe at the counter with a
damp cloth. "Pete's saying he's already under the knife.
Lyle's saying no woman's gonna take the big man
down. Then there's our own making side bets."

"Our own?"

"My Grady. Phoebe's Gentry and Delilah's Butch.
Our own."

"Surely you can't be serious?"

"As a heart attack."

She opted for annoyance. "Don't they have better
things to do? Don't they have a life?"

"Nowhere *is* their life. You're part of it now so you
better get use to it."

Harleigh wasn't sure she liked that either but Sophy was right. She'd cast off her old life for this one.
And if this were part of it, then she would accept it.

"So," she said, a twinkle in her eyes, a sheepish
grin on her mouth. "Who's winning? Me or Caleb?"

Sophy laughed with delight and gave her best rendition of a southern drawl. "Yessiree, Miz Harleigh, I think you'll do."

The noon crowd came in then and their camaraderie ground to a halt. Still, it lingered in Harleigh's mind, bringing a small smile to her lips on occasion.

These things circled around you, she was thinking. She'd been defeated, beaten down with no hope, when she'd stepped off that bus and planted her feet into the soil of Nowhere. She would've hung her head if not for the desperation that was running cold through her blood.

Now she nearly shouted, *Bring it on. I'm ready!*

And the little thing about her and Caleb, *the big man about to take a fall,* she'd keep to herself. Wouldn't breathe a word that she was waiting in breathless anticipation of their next meeting. He'd asked to take her up to the music park and show her around. Crowds'd surround them and there were lots to do there. They could go to whatever talented artist was signed on for the day. Could be country artists, he said, or blue grass or a festival of some kind. Always something going on there.

She'd said yes. Had actually said yes and now she had a real date. She felt lightheaded. Full of giddy feelings that she had to swat down every time the thoughts came bragging their way into her mind.

She'd changed. Knew she had. Owed it all to Nowhere. To the sisterhood. And Caleb.

Each day was better than the day before. She couldn't ask for more.

Sometimes, though, she wondered when the axe would fall. So much had gone right since she came here that it made her doubt the whole thing. She steeled herself, waiting for the moment when she'd wake up from a dream this fantastic and find herself locked away in that dark closet she'd been thrown for some unknown discretion against Stewart's sensibilities.

Later, in the confines of her room, out on her private balcony, she speculated, *no*, marveled at the path her new life had taken. Gazing out on that little yellow house with the picket fence, she was content. Just knowing it was there.

She heard the knock, wanted to ignore it, wanted to pretend she wasn't home. She just wanted to stand here and savor the moment. Unfortunately, whoever was on the other side of the door was insistent, refusing to go away.

The sisterhood stood on the other side as she flung the door open. Three of them, anyway. Sunny had flown home, her vacation cut short. Some crime had been committed that her expertise was needed for.

Smiles, delight, happiness. All those on their faces. How could she turn them away? After all, they were the sisterhood, her included.

"Hey guys, come in."

"This is just as I remember, Harleigh." Phoebe spun around in a circle. "Callie and I used to fight over who got this wonderful room. Naturally, him being the oldest, he won. I never let up on him, though. Sometimes he would honor me and allow me to enter his domain."

This was said with affection, love. Harleigh knew they adored each other.

"I've got something to tell you all. Breathe a word of it and you're dead meat," Phoebe told them all.

"Lips are sealed. Right, Sophy?"

"Right, Delilah. Mum's the word."

Phoebe clasped her hands together and held them tight. "I'm pregnant! I'm going to have a baby!"

The girls rushed forward, wrapped their arms around her, exclaiming. "That's great." "How exciting."

Harleigh watched, not sure what she should do. Not sure if she should stay on the sidelines or join in. That decision was taken from her.

Delilah grabbed her wrist, yanked her forward into the circle and made her a part of the celebration. They jumped up and down, rejoiced in the news, screamed with delight.

"When's the due date?"

"Boy, or girl? Do you know?"

"Do you have morning sickness?"

"Is that why Gentry's walking on clouds?"

"Have you told Ma yet?"

With that last question, the girls grew quiet. Everyone except Harleigh knew the hardship Phoebe had gone through with miscarriages, the heartbreak of losing a child. How much she wanted one to cuddle, to hold tight against her. How much she wanted one to love.

Phoebe turned away from them, walked out onto the balcony. They followed. She leaned against the banister.

"No, I haven't told Mom yet. You girls know how badly I want a baby." She turned to them with a smile, eased her bottom onto the top of the railing and sat. "This time, I have an excellent chance of going to full term. I'm past five months along, girls."

"Already?"

"You're just now telling us about it?"

"I couldn't. I was afraid of even breathing a word. Afraid if I did, something bad would happen ... still am to a certain degree. I've never been this far before."

"You're taking care, then, I take it?"

Phoebe looked at Delilah with something short of disbelief on her features. "With a husband like Gentry?"

"Silly me, I forgot who I was talking about there for a moment," Sophy said.

"I think it's wonderful," Harleigh added, a wistful note in her voice. "I always wanted a baby. Stewart didn't. Said it would ruin my body. Give me stretch marks. Make my boobs droop."

They all stared back at her in dismay. Then she realized what she'd said and felt foolish. "Sorry. I didn't mean to say that."

"No, it's all right."

"No, it isn't," she insisted. "It wasn't right of me to complain about my shortcomings when there's so much to celebrate. You girls sit down and I'll get us some tea."

"Why don't we all go to the kitchen. Mom's back," Phoebe told them. "We'll all tell her."

They marched through the balcony and bedroom doors, down the stairway and into the kitchen like they were in a parade. Phoebe was humming tunelessly and the rest gave their rendition of whatever their interpretation of the ditty was.

Kate turned, looked at the girls as if they'd all lost their minds and wondered about this group of girls that had become friends. They were a diverse group, she thought. Looks, personalities, interest. But still so alike. Warm, caring, funny.

"So, what are you little fiends up to? What mischief have you got brewing in those pea brains?"

Phoebe feigned shock. "Surely you scoff, dear woman! Us, the newly-formed sisterhood up to mischief?"

Kate tipped her head down and looked at them over the frames of her glasses. "You forget, my child, that I had you for twenty-some odd years. I know when you're up to something. What is it?"

Phoebe stepped forward, took the bowl Kate was whipping some tasty concoction up in and set it aside. She put her hands on top of her mother's shoulders, guided her to the table, pulled out a chair and offered her a seat with an elegant flourish of her right hand and tip of her head.

Phoebe held up a finger for quiet. "Just a minute." Then whipped out her cell phone, and punched in a number. "It's time. I'm in the kitchen."

She strolled back to the counter, pulled down six glasses, placed them on a tray and sat it in the middle of the table. Opening the fridge, she withdrew the pitcher of cold tea her mother always kept there and poured each one a glass.

Gentry ambled into the kitchen, spied Phoebe and walked leisurely over to where she stood. The smiles they gave each other were secretive and mysterious. He brushed his hand over her hair, kissed her lightly on the lips and pulled her into him. She paused, let his presence sink into her then stepped away and clapped her hands together.

"Okay, everybody, listen up. You guys all have a

seat while we give Mom the good news."

They all sat, sipped and waited. Breathless. Anticipating Ma Forrester's reaction.

Kate eyed her daughter, a frown dragging on her brows. Just what was the little imp up to now? What had she done? Or more likely, she rephrased, what had she gotten herself into? If Gentry was here to save her, the news must be astounding.

"Well?"

"I'm going to have a baby, Mom."

Hope. Pleasure. Happiness.

Then, all those emotions were replaced.

Concern. Worry. Anxiety.

"Are you sure, Phoebe? I can't stand the thought of you being disappointed again."

Phoebe smiled and held her hand out to Gentry who folded it into his own. "We're sure. Let's be positive about this. Mom, I'm five months, nearly six months along."

"It's okay," Gentry said softly, know the anxiety that was running through Kate. He'd had a lot of those anxious moments himself. "We're taking every precaution in the book this time."

Kate knew they were right. Be positive. What did you really have if you didn't have hope? She grabbed her daughter, gave her a big hug, sniffed back the tears and held out her hand to Gentry. He came easily into her arms. "And, here I thought you were just getting fat."

Phoebe laughed with glee, pulled up her blouse, yanked down on the waistband of her pants, and patted her stomach, proud of the little baby mound that formed on her body. "Look at this girls! Look at what I'm cooking up down there."

"Phoebe, pull your shirt down," Kate chastised. "Nobody wants to look at your body."

"Gentry does, don't ya', baby?"

Gentry felt his face burn and knew he was as red as the shirt Phoebe wore. Her sense of humor was one of the things that he loved about her.

Kate laughed, knowing the tight spot Phoebe had swept him into. She loved Gentry as her own and sympathized. "Ignore that brat of mine, Gentry," she told him, trying to alleviate his discomfort. "It's the only way."

Delilah lifted her glass. "A toast, everybody. To the new mom and pop to be."

Glasses were raised, clinked and congrats given. They chatted about names, nurseries and baby things. Of rocking chairs, stuffed toys and a new house.

Slowly, they each took their leave, allowing Harleigh to return to the sanctuary of her own room.

Stepping inside, knowing what she had to do, she took out a pad of paper, found a pencil and stepped out onto her balcony. Taking a seat, she looked out at the forest. A doe and yearling grazed at its edge, at ease at the perimeter where nature and man collided.

She put pencil to paper then and began her plan of escape. No, not escape, she corrected. She'd call it adventure. She wrote *The Road to Adventure* across the top of the yellow paper.

Pack, she wrote. Easy. Not much to shove in her bag. Had spent only essential monies.

Car. She'd keep it. It would be her pumpkin. Her means of escape. She'd see to it that Delilah got every red cent that was owed to her.

Destination. West, maybe. According to the residents of Nowhere, she was in spitting distance of the Florida-Georgia border. She got out a map she'd found in the glove compartment, checked out a route to go. Probably best if she hit a major highway first, then stick to the back roads.

"Let's see," she spoke aloud. "Interstate Ten West looks like the way to go."

She traced the line on the map with her finger then jotted down small towns off the beaten path, sure that Stewart wouldn't lower himself to step a foot into someplace that he felt was beneath him.

Timeframe? That was the clincher. When? When would she go?

She gnawed on the inside of her mouth, trying to figure that one out. Still, if she was very careful, squeezed each penny, she could do it. She'd have to find jobs that were easy to come by, no background checks, easy in, easy out. Then on to the next town on her list.

She'd have to decide length of time to stay in each location. It would probably be best if she kept a whole state or two between locations, circle around, keep moving.

That should do the trick, she decided.

She glanced down at the words she'd written and smiled. At least now she had a working plan.

She'd take every precaution. But she wouldn't run in fear.

This time would be different. Was different. This time she had a reason to run that was poles apart from the original. This time she had a purpose and that was to keep her friends safe. And Caleb.

She thought about each of them now. Thought of how each had tried to help her ... had helped her in one way or another already. Thought about what Caleb had told her about them, their spouses. It struck her that Caleb had said very little about his own life, and that in itself gave her cause to wonder.

A man as attractive as Caleb must have a horde of women chasing after him, she mused. Did he like blondes, brunettes, redheads?

What kind of food did he like? Was he a steak and potatoes man? Or did he opt for junk food? Pizza? Hamburgers? Hot dogs?

She knew a few things about him already. Knew he was dedicated to his work. Loved his mother and sister. Even held a surprising affection for his brother-in-law seeing as how he bad-mouthed his career and mode of dress every chance he got. And, if his front yard was any indication of what he liked, he was a lover of flowers. And that was a big plus as far as she was concerned.

And there was the house, of course. Her fairy tale house. The house of her dreams. That little yellow house with its white picket fence and a yard spilling over with all those glorious colors.

Now that was a definite plus.

But like her house, Caleb could only be a dream. A yearning of her heart.

She had her memories, though. Memories that she'd made from the beginning of her new life. Especially those she'd made of Caleb. His scent. His smile. His kiss. His touch.

Oh, his touch. Yes, she'd remember that for sure. Even now, her heart thrummed, pleasure skidded across her skin, sunk inward. Yes, that would forever be something she would remember.

One thing was for sure. She *would* have that date.

The object of her musings drove into the driveway. She watched silently as he exited his car, took the steps two at a time, humming all the way. The sound itself, though tuneless, was still music to her ears.

She thought she'd remained inconspicuous, but he turned back and waved up at her. "Hungry?"

She nodded her answer.

"Come on over."

He didn't give her a chance to refuse, immediately turning back to the front door.

He left it open, she noted, as she walked through, wondering what she was doing here. Knowing what the dangers were. But she wanted … needed this one more memory.

"Hey, Miz Harleigh."

"Hey, Caleb, how are you?"

"Don't you look scrumptious?" He moved in quickly but this time she didn't mind. She wanted this.

"You look scrumptious, too."

"I'm going to kiss you now." He waited for her to object, gave her time to push him away.

"I want you to kiss me, Caleb." She smiled up at him, confident in what she was doing. She brushed her fingertips across his chest, just wanting to touch. "Matter of fact, I'm going to kiss you back."

He pressed his lips to hers, took as she gave. Gave as she took. She made him crazy. Made the blood zing and rush. Pulse jumping, tumbling.

She couldn't stop the moan of pleasure from escaping. And with each twist and taste, her hunger grew.

Burned hot.

This time it was she that wrapped herself around him. It was she that had him holding on, gasping for air while her hunger drove him up and over.

Her hunger was nearly out of control. But she pressed in farther, savoring the feel of his body against her, caressing his chest to relish the beat of his heart against her fingertips.

He didn't think his body could take much more. She'd awakened things in him, he never knew were there. She made him ache, made him ache so deep within, he didn't think he would survive.

It was in the back of his mind that all he had to do was swing her up into his arms and walk down the hall. He could even see it happening. He would slowly undress her, caressing each silken inch of her skin as he went. Maybe even follow his fingertips with his mouth, kissing his way all over her.

"Harleigh." It was almost a question. One he knew he shouldn't be asking. He slid his mouth across hers one more time and let her go.

Instead of turning and making a mad dash out the door as he thought she might, she gave him a sweet smile. A smile that told him all he wanted to know.

But still he hesitated. He knew the time had to be right.

"Harleigh," he repeated, placing a kiss on her forehead. "I'd ask you to stay with me …"

"All right."

"All right?" His breath hitched.

"Yes, Caleb, I'll stay."

CHAPTER NINE

ℵ

Blatantly, in the middle of a heart-stopping kiss, Caleb's pager beeped. Startled, they jerked apart, then laughed shakily at the interruption.

He pulled her back into his arms for a moment, breathed in the scent of her then stepped away, pulling his pager from his belt and punched the button.

"Bettlyn."

"You better call."

"Yeah, probably in labor." Still he stood close, troubled, not wanting to leave her, not wanting to let the moment go. She smiled up at him then. A smile that not only was on her lips but also in her eyes. Finally.

Before she turned to go, she stood on her tiptoes and let her lips glide over his in one glorious toe-curling kiss. "Later."

Unspoken promises. Silent vows. Subtle assurances. All there in that kiss.

She turned, walked out the door and left him there before he could change gears.

She heard his truck spin gravel as he tore out of the driveway. It must be nice to have that kind of purpose, that kind of need in your life, she mused as she walked back to the sanctity of her room.

One day, she promised, one day.

"Harleigh?" Kate called from the kitchen.

"Yes?"

"Come on in and sit a spell. Tell me what you and *the* sisterhood have been up to?"

Kate pulled an apple pie out of the oven, placing it on a wire tray to cool. She pulled off her padded gloves and hung them up on the hooks by the stove. She looked exactly what she was. A woman comfortable with herself, with life.

Harleigh could only hope to be that comfortable in her own skin, she supposed. She knew it was somewhere inside her. Just waiting. Sometimes she'd feel like she was almost there. Then ... then something would happen to take it all away.

It took different forms. Sometimes a soft whisper. Sometimes a glide across her skin. Sometimes a yearning in her heart.

There was one more thing, she remembered, one more thing she wanted to investigate and explore before she left as she sat here in Kate's kitchen. She wanted to know about the *enchanted* forest. She was confident enough in herself now to ask the questions, to find out from the one person who would have the answers.

"Tell me about yourself, Kate. About the Rose House. How it chose you. And, that clearing in the forest."

"It's not something that can be told in one sitting," she replied. "So much has happened here. To this house. To others. To me."

"Then, why don't we start there. Start with you. How you came to be here."

Kate was lost in her own memories for a moment,

then smiled. "Yes, that would be the perfect place to start. The Rose House is a story in itself."

Pleased that Kate chose to start with herself, Harleigh settled in, prepared to listen to what she knew would shed some light on the mystery of this place.

"I was a young women, married, a mother of two, when I first came here." She paused, a memory of the woman she used to be flitting across her mind. "My Mitch and I had all these plans and visions of how our life was going to be. Mitch had lost his job with the company he worked for. So we decided to move the family to Texas where his grandparents were. They lived outside of Victoria. It wasn't somewhere we wanted to go but we needed a stable home environment and we had the kids. And his grandparents were all the family we had left."

"At that time, we lived in Macon, Georgia. We decided to take a short detour to the music park over at Live Oak. Mitch loved country music and one of his favorite singers was playing at the amphitheatre there so we had to go, of course. Needless to say, we never made it."

The laugh she gave wasn't one of regret, it was one of amusement and acceptance.

"So, what happened?"

"The Rose House happened. Nowhere happened."

"How so?"

"We drove off the exit ramp of Interstate seventy-five for gas. Live Oak was on down the road and we thought we'd have a look around. Driving to Nowhere the car quit on us, right in front of the Rose House. Mitch went inside to call a tow truck while I waited with the kids in the car. They said the motor blew. The money we'd saved to keep us going went to buy a car."

"What did you do, Kate? How did you survive?"

"The Rose House."

"The Rose House?"

"Yes, it was our salvation. Almost as if it was meant to be. At the time a Florida state senator owned it. He'd bought it as a pastime for his wife but she didn't like it here. It was too far from the conveniences she was use to. So he'd hired someone to run it for them. They'd just fired the gardener. Some would say it was a case of being in the right place at the right time. But I believe it was a case of the Rose House waiting for the right person to come along.

"The Dawsons let us move into the little house in the back, the one where Caleb lives now. Since Mitch was working here, I knew I had to do something to help bring in some money. School was starting. Caleb and Phoebe needed new clothes, supplies, that sort of thing. So, Mitch worked here at the Rose House and I started work at the Nowhere Café. We lived a decent life for about three years, I guess."

"So, like they say, the rest is history, huh?"

"No, it wasn't that way at all."

"What happened? I thought you owned the Rose House by then."

"Mitch was killed in a freak lightning storm."

"Oh, my God, Kate, I'm so sorry. Caleb did mention that to me."

Kate clasped the hand that Harleigh held out to her and squeezed, "It's okay ... now. Back then, I didn't think I'd live through it."

"You don't have to say anything more, Kate. Some things are too painful to talk about."

Harleigh had learned that the hard way when all her hopes and dreams were dashed by one blow of mean hard-knuckled fists.

"I was devastated. Just like that he was gone. In an instant. Mitch and the kids had been my life and now I had to go on without him. It was difficult, still is, sometimes."

Kate had stopped talking, lost in painful memories. Harleigh sat quietly, not wanting to intrude on a private moment. She was surprised when Kate rose from the kitchen table, went to the apple pie to check if it was cool then resumed her story.

"Anyway, the senator closed up the Rose House and put it up for sale. They let me stay here, rent the house, some of the residents of Nowhere pitched in and helped me much like we do anyone who passes through that needs it. Much like you."

"It's much more than I deserve. I hate being a hardship on everyone."

"Don't ever think that, Harleigh. The majority of the people who live here have hearts of gold and are willing to go that extra mile. We've all had bad times at one time or another. It's just our way of giving back."

"I know but everyone has been so generous. Take Delilah and Glory."

"Glory?"

"Oh." Harleigh turned a little red. "Glory's the name I gave the car."

"Patches. The name of my car was Patches. Every time I turned around, I had to do something to it. Seemed like I was always patching it up so that's why I named it that."

"Great name. Glory came from the morning glories

that used to hang on our fence when I was a kid."

"Ah."

"So how did you become the owner of the Rose House?"

Kate laughed, thinking back. "Actually, I'm still not sure. It's kind of a mystery to me, even today."

"How could that be?"

"Well, I continued to work at the café. I was doing okay. Able to buy what the kids needed to have at first. But everyday I would pass the Rose House and wonder about it. Once in a while, I could swear I heard things. Not ghostly noises or chains or anything like that. More like whispers, that feeling that someone's there but when you look there's no one around. Occasionally, I imagined I would see a glow in the windows. There was something about the house that pulled at me. That wrapped around me and tugged me in."

"I know exactly what you mean. I could feel it the moment I walked up those steps and onto the veranda. It was like I was surrounded by this magic."

"Exactly."

"I never told anyone because I didn't want them to think I was nuts."

"There's only a few I've told myself for the very same reason. Anyway, one night when the kids were asleep, I went inside. It was quiet, warm and welcoming. I started imagining it as my own. That I could make it more than it was. Restore it to what it was meant to be.

"That marked the beginning of a nightly ritual. The kids would fall asleep, I'd go over to the house and just wander from room to room … imagining. Naturally I kept all that to myself. Back in those days, there were still a lot of people in small towns like this that believed a woman with kids couldn't make it on their own unless they were on welfare or flat on their back, if you know what I mean."

"It must have been very hard for you."

"Financially, yes. But I had Caleb and Phoebe. They were my life. All I needed. Besides, Mitch was the only man I ever wanted. They made me the town project." Laughing, she drew circles on the table with her fingertip. "I was introduced to all the unattached male relatives they could find. There was one particular man, very arrogant. Smug. Self-important. Nice-looking. Very insistent. I'm surprised he didn't just drag me off and force me into marriage."

"Did you think about marrying him then?"

"Maybe for half a second."

"That bad, huh?"

"Not bad, just not for me. The last straw was the day he told, *told* me, mind you, that I was going to marry him or he'd see to it that I had no other choice. He was in negotiations with the Senator to buy the property the Rose House sat on. Said he didn't want the houses, was going to tear them down and build a subdivision. He was a real estate developer from Tallahassee scouting out locations. I was really down that day, couldn't afford give the kids some of the things I knew they wanted and do for them the way two parents could. I mean, I was doing okay with the bare necessities. Sometimes kids need more than that. I knew that somehow I'd lose everything if I didn't marry the man."

"Evidently you didn't. Are you sorry?"

"I have no regrets about anything I've ever done. I

was despondent. I went into the Rose House, wandering around like I usually did. That night, I saw this shadow. It was an ethereal shape, gossamer, an angel if you like. So fragile. She — I call her a she — I like to think of the entity that way. Anyway, I followed her. She walked slowly, gliding actually, checking over her shoulder, almost as if she wanted me to follow. When she got to the edge of the forest, I decided I'd had enough of phantoms for one night. Just as I turned, it seemed like she zoomed toward me and I fell backward. I looked into the face of the most beautiful creature I think I've ever seen. I could see through her and she seemed to, well, glow.

"She reached out her hand to me and I took it, she pulled me to my feet. Her touch was feather-light, warm and peaceful. She turned from me and made her way back to the forest. It seemed like she floated rather than stepped. She beckoned me to follow. We came out into that clearing where the hewn-out log, she gestured as if she were trying to tell me something. I sat on the log and she sat by me, took my hand. She reached out and closed my eyes with her fingertips. I heard this, singing, I guess. I had the most wonderful feeling seep into me. It went deep, gave me peace, solace. I was still grieving for Mitch, even though it had been a few years since he'd died. Somehow, with just that touch, she healed my heart. When I opened my eyes, she smiled, shimmered and faded away. The next day there was an insurance man knocking on my door with a double indemnity life insurance policy for $250,000."

"You've got to be kidding?"

"No, not kidding. Want to know the weirdest thing about it?"

"What would that be?"

"Mitch never had a life insurance policy. We couldn't afford it."

"Oh … Oh."

"Exactly. Now you explain that one to me."

"Yeah, I see what you mean about weird."

"For me, it was a windfall. I bought the Rose House, renovated and restored it. Added a few things, things that I thought should be here, like the Devreaux girls rooms. I've been here ever since and now, like you said, the rest is history. Through the years, from time to time, that fragile creature has appeared to me. Almost as if she were waiting for something, for someone. Like she needed someone. Like she was lonely."

"I've had things similar that happen to me for no reason that I can come up," Harleigh told her. "Sometimes when things were the darkest, when circumstances were so horrid that I couldn't stand it, I'd find myself standing on the edge of this abyss. It was where I would go when it was the worst, my safe haven. I'd watch this glow through a mist."

"Everybody needs somewhere to go when times get rough, Harleigh. Even if it is in our own minds."

"For a long time it was that way. There'd be the glow and the mist and each time it would get stronger and brighter. And closer. The closer it came to me the more the mist swirled and the more distinct it became. But I came here and it was different."

"Maybe it was different because of the location," Kate suggested. "Like you said, magic. There's something about this place, isn't there?"

"Yes, there is."

"So it's happened here, then?"

"Yes, but that's what's so strange. Always before it was when I was on the edge of desperation."

"Where did it happen? I mean, was it the house? The forest?"

"The first time was my first morning here. I wanted to begin the day by watching the sun come up. All of a sudden, I felt a warmth surround me, the mist in the distance and when I looked at my hands, it was … well, that part is really hard to explain."

Kate rose again to check on her pie. "Never mind me, go on with your story, Harleigh, while I get us a drink. What'll it be today, tea, coke, juice?"

"A coke would be nice."

Harleigh looked on as Kate pulled two glasses out of the cupboard, filled them with ice, setting them on the table and popped the tops of two cans of coke. She listened to the fizz of the cola as it hit the ice, watched it foam over the cubes while the bubbles danced.

"Then?" Kate prompted, taking a sip of her drink.

"I was standing at the edge of a void. Always before I stood waiting for a connection to the other side but that was as far as it would take me. This time it came closer than it ever did before. It was exhilarating. Then the mist that lay between me and the other side changed and the golden glow began a slow swirl upward.

"I glanced down at my hands to make sure I was where I thought I was, that I wasn't somehow dreaming this. My hands were wrapped around the railing. I was there on the balcony yet I wasn't. Then, the warm glow from across the abyss enveloped me as the air shifted and stirred. The faint light in the swirling mist became stronger.

"When I glanced back up, there were shapes inside. I'd never seen those before. They moved, outlined in the shadows. Then a figure stepped out of it. I lost my breath, knew I was hallucinating but I didn't want this to end if it was a dream. At first, I refused to believe what it was."

Harleigh breathed in deep, picking up her glass, sipping. Kate did the same, allowing the young woman a moment to get her thoughts together. She was glad Harleigh was finally talking about her life. She could only speculate on what had happened to the young woman to have devastated her so badly. Deep down Kate knew Harleigh had been abused. She was a firm believer in getting things out into the open. Knew it would take a lot of weight off her shoulders. She was content to wait.

"Me. It was me," Harleigh finally said, almost as if she didn't believe it herself.

That was something that Kate hadn't counted on, choking back the coke she'd been sipping. "You?"

Harleigh frowned as she saw again the image of herself looking back at her. "Yes, I could swear it was me. It was me but then again, it wasn't me. You've seen things that was the same but different somehow, haven't you? The same yet something about it wasn't quite right."

"Yes, I have," confessed Kate. "Many a time."

"That's what it was. The same, yet different. Even so I recognized it just the same. Then something else happened that never happened before. From somewhere inside that mist, another shadow formed and emerged to stand by me, the other me. I didn't recognize him but he was a very handsome man in a strange kind of way.

He had something in his hand, something like a palm pilot that he was constantly punching at. I could tell they were talking but I couldn't hear the words. I could see his mouth move, he turned to me, well, to my other self."

Harleigh laughed, nervous now that she was laying bare parts of her private life. "You probably don't want to hear all this. It sounds like something out of a science fiction movie."

"That's where you're wrong. I do want to hear it. I love this kind of mystic stuff." Kate reached out and patted her on the arm and laughed. "Maybe we can compare notes."

"Well, this is the real hair-raising-on-the-back-of-the-neck, goose-bumps-on-the-arms, chills-running-down-the-spine part. This other me raised her hand and reached out to me. It seemed like she wanted to come to me or for me to come to her. I was like a pillar of stone, seeing, hearing, feeling but not moving. So I just watched, wanting to go to her, then just as swift as it came it all faded away."

"Just like that?"

"Just like that."

"I wonder what that meant? Have you seen her or you since then?" Kate laughed, liking the way it sounded here in her kitchen. Liked the way Harleigh laughed, a tinkling kind of joyful sound. Liked the way Harleigh's eyes twinkled with pleasure, the way they crinkled at the corners when she let herself go. "I like that, Harleigh, you should relax and laugh more often, enjoy yourself, enjoy life."

She didn't know how to respond. She *had* been enjoying herself, she realized. This was one of the goals she had set for the new Harleigh but it saddened her that it couldn't continue. Soon she'd be on her way. She should never have gotten involved with these people. It was too hard on the heart. She didn't want to let go.

"I mean to," she stated honestly. "It's one of the things I mean to do from now on." What she didn't say was that she wouldn't be doing it here.

"It's a good feeling. Laughter. Medicine for the soul, like they say."

"Yes, it *is* a good feeling and I enjoyed talking to you more than you'll ever know. I haven't had those kinds of opportunities of late." She scooted her chair back and looked down at Kate. "Thanks for listening and not laughing. It was good to unload all that."

"My pleasure." Kate could tell she couldn't detain her any longer so she let her go, watching the slender frame that was now walking straighter, taller, more confident. She wondered what was rolling around in that mind of hers. She hoped it wasn't what she'd glimpsed in her eyes.

That soon she'd be on the run again.

Before she had time to make herself comfortable out on her own private world, Harleigh was interrupted by a knock on her door. She grumbled slightly under her breath, she didn't want visitors, she wanted to finalize her plans. Still, this was all being a part of something. Of being normal.

"Hey, Delilah, what's up?"

Delilah stepped inside the door and smiled that million-dollar smile of hers. "Just passing by and wanted to stop in, see how you were doing. Maybe talk to you a little about the sisterhood and our plans."

"I don't really think it's necessary …"

"Sure, it is. Look at all the available ways to obtain the data we need at our disposal. Grady, for sure. Sophy's already got him working on where Stewart is and what he's up to. Phoebe has Gentry going over the law books and digging into what we can do about him."

"Oh, Delilah, you don't know what you're up against."

"He doesn't know what he's up against either, Harleigh. You don't ever have to be afraid," she said fiercely. "I promise you, he'll never touch you again. Ever."

Those few words had Harleigh tearing up. She swiped them away, sniffed and reached out, giving Delilah a big hug. "You're a good friend, Delilah. I'm so glad I met you. I just want you to know I'll never forget you or what you've done for me."

"Geez, Harleigh, you make it sound like we'll never see each other again. You're not gonna do something stupid like hit the road again, are you?"

How was she to answer that one?

"I really don't know what I'm planning," she told her slowly. "I can't stand the thought of someone getting hurt on my account."

"What about Caleb, Harleigh? The man's stuck on you."

She frowned, turned away and sighed. Slowly, she walked out on the balcony, gripped the banister and gazed toward that little yellow house. "Caleb. What do I do about Caleb?"

Delilah stepped up by Harleigh and laid her hand atop hers. "You do care for him, don't you? And, when I say *care* for him, I mean more than mere friendship. I mean caring … like the be-still-my-heart kind."

Caught, she laughed. "You have me there. He does make my pulse race."

"And?"

"And, my heart pound."

"And?"

"You just don't let up, do you? And here I thought Phoebe was the bulldozer."

"And?"

Harleigh laughed again, charmed and thrilled at having moments like this. The good-natured teasing. The camaraderie.

"He makes me feel … I don't know … special, I guess. He's so different from Stewart. Stewart was cruel."

"You can't say that about Caleb."

"No, you can't. I learned that early on. I never wanted to be near a man again, let alone have one touch me."

"The man's a babe magnet, that's for sure."

"You can say that again. As much as I don't want to admit such a thing, he made my knees weak."

"I like the sound of that. What did you do about it?"

"Nothing … yet," she said with a grin. "I'm a little slow on the uptake. It's not that I don't want to. The whole thing's a little unsettling. I've never been a sexual person, or I thought I wasn't."

"Then Caleb came along and rang your chimes, is that it? I'm liking this more and more. Ever get down and dirty?"

Hot color flashed across her face, tinting her cheeks a becoming pink. "Came close. Really close, if you know what I mean. I would've right then and there.

I was ready, willing. *More than willing.* I've never been kissed like that. Never reacted like that. I was ... burning, on fire from the inside out. Then we were interrupted ... Bettlyn went into labor and he left to deliver her baby, I think. I don't know if that was a good thing or a bad thing."

"Sounds like a good thing to me. Mutual attraction. Next time, if I were you I'd jump his bones."

"Maybe next time, I will."

"Now you're talking, you wicked woman!" Delilah teased.

They looked on as Caleb drove up to the house, waited until he glanced up and waved. He grabbed his medical bag from the back seat, took the steps two at a time and entered his house.

"You know what I'm thinking I'd do if that were my Butch down there?" Delilah asked, with a mischievous smile on her lips.

Harleigh laughed. She knew what Delilah had in mind but she had to respond. It was the girl-pal thing to do. "I'm almost afraid to ask."

"Well, if it was me and that was Butch, I think I'd be in that house before another minute passes and finish what we started. What d'ya think about that?"

Why not do it? she decided. It's what she really wanted to do. She wanted to near him, to be drawn close against him, rest her cheek against that chest. So, just do it.

"I think that's a plan."

Delilah held her palm up. "High five!"

Harleigh lifted her hand, slapped it against Delilah's, felt the wonderful zing on her skin then reached out and gave her a hug.

"Get going. Take a nice long bubble bath, while I run home and bring you back something sexy. Then you go over there and give that man an evening he won't forget!"

א

Caleb heard the knock on the door, glanced over at the clock on his microwave and wondered who would be visiting him at this time. He dried his hands with the dishtowel and looped it through the handle of the fridge.

The surprise had him taking a few steps backward when he answered the door. The last person he expected to see standing there was Harleigh.

"Well, hello there."

She looked up into his face. She liked the way he looked, she decided. She liked the way his eyes crinkled just a little at the corners when his mouth curved up into a smile. A smile that had her heart beating out a rhythm against her ribs.

"Hello there, yourself. Mind if I come in for a minute?"

He opened the door wider and she stepped through. He wasn't sure what he should do now. He knew what he wanted to do but decided to let Harleigh make the first move in case he was mistaken why she was there.

He could tell she was nervous. He'd never seen her look quite this way, either. And what in the world did she have on? Where did she get that slinky body-hugging little number. It made her legs appear longer, like they went all the way up to *there*.

"So?"

"So, uh." She swung her arms forward and backward. She was so nervous her toes tingled. Never having done this before, she was unsure what came next. It was like your first dance with a boy, trying to figure out who was supposed to lead. She took a deep breath, wanting to get it out before she lost her nerve, something she was short of at the moment. "I, uh, I thought that maybe we could pick up where we left off."

Caleb was having a brain freeze. He heard every word she said but what she was saying didn't register in his head. "Where we left off?"

"You know, earlier?"

"Earlier?"

Why did he keep repeating everything she was saying? she wondered. Was she not being clear about what she was doing here?

"Before Bettlyn ... before Bettlyn, we were, uh ..."

Then, in a flash, it all came together. Came together and crashed around him. He reached out for her and folded her into his arms and breathed her in.

And his pager went off.

He groaned. "Not again."

Harleigh laughed, actually relieved. Her insides were wound so tight, the first touch of him had her jumping out of her skin. She looked up at him, the amusement playing across her features. "I think this is where I exited before."

Then because she knew at the moment she could afford to play, she tipped herself up on her toes, curved her arms around his neck and dragged him down to her mouth. She rubbed her mouth across his, a soft moan escaping her throat at the contact. Electric, Sophy had said. Electrifying, she corrected, turned and left him to answer his page.

א

"This better be good, Grady, or you're dead."

"A little grumpy, are you?"

"You could say that. You have a great sense of timing, Sheriff. There ought to be a law. What's up?"

"Maybe a broken nose, or a few broken ribs. The kind of thing you get paid for. Charlie was yelling at Bonnie again and all hell broke loose."

Caleb ground his teeth together, wishing he could get his hands on Charlie Fitch. Any man who would lay a hand on a woman in anger deserved anything he got. Immediately, he thought of Harleigh and his own anger surfaced.

"How bad is Bonnie? Is she at the hospital or do you want me to come over to their house?"

Grady's amused laugh baffled Caleb. Why the hell was he laughing? Didn't he understand how serious these injuries were?

"I don't think you understand, my man."

"What's to understand? Charlie took his drunken mad out on Bonnie, damn it, and all you can do is chuckle about it." Caleb knew he was being unreasonable but not only did his work ethic go against that kind of behavior but his personal beliefs as well.

"Gotcha on this one, Doc. Ya' want I should tell ya' what happened first before ya' blow a vessel or do ya' wanna run over here and see for yourself?" he drawled.

"Grady, what the hell's got into you? Are you going to arrest him? Can you get Bonnie to press charges?"

"Mmm. Don't think so. Not this time."

Caleb blew out his breath, knowing it was futile to try to get anything out of Grady. Ever since they were kids together, it'd had been like trying to change a tire without a tire iron.

"Okay, Grady. Why don't you tell me in lawman's terms what happened and how bad off Bonnie is? And … please, tell me you're gonna throw the asshole behind bars for smacking Bonnie around."

Grady was enjoying this, always had. Always enjoyed playing these kind of games, especially with his good friend. "Okay, let's see, where should I start first?"

"The way you're playing around, I'd say Bonnie must not be hurt too badly."

"Bonnie? Bonnie doesn't have a scratch on her."

"Grady, you're confusing the hell out of me. Will you quit beating around the bush and get on with your little soap opera."

"Well, it's like this, see. Bonnie said she got tired of his shit and hit him up side the head with a baseball bat, he fell, broke his nose. That made him madder, he started in on her again and she smashed him in the ribs with it. Needless, to say he stayed down. She called me to come and get him, she wanted him out of her house. She wasn't gonna listen to his bullcrap any longer."

"Bonnie did all that?"

"Damn straight," Grady said proudly. "I tell you true."

Good for her, it's about damn time, she defended herself against that bully."

In the back of his mind, he wished Harleigh had been that gutsy and saved herself from the soul-wrenching terror that he knew she had been through. Maybe one day, she would trust him enough to tell him the story.

They were well on their way he hoped, remembering and smiling, rubbing his fingertips across his lips where she'd planted a kiss that lifted him like magic straight off the floor. He was stilled wrapped up in her warmth. And wanted to go back to it but he guessed he better mosey on over to the Fitch's and see how badly Charlie had gotten it.

He couldn't summon up much sympathy for him, though. He'd treat the s.o.b. because he was a doctor but felt not a drop of compassion. He may not have physically abused his wife but calling her names and telling her how worthless she was, was nearly as bad.

"I'll be around shortly. By the way, heard anything about Harleigh?"

"Well, Doc, now that's another thing."

"You're not going to start that shit again, are you?"

"My, my. You're certainly wound up, ain't ya'?"

"You could say that. Tight and ready to strike like that seven-foot rattler we killed when we were fifteen. I'm about ready to plant one on your jaw, Sheriff. How'd ya' like that?"

"Threatening a law officer, are you, Doc?"

Grady bent his head and groaned then chuckled. There was no way he was gonna rile Grady. The only thing that got under that man's skin was Sophy. "You can be one irritating mean sonofabitch, Grady, when you want to be."

"But you love me like a brother, Caleb. I've got the scars to proof it from that blood pact, you, me, Butch and the Prophett boys made when we were kids."

"You got me there, brother. All jawing aside, what do you want me to do?"

"Come on out and see what you can do for Charlie. If it were me, I'd just let him suffer. Once you patch him up then I'll transport him to jail and figure out what to do with him later. Bonnie doesn't want him back so he'll need our help, I guess, to get himself straightened out."

"Isn't that carrying our neighborly *taking care of our own* a little too far?"

"He *is* one of our own, Caleb. Born and bred."

"Ah, come on now, don't tell me that. He's been a bully all his life and it's about time he was taken down a peg."

"That's true but you gotta admit, Charlie's been there for us a time or two. Time to give a little back, Doc."

"I guess. See ya' in a bit."

As Caleb cradled the phone, he realized Grady hadn't answered his question about Harleigh. He was going to jack his jaw for sure, he promised himself. He'd make knots on his head if it was the last thing he did.

In frustration, he grabbed his bag and stomped out of the house.

א

"Hold still, Charlie," Caleb told him. You're such a baby. Bonnie sure did a job on you."

"She broke my nose, Doc," Charlie whined. "Just look at it!"

"I don't think it's broken. Let me get these ribs taped up and I'll have a look at it."

Caleb wound a combination of gauze and tape around his torso to keep Charlie's ribs in place. He couldn't be sure they were broken or cracked or what. Charlie had refused to go down to the clinic for X-rays so he had to make do.

"You look like you've tossed back a few, Charlie. Want a tell me what happened?"

"She had no right doin' to me what she did, Doc. I didn't touch her."

"Sometimes you don't have to. Damn, man, you've always had a loud mouth on you. What did you say to set her off?"

"I already told Grady all that stuff," he grumbled, sulking that his better half could do this to him.

"Why don't you tell it again? Maybe it'll give me a handle on her state of mind."

"Her state of mind? She ain't crazy, Doc, she's just pissed."

"You must have done something, Charlie. Bonnie's always been an easygoing woman. I've known her just as long as you have, remember?"

"Don't know."

"Ah, come on. You can do better than that. Did your big mouth finally get you into trouble? Did you push her one step too far? Call her stupid one too many times?"

"Maybe so, Doc. I do have a trash mouth on me, I

can't deny that. Hell, you know me just about as good as anybody, know what I mean?"

"So what you're saying, or not saying, is that she just got tired of your shit and cracked your head for you?"

Charlie pulled in a swift breath as Caleb pushed on his nose, checking to see if it was really broken or not. "Dammit, Doc. Take it easy on me. I hurt like hell, man."

"You deserve it and then some so quit your whining and take it like a man. Bonnie shoulda picked up that bat a long time ago and used your skull as a baseball. I understand having disagreements and arguments but you crossed that line when you started calling her names like she was nothing but a piece of garbage."

"What d'ya mad at me for, Doc? I ain't done nothing to you."

Caleb realized where his anger against Harleigh's ex had taken him. Yes, Charlie deserved everything that Bonnie dished out and then some but that didn't mean that Caleb had the right to make it worse. He was a doctor, after all, and shouldn't concern himself about what happened. He was supposed to be a healer, not a counselor. And, he wasn't supposed to pass judgment, either.

"You're right there, Charlie. Have you tried talking to Bonnie? Other than call her a piece of trash?"

Caleb looked directly into his eyes, saw what he thought was confusion in their depths and felt a twinge of compassion enter his heart. Charlie was a good soul. He'd never had a good family life as a child, never had loving parents who cared where he was or what he did. So what could anyone expect? He was following in his father's footsteps. Except for the fact that Charlie's father had a heavy hand that landed hard up against the side of any of the kids' heads that happened to be within arms' reach.

"Is Bonnie okay, Doc?"

"Bonnie's fine. Just mad as hell."

"She didn't break my nose?"

"No, no broken nose. Just gonna be sore as hell and you're gonna be black and blue for the next few days. Probably have one helluva shiner."

"What'm I gonna do, Doc? What'm I gonna do without my woman?"

All kinds of things were on the end of his tongue that wanted to come hurling out at Charlie. But Caleb bit down on them, remembering Grady's directive to help the homegrown boy. He reminded himself that deep down Charlie had a good heart, if one knew where to look. It was an unspoken motto in Nowhere that everyone needed a helping hand now and again.

"Well, for starters, it's best you let Bonnie cool off. Go with Grady tonight. Then get counseling, Charlie. Do you love her?"

"What a smartass thing to say, Doc! Of course, I love her. I married her, didn't I? Gave her two kids, didn't I?"

"Sometimes, Charlie, you can be a hard headed bastard, do you know that?"

"You know I did, Doc. Hell, you delivered both of them."

"Charlie, Charlie." Caleb closed his eyes and gave himself a mental shake. It would do no good to give advice, he cautioned. He'd leave that to the counselor. "It takes more than a marriage and having babies for a woman to know she's loved. Do you remember when you two started dating, how it was between you?"

Charlie's eyes glazed over as his memory took him back. "Yeah, she was a cute little thing. Sassy, too. She had me runnin' after her like a puppy."

"You didn't call her names then, did you, Charlie?"

"Nah. She'd a brained me."

"Well, Charlie." Caleb snapped his bag together. "Took her awhile but I believe she did just that."

CHAPTER TEN

ℵ

Charlie laughed, a deep rumbling belly laugh. "Yeah. She did at that. Do you think she'll see me? Ya' know, let me talk to her a minute?"

"I don't know. But I wouldn't push it if I were you."

Grady stepped into the kitchen, interrupting any additional advice Caleb was about to give. "What's the verdict, Doc?"

"Bruised and battered is all, looks worse than it is. He's too stubborn to let me take him over to the clinic so I can take some X-rays. I taped up his ribs just in case. I'm done here."

Grady eyed Charlie a moment or two, letting the silence sink in, the toothpick constantly rolling from one side to the other. He was in his cop mode, Sophy would say. "Well, Charlie, whatta ya' have to say for yourself?"

The grin across Charlie's lips was a sheepish one. "I got shit for brains?"

"You got that right, buddy. As I see it, Bonnie wants you out of here and what Bonnie wants, Bonnie gets. The crap she's put up with since she married your sorry ass is enough to send any sane person over the edge. Why she loves the likes of you, I'll never know."

That straightened Charlie's slumped shoulders, had him sitting upright, a growing shred of hope in his eyes. "She told you that?"

"Yes, she told me she wanted your butt outta her house. And, I'm here to see to it."

"Not that, Grady. That she loves me!"

Caleb and Grady looked at each other, chuckled and shook their heads. Caleb headed into the living room where Bonnie sat on the edge of the couch to see if she was injured in any way and left Charlie in the sheriff's hands. He heard Grady raking him over the coals for his bad behavior as if he were nine years old again as he ushered him out to the squad car.

He looked down into Bonnie's angry face, wondering what he could say to release the tension brewing inside.

"Bonnie? You okay?"

"I'm just fine and dandy, Doc. I couldn't be better," Bonnie told him, still seething with teeth clenched.

"What brought all this on, Bonnie? What did Charlie do before you popped him one?"

Caleb took a couple steps backward as Bonnie jumped off the couch and got right in his face. "That no-good bum called me fat. Fat! Doc, do I look fat to you?"

He gulped air a couple of times, trying to hold back the laugh that wanted to start way down and erupt like Mount St. Helens. "He called you fat? That's the reason you nearly broke his nose? The reason he may have a couple of cracked ribs?"

"Yeah, then he laughed! Laughed and told me I'd lost my figure! Laughed! Did you hear me?"

He didn't dare even break a grin. In her state of mind, he'd be her next victim! "I heard you, Bonnie, but I'm not sure just telling you that you were fat and had lost your figure warrants what you did. Do you?"

Bonnie poked her finger in his chest and raised it up to shake it in his face. "Don't you even think about going there with me, mister! That man's been pure hell to live with since I married him."

Then to Caleb's surprise, she wadded her fists into the cloth of his shirt as her anger dissolved into tears. He put his arms around her, patted her on the back while she cried like one of their five year old twins with a scraped knee that had it doused with a bacterial anti-septic. He didn't know whether to laugh or feel sorry for her.

While he was holding her, it occurred to him that she was a tiny little thing. "It's gonna be okay, Bonnie."

"He's a good and decent man, most times, Doc. He tries so hard not to be like his Daddy that sometimes it just busts out of him anyway."

"And, all the name calling?"

"Hell, Doc, he don't mean nothin' by all that. I call him the same. Sweet talkin', that's all it is." She snuffled in his shirt.

"Then how is this time any different?"

"You don't understand, Doc. He could have called me anything like he normally does except fat. Anything except *fat*." Bonnie looked up at him, fat tears rimming her lashes. "I'm not fat, am I, Doc?"

"No, you're not fat. That's probably Charlie's way of saying I love you."

Bonnie eyed him like he'd lost a few marbles, let

go of his shirt and stepped back. "That's one hell of a way to say that. He coulda just said it outright. Never has, you know."

"Sit down, Bonnie, and let's chat a bit.

ℵ

Her hands were busy but so were her ears. Harleigh had heard the rumors about Bonnie and Charlie. She wanted to hear them all so she kept her ear attuned to the conversations going on around her for any tidbit she hadn't heard before.

The reasoning behind the assault especially intrigued her. If you could call it that. She'd been assaulted before, knew the physical pain as well as the mental and emotion pain of acts so horrendous that what Bonnie did was more like a slap on the wrist.

Her heart raced every time someone gave their rendition of the incident. Somehow, she drew strength from what had happened. Usually, she took the local gossip with a grain of salt but she knew for a fact this happened. Sophy had told her the details as she knew it, Grady had confirmed it when he came in for his morning coffee.

"Idiot deserved it," one of the Johnson brothers argued with the other.

"Just a love spat, that's all."

"Percy, you wouldn't know love if it bit you on the ass."

"I know about this, butthead. Sometimes a man just needs to blow off steam. Calling Bonnie a fat ass was his way. A man's under a lot of pressure these days, what with work and everything else he has to worry about in his life."

Josiah guffawed, rising from his stool at the counter and throwing down a tip for Harleigh. "Yeah, I guess Bonnie had to blow off a little steam herself, huh. A baseball bat'll do it ever time."

She'd finally heard enough to piece images together where it flowed like a video in her mind. She could almost see Charlie, the bully, calling out the names Percy thought were sweet nothin's. Almost see Bonnie pick up the bat and smack her husband up side his hard head when he got to the word *fat*. Could almost feel the power of the swing in her own limbs as the instrument of attack swished in the air as she laid into him.

She should have been so empowered, she told herself. Should have had the guts … no, what was the local lingo? Balls, that was it. She should have had the balls to give as she got from Stewart.

Stewart was in the past, she reminded herself and that's where she planned on keeping him. There was no place in her new life for the likes of him. If Bonnie, who was just a hair over five foot in a petite frame, could stand up to her six foot husband then Harleigh, who was *lots* bigger than Bonnie, could do the same if the situation arose.

Mentally, she made a note to ride on over to the local Wal-Mart store and buy a baseball bat. It would be her choice of weapons. She hated guns and knifes so the bat would be her source of protection. The next step would be making herself use it instead of cringing like a coward if she ever faced Stewart again. And she knew she would. It was just a matter of time.

"Harleigh?"

She blinked, realizing Sophy had been talking to her while she was developing a plan of defense if it ever came to blows again. "Yes? Sorry. I was off somewhere else."

"I could see that. Whatcha thinkin' about?"

"Bonnie and Charlie, mostly. Wondering how she did what she did."

"That's easy to explain. He crossed the line."

"I don't even see the line, Sophy. All he did was call her fat. I can't see how that set her off enough to lay into him with a baseball bat."

Sophy knew what she wasn't saying. Knew that in Harleigh's way of thinking it wasn't abuse ... just a total lack of respect. Maybe in time, understanding would come.

"The sisterhood is having our first meeting tonight over at Delilah's. Be there at seven."

Harleigh took one look at Sophy and knew it was useless to argue. She nodded her head in agreement. "I'll be there."

The rest of the day flew by, the local buzz about Bonnie and Charlie stirring the air, claiming everyone's attention. She barely had time to rush home, change clothes and refresh her makeup. Then she was off again to Delilah's. It would be interesting to see what mischief those girls cooked up. A more determined bunch of females, they were.

She could learn a thing or two from them, she told herself. Before she hit the road again, she'd extract as many helpful hints from those girls as she could. It could only help her along the way. Then one day she wouldn't have to wonder about Stewart anymore. She hoped.

Before she had a chance to punch the doorbell, Phoebe opened the door and dragged her inside. Still holding on to her wrist, she led her into the living room. A room that was a total surprise.

Harleigh assumed since Delilah had been a New York model that her tastes would be geared toward the more pricey décor. What she found was actually elegantly simple. It looked homey, lived in and wonderfully warm.

Simple furnishings. Couch, loveseat, recliner. A LaZ-Boy that had seen its better days, a magazine rack on one side, magazines from Cabellas and Bass Pro Shops to National Geographic and Neiman-Marcus. Alongside it all were tower lamps. Everything fit right down to the crocheted rag rugs at the doors to the afghans across the backs of the couch and loveseat. The addition of the entertainment center created an atmosphere of homespun hospitality.

"Well, ladies, what'll it be? Wine? Beer? Something stronger?"

"A glass of the bubbly for me, Delilah, please."

"Dom coming right up!"

Harleigh watched as Delilah filled glasses with bubbly champagne, wondering what and why they were celebrating. Didn't you just drink champagne when there was something special going on? Especially bottles that were that expensive, she remembered. Stewart would never spend money like that and he was rolling in money.

"So, ladies of the sisterhood. A toast."

"What'll we toast to?" inquired Sophy.

Phoebe crinkled her eyes almost shut in hard

thought. "Hmm. To the downfall of man!"

The sisterhood raised their drinks in the air, clinked glasses, toasted and sipped then giggled as the bubbles tickled their noses. They chattered awhile about this and that, babies, houses, the future.

"Okay, girls, gather round." They scooted off the couch and onto the floor, taking up positions around the coffee table. Delilah reached for a yellow legal pad and pencil from an end table, ready to strategize, plot and plan. "What's the story so far? Sophy, you got anything from Grady?"

"Stewart is having a showing in Portland, Oregon this week so we don't have to worry about his where-abouts at the moment. I checked on the internet and downloaded this article on the event."

Sophy reached for her purse, removed folded papers from it and pressed them out on the coffee table. She had printed out copies of the same article for each of the girls and passed them around.

Harleigh choked on the champagne she was sipping as she looked down at the face of her ex-husband draped around a sexy blonde much younger than he. The girl looked up at Stewart in such an adoring fashion, it made Harleigh's stomach turn. She wondered if that was the way she used to look at the man who later became her jailer. She scanned the article, looking for any mention of her. To her surprised shock, there was none. But it didn't halt the trepidation crawling along her skin ... or the fear squeezing at her chest.

"Stewart Pennington III had another outstanding turnout at the attendance of his showing at the New Times Art Gallery here in Portland of his latest creations to the art world. Attendees came from far and wide to attend this exciting affair. Dress ranged from tuxes to jeans, including the artist himself. When asked if he was fully recovered from his attack last fall when he was mugged, he indicated that he was. His injuries included a head wound that took twenty stitches and bruised ribs. According to Pennington, he never saw his attacker but recovery from that ordeal was painful.

"You have to give the man credit, though, driving himself to the emergency room to be stitched up. Authorities have been unable to find the criminal who subjected this much loved artist to such injuries."

The article continued with other showings, paintings, sketches and what to expect in the future but Harleigh had no interest in them. Her eyes were glued to the picture of Stewart and the innocent girl who stood by his side. She couldn't sit here any longer and do this. The air had suddenly been sucked out of the room and she needed to breathe.

Harleigh startled the girls by jumping to her feet, knocking her near empty glass over. She wanted to be alone. Wanted to think. To sort through things. To try to stave off the urge to run as fast as she could. "I've got to go."

Phoebe reached out and grabbed her wrist as fast as a rattler would strike as Harleigh turned to escape. "Why? What do you have to rush off for?"

"I just can't stay here now."

Didn't they see the sneer on his face? Didn't they know that underneath that handsome face lay the devil himself?

"Harleigh," Delilah said gently. "Come back and sit with us. Trust us to do the right thing by you."

"I can't explain now, Delilah. I really just need to

go be by myself for awhile."

They let her go. They saw the strain on her features, the stress she was fighting down, how pale she had become. The only thing they could do was let her go.

ℵ

Harleigh sunk her weary body down into one of the chairs on her balcony and peered through the slats at the house that sat across the way. The sun was setting and the last rays left it shrouded in pale yellow light.

She had time to think now. Time to wonder what the sisterhood thought about her now. That was a lasting impression, she was sure. Probably thought she was a coward and they were right. But there was no way she could change that. What was, was … and she was scared.

She had gotten in her car and gripped the wheel tight, all the while seeing Stewart staring back at her out of the printed paper just as if he knew she were there. That's what frightened her to the bone now. The fact that he didn't even have to be around and she was falling to pieces said a lot of how tight a hold he still had on her.

Once she'd started driving, she'd gotten her breathing under control but she was still fighting back the fear that had long been absent from her life of late. All she wanted was to get back inside her room where she felt safe.

Now as she looked out at the house veiled in the last vestige of the day, her fear began to ease but there was still the sickness it left behind. One minute she wanted to vomit up her insides and the next she fought off a violent trembling that ran through her torso, out into her extremities.

She'd turned cold the minute she saw his face and even now there was no warmth within her. She wished it were the middle of the day so she could go stand in the sunshine and let its heat sink into her.

She only knew that she couldn't look upon his face yet with her insides tying itself in knots. Maybe the day would come when she could rid herself of him. Until then her guard would go back up in full force. She wouldn't allow a day to go by where she'd forget her mission. And that was to keep herself as far away from Stewart as possible.

Something thumped and she was on her feet, ready to run. She hadn't realized she'd been so engrossed in thought that everything else had faded away.

The sound came again and she realized someone was knocking on her door. She groaned. She wasn't up to company, didn't want the *sisterhood* and their idealistic notions around. They meant well, there was no question about that. But they'd never had to face Stewart Pennington III.

Only it wasn't the sisterhood on the other side of the door. It was Caleb. She didn't want any part of him either. Trying to get rid of him was going to be hard. Especially with that questioning look in his eye. She'd found that Caleb was as bad as his sister in taking no for an answer.

"Hey, Harleigh."

"Caleb." She made the greeting short and sweet, hoping he'd get the message.

"Phebs called me, a little worried. You okay?"

"Yes."

Okay. Well, the concerned tactic didn't work. On to Plan B. He wasn't going to leave, even though she was making it as plain as day that she didn't want him there. He wasn't going anywhere until he got to the bottom of what Phoebe was talking about. "Mind if I come in for a minute?"

Reluctantly she stepped back, widening the gap to the entrance. He stepped through without hesitation, not giving her a chance to say no.

"Look, Caleb," she said snappily. What right did he have to play the white knight? It was a little too late for that. She no longer needed rescued. She did that on her own without any help from the male species. "I'm not in the mood for company. Don't you have some doctoring to do?"

The sideways grin he gave her was a glaring indication that her efforts were a waste of time. He wasn't going anywhere. "A little edgy, are you?"

"Maybe a little. I just want to be alone so I can think."

"About what?"

"Are you always this nosy and obnoxious?"

"Are you always this unwelcoming?"

He was right. She *was* being inhospitable and uncharitable. "Sorry. I just have a lot on my mind."

"Want to talk about it?"

"There's nothing to talk about." She needed to break the tie that bound them together. Things had gone too far between them the way it was. "There are a few things I do need to tell you, though."

"What would that be?"

"I like Nowhere. I like the people, enjoy them all. I appreciate the time everyone has taken to make me feel welcome and feel at home."

His blood ran cold. He didn't like the path this conversation was taking. "Where is this leading to?"

"The thing between us."

Deep in his gut, he'd known that was what she was going to say. He felt his body stiffen in defense of the things he was going to hear and not like one damn bit. "What about it?"

"I never meant to mislead you, Caleb. Or any of the residents of Nowhere. Delilah, Sophy." She took a deep breath. "I meant to stay here, to put down roots here. I needed a job until I got on my feet again. I've come to realize I can't put roots down now, or ever. I've accepted that. And, I can't have a relationship with you, with anyone."

The anger that had been brewing took hold. He held back as much as he could so he wouldn't scare her. "Why not? What we have is special, you know that."

"Yes, I do know. That's why this is so hard."

"It's Stewart, isn't it?"

"Yes and no."

"Explain."

Harleigh turned away, drew in a deep breath and walked outdoors onto the patio. "I'll start with no. I'm still scared but the few weeks I've been here have been my salvation. It's shown me I can stand up for me."

"I suppose that's Phoebe's doing."

"And Delilah and the others. And most of all Bonnie."

Now he understood. She was coming into her own. Good for her, he thought, but still that didn't solve the problem at hand. "Ah, Bonnie. Liberating, isn't it?"

For the first time, Harleigh laughed. He understood. He was a good man, this man she was falling in love with. She dipped her head to hide what she'd just discovered.

Love? She was in love with Caleb? How did that sneak up on her without her knowing it?

"Liberating, yes. I'm going to buy me a bat."

"Why?"

"You have your gun. I'll have a bat."

"I *can* protect you, you know."

"I don't doubt that for a minute. But ..." She gulped, her breath snagging on something, she wasn't sure what, on its way back out.

There was a dangerous glint in the pearl of his eyes that had her taking a step backward. Caleb took one forward. For each one backward she took, he followed her forward until her waist hit the railing on the balcony.

Slowly as not to frighten her further so she would jump for it, he gently rubbed his hands up and down her arms. "Harleigh?"

"Y-y-yes?"

"I'm going to kiss you now so don't be afraid. I just want to taste you."

She nodded her head, her body already thrumming in expectation as she remembered the last kiss. She didn't want to seem brazen but heaven help her she wanted to curl herself around his body and never let go.

She moaned before his lips brushed against hers. He took her up against his chest. A chest that was warm. She placed her palms there, feeling the rapid beat of his heart against her fingertips.

Her mouth hungered while his mouth plundered, hot, insistent, wet. Her blood zinged. If he hadn't body-pressed her against the railing, she would have ended up at his feet in puddle.

Then before she could take her next breath, Caleb released her. She stumbled and he caught her before she fell. He dragged her back to him and took her up against him one more time and tasted the sweetness of her lips, delved the softness of her mouth, telling himself the whole time, he needed to let her go.

He pushed her away. "Like I said before, good and sweet."

CHAPTER ELEVEN

א

Harleigh hovered on the edge of sleep, the remembrance of Caleb's mouth warm and moist on hers. The hot fires of desire fueled her blood. She'd thrown the sheet off her, her body overheated from memories. She felt the air stir and breeze over her.

Her eyes open now, she watched the shimmer and the shape appear. But this time, it was different. There was no abyss. No image mirroring her own.

She rose from the bed and stood before the glowing figure. It came to her then, that this was the angelic form that Kate had been telling her about. And she was right, it was the most beautiful creature she'd ever seen.

The figure turned, floated across the floor, glanced back at Harleigh over her shoulder and beckoned her to follow then disappeared through the door.

Harleigh's heart was beating so hard and fast she thought it was going to jump right out of her chest. Intrigued, she followed the figure down the stairs, through the kitchen and out the back door. The moon was full, the light from the silvery orb lighting every step of the way.

She hesitated at the tree line where the figure had entered. She could see the glow ahead of her, waiting.

244 - Cissy Hassell

- 244 - Cissy Hassell

As she continued into the forest, she heard a soft musical humming sound. When she came out into the clearing where the figure stood, she could see her lips moving and realized she was singing.

She came forward, took Harleigh by the hand and seated her on the hewn-out log. Then with a sweep of her hand images appeared. It was like watching a movie on a big screen.

A blonde haired young woman was walking along a street, three young children by her side, each holding the other's hand. All blonde, the same size, wearing the same clothes. Evidently they were sisters, possibly triplets. They looked to be two, maybe three years old.

Harleigh watched as a black van pulled up, the side door sliding open and three men jumped out. The woman was struck hard by one of the men and fell to the ground. Each man grabbed a child, jumped back into the van and it drove off leaving the young woman lying injured.

Another sweep of her hand, the scene changed. Harleigh watched in shame as her life unfolded before her. In one particular ugly scene, the tears started to flow as she relived each pain filled moment.

The angelic form next to her pulled her into her arms and held her for a moment and the emotions subsided. She ran a hand over Harleigh's hair, soothing her, calming the turbulence inside.

The scene changed once again and the abyss came into view with her image standing on the other side just as Harleigh had always seen it. This time the abyss slowly closed bringing the image closer. All she had to do was take a couple steps forward and she would be within arms reach.

Out of the shadows, another figure stepped out, the man Harleigh had seen on earlier occasions. This time he raised the instrument in front of the image that so resembled herself, pointed to whatever information showed on the small screen, then lifted his hand toward Harleigh.

It seemed that time itself stood still as they gazed at each other then stepped forward. Then the man on the other side held her back while the form who stood by Harleigh did the same. Still, their fingertips touched and the air exploded with a current so strong it shot up into the night sky. Harleigh felt it run swift and true throughout her body then the world turned dark.

With the sweep of her hand, the clearing lightened again. The ethereal being smiled and disappeared.

א

The walk back to her room was fraught with confusion and bewilderment. What in the hell happened back there? she wondered. With the touch of two fingertips, the clearing had lit up like the fourth of July. It was like an explosion within herself then everything went black.

Even so, with just the touch of those fingers, she'd felt complete.

And all those scenes of people? What was that all about? What did it mean?

What was that waiflike creature trying to tell her?

Harleigh reached the edge of the forest with no answers. Caleb's light was on and her feet took her to his back porch. Her right toe was on the first step when she chickened out. There was too much on her mind to deal with him right now.

Caleb watched her out the kitchen window, she unaware that he was there. He wondered what her intent had been, what had turned her away again.

He'd seen the flash of light in the forest behind his house, had almost ran out to investigate. Knew it wasn't lightning, since there were no clouds and the moon lit up the night sky in a luminous glow. He'd been stark-ass naked, a longneck in his fingers, gazing out the window. By the time he'd thrown on a pair of jeans and found his shoes, Harleigh had stepped out in the moon-filtered night, walked up to his back porch and changed her mind.

It was in his mind to run through the house and meet her out front. He'd make up some ridiculous story that he was going over to the big house to get something. Anything. He was halfway there when he knew he couldn't go through with it. She'd see through the whole damn thing, it was so obvious.

So he looked on as Harleigh crossed in front of the house, glanced back at the stand of trees and the house. The moonlight poured over her, bathing her in a silver light that made his blood run hot.

With a great force of will, he tamped down on his emerging desire and repositioned himself within his jeans. He resigned himself to another cold shower and an empty bed.

א

Hours later, Harleigh lay wide awake, still trying to assimilate everything that happened, everything she had seen. And, why.

She was left wondering about the young woman and three children. What did that mean? Who were they? And why was she shown those particular children?

There must be a reason.

Three little girls. Kidnapped. Mother injured or possibly dead. There had to be an account of the incident somewhere. Before she left this place she loved so much, she'd find out what the connection was to her.

The gray of the morning sky was turning pink when Harleigh finally slept. Dreams of little girls entwined with light and angels drifted in and out and through her mind.

She woke up tired and groggy. She knew it was going to be a cranky day, not bothering to style her hair after she showered. A cranky day might as well be a bad hair day, too, she figured.

Hurrying to her car, she drove like a maniac to get to work only to find the café closed. Sunday. Damn, she could have slept in and caught up on the hours of sleep she'd lost during the night. Now what was she going to do to fill the day?

The idea that she'd had during the wee hours of the morning infiltrated her thoughts and the decision was made. But where to find a computer?

As she drove back to the Rose House, she worried her lower lip with her teeth until it was tender. The light turned red as she approached and she braked. Glancing to the left she spotted an arrowed sign showing the Nowhere library down the street. She put on her blinker and turned left when the light changed.

She pulled into the parking lot, swerved into a

parking place, ready to sprint for the door. Then noticed there were no other cars in the lot.

"Don't tell me it's closed," she groaned, getting out of the car and walking to the door. "Opens at one," she read.

So much for research.

So. She would return to her own little corner of the world and piddle the day away. She'd get out her little yellow pad again and finalize her plans. First though, she'd definitely have to find out if there'd been any kidnappings and would need to go back years. She only hoped that the information would be on the internet since she was sure the kidnapping had taken place a long time back. That was evident in the clothing the victims wore. Possibly twenty or twenty-five years ago.

As she passed the driveway leading to Delilah's house, she braked and pulled to the side. Looking down the tree-lined drive, she pondered whether it would be rude of her to just drop in.

She inched the car onto the asphalt and drove slowly, giving herself enough space and time to back out if she changed her mind. Too late, there was Delilah waving at her, a twin on her hip, the other perched safely in the crook of Butch's arm.

Pulling up by the duo, she rolled down her window and perfected her best southern drawl. "Hey guys. Those are mighty pretty youngins ya' got there."

Delilah raised her eyebrows and laughed. "I see you've been working on your little southern belle drawl there. You've got it down pat!"

"Miz Harleigh." Butch nodded her way in greeting. "Car do you fine?"

"The car is lovely, Butch. I can't thank you and

Delilah enough for helping me out this way."

Butch dragged the toe of his boot in the grass and shifted the baby to his other arm. "Jes' doin' what we can."

"Why don't you drive on up to the house and come in for a visit? If you're not busy, that is."

Harleigh followed Delilah's instructions and waited for her at the front door. She surveyed the area, noting things she'd missed before. The way the border grass hugged the steps up to the stoop. The way different variety of flowers cozied right up to each other, friends and lovers.

Harleigh followed Delilah up the stairs to the nursery, standing by with a deep yearning in her heart as she watched her ready the twins for a nap. Looked on while Delilah fussed and kissed and loved them each one.

"Come on down to the kitchen while I fix us a glass of something cold to drink then we'll go out into the garden and relax."

Delilah's idea of a garden was not exactly what Harleigh expected. There was a large gazebo surrounded by brick and mortar. Circular steps leading down pathways lined with flowers, bromeliads and all types of fauna. For a minute, she thought she was in a botanical garden museum. A beautiful and aromatic sensation.

And the birds. Countless hummingbirds. Bluebirds in abundance.

Then her eyes widened in elated surprise when she stepped inside the gazebo and looked through to the other side. Butterflies. Tiny blue ones. Yellow ones. Striped ones. Ones with *eyes* on their wings.

"Oh, Delilah, this is beyond gorgeous."

"Thanks, Harleigh. This is my little piece of paradise in the country. It's my only extravagance. Oh, we could live high on the hog, to steal a phrase from the locals. I'm quite rich in my own right but Butch won't touch a red cent of it."

"I guess it's that ego thing, huh?"

"At least where that man of mine is concerned. He's one of those hard-headed southerners that believe it's a man's duty to take care of the little woman."

"That's sweet."

"Yeah but it can also cause a lot of problems. Especially if you're an independent woman like I am. And with us, it was like the immovable object meets the unbending force or some such nonsense."

"I need to learn how to be a woman of independent means."

"I'm at your disposal. How can I help you?"

Harleigh hadn't meant to say those words out loud but they were out just the same and no way to retract them. She wished she had time to figure out how best to put into words the things she wanted to know.

"Oh, I don't know, really. I envy you and your courage. And the others of the sisterhood." Harleigh laughed. "Listen to me. The sisterhood. What exactly is that, Delilah?"

"The sisterhood, Harleigh, is whatever we make it to be."

"You have a great way of not answering questions, you know that."

Delilah's smile was smug. She agreed. "It's one of my best features!"

"You're a piece of work, Delilah. That you are."

She sipped her tea, waiting for a response. "So what exactly *is* the sisterhood."

"Shoot, Harleigh. Hell if I know. Your guess is as good as mine." Delilah laughed, a tinkling kind of sound that was both happy and secretive. She twirled her frosty glass in her fingers and watched the ice move. "Seriously, though, it's newly formed as you well know and I think it's a good way to help each other. For support … for friendship … for each other. A way to be there for each other."

Harleigh scowled, worry now a better part of her feelings. She didn't want to involve Delilah or the sisterhood in her troubles. They already were to some extent but she'd see to it that it would come to a screeching halt.

She'd see to that.

Harleigh decided it was time to go. She'd taken up enough of Delilah's time. "Listen, I'm gonna go now. I'm gonna run by the library so I can use their computer. There's something I need to research."

Delilah set her glass down on the resin table and clapped her hands together. "There's no need for that. Come on, I've got everything you need right here."

Harleigh was amazed at the computer equipment that Delilah contained in her office. Everything was there for her use, right at her fingertips. Computer System. Fax. Scanner. Printer. And a few other pieces of equipment that made it a complete office all its own.

She ran her fingertips over the keyboard.

"Here, sit." Delilah told her. "What are you looking for?"

"It's hard to explain."

"Try me."

"Maybe you should do this. I'm not sure what to do."

Delilah changed places with Harleigh, booted up the computer, waited for it to load then accessed the internet. "Okay, my dear, what shall we search for?"

"Kidnappings."

Delilah couldn't hide her surprise. "Kidnappings? That was the last thing I figured you'd be looking for."

"Yeah, well. Like I said, it's hard to explain."

"Okay, kidnappings it is, then. Do you know who and when?"

"No, I have very little information to go on."

"Describe them for me then."

"Well, there were three little girls, sisters, maybe. Possibly triplets."

"Maybe we should access newspaper archives. Where did this happen?"

"I don't know that either."

Delilah's fingers paused above the keyboard then dropped them back down to her lap. "Hmm. This might be a little hard. Don't know when. Don't know where. Don't know who."

"It's useless. I have nothing to go on, do I?"

"Does this have anything to do with Stewart?"

Harleigh leaned back in her chair and sighed. "No. It has nothing to do with Stewart. You wouldn't believe me if I told you."

"Like I said before, try me."

"Promise you won't laugh or tell me I'm crazy?"

"Nothing surprises me much anymore, Harleigh. I was once a stranger in this town, too. But as you well know, you're only a stranger here for about five seconds."

"Okay, here goes. Don't say I didn't warn you. Last night, I was neither awake nor asleep. You know, when you're riding right on the edge before you fall? Well, I opened my eyes and there was this being standing at the foot of my bed."

Delilah raised one eyebrow. "I don't suppose this *being* glowed? Did it?"

"Yes, she did."

"She?"

"She was too beautiful to be a man, Delilah. Her features were so delicate and she looked so fragile. She beckoned for me to follow so I did."

"Alone?"

"What was I supposed to do? Knock on Caleb's door and ask him to be my escort?"

"Good answer!"

Harleigh was mortified at the way she spoke to Delilah, swiftly apologizing. "That was so rude of me."

"Think nothing of it, my girl, it's about time you got a bit sassy."

"Sassy?" Harleigh liked that.

"Yeah, sassy. Now, Miz Sassy, get on with your story."

"Right! Well, I followed her into the woods, there's a clearing and a hewn-out log. We sat on it, she lifted her hand and it was as if she started a reel of film. She showed me this woman with three little girls. All alike. Then this black van comes along, men jump out, shove the woman down and stole the kids."

"And, that's all you saw? Just the men jump out? Can you describe them or the woman?"

"The woman was blonde, attractive, about twenty-five, I'd say. The men were dressed in black, their faces were covered so I can't tell you what they looked like."

"What about their clothes?"

Harleigh frowned in concentration. "I don't think their clothing was like today's fashions. More like, I don't know, clothes that were worn maybe twenty, thirty years ago."

Delilah punched the buttons, entered "kidnapping of children" in the search box and hit enter. Instantly, she retrieved information pertaining to every kidnapping in history.

"Oh, boy. Better dig in and make yourself comfortable, this may take a while."

Harleigh looked on while Delilah clinked on link after link, coming up with nothing that led them to three kidnapped children. With each web page they linked to, with Delilah mumbling about finding a needle in a haystack, Harleigh's hopes sank lower.

"We'll never find out about them, will we?" she asked miserably.

"Oh, I don't know now, it's too early to give up." Delilah punched the keyboard again. "That's one thing you'll find out about the crowd you're running with now, we're like white on rice. Never give up is our motto."

Harleigh grew quiet, crossing and uncrossing her fingers as images flashed on the screen. She became antsy, had to move so she rose and wandered around the room, looking at this and that and nothing in particular. She knew this was futile, knew she was wasting time, wasting Delilah's time, taking her away from her precious children.

She returned to what she'd seen the night before. Something had been bugging her about the three little girls she'd seen. Something that was vaguely familiar. About the woman, she realized. The way she tilted her head, maybe. The curve of her jawline. It was the same as the girl in the mist.

The same as her own.

CHAPTER TWELVE

א

Caleb opened the door to the clinic and entered. The place was quiet, peaceful, soothing for a change. It was Sunday. He was trying to catch up on paperwork, needed to run by and see Bettlyn, too. See how the new little one was doing. Of all things, she'd stuck her newborn son with the moniker of Caleb. Not that it was a bad name once you were grown. But, damn, when you're an infant!

He hadn't gotten ten steps inside when the door he had just closed behind him, opened. He gave a silent curse that he should have locked it the minute it swung shut. Glancing over his shoulder, he caught Grady's image in the corner of his eye. Good, he thought, relieved that it wasn't a patient. It was high time he cornered the man anyway and dragged the information he wanted out of him if he had to tie him down to one of his examining tables and force it out of him with a scalpel in his most tender regions.

He turned, dipped his head in greeting. "Grady."

"Doc."

Caleb eyed him warily. That toothpick of his was rolling from one side to another. A sure sign that something was up.

"Problem?"

"Nah."

"Just visiting, I suppose." Caleb placed his hands on his hips, determined he was going to find out what he knew.

"Yep."

"Hmm. You giving Sophy a bad time?"

"Nah."

The more Grady circumvented why he'd stopped by, the more agitated Caleb became. He just wanted to smack him over the head with something, take a cue from Bonnie, maybe. Caleb was in no mood for his unflappable manner today. If he wanted to beat his head against a brick wall, there was one outside the office he could use.

"Dammit, Grady. What do you want?"

Grady had the nerve to look surprised. "Me? Why can't I visit my old buddy?"

"What d'ya want, Grady?" Caleb growled, then turned and walked on back to his office, "You're pushing it, here. I've got things to do."

Grady sauntered on into the clinic, following behind Caleb, seating himself in one of the office chairs in the office. "Well, it seems like your Miz Harleigh is aka Mrs. Stewart Pennington. *The* Miz Stewart Pennington III."

"That's old news, you got there, Sheriff. I know all that."

Grady reached into his shirt pocket and pulled out a printed page. He scanned it for a minute then looked over at Caleb. "You sure you want to hear this?"

All the bluster went of him then. "Is it that bad?"

"And then some."

He closed his eyes and drew a deep breath and kept them shut. "Seriously, Grady."

"There are numerous occasions that Harleigh has been to these small immediate care centers for bruises or minor injuries. Things like broken fingers, broken ribs. Never seemed to be any injuries where you could see them, though. That's suspicious in itself."

"There's more, isn't there?"

"Yes. I'm just going to touch on a couple of things. I think the whole story you might ought to get from Harleigh herself."

"I will when she's ready."

"I don't doubt that. Has she told you anything about what happened? About what Stewart did to her?"

"No. I figure when the time is right, she'll want me to know. As it stands, the man is still in control. That's what pisses me off so bad."

"How could he be in control? He's at the other end of the lower forty-eight."

Caleb tapped his fingers against his temple. "He's still here, inside her head. He's with her twenty-four seven. Always there, lurking, making her run, making her live in fear. Looking over her shoulder at every turn, every sound, every shadow. The first time you ever saw her, looked into her eyes, what did you see?"

He pursed his lips in thought, thinking back to that first day. "A wounded animal."

"That's what I mean, Grady. No one should have to live like that."

"Fear can make you do a lot of things you wouldn't normally do. I remember her fear, saw it in her eyes, could even smell it. The distress in her face that I was even there had her ready to run. She didn't want to be anywhere near me."

"In her way of thinking, you're the enemy."

"I kinda got that impression, too. I can only imagine the kind of anguish and soul-deep suffering she's gone through. But you know something else I saw that day, Doc?"

"And, what would that be?"

"In the back of all that reluctance, dislike and distrust, there's a desperation to survive. I believe Harleigh will do it, even if it means killing the bastard if he comes after her."

"You know about the baseball bat, then?"

"The baseball bat? The one Bonnie smacked Charley with? What about it?"

"No, not that one. That was just the catalyst. Bonnie hitting Charley with that bat was the best thing that coulda happened."

"Not for Charley. I don't think he'd agree with you on that."

"You never know, maybe giving him a good tap with that bat'll straighten him out. He loves Bonnie, you know."

"I guess."

"Anyway, Grady, that little incident planted a seed in Harleigh's head. If someone as petite as Bonnie can defend herself against a bully like Charley, she's decided she can defend herself against the likes of Stewart Pennington."

"Things are looking up. Can't wait for the man to arrive so I can stand by and watch her lay into him with that!" Grady chuckled.

"You wouldn't stop it? You being a lawman and everything? Serve and protect and all that shit?"

"Well, see, Doc, that's the thing," he drawled, settling back into the chair. "There's two words there. Serve … and protect."

"And, pray tell, Mister Lawman, how is standing by and watching a man getting the shit beat outta him doing your job? Serving and protecting?"

"I'd be serving the public, ya' see, protecting the wonderful citizens of our fair town, Harleigh being one of them."

"And protecting her would be …?"

"Doing unto him before he does unto her."

"You're one twisted human being there, Sheriff, but I like your way of thinking."

"Thought you would. You ready to hear about Harleigh now?"

"No, but go ahead."

"Well, hospital records indicated spousal abuse but Harleigh wouldn't press charges. Then one time, she was beaten severely, bad enough that she went to an abused women's center for protection. They helped her survive, helped her obtain a divorce. She had him put on peace bond. But according to one of the staff at the center, he kept coming after her. Something funny happened, so this person said. It was noted that Stewart had been attacked, victim of a mugging. Said it was all in the newspapers but they didn't believe it. A couple of staff persons went over to Harleigh's apartment. One has a key. When Harleigh didn't answer, they unlocked the door and went in thinking something was wrong. The place was a wreck. There was also evidence that something illicit had gone on. Silk scarves tied to the bedposts, all four of them. Bedclothes in a mess. Blood on the sheets. Broken figurines all over the place.

Seems one of the brass lamps had a lot of blood on it. A big dent.

"Anyway, the staff was afraid Stewart had done something to Harleigh. They haven't seen Harleigh since and were thinking maybe he killed her like he threatened. They searched her place but could find no evidence that he had. Couldn't tell if anything was missing or not. Harleigh didn't have much to begin with so they had nothing to go on. It was just their suspicions."

"That sonofabitchin' bastard." Caleb flew into a rage. Just the thought of what Harleigh had endured at the hands of that maniac made his blood boil. "If I could get my hands around that prick's neck, I'd kill him, Grady. As I stand here before you now, I'd kill him."

Grady pulled the toothpick out of mouth and stood up, pulling himself up to his six-two feet height. Knowing that Caleb was dead serious, he racked his brain trying to think of a way to divert the anger that was coming off the man like the ash out of St. Helen's.

"Well, now, Caleb ..."

Caleb gave Grady a frosty stare. "Don't start with me. It wouldn't be a good thing to do in my frame of mind. You know a man like that isn't gonna let it go. He'll come after her. And then, what, Grady? There's gotta be something we can do."

"I think the sisterhood is way ahead of you there, bro."

"What in the hell is the sisterhood?"

"A newly-organized party of five."

"Is that some kind of joke?"

"No. My lovely Sophy. Your dear sister Phoebe.

The ever-exquisite Delilah. The most charming Sunny. And last but not least, your very own Harleigh."

Caleb motioned for Grady to sit again while he seated himself behind his desk. "The sisterhood, huh. Now what exactly does this sisterhood do?"

At ease now that he didn't have to restrain his friend, Grady replaced the toothpick in his mouth and made himself comfortable. "Well, for the most part, as far as I can see, those fine southern belles of ours, with the exception of Harleigh, of course, formed the sister-hood for the express purpose of protecting Harleigh."

"You're shittin' me, right?"

"Nope. I tell you true."

"How did you find out about this?"

"Sophy."

"Naturally. I suppose this was pillow talk."

"Not exactly."

"She volunteered the information?"

"Not exactly."

"Don't tell me you coerced Sophy into spilling the beans?"

Not only was Grady's face turning a dark deep shade of red, but his ears were turning a nice shade, also.

Caleb's grin was ear-wide. "You old dog, you. You used sex to get the information!"

Grady glanced up at Caleb, shit-eatin' grin on his face. "It was more like she compromised me. When that woman wants something ...well, we won't go there."

"So what did your lovely Sophy want from you that she went to such extremes?"

"You'll appreciate this. She wanted me to run a

profile on Stewart Pennington. Wanted me to find out everything I could. Anything that may have been filed against him."

"Hence the info you just shared with me."

"For my lovely Sophy, Doc, I went the extra mile and found out the other information that I shared with you. She, excuse me, *the sisterhood,* wants me to keep tabs on him, his whereabouts, what he's doing, where he's going."

This gave Caleb food for thought. What were those girls up to? "In other words, they want you to keep tabs on the bastard and if he comes this way, you're to alert them and they're gonna do what?"

Grady inhaled, blew out his breath and shook his head. "Damned if I know, Caleb. You know how hard-headed those girls are. They get something in their heads and it's like shaking a dog off a bone. Forget about getting anything out of them, it ain't gonna happen."

"Hmm. I guess we've got our work cut out for us then. Keeping an eye on those five is gonna be a full job in itself."

"You got that right. Luckily, Sunny's gone and Phoebe will be leaving soon, too."

They stood, both bent on protecting their own. Now they had five to look after with special care.

ℵ

"Damn!"

Harleigh jumped at Delilah's exclamation. "What is it? Did you find something?"

"We're going at this all wrong, Harleigh! We need to go to the source!"

"But we don't know where that is."

"Sure we do. Let's go have us a visit with our little Sophy. She'll know what to do. Follow me." Delilah grabbed her purse, headed out the door, kissing Butch on the top of the head as she passed by him reading the newspaper in that beat-up old recliner of his. "Be back in a bit, love, we're running over to visit with Sophy a minute. Keep an ear out for our little darlins."

Harleigh could do nothing else but follow. As she trailed behind Delilah, watching as she whipped precariously down the road in her SUV, Harleigh mentally tried to keep up with all that had transpired within the last hour.

Okay, they were searching for the kidnapped children, Harleigh deliberated. Delilah was intent on the computer screen, while she, Harleigh, walked around the room worrying about this and that then Delilah had a brain storm which she didn't bother explaining and here she was flying down the highway like they were trying to win the Indy 500.

So, what happened? What had Delilah thought of?

Delilah signaled a left turn, swung down a fenced driveway to a ranch-style house. In minutes, they were inside enlisting Sophy's help.

"So what you're saying, Delilah, is that we need to access police files to find these kidnapped kids?"

"That would be the fastest and easiest way we could trace them. Harleigh thinks this happened years ago. So it being on the internet is like looking for that damn needle in a haystack. Nearly impossible."

Sophy chewed on her lip, standing before a large

window that looked out into the back of their house. Horses with colts grazed in a far pasture. An old hound-dog that looked like it hadn't moved in a hundred years lay on the back patio.

"It's gonna be downright impossible, Delilah, not *nearly* impossible. We don't know anything. Don't have a thing to go on. Who. When. Where."

Harleigh knew they were trying to help. But she could see how hopeless it was. She had little to offer. "The only thing we do have, Sophy," she put in, "is the pictures in my head. We may not have names, places or times but I know what they look like, what they were wearing."

Sophy turned to Harleigh, saw the last vestiges of hope lingering in her eyes. It was on the tip of her tongue to tell her it was like beating a dead horse but she didn't. If Harleigh needed this, the least she could do was try.

"Okay, here's what I'll do. I'll page Grady and work my womanly wiles on him. You girls run on home now and I'll be in touch.

ℵ

Grady pulled his pager out of his holder, looked at the number, gave Caleb a grin and wiggled his eyebrows. "The little woman calls. Mind if I use your phone?"

"Nah, go ahead."

Caleb busied himself with paperwork while Grady talked with Sophy. He tried not to listen. In fact, it wasn't the words he was hearing. It was the way Grady's voice dipped soft and low. The quiet gentleness, the unspoken, the underlying emotions.

Oh how he envied his friend right now. What he'd give to have that. To be speaking in hushed gentle tones with Harleigh. To express just in that tone so many things that didn't need saying, yet somehow known.

Grady placed the receiver back into the cradle, a studied frown on his face. He was in his cop mode now, Caleb could see. He just stood there, hands on hips, toothpick rolling furiously side-to-side.

"Trouble?"

The smile Grady gave Caleb told him different. "With a capital T!"

"You like this kinda trouble?"

"Ya' have to know my woman, Doc. Something's in the air and I gotta run on home to find out what she's up to now."

With that said, Grady hitched up his duty-laden belt, turned and walked out of Caleb's office, whistling.

Caleb knew he'd never get any work done now. He had the biggest urge to plant flowers which was the most ridiculous thing he could think of doing. But there it was anyway.

It was for Harleigh. He knew it just as he knew he'd stop by the nursery and grab a full plat of flowering plants and head out to the gazebo, ring the structure with what he brought home. Then he'd invite Harleigh to see what he'd accomplished. His chest puffed out with showing-off-pride.

That's where Harleigh found him, digging in the dirt. She stood back, content to just watch this man who awakened such powerful feelings inside her. He was on his knees, humming lightly under his breath. He wore an old pair of jeans. Jeans that hugged his backside as he moved around on the ground, repositioning himself for the next job at hand.

He straightened a little, stretching his back, massaging away an ache that had started with the strain of being bent over for a long period of time. That's when it hit her that he was bare-chested. She'd concentrated so hard on those skin-tight jeans of his that she missed that until his body lengthened to work out the kinks. But now, now she noticed. Not so much that he had a perfect muscled body, but that there was so much flesh exposed for her to drool over.

There was an untidiness about his usually-well-groomed hair that drew her to take a couple steps forward. She wanted to smooth it back into place then mess it up again.

He must have heard her. He turned toward her and smiled. She felt it all the way to the tips of her toes. Desire ... warm, fluid, welcoming. It ran throughout her body as he stood and turned her way with his hands on his hips, smiling that smile of his.

And for the very first time, he knew what Grady felt. It was there between them.

The unspoken, the underlying emotions. The want, the need. The desire.

It was all he could do to keep from yanking her to him and taking her mouth like he wanted to take her body.

They stood within inches of each other. Just looking. Wanting. No words needed. Unspoken need in their eyes. He was hesitant to carry out the yearning that had taken hold of him.

The decision to carry out that gut-aching need was taken away from him as Harleigh closed the distance, brushing her body against his, curling her arms around his neck, dragging his mouth down to hers and answered his body's call. The flame spurted from his heels to the top of his head. A ball-busting wildfire. Hot. Out of control.

"Jesus, Harleigh. We can't … not here." He shivered as the warmth of her lips followed the line of his jaw, breath, soft, moist.

"Then we better find a place, don't you think?" she whispered against his neck before letting her lips trail a kiss down to his collarbone. "You don't want anyone to find us here in compromising positions, do you?"

She stepped back and held out her hand. He didn't need any prompting. He was about to pop the way it was.

They ran for the house, barely managing to make the steps to the back door without tripping. He shoved her up against the door, thinking only to staunch this poker-hot blaze that was burning him alive. Somewhere, somehow, his brain kicked into gear, made him realize how violent he was treating Harleigh, leaned into her and rested.

"Caleb?"

"Hmm."

"What is it? Why did you stop?"

"Trying to catch my breath. I didn't want our first time to be this way. I wanted it to be gentle after all you've been through."

Harleigh breathed in deep, aware now that her own desire was as widespread as his. "No, Caleb, don't back off now. I need this. I need you."

In minutes, his mouth back on hers again, taking, giving. Need mixed with want. His hands wandered.

Searching. Found what they were looking for. Her breast fit as if molded specifically for his palm.

She twisted. Now it was he that was body-pressed against the door. The fire raged when she arched, pressing herself more against his hand, his body. She smoothed the hair on this chest with her fingertips, sending another wave of desire through him. She felt it and her own knees nearly buckled with the force of it.

He fumbled for the doorknob cutting into his back, wrestled it open and they fell through the opening. He gave it a kick with his foot, heard it slam, heard his own ragged breath, tried for control then gave it up as she fumbled with the snap on his jeans.

She had too many clothes on. He dragged her up on her knees, stripped her of her shirt, her shoes, jeans.

"The bed," he breathed raggedly, holding her tight against him, planting kisses on her shoulder then moved to nibble on her chin.

"No, here, Caleb. Love me here. Now."

"The floor," he whispered into her mouth. "We're on the kitchen floor."

"Doesn't matter."

"You're right, it doesn't."

The room was quiet except for heavy breathing, erotic sighs and needs answered. He stripped her of her final bit of clothing, threw the lace front panties across his shoulder as he shoved her back to the floor.

He balanced himself on his elbow as he ran his eyes the full length of her body. He trailed a fingertip down the soft column of her throat, down between her breast. He reached out with strong capable hands and touched her. She shivered in anticipation.

He ran his hand upward to her shoulder, letting his

hand glide across the smoothness of her skin. A thrill of discovery passed over him as he ran his hand down her arm and raised her hand to nip at her wrist then brushed it with his lips.

She let her eyes wander over him. His face. Mouth. Down onto his chest where the crisp hair marched downward over a tanned farmer's tan to his desire. Her eyes closed, wondering, hoping. Afraid even that what he was feeling was only a momentary thing. That it would pass as quickly as the sun moving from morning to night. But the warmth of his mouth on her skin, slithering upward and over told her this was a lasting emotion.

She felt her heart beating fast and hard in her chest and raised her hand to touch him, felt his own pounding the same rhythm against her palm. His mouth hesitated over her breast. She arched upward, curled her hand around the nape of his neck and pressed him down. The touch of his lips melted the rest of her fears away.

She pulsated from his touch, his warmth. Her need. An explosion waiting to happen. Bursts of it surged like a storm-ridden tide, coils of intense heat expanded until she was so needy she wanted to jerk him under her and rid herself of this force running through her out of control.

But his mouth was persuasive, holding her in its power. She didn't mind, she wanted more. Her body was thrumming to a tune all its own and a desperate need to be fulfilled. Her head was spinning. And it was all so wonderful.

And she wanted more.

"Caleb."

His name was soft on her lips. And he heard everything she wasn't saying.

He sunk into her softness, forgetting all the promises he'd made to himself. All those absurd ramblings of being gentle, of taking it slow. Her body was having none of it. She knew what she wanted, what she was asking. She took him into her, a warm safe haven that surrounded him and gripped him in a flashing blindness that made him nearly cry out.

And he heard the soft gurgling in her throat, a gurgling that pumped his blood and started inching him toward the edge of a madness that he'd never envisioned. He felt her shudder, felt her crest and it blinded him to all else.

Harleigh thought she'd never felt such wonders. Pleasure was everywhere. She felt like she was tumbling through space and any moment would fall through the atmosphere. She wrapped her legs around Caleb as she fell, pleasure ripping in her throat. Caleb heard, felt her pleasure, felt her falling and hung on while he fell with her.

Caleb lay panting, trying to catch the breath he'd lost while he hurtled back to earth with Harleigh clinging to him. He'd never before experienced this kind of body-numbing, mindless, energy-zapping sex before. Vaguely he wondered if he would ever be the same again.

He felt Harleigh's heart beat slow and return to normal. Knew he was crushing her but for the life of him not a muscle in his body responded to movement. "Give me a minute. I'll move in a minute."

"Don't. It's lovely."

That made him laugh. "Me crushing you is lovely?"

She tunneled her fingers through his hair. "Lovely." She nipped at his chin.

"Sorry about the floor."

"Hmm. Don't be. It was my idea. It was lovely, too."

"I still wish we could have made it to the bed."

"Anywhere would have been fine."

"Still. I wanted our first time to be special. Not rolling you around on the floor like I couldn't wait."

She smiled up at him, placed her forefinger on his chin, then raised herself and brushed his mouth with hers. "I couldn't."

"Shall we take it to the bedroom now?"

He managed to get himself to his feet, bent and picked her up off the floor with a groan. And groaned all the way to his bedroom where he threw her down across the covers and fell face down beside her.

"A man not ought to try anything physical after making love to a woman that empties him out and leaves him with nothing," he muttered into the bedspread. "No strength. Not one shred of thought."

"It was that bad?" she teased.

He managed to open one eye to stare at her then closed it again. "Bad? I wish. Then I could think. I could hear. I could move."

"I thought it was nice."

He did the eye-opener thing again, this time with a moan. "I'll never be the same."

She righted herself to sit in the middle of the bed. "I still thought it was nice."

He gained enough strength to raise and nibble at her knee. "You thought it was lovely."

She brushed his mouth, hers still warm and passion-kissed. "Yes. I had been thinking that for a while. Especially since I saw you all decked out in your doctor suit when you had me in the clinic that day. A man in a white coat, stethoscope around his neck, checking me out until I couldn't breath. Staring at me with those pearly eyes. Concerned. Caring. Making me want things I shouldn't be wanting. Making me want you."

"You make me want you just by being in the same room with me. That night at the house when all of us were together and you were across the room? All I wanted to do was cross that room, grab you and haul you over here and make love to you all night long."

"My, my. The truth comes out."

He saw a subtle light of desire enter her eyes and reached out to stroke her cheek with his fingertips. Just touching her made him feel good.

"Just look at you. You're beautiful."

"And look at you, Doc Forrester. You're beautiful, too."

"Come over here and let me hold you."

A new light flashed across her face. Mischievous. Daring. "Hey, ever made love outside? Out in the open before?"

"No. I can't say I have."

"Well, do you wanna?"

He scrambled after her when she went flying over him, grabbed one of his shirts out of his closet and out the door she went. He grabbed his jeans off the kitchen floor, jumped up and down on one leg as he turned in circles trying to shove the other into them. She was long gone when he made it to the back porch.

He ran to the gazebo, thinking she would be hiding there. But she wasn't. He knew she wouldn't take her bare bottom into the Rose House. There was only one other place she could be.

She was there. Waiting. Waiting for him. Standing naked in the clearing, his shirt thrown over that old log as if that's what it was made for. She stood in a spray of sunshine that filtered through the trees. A happy laugh escaped her lips, a tinkling kind of echo that bounced back from the edge of the enchanted forest.

Then she stretched her arms wide, raised her face to the sky, closed her eyes as the warmth of the sun washed over her and turned three times. She'd done this the first time she'd ever stepped into this whimsical place. And oh did it feel good. The sun was warm on her bare skin. The breeze blowing soft through her hair.

"Did you ever do this, Caleb?"

"Run naked through the woods?" He sat down on the log and just watched the enjoyment that seeped from her. "Can't say I have."

"No, you silly man. Go around three times in a circle. I read somewhere that if you found a magical place like this, if you turned three times with your face skyward, good luck would find you."

"Hey, I didn't have to stand naked in the sun, going in crazy circles to find you, my love."

She caught him staring, the desire for her open for anyone to see. Like the way Gentry looked at Phoebe. She liked that. It made her take steps toward him.

With each step she took, the breath backed up in his throat and he couldn't tell if he needed to breathe in or breathe out. When she stood before him, he knew he'd do anything she wanted.

Placing her hand on his cheek, she bent down to him and brushed her lips over his and his eyes closed in the sheer pleasure of it.

"Open your eyes, my love," she softly whispered. "Let me see how you feel when I kiss you."

So now his eyes were open. Filled with all the things she wanted to see.

"Make love to me here, Caleb. Here in this magical place where no one can touch us."

He stood, willing to grant her anything she asked and spread his shirt out upon the soft grass. He drew off his jeans and tossed them aside, eager to be in her arms.

He eased himself down on his shirt and held out his hand to her. Without hesitation, she took it and dropped down beside him.

The kiss she gave him was soft and tender. Not the mind-blowing, ball-busting burst of pleasure she'd given him before that carried enough power to wipe the town of Nowhere off the planet. Even so, it had power of its own. Power that came out of the blue and dropped him like he was nothing. A kiss so sweet and tender that it seeped right into his heart and laid claim to it.

And when Caleb folded her into his arms, she felt as if she'd just ended a long journey and was finally home.

א

Harleigh thought she was dreaming. But she'd never dreamed with her eyes wide open before. She looked above her, around her, watched a swirling glow stir the leaves. And smiled.

It was an approval, she thought. An approval that this wonderful place should be used for this. For love.

For sharing.

She felt Caleb stir beside her. They should get up and dress, she supposed, before someone happened by but at the moment she felt so content that she was beyond caring.

She marveled at the different ways he'd loved her. Hot and driving. Then warm and tender. She would have no regrets that she did this, she told herself. This was one memory that would last her forever. Last until the end of time.

Nothing, not even Stewart and the evil he carried inside him could taint this.

She sat up, knowing now that she had to go before he woke. Before she allowed herself to love him again. Even now, the hunger for him licked at her belly.

She picked the sleeve of his shirt that had wrapped itself around her, off her ankle. She glanced down at him, making another memory then softly walked away, pulling his shirt around her.

She entered her room with a soft smile and a warm heart. She walked to her balcony and just looked at that edge of the forest from where she'd just come, wondered how long he would sleep.

She had things to do, things to think about and plans to make. She knew she couldn't walk away from Caleb just yet. Not after being loved so wondrously, lying beside him and held in the safe haven of his arms. She wanted more of him. To taste more of what he had to offer, fleeting as it was. He'd gotten under her skin and into her heart. And she loved him. That was the bottom line.

As she stood in the stinging spray of her shower, she remembered his lips, his hands. And wanted more.

She would have more, she knew that without a doubt. Had to have more.

He was as addictive as any drug. She'd never be able to have enough of him. It'd taken her by surprise that she could experience such emotions and still remain whole.

She turned off the shower and stepped out, still working things out in her mind. She dried off. Dreams and hopes twining themselves inside her.

She couldn't hide the smile that turned up the corners of her mouth every time she thought of Caleb. The clearing.

She hugged herself close. Savoring. Wondered if he was still there sleeping. Even thought about running back, stripping down and kissing him all over again.

She wanted him. Badly.

And if the heated experiences she'd just had were a true indication of his feelings, he wanted her just as badly.

Just thinking of it heated her blood.

Did he love her?

She knew he had feelings for her. But was it enough?

She wouldn't worry about that right now. She assured herself that it was enough for now. She'd worry about the other later.

She heard a door slam and a car start, knew it must be Ma Forrester as most of the guests were out and about.

She was hungry. Had a sudden urge to eat. She dressed, pulled her wet hair back with a scrunchie and all but floated down the stairs she felt so light.

She was making a sandwich for herself when she

heard the back door slam and her heart tripped. She knew it was Caleb. She didn't have to turn around to face him to know. She could feel every step he took. Could even feel him breathe from across the room.

He jailed her inside his arms, blocking her escape and nuzzled her neck. "Hmm. You sure taste good, Miz Harleigh."

She smiled. He pushed himself against her backside so she could feel his arousal. Her smile widened.

"I could take you like this, Harleigh."

Fear clogged her throat. She couldn't help the terror that clawed its way up her belly as he ground his erection against her.

Caleb felt her stiffen and stepped back from her, giving her room. He felt her drag air into her lungs, realized it must have something to do with what he said, what he did. And it fueled his anger. It was all he could do to keep it inside.

He wasn't angry with Harleigh. He was angry at that bastard ex-husband of hers. He'd never been a violent man. Never thought of himself as such, but since Harleigh had entered his life there were a lot of things he was finding out about himself. One of those things was the ability to kill with his bare hands if he ever had the opportunity to come across Stewart Pennington.

"Harleigh?"

"Yes?" Her voice was shaky and it hurt that he was the cause of it.

"Turn around."

She tried to be brave. Tried to hide the fact that she was afraid. Afraid that he would hurt her the way Stewart had. She didn't think she could stand it. She turned in the circle his arms made around her.

"Look at me, Harleigh."

Warily, she raised her eyes to his. Lifting her chin with his fingertip, he kissed her on the forehead then gave her a direct look. "I'll never hurt you, Harleigh. You're safe with me. You'll always be safe with me."

And she knew that. It was just Stewart's way of never letting her forget. Never let her forget his hold over her. And she wouldn't let him do this to her. Or Caleb, the man she loved.

Caleb was a good man. There was no comparison between the two.

"I know," she assured him shakily. "It's just sometimes … well, you know how you can hear a song and it will take you back to a place or time in your past that something happened. And it triggers a memory."

He raised a hand slowly to see if she would flinch. When she didn't, he tucked the strand of stray hair behind her ear but didn't touch her otherwise. "Yeah, that happens a lot as the years go by."

"Sometimes I can't stop the bad from coming through."

He leaned forward within a breath of her lips. "He'll never touch you again, sweetheart. I swear it by all that I am. And I will never hurt you."

"I know, it's just sometimes I wish he weren't there," she whispered. "No matter what I do, he's always lurking in the back of my mind."

"Broken wings can be repaired, my love." He leaned into her then and kissed her. "Let me heal you."

"You can't fix me like a broken arm, Doc. There's too much damage. Inside."

"Just let me try, then. Give me a chance to get inside to where the damage is. Let me see the real you."

He took her face in his hands and held her there while he looked deep into her soul. "Give yourself into my capable hands. I'll take care of you."

He already held her heart in his hands, didn't he know that?

To erase the shakiness in her belly that was invading her perfect world, a bouncing light came into her eyes. She arched into him, wiggled her eyebrows and thrust the sandwich in his face. "Wanna bite?"

"As long as it's you, babe. As long as it's you."

She giggled, dropping the sandwich and threw her arms around him, her hunger for food forgotten. The hunger for Caleb blocked out everything else. He picked her up and her legs curled around his waist.

Yes, he would heal her, he thought as he carried her up the steps and into her room. As he kicked the door closed, clicked the lock, he flew to the bed.

No doubt, he'd be able to reach deep within and erase all the misery and pain that lived there.

Yes, she would let him heal her, she thought. He was already on the right path.

א

It was good to be back at work. She'd had such a good day yesterday and on up into the night. It was so good, she was afraid to think about it. Afraid that she'd never have another. But she'd allowed Caleb in. She'd given him her heart, her trust. There was no going back now.

Today, she was overflowing with a happiness that spread fast. Everybody noticed. Even old man Pritchett.

"Have I lost ya'?"

"Lost me? What are you going on about?"

"Just look at yourself, girl. You're floating around here on a cloud. That Forrester boy got to ya, did he?"

Harleigh felt the hot flush of embarrassment slide into her cheeks. She swept it away because she could do this now. She could take and give back. Besides Mr. Pritchett was eighty-two years old. "Now, you sweet man, you know I don't kiss and tell."

He gave her a toothless grin of approval, reaching out to pat her arm with arthritic fingers. "That's my girl."

She took another swipe at the already clean counter and turned to check the coffee and ran right into Sophy.

"So, did he?"

Harleigh saw the corners of Sophy's mouth wanting to turn up. She was learning how to do this. How to cope with this everyday stuff she'd longed to do seemed like forever ago.

"Did he what?" she deadpanned.

"You know very well who and what, Harleigh Bleu. Did that Forrester boy get to you? Sweep you off your feet? Is that what's got you all smiling and happy and mysterious?"

Amused, Harleigh raised both brows and turned her head. "Didn't I just say, I don't kiss and tell?"

"I got news for you, Harleigh," Sophy teased. "You don't have to say a word, it's written all over your face. I can't wait to see Caleb. I bet it's the same with him."

"Maybe. But you'll have to pull my fingernails out by the roots to get the goods on that!" Sophy glanced over her shoulder. "Well, if it isn't that man of mine.

Don't ya' just love the way he drags himself out of that squad car and walks like he owns the universe."

"Yeah," Harleigh replied dryly, "it really gets my juices flowing."

Sophy looked over at her in surprise. "Harleigh! You made a joke. Wow, am I proud of you or what!"

Grady walked in, his eyes searching. Finding what he was looking for, walked up to the counter and removed the toothpick out of his mouth.

"Miz Sackett." He tipped his hat.

"Mr. Sackett."

Harleigh thought they looked like they were the only two people in the world. Grady was looking at Sophy as if he wanted to eat her up. Sophy's return look was one of a cat waiting to lick up a saucer of cream.

There was heat flowing between them, hot and heavy. Harleigh couldn't resist.

"Get a room, guys, unless you want me to douse you with a bucket of cold water."

They both returned to reality on a slow path. Then aware of where he was at, Grady managed to brush away the beginnings of embarrassment.

He was caught. His hand was in the cookie jar. He couldn't help it. He loved this woman. He didn't care who knew.

He grinned over at Harleigh, noted the glowing look on her features, knew what happened and returned the favor. "No, ma'am. How about you?"

Harleigh clamped her mouth shut. She could see the merriment in his eyes. Knew she had to respond. "Does it show?"

"Kinda. Shows a lot on that old buddy of mine, too."

"You've seen Caleb this morning, then?" Just his name caused her heart to trip.

"Yeah, I had him come over to the jail to make sure Charley was doing okay. I'm releasing him today. No reason to keep him anymore. He didn't commit any crimes."

"You need coffee this morning, Sheriff?" Harleigh asked, thinking to give him one more dig. This was the way it was done and she could do it. "Or is it already hot enough for you?"

Grady chuckled, bent down and smacked Sophy on the mouth. "You're learning, Miz Harleigh. I think you'll do."

On his way out, he met Delilah, tipped his hat. "Morning, Miz Delilah. Great day, ain't it?"

Delilah eyed him like he'd lost his mind. What was with these people? Had they all lost what little sense they had? First Caleb, now Grady.

She'd taken the twins in early for their well-baby exams and hurried back home, called Miz Clancy over to watch them for an hour so she could talk to Sophy, see if she'd learned anything. And everyone she met seemed to change overnight.

Delilah took one glance at both women and looked around. "Is this a sauna or something? Is there steam rising off you two?" To make her point, she pulled a napkin out the holder and touched her forehead with it. "So, Harleigh, want to spill the beans about you and Caleb?"

"Hey, like I told Mr. Pritchett and Sophy, and countless others, I do *not* kiss and tell."

"So, you did kiss the man then?"

Harleigh busied herself with wiping down the

counter. "You're one incorrigible woman, Delilah Cassidy."

"That's what Butch tells me at least once a day." She turned to Sophy. "Where was Grady off to?"

"Going to see Doc, I imagine. He's got to file that report on Charley."

"Was he able to find out anything about Harleigh's kidnapped kids?"

"He's looking."

Delilah waited a heartbeat. "So … Harleigh, how was he?"

Harleigh looked at Delilah, over at Sophy and back again then grinned, a big happy secretive grin. "Damn good!"

א

"Got that report ready for me, Doc?"

Caleb raked his eyes over Grady in exasperation. "What report?"

"Whatsa matter, Doc? The little woman turn your brain to mush?"

"Did anyone ever tell you that you're a nuisance? Go out and solve a crime or something, Grady, I'm kinda busy here."

"Busy with what? Nobody in the waiting room."

"There are other aspects to my job besides setting bones and sewing up gashes."

"Missed you yesterday."

"Missed me? What was yesterday?"

"We were supposed to go over to Butch's and practice horseshoes, remember? The yearly ball is coming up soon and we want to be in top shape for the tournament this year, ya' know. Coulda used ya'."

"Yeah, yeah, yeah. I had more important things to do besides playing horseshoes."

"What? Playing spin the bottle with Miz Harleigh?"

"It's none of your business, Grady, how I spend my days off."

"My, my, my. Aren't we a bit touchy today? What happened since you were over at the office? You were walking with your head above the clouds."

"Nothing happened. Just started thinking things I shouldn't be thinking is all."

"What do you know about this kidnapping thing the sisterhood is all hot and bothered over?"

Caleb laid down the paper file he'd been going over and looked up at Grady. "Kidnapping? Maybe you better sit a spell after all and tell me what you know?"

"Not much. I was being taken advantage of by my dear wife again. Big advantage to seduce me like that." Grady cleared his throat as he sat. "As near as I remember something about an angel showing Harleigh movies about a woman out walking with her three children and they were kidnapped."

"When did this happen? I haven't heard anything about any kidnappings lately. She know who they were?"

"Don't know who. Don't know when. Don't know where."

"Sounds like a lost cause to me."

"Only thing is there was a kidnapping twenty-five years ago. A four year old and her two twin sisters. Their last name, so it seems, was Bleu."

"What?"

"Yeah, that kinda shakes you up a bit, doesn't it?"

Caleb ran his fingernails over his chin, noticed some whiskers he'd missed that morning, and wondered if he'd scraped Harleigh's tender skin. "Have you told her?"

"Not yet. Still checking out facts. Want to get them straight. Get it right."

"I agree, we've got to do everything we can."

"I was right, wasn't I?"

"Will you stop jumping from subject to subject like some damn bee on a flower? It's hard to keep up." He rubbed his hand over his face, needing to clear his head. "Right about what?"

Grady removed the toothpick from his mouth and jabbed it in the air to make his point. "That Harleigh's one of your crusades."

"I'm in love with her, Grady. I've waited forever, it seems, for her to come along and make me complete. She's made me more than I ever dreamed of being."

Grady shoved the toothpick back in his mouth, stood, looked down at Caleb and planted his hands on the desk. He looked directly into his eyes and grinned. "You got it bad, boy. Real bad."

"Don't start with me now, Grady. Just don't start."

"Didn't I tell you one day you'd take a fall? Remember how you use to point your finger and laugh at me about me making moon eyes at Sophy? Well, the shoes on the other foot and now, my man, you're about to take the fall of your life."

Caleb laughed. "Grady, you are so full of shit!"

"And, didn't I tell you she had you wrapped? I love being right!"

"You know, sometimes I wonder why I call you friend. It can't be because of your sparkling personality."

Grady wiggled his eyes and walked away then turned back. "Just for your information, Stewart's coming this way. He's supposed to be in Atlanta some time this month then Orlando."

Caleb rose from his desk and walked to the doorway of his office where Grady stood.

"He's looking for her, isn't he?"

"I can't honestly tell you that. It's something I don't know. There's no reason he should come to such a small town like Nowhere, though. In his circle, that'd be beneath him."

"But what if he does?"

"Then the only thing we can do is be ready."

CHAPTER THIRTEEN
א

Okay. This was a load of crap, she knew it just as she knew that she was five foot six.

Nevertheless, here she was. Standing like an idiot in the middle an empty parking lot watching this ... *alien*? ... that's the only thing she could think of calling him. A living breathing E.T.

Thank goodness, it was nearly dark. If anyone came along that she knew, she'd just say her car broke down and she had elicited help from this ... *stranger.*

She'd never believed in such things before he came along. And he'd changed her mind in a hurry. Something about a full moon and flowing currents and finding a lost soul.

She may not understand about the moon and currents but she did understand everything about lost souls. She'd been searching since she was thirteen years old for the other part of hers.

At an early age, Caileigh knew there was something wrong. Not so much as wrong, she corrected. Just not right. She'd felt different. Knew that she was different. That part of her was out there. Somewhere. Then when she found out she was adopted and had a twin, that's when the search began in earnest.

A long futile search that had gotten her nowhere, until, bless the electronic highway, the internet came along and you were privy to anything and everything. She'd been digging through the newspaper archives, came across an article, a very small article about a wealthy family losing their three children to kidnappers. The ransom had been paid but the children never recovered.

She'd always wondered about her middle name. Always thought it a little weird. As it turned out, Bleu, like the color, was her real last name. Her adoptive parents had told her they knew nothing about her biological parents. Only that her name couldn't be changed. Almost as if whoever had taken the girls knew that this day would come. Knew that one day all the dirty details would be known.

Then before she'd had time to act on the information, wade through the facts, separate truth from supposition, she'd been contacted by an investigator, then an attorney. She'd gone through DNA testing, it proving she was one of the daughters and she was the heir to a massive fortune. Then the circle that surrounded her closed a little more.

Her mother never gave up, it seemed, insisting she'd know if her children were dead. But her heart never grieved for dead children. Her heart grieved for lost children.

And, an indulgent and rich husband did everything possible to please his wife.

She was grateful for that. Her mother was no pushover. She supposed that's where she got it. She herself was full of the determination and strength of character that her mother exhibited.

Even before it was proven that she was Caileigh Bleu, her mother insisted she was. She'd known it the moment she'd looked into her eyes, she said. Those were her own mother's eyes, she persisted. Adamant that she knew her own daughter.

Sure, there'd been many before Caileigh came along. So many paraded before her that she'd lost count. But her heart had never recognized any of them, she was fond of saying.

Until Caileigh. And things had changed at such a rapid pace, she felt like she was in a whirlwind, her mother in the center of it.

Caileigh laughed to herself.

Her mother. Her mother was too serious, by far. Guess she had to be when your children were stolen right before your eyes and you were helpless to do anything about it. But she needed to loosen up. She'd been telling her that for years.

And Elizabeth Bleu would go ballistic if she knew what she, Caileigh was doing now.

She wasn't sure herself what she was doing now.

She looked out through the windshield of her truck at the man pacing back and forth across the asphalt. He was a hottie, that was for certain. There was that look about him that made you drool and your blood run hot. Made you just want to throw yourself at his feet and say take me.

But there was that other side to him that drove her up a wall. The side that was doing the pacing. He was always pushing at that damned gadget in his hand and that made her crazy. Said he was looking for currents, traces of bio emissions, and some nonsense about why he was here.

At first, she thought he was some idiot making it all up just to hit on her. From the first moment she'd met him on a street corner and he looked at her with fire in his eyes, she was hooked. On him, on what he was doing.

Of course, she'd never let him know that. He was a man, after all, transient being or not. Just as hardheaded and pea-brained as any Earth-bound male. His body parts ruled his brain.

Only when that gadget thing started pulsating and vibrating did he give up his quest to get himself into her bed, did he become focused as if she didn't exist.

And right now was one of those moments. That thing was flashing and emitting small beeps as he turned. Then, all the lights went out, the noise stopped. And like any Earth-bound male, he threw the gadget against a light pole.

Caileigh laughed at the tantrum he was having and couldn't let the moment pass. "Hey, hotshot, you having a problem with your toys? Got a mad on, do you?"

He hated it here, he decided. This noisy damn planet where there was so much racket it hurt his ears. Where there was so much pollution, it interfered with his breathing. And most of all, he hated Earth people.

And especially, the female of the species, one being Caileigh Bleu sitting in her black Ford Explorer truck that she thought was made of gold, laughing at him.

He stomped her way, wondering how he had gotten so out of control on this planet. That's why he was sent here. Because he never lost his cool. But, this … this Caileigh female, got under his skin and into that cool reserve to interrupt his purpose, his thoughts, his control. Seems like anger, an emotion he never knew existed inside, was always there in front of him. Seething. Flaring up at a moment's notice. Raging on. No matter what he did to stop it.

He pushed at the transor in his ear. Hated that thing, too. He was learning the English language but when he had a mad on, as she called it, he preferred having it translated for him. Now was one of those times. If it weren't for the fact that she knew her way around this abhorrent and foul-smelling place, he'd go it on his own.

As it was, he needed her. Things had changed so much since Shera was left behind. And he had to find her at all cost. Time was running out. Her time. And he had to get to her before that happened.

For now, though, he had to deal with this female.

His breath was coming hard when he stopped before her. Then, like always, his olfactory senses clicked in within smelling distance of her and he immediately forgot he wanted to ring her neck. His desire rose like that orange ball they called the sun. Rose hot and searing.

Then he reminded himself of his purpose here. Of Shera. "It's not a toy," he sneered, baring his teeth like a feral animal.

"Oh, that's why you smashed it against that pole over there! Hey, by the way, that was a great tantrum. A two-year old couldna' done better."

What was it about this earthling female that boiled him over like hot lava out of a spewing volcano?

"It was *not* a tantrum! It was a malfunction!"

"Uh, huh. Malfunction. And the malfunction is laying all over the pavement over there in pieces. Why is that, you suppose?"

He stomped back and picked up the pieces of his emission identifier and threw it in the bed of the truck. In frustration, Aidan Cain stomped around the nose of the truck and threw open the passenger-side door.

"It was *not* a tantrum, earthling female," Aidan insisted.

"That's what they all say, sweet cakes. Get in and let's hit the road again. Maybe when you get your little thingy fixed there, we'll find one of those current things you're always going on about."

א

Harleigh stirred her body in wakefulness. She'd been covertly watching for Caleb, laying in wait, so to speak, her private patio in a direct line to the front of his house.

His truck was not in the driveway.

She'd wait, she decided, and pillowed her head back against the wicker chair. She heard a soft sound and slitted her eyes.

Through a fringe of lashes, she saw movement. Saw a black truck, moonlight falling through a window silvering a head of long hair. Saw a man tread heavily to the window, his mouth moving.

From his stance, he was angry. From his face, that same anger lashed outward like a whip. His fingers curled into fists when the woman laughed. Then like an obedient little boy, the man walked back to retrieve the litter, throwing it in the back of the pickup and got in. The silver-haired woman roared out of the parking lot with a punch of the accelerator and faded away.

The laughter, however, remained behind.

It was like seeing something in your peripheral vision, then you blinked for a better look and it was gone. Then the only thing that lingered was in your memory like the echo of the laughter she heard.

She rose from her chair, rubbed the chills off her arms and went inside. As she freshened up, she heard the slowing of a vehicle, tires on gravel and smiled. Caleb was home. Her time was now.

She was so enjoying this place, this day, this time in her life. There was so much going on, some explainable, some not but her life was fuller than it had ever been. Her life had been cracked and those cracks were slowly filling in making her whole, making her complete.

She'd been in Nowhere now for four months. The best months she'd ever known. Soon she would move on. She'd wait for the end of summer. She still had things to do … like that *real* date Caleb had asked her to go on. Of course, now that she was his bed partner, maybe, that was no longer under consideration.

Still, she would hold out for it a little longer.

Her favorite time of day was fast becoming the evenings where she could sit in the cool of the twilight waiting for Caleb. He'd become habit-forming, she watching and waiting for him if he hadn't come home by the time she did. Then she'd slip over to that wonderful house of his and share whatever the night would bring.

Sometimes, he'd cook those wonderful meals his mother had taught him. If it were left up to her, they'd starve. She couldn't even boil water. So, he'd cook for her, instruct her on down-home, southern cooking.

Sometimes, they'd sit inside the gazebo and watch the shadows of the moonlight twirling around the edge of the forest. He'd nibble on her neck, breathing in her scent.

And sometimes, they'd make love wherever they were. Wherever the passion took them over.

And it was wonderful. Heaven.

And that's where she was going now. Heaven.

She knocked softly on his door. When he filled the doorway, her heart skipped and tripped.

He leaned against the door edge and crossed his arms, his eyes greedily devouring her. "Well, look at what we have here." Caleb leaned forward and sniffed. "Mmm. Sweet. Good enough to eat. Where would I start?"

He pulled her inside, closed the door and pulled her into his arms. Into safety.

Lately though, she'd sensed a restlessness about him. Sensed that somehow he knew what she was planning. Sensed that he needed more from her than she could give.

Oh, she knew, he'd protect her. There was no doubt about that. Knew he'd try but she couldn't be responsible for spilled blood. And there would be. Didn't know how she knew, she just knew.

He'd once told her she could tell him anything but if she told it all, down to the last dirty detail, he'd never touch her again. Stewart had tainted her, made her dirty. Then little by little Caleb had cleansed her. But Stewart still had his grip on her, not because of the past but because of Caleb. He was her weakness. She couldn't bear to have him harmed.

She knew she should tell him everything. Many a time during the last few months she was tempted. But in the end, she couldn't do it. She didn't want him to know how deep her humiliation went so she'd kept her shame hidden inside.

The truth was her little corner of the world was going so well that she didn't want anything to interrupt it. And coming clean would cause a tidal wave.

She didn't like it, of course. It ate at her at times. These things she kept from him. The deceit with which she laced her well-chosen words. The lengths she would go to keep it covered up.

One thing was for sure. A promise she made herself. She would *not* go back. She'd kill Stewart first. If petite Bonnie could weld a bat, then so could she.

Even now, in the quiet, when everything was so good, when Caleb had loved her with a sweet tenderness, Stewart would intrude on what they had. And she hated it. Hated him even more.

She felt Caleb move beside her. He pulled her close and she curled around him, held him, and kept Stewart at bay.

א

There was more of a crowd than usual today at the Nowhere Café. The Summer Jam Festival was beginning its weeklong event and people were coming out of the walls to see the stars.

Harleigh's feet hurt but she went on. No one had been able to take a break to rest. She and Sophy were scurrying around in their haste to serve the customers, barely missing each other on their way to and from the serving window. Just when they thought the crowd was thinning, here came another throng of people.

On her way back to the counter, she stopped to pour coffee into a cup of one of Sophy's customers. She glanced up with a smile and froze.

Her perfect world had come to an end.

"Harleigh! What are you doing in Podunk USA?"

The fear was back. It clogged her throat, knotted her stomach and drained every ounce of strength from her body. She swallowed back the bile that spewed upward into her throat.

She was caught with nowhere to run. Stewart's cousin, Adele Pennington, was sitting right there before her. The minute Adele returned to New York, she'd be on the phone to Stewart.

She straightened her spine and swallowed her fear. This was not the old Harleigh they were dealing with here. She smiled. "Hello, Adele. How are you?"

"Have you gone mad, chickie? Working in a place like this when you have all that money at your fingertips?"

Harleigh thought long and hard before she gave her an answer. So she smiled while the wheels turned. She needed to buy time. "No, I'm not mad, Adele. You know how it is. You have to go slumming now and then, have to see how the other half lives, don't you?"

Harleigh knew Sophy heard her, hoped no one else did, but right now she had to get rid of this parasite. She hurried away before she had to waste any more words on a woman she detested. A woman who looked down her nose at anyone less fortunate.

Sophy looked at her oddly as she set the coffee pot

onto the warmer and marched straight back to the kitchen. She bit back the tears. She couldn't break down now. They depended on her here and she couldn't let them down. Wouldn't let them down.

She leaned against the door, her stomach roiling, tremors shaking her body. She felt a hand on her shoulder and stiffened.

"Here, you better sit down," Sophy told her and pushed her down. "You're white as a ghost. Are you okay?"

"Y-y-es," she replied as the tremors worsened. "I'm having a panic attack. Give me minute, will you?"

She welcomed the cold cloth against her skin. It would pass, she told herself. Gave strict orders to take deep even breaths.

The shakes began to subside with each ragged breath she took. Periodically, Sophy would run back to check on her. The guilt that wrapped itself around her made her feel that much worse. Thankfully, the crowd had slacked off and Sophy didn't have to do double duty.

She opened her eyes to find Caleb standing before her and her trepidation dragged the guilt deeper. The storm brewing in his pearl gray eyes warned of more turbulence ahead.

His voice carried a bit of early morning frost on a windowpane. "Want to tell me what that was all about?"

"What was what all about?" Harleigh knew exactly what he was talking about. But she couldn't bring herself to say the words. Her emotions were too raw, too close to the surface and she needed to distance herself from it. From everyone. From Caleb.

She was losing her breath again, her airwaves constricting with each breath she tried to take. She was frightened. More frightened by the revulsion she saw in his appearance than by the thought of Stewart breathing hot and heavy down her neck.

He could see the lies in her eyes. Could see the deception clearly written on her features. "Don't even try to lie to me, Harleigh. You know damn well what."

She tried another tact. "If you'll just tell me what it is you want from me, I'll try to give it to you."

"How about a little honesty on your part, then? How about telling me and the good citizens of Nowhere, people who have gone out of there way to help you, I might add, to protect you in this Podunk little town, why you're even bothering to lower yourself to our level and rub elbows with the local scum. What was it you called it?"

She dared not look at him. Her heart was already breaking from the coldness of his voice. If she looked into those eyes filled with loathing, her heart would shatter.

The slamming of his fist against the wall above her head got her attention and she forced herself to look fully into his face. What she saw made her shudder.

"It was the only way I could get away from her, Caleb. I had to say what she wanted to hear."

"Just like you're so willing to give me what I want? Are you still walking down that path?"

"I don't know what you want from me, Caleb. Adele is Stewart's cousin. If you'd let me explain … "

"Explain what? That this was just a stopping over place for you? Somewhere where you could go slumming then run back to wherever the hell you came from

so you can tell your high society friends about your little side trip?"

"It wasn't like that."

"No? Then what was it like? Was I a big joke as
well? Just something to tell all the girls about a roll in
the hay with the country doctor?"

Somewhere deep, there was an anger that took
hold of Harleigh and wouldn't let go. He was taking
something beautiful and soiling it.

"I'm not going to listen to another word, Caleb."
She drew herself up and looked him straight in the eye.
"You've taken everything and twisted it to suit your-
self."

"Why, Harleigh? Why aren't you going to listen?
Because I'm right? Because I'm too close to the truth?
What about me, Harleigh? What about me?"

She had no answer to give him. She walked away
without looking back.

He didn't want to leave it like this, knew he
shouldn't, but what choice did he have? He did have a
choice, he realized. He would get to the truth.

"Harleigh."

She didn't stop, kept right on walking out the door.

He grabbed her arm and held fast. "Dammit, Harleigh, I want answers."

Panic was raking her insides raw with sharp talons.
"You won't listen, so why should I even try? You don't
want to hear the truth."

"Truth? You wouldn't know the truth if it was staring you in the face."

That rankled. That anger that was simmering below the surface exploded. "What do you want to know,
Caleb? How many times he locked me in the closet?

How many days he made me run around with soiled clothes? How many of my body parts did he break or burn? Is that the kind of truth you want to hear?"

That stopped him cold and his insides recoiled like a rifle from the revulsion. He saw the anger but he heard the pain. He stepped forward. "Harleigh."

"Don't." Harleigh held up her hands to hold him off. She wasn't that scared little rabbit anymore. "I don't want to be near you right now."

Helpless, Caleb watched her climb into her car and slam the door so hard he was surprised the glass didn't shatter.

א

How long was he going to let this go on? It had been three days since Harleigh had walked away from him. It had been his fault for not trying to understand.

Phoebe had raked him over coals so bad he felt like his skin had been peeled back. She'd explained to him the why of it. It was another survival tactic, she told him while punching his chest with a sharp-pointed fingernail.

Delilah had sent the whole sisterhood down on his head. When Delilah appeared at his door near midnight, eyes blazing, he knew he was in it deep.

She knew all about this Adele Pennington. She was a viper, she'd told him. Thought everyone ought to bow down and kiss her feet. She was shallow to the core.

And, Harleigh did the only thing she could. Why were men so pig-headed?

On and on she went till she'd flailed all the hide from his body.

And the last thing, thank God, she was on her way out, was to say he'd better get his butt over there and apologize to Harleigh big time. Even if he had to grovel.

If he didn't, he'd have the sisterhood to answer to. Understand?

He understood all too well. That was why he was standing beneath her balcony, chunking rocks. He'd thought about entering the house and knocking on her door but his mother wasn't speaking to him either. She'd cut off his supply of desserts.

No telling what Harleigh was going to do to him. He'd rather be standing in front of a firing squad than what he was doing now.

He was about to walk away to try another day when he heard her door open. She looked down on him as if he were slime.

"What dya' want, Caleb. I don't have time for you or your wise-ass remarks."

And he grinned up at her. That boyish grin that teased the corner of his mouth before turning upward. That damn grin that made her pulse pound in her ears.

She was in one hell of a snit, he could see that from where he stood. Well, he might as well get this over with.

"Hi, Harleigh." He paused, waiting for her to throw something at his head, if that was her inclination. "Please don't be mad at me. Everyone else in this town either has a piece of my hide or given me a piece of their mind."

"You've given me no reason *not* to be mad,

Caleb."

"Will you come over to the house a minute so we can talk? I've missed you."

She stared down at the man who held her heart. Knew she shouldn't give him the time of day but felt herself relenting.

"You didn't miss me, Caleb. You missed having somebody to roll around your kitchen floor with."

He looked down at his feet where he was kicking at the grass. "That, too. But I need to talk to you. Please, come listen to what I have to say."

"Why should I?"

She sure wasn't making this easy. "Because I need you to."

Now why did he have to go and say that? He could of said anything but that. Said that he had a need for her.

"Give me a minute."

She didn't have to pick up her perfume bottle and squirt a couple of sprays on her brush and swept it through her hair. Didn't have to check out her appearance to make sure she looked good for him.

And Caleb. He fairly skipped back to the house, splashed on a dab of cologne and breathed in deep to try to calm down. It wasn't as if this was his first date. But it might as well have been from the way his testosterone level was rising.

She was at his door before he had a chance to do much else. When he opened the door and she entered, got a whiff of her scent his hormone level went right off the scale.

"Look, why don't you come in and sit down? I'll talk, you listen." The heat of her anger poked at him and it smarted. But she had every right. "You've got every right to be mad at me."

The step she took made him retreat. "Mad? You think I'm mad?"

"You seem to be."

"I'm pissed, Caleb. Pissed off, big time." She picked up a book and hurled it at his head. "Do you hear me?"

Caleb put his hands to defend himself, delighted that she was finally letting go. "Harleigh, you're taking this all wrong."

"I'm taking it just the way you took it."

"Okay, okay. You win."

Harleigh lowered the newspaper she held in her hand. "And?"

"And, I'm sorry."

"But?"

"I wanted to take care of you, Harleigh. I wanted you to let me in so I could help you."

Harleigh sat heavily on the couch and sighed. "What am I going to do with you?"

"Let's start all over at the beginning. Let me in."

"You ask too much of me. There's more to it than I'm able to give you. I have nothing more inside me that I can give."

"Don't tell me the things we've shared over the past few weeks have been just fun and games for you! They were real … the things we shared were real."

"Yes, they were."

"What we had was good and pure."

She gave him a smile, one that swept into his heart and spun it around. "I think you called it good and sweet."

"Then it's settled between us?"

"No, it's not settled. There's so much you don't know. Some things I can never tell. Things I don't want to remember."

"I understand."

"No. I don't think you do. You don't understand why I stayed. Why any of it."

This wasn't going the way he envisioned. Not at all. What had happened to that pliant terrified girl that had stepped off the bus and into his heart?

"I do understand. You were trapped. What else could you do? You finally got out, didn't you?"

"Yes, it was stay and be killed or run. I elected to run and live." She knew he deserved details but she wasn't up to spilling her guts at the moment. "Stewart is an evil man, Caleb. He hurts people for his own perverted pleasure. Just for the sheer joy of knowing he can."

"I'm glad you ran." He allowed himself to run his fingers through the fine strands of the hair draped on her shoulder. "I'm glad you came here."

"I should have kept my guard up. I should never have gotten involved with any of you. I just wanted a real life for a change. To feel and to know how it was. No matter how brief it was." She bit down on her lower lip and frowned. "Don't make me sorry I came."

"Sorry? How could I make you sorry?"

Exasperated, she jumped up and paced. "By pushing and poking. I know you want to know about my past but I've told you all I can. I want to forget the rest and go on from there. And now, he's going to know where I'm at as soon as Adele gets to him."

"Bring him on, Harleigh. We'll take care of him."

She walked to the window, hugged her arms to herself and stared over at the Rose House. "I know you will and that scares me more than Stewart does."

"You've come a long way, Harleigh, from that girl I picked up off the café floor. You were so terrified of me and look at you now." He rose and stood behind her, wanting to reach out and pull her back against him. To breathe her in and make it better. But he knew it would be the wrong thing to do. "Now, you throw things at me. You can't get more normal than that."

She turned around to face him. There was that grin again across his mouth. The one that made her tingle. She looked away quickly before she found herself up against him and kissing that mouth.

"It felt pretty good, too. I'm going to have to improve my aim because I missed your head."

"Butch can help you there. Early on he was destined to be a baseball star."

"What happened?"

"Threw his arm out."

"That's terrible. What a career he would've had."

Caleb made a clicking sound at the corner of his mouth and twisted his head in a negative fashion. "I don't know. I really don't think he was all that broken up about it. He's a small town boy at heart. Not one to roam outside of our little piece of paradise."

"I like this piece of paradise, Doc. It's calming."

"Are we okay now?"

She placed her palms on his chest as she stepped forward to brush up against him. "I don't know about that. I think I'll make you pay for a long time to come."

He enfolded her loosely in his arms in case he was reading her wrong. Since she gave no indication of moving away, he brought his right hand up to cup her cheek, caressed her lower lip with his thumb.

She was the one who moved first. She inched into him, running her palms upward to tunnel through his hair and circle them around his neck. She drew him down to her, rubbed her lips against his. A kiss that began sweet and tender then burgeoned into a scorching, blistering merging of senses.

"Are we okay enough for me to make mad passionate love to you?"

He found himself on the floor before he'd even finished asking. "Only if you'll be my love slave," she teased.

They were all right. Were going to be all right, he thought as the pleasure of her response to his touch heightened.

This was sweet, she was thinking as he tucked her under that body of his that could play hers like the sweet strains of music. And, speaking of sweet, he was that. And her body thrilled as he moved against her. Thrilled. Wanted. Needed.

He gave her all this and more. He gave himself.

His hands trembled against her skin as he fumbled with her jeans. He swore. "You've got too damn many clothes on. I need to feel you bare against me."

Looking into his eyes, she saw everything she wanted and needed. "Here," she whispered softly. "Let me help."

Harleigh raised herself upon her knees and stripped off her clothes which went flying everywhere. She was in no mood for slow.

His were off just as fast.

As if it were a written script, they moved with each

other. Skin brushing skin. Kisses upon heated flesh. Fingertips caressing.

Her body vibrated with each touch of his glorious hands sliding across her skin. And she gave everything she was in response. She felt it begin deep within her and expand and swell until she thought she would burst from it.

His mouth seemed to be everywhere. Tracing patterns down the column of her throat leaving a trail of moist kisses behind. She could only sigh in approval and let him do what he did best.

"Too slow," she murmured against his throat. "You're going too slow."

"I want to love you," he murmured back.

Impatient now, as the blood surfed through her body, heart pounding, pulse rushing, she moved against him and on an intake of breath, he drove into her with a blinding passion.

She gasped as the heat built and she thought she'd surely combust from the blazing inferno churning inside her. She could do nothing but hold on.

Caleb had never felt such fire. Never felt such need. Never felt such a wild intensity to touch, to taste, to have. A blinding wave of heat hit him with such force he lost his breath and felt like he was falling through space.

She cried out with intense pleasure as he took her up to the top of the world and held her there and let her fly.

א

The committee for the annual charity ball met in the community center. The Nowhere Café supplied the refreshments. Ma Forrester had baked a few goodies which everyone was grateful for.

"Okay, ladies, let's get this show on the road and come up with some ideas of how we're going to make this years ball the best ever." Pauline Hayes, this year's chairwoman, pounded her gavel on the block in front of her for attention. "We have to raise enough money to go around."

"Are we still going to start with a picnic?" Myra Warren asked. "You know food always gets the men out."

"That's for sure," put in Vera Ward. "My own Arthur won't go to things unless there's food and beer."

This brought a chuckle to the group as they got down to what they considered serious business.

"Any discussion on that, besides the food?" Pauline asked the members.

"No discussion needed, Pauline," Kate pointed out. "Just decide who's bringing what and how much. And how we're going to get their money."

"Okay, Kate, why don't you circulate a list to all the women, have them jot down what they want to prepare. We'll meet one more time, a week before the date and finalize all those plans. What's next on the agenda?"

"After the picnic, after the food's settled, it's game time," Sally Ann Talbert reminded them. "The men expect that. From what I hear, they're all geared up for the horseshoe tournament."

"Okay, Sally, that'll be your department," Pauline told her. "Get together a list of activities for the men, a list for the women, for the kids. What else?"

"Beauty pageant? Talent contest? Arts and crafts show?" The oldest member of the group banged her cane against the floor for effect and straightened her signature beribboned straw hat. "We need to get a crowd out there."

"Well, now, Miz Justine," Pauline drawled, "you sure have been thinking, haven't you?"

"Yessirree. Still thinkin', too. What happened to our bakery competitions. Cakes. Pies. Then we could sell the portions to the public. Instead of us feeding everybody at the ball, let's fancy up a box social for the men to bid on. If they wanna eat, make 'em pay for it, is what I say."

"You are one hot momma, Miz Justine!" Kate teased.

Miz Justine harrumphed but she sat a little straighter with a sparkle in her eyes.

She was the matriarch of the community, so to speak, eighty-five years old and made the citizens of Nowhere tired. She only had one speed and that was fast. She had a car but she walked as much as she rode. That's what legs were made for, she pointed out. That's what was wrong with the people of today, she claimed, not enough physical activity. Fat and lazy.

Caleb called her spunky. She said he was full of piss and vinegar.

"Yessirree, ma'am. Make it more interesting that way."

"Who could we get to do something like that?" Myra asked, looking around the table. "We don't know anything about beauty pageants."

Kate glanced at each individual and chuckled.

"We've got it all right here, ladies. Right at our finger-tips."

They all stared at her as if the craziest thing had just come out of her mouth. "What dya' mean, Kate? We don't have much of anything here."

"Ladies, ladies," she scoffed. "We've got Delilah. Need I say more?"

There were gasps of understanding around the table amid murmurs of approval. Delilah was a home girl now and gave everything to the community.

"Smart move there, Kate," Miz Justine praised.

"Thank you, ma'am."

"What about the talent show? Arts and crafts, I think we can cover without any problem. Everyone here does that."

This one stumped everyone.

"Well, seein's as how our Miz Delilah is heading up the beauty pageant, maybe she'd do the talent show, too."

"Wouldn't hurt to ask."

"Okay, then," said Pauline. "We got daytime activities covered except for the baking competitions. That should be easy. Just need judges for that, and advertise for entries."

"I'll make up flyers," Kate volunteered. "I'll put one in my window and around town."

"Sounds like a plan. Let's move on to the ball itself. Any ideas?"

"Well," Kate said, pursing her lips "I was thinking that this year maybe having a masked ball. Costumes and things. Keep it simple, nothing fancy. You know the men don't go for that sort of thing."

"Hmm," contemplated Pauline, "It'd be different.

Ladies? Yea or Nay?"

Vera tapped her finger across her lips in thought. Sally Ann tapped the table. Myra tapped her arm. Miz Justine tapped her cane on the floor.

"I like it," Miz Justine said. "We need different."

"Then," Kate added, "with Miz Justine's suggestion about a box social to feed everyone. I think it'll go over nicely."

"Let's wrap this up then," Pauline commented. "We've got work to do."

א

On the other side of town, another meeting was taking place. The sisterhood had called a short one of their own. They left Harleigh out of this one as it affected her and it was their sworn duty to protect her.

Phoebe picked up her cup of tea, sipped and turned to the other girls. They were waiting for Sunny to call them back, waiting on the back patio to pass the time. "I won't be able to stay much longer, guys. Gentry has to get back to Atlanta. He has a case coming up that he has to get on track for. We have to figure out what to do about Stewart."

"He won't hurt her," promised Sophy with fire in her eyes.

"He's on his way, girls, and we have to act now. His next show is in Atlanta. Your neck of the woods, Phebs."

"I'll check him out when he gets there, that's a start."

"There'll only be you and Delilah here to pick up

the load."

The girls looked over at each other and grinned. "We've got big shoulders."

Phoebe frowned over at them, silently saying they were a bunch of nutcases.

"Okay, we've got Butch and Grady's big shoulders," Sophy amended.

"And, Caleb," added Delilah.

"Put them all in the mix and it's safe to say, she'll be okay."

Phoebe wasn't so sure. "Harleigh knows what she's talking about, though. We all know she's been through hell. All you have to do is look into those eyes of hers and see what she's not saying. I'd like to get my hands on the bastard and make him pay for what he did to her. I think it's much worse than what she told us."

"Me, too." Delilah had seen the man up close and personal. What she saw made her skin crawl. She just wanted to run the other way. "I met him on several occasions in New York. I've gone to a couple of showings he had. He's not as good as he thinks, he's just got the money to back it up."

"What was he like?"

"It's hard to explain. There's a darkness there under the surface. I could sense it. He's very handsome, self-assured, full of himself. If you want to know the truth, I thought he was repulsive."

Sophy slammed her glass down on the tabletop. "Well, that does it for me. There's enough backwoods around here that we can just take him back there, stake him out and let the animals have him."

"We need to get serious about this, girls." Delilah interjected. "We can't allow that man to come into our town and hurt one of our own."

"There's plenty of alligators and wild hogs in these backwoods to take a bite out of him."

"We can always throw him in the Suwannee River. You know, give him a pair of cement shoes."

"Not good enough," Phoebe said. "We need to make him pay."

The phone rang. "Let's put a plan into action and make that bastard pay." She reached for the ringing phone while they nodded in agreement.

א

Restless, Harleigh was drawn outside. She felt it, as surely as if she were shavings and the forest was the magnet. She walked to the edge and peered in. Whatever was tugging at her was inside. She wasn't sure she wanted to enter but she had no choice. The pull was too strong.

The clearing was the same but different. The same clearing where she and Caleb were drawn into the magic circle of love.

It seemed ... well, sad. Almost as if its magical quality was fading away. The light was losing its glow, she noticed. The shadows darker.

Harleigh sat down on the hewn-out log that always seemed to give her comfort and waited. For what she didn't know. She wasn't afraid, not for herself. But she knew something was going on. The last time she sat here, she was shown the children, and pieces of her life.

The moon rose higher as she waited. The night was unusually quiet. No serenading of crickets. Or ribbetting of frogs.

Just a soft rustling of leaves.

And footsteps upon the cushion of dried foliage on the forest floor.

"Harleigh. You okay?"

"Hey, Caleb. What brings you out here?"

"You." He moved in on her and pressed his mouth against hers, drew back and smiled. "I couldn't find you."

"I didn't know I was lost." Her stomach did a slow roll. He was here where she needed him to be. "I have something I need to say to you."

"You don't have to say a word. I just want to keep you safe."

Harleigh linked her fingers with his. "No, I need to say this. It's something I've been thinking about for awhile. Something I want you to know."

"Okay."

"I think I'm in love with you, Caleb. It's been rolling around in my brain for weeks like a little silver ball on a track but I never allowed myself to dwell on it overmuch. Not until now, anyway."

Her words ripped the breath right out of his lungs. He felt frozen in time then with the next beat of his heart, the rhythm began again. And he stared, not sure his hearing was working properly.

"You … you think you love me?" His hope soared as he waited for her answer.

"No, Caleb, I don't *think* I love you."

His hope plummeted in his stomach faster than a stone dropping from the top of a tall building. "Oh."

"I do love you. You love me, don't you?"

He shook his head to clear the ice that had frozen

his brain. "Of course, I love you! I love you so much it makes me crazy."

"You make me crazy, too."

He laughed, that deep rumbling sound she loved as much as she loved him. She was glad she'd finally told him.

"We're a pair, aren't we?"

"Yes," she conceded, "we are indeed."

He gazed into her eyes and saw everything she offered. Her love. Her trust. Her life. With gentle hands, he brought her close, held her against him and breathed in her scent. Roses, he thought. Naturally.

"It's for the long haul, Harleigh. You know that, don't you?"

She drew back out of his embrace, pressed her lips against his eyelids in a tender kiss. "Forever," she whispered.

For a moment, she felt that familiar curl of trepidation of giving herself over into his care, a man's care, then brushed it away with the strong conviction that it had no place in her life any more. No place for it to live within her.

א

Adele Pennington strode into the hi-rise on spiked heels, clacking hard against the marble floor with each step she took. Her movements were quick and fluid. She had no time to waste. She had to get to Stewart and inform him of what his bitch of a wife was doing. A woman of her stature working in a place like that!

What if someone else had recognized her? That

slut was right out in the open shaming the Pennington name where everybody could see. Stewart had to put a stop to it and had to do it now.

Impatiently, she punched the elevator buttons and tapped her foot. With a whip of her head, she entered the elevator and punched more buttons to take her to the penthouse suite.

She pounded on his door, placing both arms on each side and hissed her breath through her teeth.

Stewart opened the door with a curse on his lips but let it pass when Adele stormed into the room. "Nice to see you, too. Adele."

"Do you know where your wife is, Stewart? Do you know what that tramp of yours is doing?"

"Careful, Adele. Those words are reserved for me."

Adele ignored him. She was on a roll and had to get the words out before she exploded. "She's working, Stewart! Working! A Pennington doesn't work!"

"Calm down and tell me what you're talking about. Take a load off while I get us a drink." Adele, he thought, as he scooped ice into two old-fashioned glasses, what a pain in the ass she was. But if she'd found Harleigh, well, the least he could do was find out where. And when he did, well, she had it coming. His head still hurt.

He shoved the glass in her hand and waited.

"She's in some miserable, run-down place called Nowhere." She drank deep of the whiskey, nearly draining it on her first sip. "A dusty ghastly hole-in-the-wall."

"First, Adele, I need to point out that Harleigh and I divorced. She can go where she wants and do what she wants."

"And, you're just going to let her stay there? Let her smear the Pennington name?"

"No one even knows us there, Adele." He needed to get rid of her so he could start making plans to go to that run-down place she spoke of. "I do appreciate you informing me of her whereabouts, though. If it will make you feel better, I'll go talk to her. How about that?"

"Yes, Stewart, that's an excellent idea." In her excitement, she jumped up from the sofa where he immediately removed the empty glass in her hand. "You'll do it right away?"

"You can count on it." He nudged her toward the door. "Run along now and I'll make plans."

Stewart called his assistant, gave him the information and began pacing the floor. He itched to get going, everything else was of no consequence. Harleigh was within his grasp and that's where she would stay.

He poured another drink and gulped it straight down. It burned but he didn't care, it would be one more thing that she had to atone for.

Harleigh. Finally. She would be his again. The only thing she knew how to be.

He only had to close his eyes to see her, to smell her, to taste her. He curled his hands into fists as he envisioned how they would feel pounding against her flesh when he punished her.

And punish her he would.

It's what she deserved for running away from him, after all.

His friends believed he was consumed with grief. And he was. But it was grief for the loss of one who had been trained and fine-tuned to meet his every need. It certainly wasn't because he loved her. That was such an over rated emotion. It wasn't something he'd ever felt. Definitely not that skinny little bitch. He gave her what she wanted.

And he gave her all of him she wanted. She wanted the pain, he knew she did. Why else did she deliberately fail him time after time?

But she had hurt him that last time. She'd drawn blood. His blood. It was an unforgivable act on her part.

The phone rang and he turned to answer the call from his assistant. No one else had his phone number.

"Yes, George. What have you got for me?"

George Tanner was a good assistant. Sometimes, too good, he told himself. The information George had he really didn't want to relay to Mr. Pennington. Especially any information concerning Mrs. Pennington.

Mr. Pennington was a deranged asshole as far as he was concerned. There was no other way to put it. George knew he mistreated the lovely Mrs. Pennington. She'd always treated him with respect and in turn George did his best to keep her out of harm's way. Out of Stewart Pennington's way. As far as George was concerned, he was the devil himself.

"George? I asked you what you found out."

He heard the underlying threat in that voice that grated on his nerves and not for the first time did he remind himself to look for another job.

"Nowhere is located in North Florida near the Georgia-Florida border. It's a very small town, a little off the beaten path. A little country type town."

"That's it?"

"Well, sir, it's not your style. Someone of your

stature and importance wouldn't be caught dead in a place with no significance."

George knew he was laying it on thick but he was afraid for Mrs. Pennington. He was one of the few people who really knew the true Stewart Pennington III. And he hated the bastard. If he were making plans to go there to drag her back, he was more than happy to do what he could to prevent it.

"I'll be the judge of that, George," he snarled. "Get me a car and keep it quiet. I don't want it traced back to me."

George had no choice but to do what he said. It was in the back of his mind as he hung up the phone that he could call and warn her. Surely someone there would know her, it being such a small place and all.

Stewart replaced the receiver thinking he was going to fire that little toad one of these days. He fixed another drink. This time something a little more bracing than brandy. He tossed it back and hissed through his teeth as the burn slid down his throat.

One more, he decided, then he'd throw some clothes together for a short trip. He'd be there and back before anyone would know. And he'd bring that bitch of a wife back with him.

And then, he would give her everything she deserved.

That in itself was cause to celebrate. He found himself pouring another one. He liked the hard liquor when he was in a mood. And he was in a hell of a mood tonight. Too damn bad he couldn't get his hands on her now.

Oh, the ecstasy of having her flesh under his hands where he could manipulate her body to suit his needs.

He felt the first tightening of an erection. Something he hadn't felt for such a long time. Hadn't felt without … no, he wouldn't think of that. His inability to maintain an erection was her fault, too. It really wasn't his failure, he reasoned. Harleigh should have seen to it that he was serviced properly. She should have been more sexy, more intuned to his needs, more willing to respond to his wishes.

Just the thrill of having her again the many ways he wanted mushroomed until he had to have relief. He called George again, told him what he wanted and tossed back another one in anticipation.

Chapter Fourteen

א

Miz Justine had called the café for Kate, said she was feeling under the weather and could someone bring her a bowl of that wonderful chicken soup of hers. She didn't feel up to coming downtown today, she said. Her old bones were acting up and walking would be too much for her. Her old '74 Caddy didn't feel up to making the trip either.

Everybody knew that old car should've been assigned to the junkyard years ago. It was held together with bailing wire, as it was. But every time, a mechanical problem came up, she'd slap a little more wire around whatever it was or duct tape it back together when the wire didn't work. Duct tape was man's answer to any fix-it problem, she was fond of saying.

Harleigh had been chosen as the courier for the task of making the soup run. She'd been driving down this dirt road for what must be miles, she figured. The road was sparsely populated. Homes two or more miles apart.

Finally. She knew she'd come upon the right place. Several mailboxes sat in a row waiting to be filled. One of them told it all.

A large-brimmed hat made of sheet metal surrounded an opening where the mail went. Like Miz Justine, it was unique.

She turned down the driveway. Well, it wasn't really a driveway. Just a strip of grass in the middle and bare spots where the tires had worn the grass down.

Another mile brought her to a small red-bricked home surrounded by a wooden fence. On the top of each fence post were small wooden hats each painted a different color.

The lawn was strewn with several large painted rubber tires that had been turned inside out with massive amounts of flowers inside. Out front sat her pink Cadillac with a couple of pink-dotted fuzzy dice hanging from the mirror.

Harleigh opened the door, careful that she didn't spill any of the soup that was in her care. Before she even got through the gate, Miz Justine came swinging out the door. For a woman who was supposed to be sick, Harleigh was thinking, she sure was a spry old bird.

Her clothes were layered. A slate gray crocheted topper covered a dark green ankle-length dress. Over this, she wore a woolen shawl on her bent shoulders. Harleigh tried not to laugh as she glanced down at the lady's feet. Basketball shoes, the old canvas kind.

And on her head was the most atrocious straw hat, Harleigh thought she'd ever seen. Fruits of different varieties seemed to be growing out of her head.

She bit down on her lower lip as that laugh she'd tried to hold back, bubbled out. She smiled down at the elderly lady. "Heard you were feeling poorly. Brought you some soup, Miz Justine."

"You come right on in here, Miz Harleigh, and set

a spell." She opened the screen door wider so Harleigh could maneuver through with the crock-pot.

Harleigh made her way through the living room to the kitchen, taking note of the ceramic collections displayed in various places throughout the house. Statues of Indian maidens, warriors. Animal figurines of kittens, puppies, owls, wolves and numerous miniatures. In a tall glass enclosed case, were rows of tiny hats on pedestals. Beside each one was a miniature handbag with a little gold chain for a handle and a matching pair of shoes.

On a small corner desk were photographs. A young Miz Justine was wrapped around a handsome young man. Another was of a family of three, then four then five. Several were with those children grown with children of their own.

"Nice pictures. You were a fine looking lady," Harleigh commented as she passed them by.

"Had good looking kids, too. Lost my Jacob back in '98, though." Harleigh heard the loneliness. "We been together nigh on to seventy years when he passed. Been that way since I was just a girl of fifteen."

"Do they live close by?" Harleigh sat the crock-pot on the counter and plugged it in. "Your children, I mean."

"Up the road a piece. Big city roped 'em in, it did." She squinted at Harleigh through sharp eyes. "Tried for Caleb, too, but couldn't keep him. He came home."

"Where did Caleb go from here, Miz Justine?"

"Why, he took himself off to Atlanta. Went down to Gainesville to that university then went on up there and hung out a shingle. Was there, let's see, nigh on to three, no, two years it was."

"What brought him home?"

"Phoebe. She got herself all tied up with that lawyer man of hers. She chased until she ran him aground." Miz Justine chuckled, thinking of that incident. "Seems Mr. Gentry was resistin' her advances causin' Miz Kate's hair to turn gray. Miz Kate called Caleb back from the big city to straighten her out which was total hogwash, if you ask me. Ain't nobody gonna straighten that little gal out. Got a head as hard as a brick."

"She does seem like a determined young woman."

"Mr. Gentry never had a chance. Would've saved himself a lot a time and trouble if he'd a just given up early on." Miz Justine clicked her tongue. "Gave her a merry chase, he did."

Harleigh noted that she didn't seem under the weather at all. A lonely person in need of a little company. It was a slow day at the café and it wouldn't hurt to visit for a while. She elected to take the lady's suggestion. *Take a load off and sit a spell.*

The day was perfect. A slight breeze rustled the leaves around the back porch where they sat overlooking a small goldfish pond with elaborate statutes standing watch. A big yellow cat lay stretched out on the tiles along the edge of the pond lazily watching the gold fish swim in circles.

Off to the left was a flourishing vegetable garden with neat little rows of corn, beans, onions and potatoes. Several red hummingbird feeders hung from various trees while a monarch butterfly tasted of the nectar from the flower garden.

Harleigh listened while Miz Justine talked about her family and the goings-on around the community. Occasionally, she would make a sound, murmur or nod her head in reference to whatever topic they were discussing.

"So, the big city never pulled at you?" Harleigh asked when there was a lull in the conversation.

Miz Justine sat straighter, her eyes cloudy, remembering days when she was young. Then she chuckled. "No, can't say it did. Everything I always wanted was right here so why should I wander? My Jacob was here. We had a good life right on this little farm. Used to call it our little corner of paradise, he did."

Mentally, Harleigh counted the years, thinking maybe she could kill two birds with one stone. Indulge Miz Justine with her need for company and delve into her memory banks about the Nowhere.

"What's the mystery behind the Rose House, Miz Justine. You know anything about that?"

"Miz Kate's a fine woman. Never let that fellow from Tallahassee railroad her into marriage. Can't say I blame her. Once you find that one man that holds your heart, there's never another."

Harleigh thought of Caleb and silently agreed. "What about the earlier years? Do you remember any of the rumors that it was haunted?"

"Hmm," she grunted. "Wasn't haunted. Just occupied."

"Occupied?" What was that supposed to mean? Harleigh wondered. "With what?"

"Some folks say it was a haint. Me, I don't believe that kind of hogwash. As far back as I can recollect there was something almost sacred about that place. Used to play there when I was a kid."

"You did? Did you see anything?"

"Can't say I did. But, there was always something.

One of those feelings if you look over your shoulder there'll be somebody there. That place always felt safe, kind of a warmth that settled around you when you walked inside. Back then, most folks around these parts was scared of their own shadow. It's not like it is today.

"Oh, through the years growing up, there was always this and that been said. Of hearing things, seeing lights. Some folks said it was creatures from another planet landing to eat us."

Harleigh chuckled at her description. "What about in the beginning, when the Rose House was built?"

"Can't really say. A lot of stories have trickled down over the years. Small town scandal has it that Faire Sabra was smitten by a man that walked out of the forest one day. The town never approved of him, tried to hang him so the story goes. But the strangest thing happened that made them run. They had the rope around his neck and he looked skyward, his arms outstretched and closed his eyes. The next thing they knew he was gone. Disappeared right before their eyes. Scared the bejesus outta them. Thought he was the devil and they would all go to hell for what they'd tried to do.

"The Faire Sabra had a baby that the town folk wanted to take from her and raise proper. She was a tainted woman, shameful that she had lain with a man and got herself with child. Bunch of idiots if you ask me."

"Does seem so, doesn't it?"

"Yessirree. That baby grew up into a beautiful young woman, married a man who was as mysterious as her father. Lived in that house for a lot of years. They had three girls, I remember."

"You mean you knew them?" Finally, they were getting somewhere, Harleigh thought. Caleb had told her all this before. Now here was new information, another link in the chain welded together.

"Sure, I did. Wonderful girls they were, too. Course there was always a ruckus with those girls. They were several years older than me, guess I was about four or five then. They'd be in their teens, fourteen and up, I reckon. Rowdy bunch of girls, another thing the snooty women of Nowhere didn't like. Weren't raised as proper ladies. Had a mind of their own and wouldn't tolerate anything being said about their daddy. Worshipped him, they did.

"Well, one day, Esther Ridgeway, Althea Simons and Lydia Bishop started up about the girls' daddy. Saying he wasn't a real daddy, always coming and going and leaving them alone. All three girls rounded on those three girls and nearly yanked the hair from their heads. Saw it with my own eyes."

Miz Justine's laugh was deep, her eyes alight in pleasure from that incident.

"So what happened?" Harleigh prompted, hungry for every detail.

"Pounded them girls into the ground, such a catfight you never seen. Justice turned, angry eyes lighting on me then she slowly walked up to me, sucked on her front tooth, she was a kind of a tomboy, you know, and asked me if I was spying on them. I was frozen on the spot until Liberty told her to leave me alone, that I had nothing to do with this. Harmony came over, pulled on one of my pigtails and asked me how I was doing. She'd sat me a couple of times and I adored her.

"After that, they let me hang around them. Then

one by one they up and got married and eventually left. After a time, they quit coming back, sold the Rose House. They gave me things now and then, barrettes for my hair, trinkets they'd picked up here and there, books."

"That's wonderful. Sounds like they led an exciting life."

"Yeah, yeah." Miz Justine looked around her, saw the shade of the sycamore tree stretching to afternoon and realized she'd kept this young woman here for hours. "Oh my, Miz Harleigh, you let me go on and on about nonsense. Didn't mean to take up so much of your time. I sure appreciate you sittin' here with me like this. I know you're busy and got things to do. Gets kinda lonely out this way at times."

Harleigh picked up the old woman's hand and covered it with her own. She genuinely liked this woman and would have sat with her for any reason. "I don't mind at all, Miz Justine. It's been wonderful for me to sit and relax, to just take time out. I hope you invite me back again."

Miz Justine rose, a happy smile on her face and in her eyes. "Welcome anytime."

Harleigh followed her back through the house and out onto the front porch. Miz Justine seated herself in the porch swing hanging from the roof by chains. She picked up a fan lying beside her and gave it a couple of fast swishes in front of her wizened face.

Harleigh stepped off her porch onto the flower-edged path. A loud thunderous bang ripped through the air and she jumped. Miz Justine leaped up, stepped forward, and laid a hand on the railing to steady herself.

"Damn idiots."

Harleigh glanced back to where Miz Justine stood. "What was that?"

"Them damn Wilbur boys at it agin. Sheriff oughta put 'em in jail and throw away the key."

"But what was it?" she asked again, thinking if it was an explosion someone needed help. What if that someone were lying injured?

"I been tellin' them for nigh on to twenty years that one day they'd blow that contraption to smithereens."

Before Harleigh could voice her next unanswered question, she heard sirens heading her way. In a few minutes, Grady went whizzing by in his squad car as fast as the road conditions would allow.

"They must be hurt, Miz Justine. Wonder if I should run up there and see what I can do?"

She stepped through the gate, watching the dust boil up as he disappeared around the curve in the road. She waved goodbye to her sick friend as she reached out for the door handle. She recognized the truck that was coming at her in the distance.

Caleb braked, stopping directly in front of her. "What you doing out this way, Harleigh?"

"Miz Justine was feeling poorly so I ran some soup out to her." She winked at him, a faint impression of a smile curving her lips.

He glanced at the lone figure standing on the porch and gave a nod of understanding. Miz Justine was famous for her *spells*.

"Hop in. I'll show you a sight you'll probably never see again."

She climbed in beside Caleb. He beeped the horn and waved to Miz Justine, shoved down on the gear-

shift, popped the clutch and headed up the road where
Grady had gone.

She held on to the handle as Caleb navigated the
precariously narrow road. "Where are you going in
such a hurry?"

"You heard the explosion?" He glanced over at
Harleigh for a response.

"I heard something. I never did get an answer from
Miz Justine, though. She went on and on about the
Wilbur boys and some contraption she'd been telling
them for twenty years that it was going to blow up. And
something about how the Sheriff should lock them up
and throw away the key. Are they dangerous?"

"The Wilbur boys?"

"Yes, are they very dangerous? Are they a threat to
the community?"

Caleb laughed, his eyes crinkling from the movement. "Nah. They're more dangerous to themselves
than to others."

"So what did they do?"

"Blew up their still, I imagine." He grinned over at
her, watched her gather her brows down in concentration.

"A still?" The frown grew, drawing her forehead
into the action. "You mean like moonshine?"

"You got it!"

"I didn't think those things existed anymore."

"Makes the best corn whisky in these parts. It's
tradition, I guess. When we were teenagers, we'd hit up
the Wilbur boys for a pint. Me, Grady and Butch and
the Prophett boys would find us a little spot down by
the Suwannee and get skunked."

"You mean drunk?"

Caleb laughed as memories drew him back. "Drunk on our ass, babe."

"You sound as if that was a good thing."

He was silent for a moment, letting those memories walk across his mind. "Yes, it was," he finally said. "Had a lot of fun, we did, down by that river. There's a big old willow down there with a rope tied to it where we use to swing out over the water and drop in."

Harleigh had no such memories. She loved her adoptive parents but they were already in their late forties when they adopted her. They'd led a hard life before she came along. Not having a child of their own, they took her in and gave her all of themselves they could. She was grateful that they had, at least she had people who cared about her in her life.

She hadn't made friends easily. She'd been shy, her tongue froze when she'd meet strangers and just couldn't seem to say the right things. Still, she had a good life. Up until she married Stewart.

Thinking back, maybe she was just swept up in the romantic idea of marriage and happily ever after. She'd never figured out why Stewart had picked her out of the crowd that day. Maybe he knew she was an easy snow job and could bide his time to get her under his thumb. To do with as he wanted. She shuddered as her body racked with the remembrance of what he wanted and closed her eyes against it.

Caleb saw it, somehow knew her mind had wandered to a place and time she didn't want to go. "Harleigh? Something wrong?"

When she finally opened her eyes and looked at him, he still saw the traces of humiliation she tried to hide from him. The fury of his displeasure with her inability to confide even that dark part of her raced through him.

He knew what his mother would call it. Righteous anger, she'd say. And she'd be right but it was a hard thing for him to swallow. Couldn't Harleigh see how much he cared for her? That he would stand by her, no matter what had transpired in her past life?

He shook off that dangerous emotion on the verge of an explosion of its own. "Harleigh?"

"I'm fine, Caleb, really. Just sometimes, things hit me without warning."

"I could help, if you'd let me," he offered.

She laid a hand on his forearm and squeezed. "I don't need counseling. Time will take care of it. Isn't that the old adage?"

He didn't want to tell her that sometimes time doesn't heal all wounds. There were those wounds that were too horrendous to heal. They'd just fester over and when least expected they'd erupt, leaving an ugly scar behind.

He didn't want that to happen to her. He wanted her to come out of this clean. She'd already been scarred enough. Scars that went deep into the soul and would never outwardly show.

He thought a change of subject was the thing to do at the moment. "That's what they say. How was your visit with Miz Justine?"

That brightened her face, he noted. "She's a wonderful lady. Just lonely and I don't mind visiting at all. We talked, or rather, she talked about her husband and family. The people she's known. Told me a little about the Devreaux girls. She knew them personally, did you know that?"

"Yeah. Although the girls were about fifteen or so years older, they seemed to bond, made a great team, she told me."

"Then she should know all about the Devreaux family, their history, and their mother and grandmother, don't you think?"

"Yes, I'm sure she knows a lot. But she's never talked about them much, just that she knew them. Never divulges anything of their personal lives. The girls had children that come and visit Miz Justine on occasion."

Caleb maneuvered his truck up another back road then pulled into a stand of trees beside Grady's car. "We walk from here."

He jumped out, and met Harleigh on the other side of his truck. He pulled her close and kissed her. "Maybe that will keep me for awhile. Just so's you'll know, there's more where that came from, if you want it."

"Maybe."

He took her by the hand and helped her through the brush coming out into a shaded area. Two men sat on the ground, leaning back against a tree trunk while Grady lectured them on the dangers of firing up a still they way they had.

"I ought to drag your sorry asses into town and lock you up."

"Aw, come on now, Grady boy. Ain't no need for you to go on like that. I done tole Marsh what a idiot he is. He knows he put too many logs under that thing."

Harleigh looked around at the debris from the explosion. A cylindrical vat lay on its side, a hole in the bottom where it'd been blown out. Copper tubing lay at various angles. A large tub was upended, it contents spewed over the ground.

"Harold, are you hurt anywhere?"

"Nah, Doc."

"Marsh? How bout you?"

"Nah, me either. Weren't near it when it blowed."

"Okay, then. Grady, we're gonna head back to town. You boys be more careful."

Caleb took Harleigh's hand and started walking away.

"Is that your woman, Doc?"

He glanced over at her to gauge her reaction, saw a merry glint in her eyes and turned back to the Wilbur brothers. "Yes, Harold, this is my woman, Harleigh Bleu."

"Right perty little thing you got there for yerself, Doc," Marsh commented.

"If I were forty years younger, she wouldn't look at you twice," Harold teased. "She'd be on my arm."

Harleigh looked at the two men she gauged to be about sixty-five, their eyes creased with laugh lines, their faces wrinkled with life. She decided to tease back. "You can bet on that, Harold. I bet you were a mighty fine looking man in your younger days."

"Bull hockey, Miz Harleigh," Marsh put in. "Youdda been mine. I was better lookin'."

Caleb chuckled deep, grabbed his woman of her own admission, and left Grady to it.

ℵ

It was an unspoken agreement that Harleigh would

spend the evening with Caleb. She'd gone to her place to freshen up. Now she stood on her balcony, watching the sun sink into the horizon. She looked down at that little yellow house, the one the daises told her would be hers one day.

She saw the flash of light against the glass of the screen door and knew Caleb was wondering what was keeping her. But it wasn't Caleb she saw walking to the edge of the porch. It was Stewart.

She gripped the edge of the railing that kept her from falling, a scream of terror sliding high in her throat. "You bastard, you stay away him!"

The sneer on his face froze her blood. She knew that somewhere inside that house Caleb was lying injured, his life's blood draining from his body. She saw it as clearly as if she was standing in the room before him.

There was no stopping the images that danced before her eyes. The pool of blood at his head grew larger, darker, until Caleb was surrounded by it. His eyes were open, dull, lifeless as his body.

She wanted to scream again as Stewart stepped off the porch. But darkness took over and in a long slow boneless slide, she floated down into a soft velvet cushion of blessed oblivion.

א

Caleb's heart caught in his throat as he saw Harleigh standing on her balcony, a look of horror so disturbing it made his blood run cold. He called out to her but she didn't answer.

Then she screamed and knew she was locked in a nightmare of her own. He could swear that she was about to topple off the balcony and hit the ground before he could get to her. But by some miraculous force, she was pushed back and slid downward. He stepped off the porch and ran like wildfire was licking at his backside. When he got to her, she was out like a light. Her face far too pale to suit him.

Kate had seen him run through the kitchen and wondered what had his pants on fire. He didn't even acknowledge that she standing there mixing up a batch of his favorite cookies. Then, thinking about the expression she'd seen on his face, she decided she better follow after him and find out for herself just what was going on.

She got there just as Caleb lifted Harleigh in his arms. He carried her to her bed and laid her down on the coverlet. Kate hurried to her side, not liking the alabaster color of her skin.

He was in the bathroom, found a washcloth, ran it under cold water and rushed back to Harleigh's side before any time had elapsed. He wiped her face down with the cloth, then folded it and laid it against her forehead.

"Son, is she okay? What happened?"

"I don't know, Mom. I was standing on the porch looking up at her when she seemed to freeze. I thought for sure she was going to topple forward off the balcony but, I know this is going to sound a little off the wall but I swear, it was like something pushed her back and she floated. It was as if someone was there helping her down. She has no bruises that would indicate she hit her head or anything. See what I mean? Weird."

"It's not weird at all, son, stranger things have happened."

He lifted her hand to his lips and kissed her fingertips. "Harleigh, love, open your eyes and talk to me. Tell me what happened."

She heard him from miles away. As if she were standing inside a cavern and he was calling to her from the entrance. Finally able to open her eyes, she stared at him in disbelief, unable to comprehend that he was sitting next to her.

"But, you're dead! I saw it."

"I'm okay, honey, tell me what you saw and maybe we can figure out what happened to you."

She reached out her hands and placed them on his face, examining his features to make sure he was still there. "But I saw you."

"Where, Harleigh? Where did you see me?"

Harleigh moved her eyes to the left, saw Kate standing over Caleb's shoulder and wondered what she was doing there.

"You were lying on the kitchen floor in a pool of blood. Stewart must have been waiting for you. He hurt you but …" The terror was clawing its way up her throat and she was choking back sobs. "Stewart, where is he? Why aren't you bleeding? I saw you."

He pulled her close and ran his hands up and down her back in comfort. She felt so fragile in his arms, shaking hard, her breathing rapid, small sobs escaping. He needed to get her to relax.

"Mom, why don't you go get Harleigh a cup of your famous tea."

"Of course, why didn't I think of that. Be right back."

Little by little, Harleigh's tremors lessened. "There, love, it's all better now," he soothed. "I'm here with you and Mom's here. Everything's okay."

Harleigh hiccupped and pulled herself from his embrace, frowning. Then asked hopefully, "Stewart wasn't here, was he?"

Caleb reached out a fingertip and touched her nose. "No, love, he wasn't here. Is that what you saw?"

"Yes. The door of your house opened and he walked out onto the porch. In my mind, I saw you lying on the kitchen floor in your own blood. He looked up at me with all that evil inside of him and I screamed down at him but all he did was laugh. That maniacal laugh of his, that's all I could hear. The next thing I know is that you and your Mom are standing over me."

Kate bustled into the room, a tray laden with a pot of hot tea and cups. She poured a cup for Harleigh, stirred in a teaspoon of honey and handed it to Caleb.

"Is there anything I can do, son?"

"I don't think so, Mom. Thanks for the tea."

"What about tonight, son? You shouldn't leave her alone. She's been scared out of her wits."

"My thoughts exactly. I'll take her over to the house and keep her under observation for tonight. Okay, Harleigh."

Kate didn't wait for her to answer. She slipped out of the room, confident Harleigh was in good hands. Caleb was a doctor, after all.

א

Harleigh was still a little shaky as she walked with

Caleb over to his house. She tried to tell him that she was all right now but it was as if he had suddenly lost his hearing.

The phone was ringing off the hook when they stepped inside and rushed over to answer it. "Mom? I just left there."

"Yes, I know, saw you walking over. Have you two eaten?"

"No, ma'am. I'll rustle up something."

"I'll bring over what was left of dinner. You and Harleigh can nibble on that the rest of the evening."

Before he could say yes or no, she'd already hung up the phone and he was listening to static.

"Make yourself comfortable, Harleigh. Mom's bringing us some supper. Are you hungry?"

There was a knock on the door before she answered. Caleb turned to answer but Phoebe had the door open and was through it before he could move. She thrust the tray of food at Caleb.

"Here, take this into the kitchen. I'll see to Harleigh."

She hadn't even looked at him, her eyes were on her charge. Inside her stomach was jumping and her nerves were tingling. One look at Harleigh's wan face made her heart trip. She grabbed hold of her hand and held fast.

"You look like shit, Harleigh. What happened? Did that stupid brother of mind do something to you? Just tell me what it was and I'll put knots on his head."

Caleb had stepped back through the door but didn't approach the girls. Maybe this was what Harleigh needed, more than she needed him hovering.

And for the first time since she started her tumble,

he saw her face become lighter and a smile on her lips.

"No need to go beat up on your brother."

"Ah, come on, now. Let me at him. I can still take him."

Harleigh laughed. Phoebe always made her feel better. "No, leave making knots on his head to me, if it ever comes to that."

Caleb slipped back through the kitchen and out the back door, giving them some time alone. It looked like Harleigh needed a woman's touch. Sometimes a doctor just wasn't the answer.

"You want to tell me about it?" Phoebe needed to get it out of her, what she'd seen, what made her go sliding down the balustrade like water off a duck's back.

"It seems so silly now, Phoebe. What must you guys think of me?"

"It can't be that silly to have affected you the way it did. Mom said you saw Stewart. Was that what happened?"

Harleigh relayed everything she'd seen, felt, feared. The terror was still there but she was able to control it now. Able to shove it away now that she knew Caleb was all right.

Phoebe decided to be straight with her. "He's going to come for you, Harleigh. I don't want to scare you."

"I knew someday he would. I'll have to get everything together so I can slip out of town quietly."

"What the hell for?" Phoebe exploded.

"What do you mean, Phoebe? It's the only way." She didn't understand why her leaving should affect her friend so.

"The only way for what?"

"To keep everyone safe. To keep your brother safe."

"There's no need, Harleigh, believe me. There is safety in numbers. We'll watch your back. The sisterhood. Grady. And naturally, Caleb. You won't be able to pry my stubborn brother from your side. He's there to stay."

"But I don't want Stewart to hurt Caleb."

"He loves you, too, you know."

"Oh, I don't know about that. Your brother thinks he's my protector, nothing more."

"Hah!"

"Hah?"

"Yes. Hah!" Phoebe repeated. "You've stolen that boy's heart. He's nothing but putty in your hands. You're the reason he acts like a lovesick fool. Gotta say you did a great job of getting him wrapped."

"You're funny. He's not the pushover you make him out to be. I'd like to think he loves me, though. He told me he did. But I mean a real love, not like before. Not like with Stewart."

Phoebe reached for her hand again. "I believe you when you say Stewart is a monster. I saw an interview a few years back he did for a local Atlanta show and he didn't impress me at all. As a matter of fact, he made my skin crawl."

"I guess you recognized him for what he was before I ever had a clue."

Delilah knocked briefly, flung open the door and breezed right on through. "Harleigh, are you okay?"

Harleigh was beginning to feel like an invalid what with everyone hovering and fawning over her. First

Caleb and Kate, and now these two.

"I'm fine," she assured her. "There was no need for you to come all the way over here."

Delilah blew her off as if she hadn't said a word. "I had to pick up something from Ma Forrester. She was telling me you had a near fatal accident."

"Oh, for heavens sake, you guys. I just passed out. It wasn't a big thing."

Delilah drew her brows down and narrowed her eyes. "When one of the sisterhood is hurt, all of us are hurt. Right, Phoebe?"

"Right, Dee." She laughed, watching Harleigh's cheeks redden. "Where did that brother of mine get off to? You see him outside?"

With a shake of her head, Delilah walked on through to the kitchen and peeked out the window above the sink. "He's sitting out in the gazebo, girls."

"Well, first of all," Phoebe said, "since we're here together, we can clue Sophy and Sunny in on our conversation later, we should make plans."

Delilah nodded in agreement as she returned to the living room and sat across from the members of the sisterhood. "Did you tell her then?"

"Tell me what?" Harleigh wanted to know.

"Partly." Phoebe glanced over at Harleigh, glad to see her color was coming back. "We've been following Stewart's whereabouts. He should be in Atlanta about now."

Harleigh felt her chest tighten, that clawing again in her throat. With a force of will, she tamped it down. "You mean *the* Atlanta?"

"Yes. *The* Atlanta."

"Oh, dear God, that's only hours away." Her

breath hitched, fear dropped like stones in her belly, and terror clawed with talons that were razor-sharp across the surface of her skin. "He could already be on his way here."

She jumped up and stumbled, catching her toe on the leg of the coffee table. Delilah caught her before she fell face down in a small tub of philodendron.

"Whoa, girl. Steady, now."

"I've got to get out of here now," she said shakily, panic ripping through her so fast her vision was going, heart pounding so hard she thought it was going to explode. "Please, let me go."

"Go get Caleb," Phoebe instructed. "Maybe he can give her something to calm her down."

Delilah leaped over the coffee table in a dead run, headed for the kitchen and yelled. "Caleb, get your backside in here now!"

Before she barely turned to hurry back where the girls were, Caleb slammed through the door and passed her on the way.

"What is it?" he breathed, his chest heaving from the mad sprint to get inside.

"It's Harleigh," Phoebe told him, moving aside from where she sat so he could take her place. "I think she's having a panic attack. I thought you could do something."

Caleb folded his fingers around her wrist feeling for a pulse. It was racing like a runaway train. "I can give you something to calm you down, Harleigh. It'll make it better. Phoebe, get my bag."

"No, no." Harleigh grabbed his hand. "Please. I'm okay. Really. My brain just scattered for a moment."

Phoebe and Delilah stood behind Caleb as he finished a preliminary check of Harleigh's vitals. Looked on as he wrapped the cuff around her upper arm, pumped it up with air and read the dial.

Phoebe poked Delilah in the ribs, pointed to the door and they eased themselves quietly out of the room, leaving Caleb and Harleigh alone. They might as well, Phoebe thought, those two didn't even know they existed at the moment.

Caleb coaxed Harleigh into the bathroom where he drew her a hot bath. He improvised, using shampoo for a bubble bath. He slowly undressed her, taking care not to allow himself to become aroused by touching her, or wanting her.

He held her hand, steadying her as she stepped into the tub and slid down into the soapy bubbles. He picked up a sponge his mother had given him that he'd never used and dipped it into the water and squeezed gently, letting the warmth and frothy suds spill over her arms she had propped along the edge of the tub.

Inch by inch, he applied his nurturing care until he saw her visibly relax. In the distance, he heard the frantic barking of Wilbur's foxhounds as he gently lifted her out of the bath and set her upright. She held on to his shoulders as he toweled her dry.

Under his fingertips, he felt a pucker of skin on her shoulder, started to turn her to take a look but he saw how weary she was, and checked himself. His curiosity could wait. Other things were on his mind and examining her body for flaws was not one of them.

He tried his best not to notice the silky smoothness of her skin. The gentle swell of the slope of her breasts. The fragrant natural scent of her body.

How was he going to make it through the night

with Harleigh within breathing distance?

He picked her up in his arms and took her to his bed. He should put one of his tee shirts on her, he thought, but for now, she needed rest. With one hand, he tugged back the covers, laid her inside and tucked her in.

Harleigh hadn't uttered a word since they entered the house. Between her back-to-back panic attacks, Ma Forrester's special blend of tea and Caleb's tender care, her body was as pliable and malleable as a chunk of fresh out-of-the-can silly putty.

All she wanted to do was close her eyes and sleep the sleep of the dead. Within minutes of being wrapped in a loving cocoon, she drifted down into a peaceful slumber.

א

Caleb sat in a chair, watching the rise and fall of Harleigh's chest. Confident she was resting peacefully, he rose and slipped out of his bedroom. He picked up his cell phone and punched in Grady's number.

Waiting for him to answer, he paced. He pushed on the screen and strode out onto his front porch. He lifted his eyes to where Harleigh had nearly taken a headlong dive off her balcony and shuddered. Even though it was only a three-story fall, she would've been hurt. He closed his eyes against the image that waited in the shadows and shook it off.

"Hey, Doc. What's up?"

"Just checking on the progress of the whereabouts of Stewart Pennington."

"I got it covered, Caleb, don't worry."

Grady didn't like the hard edge in Caleb's voice. He'd only heard that reaction in moments where there was an upheaval in his life eating its way down to his gut.

They'd been together since they were boys and Grady could read him like a book. It was there in black and white. From the curt way he'd made his statement to the absence of a greeting. Something was up.

"You tell me not to worry? What the hell are you doing to protect her, Sheriff?"

"Back off, Caleb," Grady said, an edge now to his own voice. He allowed no one to put a smear on his occupation. "I know my job and I know how to do it."

Caleb slammed the phone down, harder than he intended. Even that show of forceful anger, didn't eliminate the prickly restlessness crawling his insides.

Before Grady had a chance to punch in the numbers to call Caleb back and chew his ass for being a prick, his DDT alert went off. He punched in the button, irritated still from his non-conversation with Caleb.

"Yeah."

"Sheriff, we got a strange phone call a moment ago," Phyllis, his dispatcher told him.

"Go ahead."

"He didn't say who it was. Asked if we knew Harleigh Pennington and if we did, could we get a message to her, that it was an emergency."

"What did you tell him?"

"Nothing. He didn't give me a chance. Said to tell her to hide, he was on his way. '04 White Lexus, rental, license number, AH123T. Said to tell her that and she'd know."

"That's it, Phil?"

"Yes. Then he hung up."

"Thanks. Listen, do me a favor and call Rowan Colby up in Valdosta and tell him to be on the lookout for that car. It's not an APB, mind you. This is personal. Give him the description and have him call me when the car passes through."

"Where should he be looking, Sheriff? There's too many roads for him to cover. Interstate seventy-five would be easy but there are a lot of back roads in and around the city down to the border."

Grady sighed. Maybe he didn't have this damn thing covered after all. "Just tell him to do the best he can for an old friend. Tell him it's urgent. I'll explain later."

Okay, Grady told himself, maybe Caleb had cause to worry. He'd position someone, if not himself on the outskirts of town. The picnic was coming up on Saturday and he didn't want anything to interfere with that celebration. Hopefully, they'd catch the bastard before then.

א

"What's the plan, girls?" Pauline Hayes asked the members of the committee. "The festival is just days away."

"Covered dishes for the picnic. An old-fashioned dinner on the grounds. The men will set-up the tables for us and we'll put the dishes on as they arrive."

"Sounds good. Thanks, Myra. How 'bout you, Kate? What've you got?"

"Delilah agreed to do the pageant and talent show. She wants to do a pageant for kids rather than adults. Have a prince and princess crowned for the festival and lead off the dance for the ball. She's organized the locals for a show for us after the pageant. The flyers are already up and out to the public."

"That's great, Kate. Who's next?"

"Me," Vera volunteered. "The booths for arts and crafts are ready. We have a total of thirty or so entries for that. The horseshoe tournament's all set-up, too. The men took care of that and some of the other tournaments, too, like archery and the like."

"And, I've got the cake and pie baking entries taken care of," Sally Ann told them. "The only thing that leaves is the night time activities. Pauline, that's you and Miz Justine, I think."

"We thought just an old-fashioned barn dance type of thing. Western wear. Cowboy hats, six-shooters, chaps, that sort of thing. Then for masks, simple black masks, Lone Ranger style. Hand them out at the door for twenty-five cents. No reason to hide faces around here, everybody knows everybody. Then, we could have Judah Prophett call the dance. He used to be pretty good at that."

"Kinda young, ain't he?" Miz Justine asked.

"Judah's pushing thirty, Miz Justine. He started calling square dances when he was fifteen. Just because he went off and had himself an adventure and has more money than God, don't mean he's changed. He ain't, has he Kate?"

"No ma'am. He hasn't changed a bit. Still the same mean-streaked Prophett boy he always was."

"Well, then, I'll call his momma and see what he's

about these days. See if he'll be our caller." Pauline looked down at the tablet she'd taken notes on. "That leaves the box social."

"I think," Sally Ann began, "that we can get a few of the wives to help us box up what's left of the picnic and make a box dinner. When it's time to eat, the dinners can be sold for a couple of dollars for the benefit."

"I figure the cake and pie entries can be sliced and sold separately, say for fifty-cents or so a slice. What d'ya think of that?"

"I think we got us an annual picnic and dance, ladies!"

א

"Damn it, Phoebe, I want you home!"

"Don't you curse at me, Gentry Beckett! I'll do as I damn well please." She knew this had been coming, knew it just as soon as she'd told her husband that she planned on staying in Nowhere until the issue of Harleigh had been resolved.

"No, you won't! Not this time!" Gentry knew he was wasting his breath, knew that his wife was immune to threats and browbeating. But he had to try. "This time we have too much at stake. This time we've come too far."

"Oh, Gentry, that was hitting below the belt." Tears welled up in Phoebe's eyes. "You're not playing fair."

He reached out and pulled her into his arms, pressing her tightly against him. "I wouldn't be able to stand it if you lost the baby."

Any other woman would have taken offense to that statement but she knew her husband too well. "I'll be safe."

He released his hold on her, looking down into her face, caressing it with his fingertips. "I love you more than life itself and it hurts me when I have to stand by and watch you suffer when it's not in my power to help you. I couldn't stand seeing you broken again, my love. I know how much this baby means to you, it means a lot to me, too. But you're my first priority, babe. I don't ever want to see you so bruised again."

She pulled herself back into his arms and held him. She ran her lips across the exposed skin on his throat and murmured. "I love you, too, Gentry Beckett. More, I think than you know. And, you help just by being."

He laughed into her hair, breathed in her scent. He loved this about her. The way she smelled, the way it drifted up his nostrils and seeped under his skin. She was everything he'd ever wanted and needed. And the thought of her sinking into a state of depression after the last miscarriage, ripped at his insides.

"Being what?"

"Being you." She drew back now to look directly into his eyes. "Just by being you. By being my husband, by loving me and letting me be me."

"I could love you no other way. Now, why don't you forget this silly thing with the sisterhood and the silly pact you've made."

"Silly!" A trace of annoyance took a bite out of her. "Gentry! That's the most bigoted statement you could've made. I thought you understood."

She pushed, trying to step back from his embrace, torn between two needs. Her need to help Harleigh and her need to make the man she loved happy.

He wouldn't allow her to step away, holding on tight. "Look at me, honey."

She refused. She didn't want to be mollified. She wanted him to realize the danger to Harleigh. "You'll never understand about Harleigh. He's going to hurt her, Gentry. You don't know the horror she's suffered at his hands."

"No. I can't say I do know, Phoebe, but you're my main concern. Not that damned sisterhood of yours."

She broke contact with him and turned away. "Gentry, how can you be so blind to this!"

"I'm not blind to it. I know that she's on the run from that pervert. But you're not responsible for her."

She rounded on him then, with teeth fanged and eyes flashing. She flattened her palm and tapped herself on her chest. "Well, mister, for your information, *I'm* making her my responsibility!"

Gentry could see she was beginning to boil so he stepped back, not wanting to upset her more than he already had. He'd let her chew on his ass another time.

He held up his hands and laughed. "Okay, okay! Uncle!"

Not easily pacified, she blew out her breath, knew she had to calm down. It was hard to stay mad at him, anyway, especially when he was standing there with that devil's grin on his lips. Lips she loved to kiss. Lips she loved having on her skin everywhere.

She smiled, blinked her eyelashes rapidly and said in her most southern belle voice. "I swear, sir, that sexy smile of yours shore makes mah heart fast."

"Come over here," he growled low. "Let's see what else I can do for you."

She went flying into his arms without further invitation.

Chapter Fifteen

ℵ

"**O**kay, hotshot, now which way?"

Caileigh glanced over at Aidan, eyebrows raised, sneer on her lips and an I-told-you-so look in her eyes. She wanted to rub it in. This man had to be the most infuriating man in the world. Why did she have to be the one saddled with him?

He stared back, not quite understanding what she was saying. He knew, though, by that haughty appearance on that exquisite face that she was making some kind of cutting remark against his character and why it should matter, he didn't understand. He wasn't here for her!

He touched his transor to bring in the frequency of her voice, of the English language. "You were saying?"

Her mouth quirked in derision. "I said turn up your Beltone, you moron."

"That is not the way your mouth was moving, lady."

"If that's the case," she clawed deeper, "then you should know this road is a dead end. You can't go right! You can't go left! So, Mis-ter Navigator, which way do you propose we should go? Hmm?"

Aidan sneered, his lips drawn back to show his

sparkling teeth. Lips that made Caileigh wonder how they would feel against hers. She couldn't dwell on that, she decided, he wasn't for her.

"Pay attention, female earthling, your mind is wandering. How do you Earth people ever get anything accomplished? Your species have the attention span of a rock."

"Just a little tidbit for you there, E.T., you're the one that needs help, here. I can take myself right on back home and leave you to it."

Aidan knew he better do some, what was it these genus of humanoid males said? Ah, yes, fast-talking. He'd better do some fast-talking and get this ... he searched his thesaurus for the words ... get this show on the road.

"The paper directory you have in the hole box should ..." Fritshin! He hated having to scan his phrase list, "should put us on the right track."

"Paper directory? What the hell is a hole box?"

Exasperated at always having to explain himself to this female, he tapped his transceiver rod against the glove compartment. "This contrivance."

Caileigh couldn't help it. The laughter bubbled up out of her throat before she had a chance to catch it. She knew Aidan hated being the brunt of her laughter but he was such an easy mark ... and it was so much fun.

She coughed and slammed her hand over her mouth to stop it but all that did was bring tears rolling down her face. Finally, she put up her hand, fanning her now red face, choking back more laughter.

He stared at her in a strange way. As if this was the first time he'd ever seen a tear. He hadn't.

He wanted to feel the sensation of the substance running down her cheek. He'd like to take a droplet and sample the taste and texture of this foreign matter on his tongue. He reached out his forefinger and trapped a bead on the tip. He studied the ball of moisture, lifting it and peered through its transparency, watched the light form a prism within it.

He raised his finger again and stole another droplet. This time he brought it to his tongue, closed his eyes, and let it sink into his taste buds.

Aidan wasn't sure what he was trying to achieve by these acts, he only knew that he was compelled by a greater force than his unbendable will.

Caileigh was shaken by the reverence of his touch, almost as if she were a mystical being and he were worshipping her. A slow roll of pleasure shimmied up her spine, catching her by surprise. Her breath seemed to catch somewhere between an inhale and exhale.

"I think we should get that paper directory out of the hole box, Cain," she said softly. "Push the button."

Aidan glanced from her mouth up to her eyes and back again. His desire for her was yanking at his insides as it always did, always able to down his defenses when he least expected it. The roaring of his blood thrashed against his eardrums, blocking out any other noise. He knew he was out of control when he tried to hold back from dragging her across the seat and lost the battle.

He was on her before he could take his next breath. Her mouth was hot and moist against his. And his blood raged that much faster through his veins.

He was panting and it made no sense to him that he was so far gone. That he was unable to pull back, to eliminate this engulfing desire that was racking his body. He was a master of this kind of emotion. It had never hindered the performance of his duty before. And now, his brain was so fuzzed with craving for this female that he had no other thoughts.

Caileigh thought she'd never felt something as soft, or as glorious, as the mouth that covered hers. It robbed her of all rational thinking, rendering her incapable of doing anything but respond like some love-starved nitwit.

She tried to stop the devastating swamping of her senses. But there was no way to put on the brake. So she rolled with the emotions that were destroying her, demolishing, ravaging.

She didn't know what stopped her from ripping off his clothes. It's what she wanted to do. Her hand was already on the top button on his shirt.

She'd like to think it was her sense of propriety. Good Lord, it was still broad daylight out, and they were out in the middle of God's country and she was ready to strip and be stripped of every stitch of clothing they wore. More than likely, it was the truck that rolled by blasting its horn, whooping and hollering at catching them in a hot, mind-bending lip-lock.

Startled, she shot back out of his embrace, smacking her head against the edge of the door. Thank goodness, the window was rolled down or the force of the impact would have smashed the glass.

They stared at each other long and hard as their breathing slowed.

Caileigh blinked and cleared her throat, found the ability to speak, shaky at best. "I think you should get that paper directory out of the hole box now, don't you?"

א

His breath was soft and warm against her neck. She didn't know when Caleb had crawled in bed but it was fine with her. With him beside her, she'd slept the whole night through, the nightmare that had thrown her into panic attacks dissipating with the night and his loving care.

She wasn't quite awake yet, just sliding on the edge of sleep before stirring to full awareness. He was warm against her where they lay like spoons in a silverware tray.

She felt his lashes flutter against her check and his lips slide down the column of her throat. She groaned softly, a sound of approval.

Caleb brought his lips down the silken slope of her shoulder, nibbled and wandered. The pucker of skin stopped further motion. He propped himself up on his elbow to get a better view. What he saw brought bile shooting upward through his throat and it was all he could do not to gag.

"God dammit, Harleigh! What did that prick do to you?"

The explosion of his anger burst upon him before he could stop it. The only thing he could see was the red haze of fury that blocked out everything else. Blocked out everything except her scarred delicate skin. Blocked out Harleigh's distress-filled face. Blocked out that she'd scrambled upward to a sitting position to press herself against the headboard.

She didn't know what to do to diffuse the situation. She could feel the anger boiling off him like steam out of a teapot. She wanted to tell him to calm down but was afraid it would make the situation worse.

"Are you going to tell me what happened?"

"I-I don't think I can."

"Or won't!" Caleb shot out in a pained voice. He couldn't stay still, could still feel the pucker of scars on her soft skin, could feel the revulsion boil up and over. The nausea crawled thorough him in a slow torturous curl. "Dammit it, why can't you trust me enough to share this with me. I love you. I want to be with you. I want us to have a life together."

She should have known it would end this way. Under the anger, she could see the hurt she caused by not being able to tell him about her past. Things she wanted to forget. He would never understand. But she could try.

"Please don't be angry with me," she started to plead, trying to slip through his anger. She resisted the urge to fling the sheet back, grab her clothes and make a mad dash to the bathroom where she could dress and run for cover. She was past that, she told herself. She would *not* run. Ever again.

Caleb tried to tamp down on his anger. He'd be the first to admit it was out of hand but trying to control it was like pulling a semi full of concrete up a hill with a yank rope.

"What happened to your shoulder, Harleigh? At least trust me enough to tell me that."

She labored against the conflict of emotions that seemed to fling themselves precariously like knives against her heart. She had no defense against him. She wanted to wrap her arms around him and hold him tight. But his anger held her back. She had nothing to tell him that he'd want to hear.

She drew a deep ragged breath. "You don't really want to know, Caleb."

"I wouldn't be asking if I didn't," he answered, a stubborn turn to his jaw.

She finally got up the nerve to get out of bed. She threw back the covers, not caring whether he saw her naked or not. She was damn tired of his attitude. If she didn't want to talk about it, she wouldn't talk about it!

Through a shimmer of tears, she reached for her clothes. She had to get away from him so she could think. She needed to think about what to do about this latest disaster in her life. She knew he deserved the truth but she didn't have it in her to tell him. Not all of the horror tales. Not what happened to her shoulder.

"You don't want to listen. Not to what I have to say anyway. What good would it do you to learn every filthy smutty detail?"

"What? You think I haven't heard those kind of things before? I'm a doctor for God's sake!" What the hell was wrong with her?

"A doctor you may be but you wouldn't be able to remain objective," she told him quietly, the cut of the knife going deeper. "Besides, I don't need a doctor."

"I thought loving you would make a difference. Evidently I was wrong!" It was all he could do to keep from taking her by the shoulders and shaking some sense into her. But he knew that was not the way to deal with a situation this serious.

"No, you weren't wrong, Caleb. Loving you is the best thing that ever happened to me and for that I'm grateful."

"Grateful!" That stopped him cold. "What kind of dim-witted comment is that?"

"Call it whatever you like." She knew it was hopeless to try to explain any further. That thought itself was breaking her heart.

His eyes turned cold, his features rigid. "Tell me one thing, then. I have a right to know."

"What would be the point to tell you anything? It wouldn't change what happened to me!"

Without thought, Caleb reached out and swept his dresser clean of the contents, bottles shattering, pocket change scattering. Across the hazy fury, he saw her jump, saw the color drain from her face, saw her hands fling up in front of her face.

He turned from her and hung his head, blew out his breath, hoping that with it his anger would go, too. Distancing himself from the situation for a moment, eased the strain to his heart. Maybe it would be best to let it alone for now, he told himself.

"No, it wouldn't change a damn thing," he admitted. "But what it would do, is relieve you of some of the burden of the suffering you've been through." He harnessed his anger, breathing deep, telling himself that taking his anger against Stewart out on Harleigh wasn't going to help matters. "Why won't you let me help you?"

"What help could you give me, Caleb?" she all but shouted. "It's in the past and I want it to stay there! I don't want it to enter into my life here. Into what we have together."

"We don't have a damn thing together, Harleigh, if you can't trust me to do right by you."

"It's not a matter of trust."

"Then what is it, dammit? What is it?"

"It's a matter or survival."

She said it so quietly, it took him by surprise. He'd never thought of it that way before. Still, it rubbed him raw to think that he wouldn't take care of her.

"That's a cop out, Harleigh. I'm here for you."

"It's not a matter of my survival." She turned from him and walked to the bedroom door. She needed to make space between them and pick up the pieces of her broken heart. "It's yours."

He stared after her, his mouth open but he clamped it shut again. There were no parting shots to make. She just didn't want him enough for it to make a difference.

Harleigh walked into her bedroom and flung herself down on her bed. She felt like there should be a flood of tears streaming down her face. But she was too numb for that.

Her mind kept running back to Caleb. How could she explain to the man she loved about the humiliation and degradation she'd been through?

He was right in one respect, though, she did need to talk about it. It'd become more than she could handle alone, now that there were others so involved in her life. Now that there was Caleb.

She knew that Phoebe had gone into Nowhere with Kate to run by Delilah's to help finalize the pageant plans. Delilah!

She rolled over, yanked the phone off the hook, and punched in her number. She chewed on her lower lip, waiting for a hello. When it finally came, she didn't know what to say.

"Hello? Is anyone there?"

The soft tone of Delilah's voice somehow gave her courage. "It's me, Delilah."

"Hey, Harleigh." She heard the tension in her voice. It gave her pause, she knew something was in the air.

"Listen, I, uh, I need a favor."

"Done." Delilah told her. "What is it?"

"I am a member of the sisterhood, right?"

Uh, oh, Delilah thought. Trouble. "Yes, you are that, a full-fledged member."

She blurted it out before she changed her mind. "I need to call an emergency meeting of the sisterhood."

That was not exactly what she thought Harleigh was going to say. Surprise mingled with curiosity then lengthened into concern.

"Sure, Harleigh. When?"

"How about now?"

"Now?"

"Yes, if you guys don't mind. It's really important. I—" She was talking into a dead phone.

א

Harleigh decided the best place to wait for the members of the sisterhood would be the veranda. She stepped out, closed the door quietly behind her and seated herself at one of the wicker tables to pass the time. She ran what she wanted to say through her mind. It sounded good in theory but she wondered if she could actually tell them anything without becoming tongue-tied.

She had no choice now. She had set the wheels in motion. A car pulled into the driveway and three existing members of the sisterhood poured themselves out the doors and pounded up the steps.

"Harleigh, what is it?" Phoebe kneeled in front of her, and held out her hands. Hesitantly, Harleigh placed her own inside and received a squeeze of courage.

"Guys, this seems so silly now. You probably'll think I'm an idiot when you find out what it is. It's so trivial and I want to say I'm sorry up front for inconveniencing you."

"Cut the crap," Sophy spoke up. "There's no such thing as being inconvenienced when you need us."

"It's Caleb, isn't it?" Phoebe asked.

Harleigh blinked back her astonishment. "He told you?"

"No, he hasn't. There's just this haunting lovelorn look about you that sings of a broken heart."

"Why don't we take this inside, girls?" Delilah suggested. "We won't be out here for all the world to see, especially if the subject of our discussion happens along."

She pulled on the door, holding it open while the sisterhood filed inside. Then she followed suit.

"Where's the best place for privacy, Phoebe," Sophy wanted to know. "If this is as serious as I think it is, we need to be behind closed doors.

All three glanced over at Harleigh's pale face.

"I think you're right. Why don't we just go on up to Harleigh's sitting room," Phoebe suggested." We'll lock the door behind us to assure us of all the confidentiality and quiet space we need."

Like chicks following a mother hen, they trooped up the stairs, in her door, into the sitting room and took a seat. Harleigh was left standing, her visitors comfortable and ready to listen.

Now that the time was here, she didn't know how to proceed. What could she say? They already had a few of the sordid fine points of her trip down insanity lane. She inhaled deeply, the words she'd planned on saying flowing like a waterfall over her brain. Except now, they seemed inappropriate.

"Why don't you start with Caleb, Harleigh?" Phoebe could see she was struggling within herself, making a great effort to get her thoughts together so they'd come out right.

She clasped her hands together in front of her and paced. "We had a fight."

Sophy breathed a sigh of relief. "It's normal for couples to fight. It's just the natural way of things."

"Harleigh, I think you need to tell us whatever it is that is so bad that you called us in for support. That is why we're here, isn't it?"

"Yes," she admitted. "I need your help, your advice. Each of you has such a great relationship with your husbands. I just kind of wondered how you handled their anger. How you found it within yourself to share the most intimate of details."

Phoebe could see where this was going. Harleigh was comparing Caleb with how Stewart was. How could you give advice on something like that?

"First of all, Caleb isn't like Stewart. He gets angry, sure, everybody does. It's just human nature to do it. But his anger is a different kind. He'd never hurt you. And, then you have to deal with what made him angry. What was it?"

She licked her lips, suddenly finding that this was harder than what she'd first thought. The telling of it should have been easy but this was like trying to color inside the lines when you were dizzy.

"Okay. He was angry with me because I wouldn't tell him all the bits and pieces of my life with Stewart. But, uh, there are things I can't tell him, things I don't want to remember or think about. Things that are best left alone and forgotten."

"I can certainly understand that," Sophy replied. "We're of the same mind there."

"Well, apparently, Caleb sees it differently."

"Wait a minute. What brought all of this on? Something had to trigger it." Delilah looked up at Harleigh for confirmation. "Right?"

Harleigh sighed raggedly. There was no other way. Before she allowed herself to change her mind, she began to unbutton her blouse.

"What are you doing, Harleigh?"

"Yeah, this isn't a strip show, you know."

"That's for sure," Sophy giggled, "None of that I'll show you mine if you'll show me yours and see who's bigger!"

The girls started laughing harder when Harleigh got to the last button. She hesitated but for a moment. The laughter died in their throats as tears welled up in Harleigh's eyes when it was time to do what she needed to do.

She sucked on her lower lip in despair. This was something she didn't want anyone to see. Caleb was the first and only person that had seen her disfigurement. But, the only way they'd get the picture was to show them.

She turned away from them and pulled her blouse down from her shoulders, exposing Stewart's handy work.

Phoebe's intake of breath was an audible sound in the unnatural stillness of the room, the strangled gasp at the mutilation of otherwise flawless skin. Sophy and Delilah sought each other's hands in horror. They couldn't get their minds around what they were seeing.

The initials were letter perfect. S.P. sitting on top of the Roman Numeral, III. The puckered scar told the story. The initials had been burned into her skin with a cigarette.

All three girls leaped to their feet, tears streaming down their cheeks and enveloped Harleigh within their embrace. They wept for her, for the trauma of their sister and for all women who'd ever been subjected to such brutalization.

No words were spoken. There was no need. Just a solid comfort to those in the circle of an embrace.

"Come on, girls," Phoebe said softly. "Let's get a cup of tea. Momma swears that it's the cure-all remedy for soothing a bruised soul."

In the kitchen, Phoebe ran water into the teakettle and set it on a back burner to heat. She pulled a tray from under the counter, placing it near the stove for easy access. All the while she methodically pulled tea bags, cups, sugar and creamer from their locations, her mind whirled, still in shock from what she'd seen on Harleigh's shoulder. How could anyone survive such brutality and come out of it like she had?

Damn Caleb, she cursed silently. What was wrong with that brother of hers? Couldn't he see what he was doing to Harleigh? She didn't need this, especially with that pervert breathing down her neck.

She smiled to herself as she ran her eyes around

the kitchen. The ceramic roosters perched on the windowsill. The cookie jar with a crowing bantam on the lid. Fridge magnets of just about everything. Not much had changed here and that reassured her to a certain degree. Sometimes it was best for things to remain the same.

Evidently Harleigh hadn't had much of that.

She sighed as the teakettle chirped that it was ready. She placed the bags into the brewing pot, poured the hot water over them and set the empty kettle on the warming pad.

She set everything in the center of the table, doled out cups and passed the pot around. She wasn't sure where to go from here. Evidently no one else did either.

"I know my brother well, Harleigh. As a doctor, he'd be concerned about health issues, mental and physical. As a man, though, he would be hell-bent on getting answers. I know he's in love with you and that makes him helpless. That in itself is probably tearing him apart. He's not the kind to stand by and let crimes go unpunished, especially against someone he deeply cares for."

"I'm not up to giving him answers, Phoebe. There are things I don't want to drag out after I've managed to lock them away."

"As a woman, believe me, I understand." She watched Harleigh over the rim of her cup as she took a sip of tea. "But Caleb has always rooted for the underdog."

"I don't consider myself an underdog."

Phoebe smiled, glad to see Harleigh was not defeated. "Of course not. Let's say he goes out of his way to help those less fortunate, those in need."

"I'm not needy, either."

She glanced at Sophy and Delilah who hadn't said a word since they sat down. They were closely following Phoebe's lead and the conversation.

"Maybe not now, sweetie," Phoebe said gently. "Caleb is a good man. He doesn't take these kind of things lightly. There's only one way I can explain him, I guess. He'd make a great white knight, don't you think?"

Harleigh shrugged, not sure where she was going with this. "I don't need a white knight. I'm not a damsel in distress."

"Maybe not to you. But in Caleb's eyes you are. What gets to him is that he failed you. You needed to be protected from that lunatic you were married to. It's a reality that is hard for him to deal with. Our father died when we were young and he took over being the man of the house. To him it was the biggest job in the world, protecting his momma and his baby sister from the rest of the world. That's a heavy load to carry when you're seven years old."

"Yes, it must be." Harleigh twirled her cup in anxious fingers. "But he didn't know me then. There's nothing he could've done."

"That's true but he doesn't think in those terms."

"I just need to find a way to correct this. Any ideas?"

Delilah looked across the table at Harleigh. "Well, the easiest out would be to just tell him what he wants to know."

"That's true," Sophy added, "but sometimes that's easier said than done."

"You're right but every now and then the toughest

things for you to do are always the best."

"I might agree with you, Phoebe," Delilah told her, "if you can give me a good example."

"I've a perfect example. Harleigh."

All three pair of eyes were riveted on Phoebe for an explanation.

Sophy raised one eyebrow. "Explain."

"Harleigh found a way to get herself out of an horrific situation. Now tell me that was an easy thing to do?"

"Point taken," Sophy replied.

"It was an extremely hard thing for me to do," Harleigh conceded. "But I really didn't have a choice. It was stay and die or run and try to stay ten steps ahead."

Phoebe covered her hand. "What you did took guts, girl. I'm glad you did it. I'm glad you're here with us."

"I'm glad, too."

They formed a circle, holding hands, feeling a sort of electric surge of power run through them at contact.

"It's a good thing, too, that we can meet like this. We need to decide what to do about Stewart. I know he's going to try to get to Harleigh once he knows where she is."

They saw her shudder at the mention of his name. To those who held her hands, they felt them tremble.

"I, uh, I know you're trying to understand about Stewart but he'll hurt you if you try to help me. He won't even hesitate to do it. Nothing will stand in his way to get what he wants and if that means hurting you in some way, he'll do it. Or, even kill you."

"There's too many of us, Harleigh. He has too many barriers to penetrate. He won't get to us and he won't get to you." Phoebe wasn't one hundred percent sure of this but they'd try their best.

"I don't know. He has no conscience."

"He's never come across people like us before. And by that I mean, we, the sisterhood, along with our guys and the good citizens of Nowhere."

"Let's get a solid game plan then and put it into action."

א

Grady found Caleb at the clinic. He'd made the evening rounds, saw his light and wondered what brought him down here at this time of day. He'd been looking for him anyway to tell him about one Stewart Pennington III.

Finding the door locked, he rapped on it in an insistent manner to get his attention. When Caleb opened the door, he had a sour look about his features. He might as well have said, *I don't want to be bothered.* It was written all over his face.

"Who got your dander up? You look like you just ate a bunch of sour candy."

"Go away, Sackett. I'm not in the mood for you tonight." He wasn't in the mood for a damn thing, he thought.

He couldn't make any sense of it. What was the problem, anyway? All Harleigh had to do was talk. Isn't that what women liked to do? What was wrong with just giving him a few answers? Didn't he deserve that?

He growled low in frustration, having no idea

where to go from here. All he knew was that he was pissed. And he had Harleigh to blame for that.

"What's crawled up your ass, Doc? Got yourself a problem there, do ya'?"

Caleb rounded on Grady, a glint of warning in his eyes. The snarl on his lips feral. "Is there something you want, Sheriff? I've got work to do."

"Uh, huh." Grady allowed a half smile to grace his lips, sauntering to plant himself in front of Caleb, toothpick busy.

Caleb's cell phone rang just as his hands curled into fists. His glare was hard and cold. Grady held his grin simply because he knew it was a great way to push his buttons.

He flipped open his cell, saw it was Phoebe and answered. "What dya' want, Phoebe?"

"Don't be snippy with me, Mister, I want to have a little chat with you and I want to have it now. Where are you?"

"I'm at the clinic, not that it's any of your business."

He might as well be talking to the wall. She was gone and probably already on her way.

What was wrong with these people? He just wanted to be alone. He needed to think. He wanted to get to the bottom of what was really bothering him.

He knew it was Harleigh. Knew that he cared more for her than he had ever cared about another woman. The bottom line was he was more than pissed because Harleigh wouldn't share her secrets. He was hurt. A lot more than he ever dreamed he could hurt.

"Doc, when you get over your snit, I need to talk to you about Harleigh and Stewart."

Before it was out of his mouth good, Caleb rushed Grady, knocking him back against the wall of the clinic.

"You bastard, don't ever, ever, link her name with that slime in the same sentence again."

He released his hold on Grady, wishing he had something stronger than water in his cabinet. He needed to knock back a few, maybe that would kick him over the obstruction pressing down on his heart.

"I'd run you in for that if it wasn't for the fact that I know what's eating at you. Got something else to bend your ear if you've got a mind to hear it."

"You don't have a damn thing that I want to hear about."

Grady was getting nowhere with Caleb and wouldn't in his stubborn frame of mind. He'd just have to spit it out.

"Stewart Pennington's coming after Harleigh, Caleb." Grady saw the blood literally drain from his face. "You better sit down, ole buddy, you're lookin' a little peaked there."

He shoved the hand off his arm and stepped away from Grady. That bastard was coming here. Coming after Harleigh. "I want all the details. When you expect him. What your plans are to protect her."

Grady hitched up the heavy weight around his waist. Never could understand why you had to wear all that gear anyway. "Don't step over the line, Caleb," he warned. "It's my job to serve and protect the citizens. That includes Harleigh."

His next words were cut off as his DDT buzzed loudly. He pulled it off his belt, pushed the button, staring hard at his friend.

"What is it?"

"Grady, Trace here. The Prophett brothers are at it again down at the Hometown. The moon's full, you know. Might better bring the Doc."

"Gimme a minute." He switched off, put his hands on his hips trying to figure out the next course of action.

Vaguely he heard a door slam. "Caleb, I want to talk to you!"

Phoebe stepped into the room, the currents so strong they nearly knocked her backward. She took one look at her brother and knew he was passed the point of reason. Still, she had to do something to diffuse the situation before it exploded.

Grady glanced over, tipped his hat down. "Phoebe."

"Grady."

Then it was as if she wasn't even there. They were so intent on each other and whatever had been said or done before she arrived. Whatever it was, it was still alive, seething and swirling in the room.

Anger boiled over and Caleb couldn't stop it. "Well?"

"I know my job, Caleb." For one of the few times in his life, he felt his own anger stir to life. That took him by surprise. It'd been awhile since he'd felt such deep-seated fury licking at his belly. Sophy had and still was, the only one that could bring it to life.

Caleb raised his hands and shoved Grady backward, dark rage on his face and a sneer on his lips. "Then, I think you better get your ass out and do your job, Sheriff."

"You touch me again, ole buddy, and I'll forget I

am the sheriff."

They were in each other's faces, waiting for the next move.

"Why don't you just do that?" Caleb said the words slow through clenched teeth. "Afraid I'll beat your ass like I used to when we were kids?"

By a sheer force of will, Grady kept his cool. He summoned his good-old boy grin. "Got it backward, don't ya'? I used to beat the shit out you."

If Caleb's pearl gray eyes turned any colder, they'd crack, Phoebe thought. She could only stand by and watch it unfold. "Guys?"

"Better get on back to that pretty boy of yours, sister."

"Stay out of this, Phoebe."

"Cute doesn't wear well on you, Sheriff. If you're not going to tell me what I want to know," Caleb said in a voice grounded low in dangerous warning, "then, get out of my way, I'll see to it myself."

He made to step around the sheriff but Grady grabbed him by the arms to hold him. All the anger that had been simmering unleashed itself in a red fury and Caleb clenched his fist, bringing it up to punch Grady on the chin. He dodged the flying fist coming at his face, snatched Caleb by the shirt, and slammed him up against the wall, his forearm across his neck.

Phoebe sprang into action, taking a firm hold on the arm shoved under her brother's chin. "Let him go, Grady. Let me talk to him."

He looked down into her face, then back at Caleb. "It's a good thing I'm your friend, Doc, or your ass would be in jail."

With that said, he released him, and walked out of

the clinic.

Caleb straightened his clothes and rubbed at his throat. That little action by Grady had taken him by surprise. He'd tried to pull back on the seeping rage that had taken hold and snatched all his good sense out of his head. Even now, it still simmered.

"What the hell do you want?" Phoebe was closest so he'd take his anger out on her.

"What the hell's got into you?" She'd fight his anger with anger of her own.

"Stewart's coming for Harleigh."

"I know that! What's your problem?"

"What? I'm the last to know something this damn important!"

"A lot you care, brother. If you did you wouldn't be acting like a dickhead!"

"Lay off, Phoebe, I don't need you chewing on my ass, too."

"Apparently you do," she persisted. She felt a flicker of anger with her brother. "Your attitude is not accomplishing a damn thing!"

He walked to the window, looking out into the parking lot, seeing nothing. He needed to calm down so he could think rationally. Phoebe was right about that. His attitude needed an adjustment.

Phoebe closed the distance between them. "Harleigh needs you now more than ever, Callie. She needs all of us."

"She's keeping things from me, Phebs. Important things."

"Important things for you, maybe. There are some things that need to stay dead and buried. I think this is one of them."

He didn't need to hear this. Caleb pushed away from her and walked back to his office. Taking a seat behind his desk, he shuffled papers. He looked up when she pulled a chair close.

"I need to know what happened," he ground out, the anger in his voice like wet sand.

"Why, Caleb? For your own sense of honor? For duty? Why? What's it going to accomplish?"

He gave up all pretense of working. "I don't know. There's so much she has buried inside her. Horrible, unthinkable things."

"And, that's where it should stay, brother. What good will it do to bring it alive again?"

"I was thinking that if we got it all out in the open, talked about it, we could start off with a clean slate."

"Brother, you are a dickhead! You've already got a clean slate. You're in love with her, aren't you?"

"Yes, I'm in love with her. So what?"

"So why do you want something from her past to enter into the relationship you have with her? She doesn't need to be reminded of her past, Callie. She's trying to forget it. She got away from it before it totally destroyed her. Keeping it fresh will not help the situation. She needs your total support here. Your help and protection."

He peered up at her as she rose and came to sit on the edge of his desk. "I will help her. I will protect her. I need to know what I'm up against."

"The devil, brother. You're up against the devil."

Caleb stared at Phoebe as the blood ran cold in his veins. She jumped as the phone rang.

"Doc."

Grady growled into the phone. "You coming over

here or what?"

"How bad is it?"

"Four of 'em in the fray this time. Mostly split lips and cracked skulls. Need you to stitch a couple up. That is, if you quit playing lawman and are back to being a doctor."

"You sonnaofa …."

Caleb was talking to an empty phone. Evidently, he'd stomped all over Grady's ego when he had his mad on. He clutched the handle of his bag, marched over to the medicine cabinet, opened the door and withdrew extra supplies. Placing them inside, he snapped it shut and turned to Phoebe.

"Keep your eyes and ears open, Phebs. I know you girls have formed this sisterhood thing, thinking you can go up against this guy but if he's the devil like you say then you girls are no match for him. You'd be in as much danger as Harleigh is."

She put her arms around him and hugged him tight. "You need to go to her and talk it out. She's hurting, too. The incident this morning ripped her up. She thinks it's over between you two."

He pressed his cheek against the top of her head. "It's never going to be over, little sister. There's too much between us. Almost as if it were destined, you know?"

"Yeah, I know. Been there, done that." She gave him one last hug. "Go before those boys bleed to death."

"Shit. Those Prophett's are too ornery to bleed to death."

"Don't forget to swing by to talk to Harleigh. It'll mean a lot to both of you, if you do. Besides, the festival is tomorrow."

א

Caleb took one look at the Prophett brothers and shook his head. Grady had them all handcuffed to bar stools.

The Prophett boys were a rowdy bunch. Had always been. They butted heads with each other more than any other family he'd ever seen. They never needed much prodding to fight. It came as naturally as breathing.

He took a moment and walked up and down the bar, stopping and appraising each one. "Getting' a little old for this, aren't you, boys?"

"He started it," growled Jonah, tipping his head at the brother on his right.

"You little snot-nosed shit head," exploded his brother. "If I could get loose, I'd put another knot on your head."

Grady stepped in. "Knock it off. Let the Doc take a look at you."

Caleb started with the most injured. Jubal Prophett was the youngest of the bunch and just as hot headed. Opening his bag, he took out supplies to clean the cuts and abrasions to see how bad they were. Swabbing of the cut over his brow that was bulging out like a third eye, he assessed the damage.

"Gonna need stitches there, Jubal. This is gonna hurt, so hold still and don't flinch."

Jonah, Judson and Jacob Prophett looked on as Caleb cleaned up the injury and sewed him up. Now that the heated discussion that had lead to trading blows was dissipating, their next worry walked in the door.

Judah Prophett, the oldest and meanest brother, advanced through the door and stood over them with a glare in his eyes.

"Acting like children again, are we? Don't you ever get tired of this kinda crap?"

All four boys bowed their heads, caught by big brother. They were as silent as a gentle snowfall at midnight in the dead of winter.

He eyed Caleb as he moved on to the next brother. "I'd let 'em bleed out, if I were you, then we wouldn't have to put up with this shit."

"Aw, come on, Jude, Brother Jacob was maligning your good name."

With a sardonic lift to his lips and a mean-assed glint in his eye, he placed his six-foot four frame before Jacob, his thumbs braced inside the Harley Davidson belt that surrounded his lean hips.

"Let him go, Sheriff." The smile on his face was deadly, his brows arched in demonic implication. "Got something to say, Jake?"

Jake knew better than to tempt fate. Knew that lean whipcord body of his brother's was a weapon in itself.

"You went away and left us, Jude. We needed you here to take care of things."

The guilt that Judah felt never showed on his face. "I'm not your keeper, Jake. You're a man grown, dammit."

"We took care of things the best we could," put in Jonah, his twin brother.

"Yeah, it was Ma who needed you," added Judson. "It was Ma."

"We was never enough." Jubal's hands fluttered helplessly. "You were too big for us to fill your shoes."

Judah closed his eyes in frustration. He never

wanted this. Never wanted this dissension with his brothers. He wished he'd never gone off. He'd had a head for figures, got a fast-paced job in real estate, became a flipper and made tons of money on other people's misery.

Then his father had died unexpectantly and his mother was nearly unconsolable. They'd been together since she was fourteen years old and she knew nothing else.

So he had given it all up and come home. And here was the last place he wanted to be.

In his momma's eyes, he was a heavenly light, her shining star. Oh, she loved them all, no doubt about that. But he'd come home rolling in money, set each of his brothers up in a business of their choosing and it rankled them that they were in his debt. And that made the difference to her. He was looking after his own.

He turned and stomped away.

"I'm gonna let you loose now. It's best you behave." Grady drew his brows down in thought. "I don't think the new owner of this establishment is gonna take kindly to you busting up the inside like this. All done, Doc?"

"All done. Now, how're you gonna explain this to your ma, boys?"

They glared at each other, then when realization dawned that there was no way they could hide what they did from their mother, they became little boys with "aw-shucks-shuffling-feet" again.

Caleb left them to it. He had things to do. Had repairs to make to a heart.

א

She didn't know what she was doing in his house. She just wanted to be inside it again. Take in his scent and remember. Running her fingertips across his shirt that was flung over the back of a chair brought an ache to her heart.

She'd had it all, she thought.

It had been the best of times. Period. The best that life had to offer.

Love. Happiness. Joy.

A joy that filled her very soul, brimming over and making her whole again.

And life.

The life that dreams are made of. She'd had it all in her grasp. Her second chance, so different this time around.

And yet ...

She'd lost it all in the blink of an eye.

She'd let it slip away like fine-grained sand swirling through the small opening in an hourglass because she was too much of a coward to allow herself to trust.

She knew deep in her heart and soul that given the option, she would jump at the chance to do it all over once again. For the sheer joy of just being.

The happiness she'd felt in the safe haven of his arms was heaven itself. She'd walk the same path a million times if need be, even knowing that in the end she'd lose her heart.

She started as she heard the squeak of hinges, held her breath as she watched the knob turn. She had nowhere to go, caught like a thief in his house.

Caleb halted his entrance into the room when he spied Harleigh standing there. His heart sank deep into his soul. He didn't like that trapped-animal look that crossed her features.

He dropped his hand from the knob, closing the door behind him with a light push. "What are you doing here, Harleigh?"

Right now, what she wanted to do was bring him close to her and touch him. The compulsion to do just that had her taking a step forward before she could stop her feet from moving. She longed to run her fingertips along his jaw line. Longed to kiss his closed eyelids, to feel the texture of all that dark hair, so thick and full it made her fingers tingle.

But she couldn't tell him that.

He raised an eyebrow when she didn't answer.

"I just wanted to see you, that's all."

There was still residual anger in those pearl gray eyes, she noticed. But at least his tone of voice wasn't so hard it would crack a block of ice.

She knew it would be futile to begin any kind of explanation of her past. If she couldn't explain it to herself, how could she explain it to anyone else?

"Is that all?"

"All?" What more could there be? She wondered. Wasn't being here enough?

"So you didn't enter my house without invitation for any other reason?" He heard the accusation in his voice and wanted to give himself a swift kick in the backside. Hadn't he been on the lookout for her anyway?

His condemnation hit and sliced, cut deeper. Bruised by his direct insult, she breathed deep, drew herself up and put on a brave front, hard as it was. It was going to take everything she had to get over this obstacle in her path.

"I wanted to clear the air a bit ... you know, try to explain some things to you."

This was what he wanted, wasn't it? What he'd carried on like a crazed lunatic about, and now that Harleigh was here, ready to bare all, suddenly he wasn't so sure he wanted to know about her past. About her life with Stewart Pennington III.

"Maybe we better sit down for this." He trembled inside and his knees had suddenly grown so weak, he doubted he could make it much further than the sofa.

Reluctantly, Harleigh took the chair opposite where he was sitting. As hesitant as she felt, she wanted to look him square in the eye and tell him what he wanted to know.

"I'm not sure where to start, what exactly it is you want to know about my past. I've already told you bits and pieces."

"The shoulder, Harleigh. Tell me about the back of your shoulder."

God, give me strength, she prayed. She closed her eyes against the avalanche of nausea that racked her body and licked her dry lips.

"Stewart was ..." Her voice cracked as she started to talk. She cleared her throat, felt tears burning the back of her eyes. Tears, that even now, clogged her breath but she gathered her strength and went on.

Caleb sat back and waited, chewing on a thumbnail while Harleigh composed herself and related the horrifying details of her abusive past. He saw her struggle, wanted to stop her, say to hell with it, that it didn't matter anymore. But his need to know overrode that objection.

It took all his strength to stay seated and listen to a story so horrific it made his blood run cold.

"Stewart was," she began again, "after we were married for a few months, he had trouble ... he couldn't ... he, uh ..."

Her face grew a bright red and it dawned on his thick skull what she was trying to say.

"He couldn't get it up? Is that it, Harleigh?"

Her body sagged in blessed relief that he understood. "Yes. He needed things to make him ... uh, in order for him to, uh ..."

"Get it up?"

"Yes. So he used visual aids to make that happen."

"And, by visual aids, you mean?" he prompted.

"Hard core porno flicks, adult toys, he was into leather, whips, collars with leashes, things, just things." Finally she tore her gaze away and dropped her head in shame. She couldn't bear to see the censure in his eyes.

"Sometimes he'd bring in a, uh, fluffer and make me watch. If I closed my eyes, he'd hit the bottom of my feet with a spatula. He'd have the fluffer perform oral sex only, not allowing them to touch him anywhere else. Said that was the way it had to be. That he had to remain clean for me, whatever that meant. Even though I was being ... abused, I was thankful that he never forced himself on me that way.

"He liked to act out whatever movie he watched. The kind of movies he chose bordered on deviant behavior rather than on your normal, if you can call that normal, porno flicks. If they used candle wax, he'd light candles and pour the wax over my body making sure it was dropped on the most sensitive parts. If they were master and animal, guess who wore the collar? If they were riding each other like horses, he'd use me as his ride."

She clamped down on her emotions. She'd gone this far. She could end this here and now. "That's why his initials are branded into my skin. I fell under his weight and he was so outraged that I was ruining one of his best-ever fantasies that he had to punish me for my weakness." A blur of tears entered her voice. "He thought it was rather clever of him." She paused, gave herself a moment to get back in control. "Said it was the best sex he'd ever had."

Hearing of the humiliation and degradation she'd been subjected to, made him forget he was a doctor. For the first time in his medical career, Caleb wanted to take a life, not save one. Wanting to kill Stewart Pennington for bruising her soul tugged on his sense of honor with sharp talons. His need for justice tore at his insides. His desire to make things right, strong. He steeled himself against the rage that was building as she continued.

"I started making plans then to get away. The night he beat me so badly that I nearly died, I knew it was run, or stay and let him kill me. My desire to live was greater so I went to an abused women's shelter. They took me in, got me straight. I was able to obtain a divorce but that didn't stop him. I had him put on peace bond and that was laughable. He still came around. He was Stewart Pennington III so who was going to stop him? He could do anything he wanted.

"He came over to my apartment one day, broke in and waited for me. He tied me to the bed and raped me.

Told me it was my fault, that I had no business divorcing him. That I was going to be his forever. He kept me there all day and part of the night. Each time he raped me, he'd pull up a chair at the end of the bed, sit there smoking a cigarette and tell me what an ugly ..." She stopped, groping for the right words. She couldn't bring herself to say the words Stewart had said.

"Let's just say he'd tell me my body parts were ugly, wretched and useless. Couldn't understand why he wasting his time with me. Finally, he tired of his little game. He untied one of my hands and started dressing. I was so filled with hate and fury that I didn't stop to think. I reached out, grabbed the lamp on the nightstand and hit him over the head with it. Blood gushed everywhere but I didn't care. I threw a few things in a bag and ran. I've been running ever since."

Caleb didn't know what to say. He'd wanted to hear it all, hadn't he? But hearing it all, had sickened him with loathing against the man who did this to the woman he loved.

"Do you love me, Harleigh?"

"Yes." It was out before she had a chance to think about it. "Yes, Caleb, I do love you."

"Was it so hard for you to tell me those things?"

"Yes," she said evenly. "It was hard. I didn't want you to know those things about me. I didn't want you to know the things I allowed him to do to me in order to survive. I didn't want you to know the depth of depravity into which I allowed him to drag me." She leaped to her feet and started to leave but turned back. "I didn't want you to know how corrupt I was. That you were dealing with tainted goods. Used goods."

There was a part of him that wanted to take her in

his arms, wrap her in the warm comfort of his love. Then that other part, that bad-tempered irrational side of him, wanted to shake her until her teeth rattled.

He did rise to his feet, though, ready to tell her something, anything before she walked out that door, out of his life. "I love you, too, Harleigh. You're more to me than a roll in the glade in the forest."

He tried to smile, to reassure her. But that bruised look was back in her eyes. Maybe he had made her go too far. So, this time when she turned away, he let her go.

"Are we still on for the picnic tomorrow? I mean, we've never had that date yet."

Pleasure streaked across her features and her eyes filled with hope.

"Yes, Caleb, we're still on for the picnic."

CHAPTER SIXTEEN

ℵ

Rowan Colby picked up the phone to put a call through to Grady Sackett. He knew his friend wasn't going to like what he had to say. But there was no help for it. It had happened, they had to go from there.

"Hey, good lookin'."

"Is that you, Rowan Colby? I oughta report you to the sheriff for sexual harassment," Phyllis told him with a soft laugh.

"You love it, beautiful. Where is the sheriff?"

"We're getting' ready for our annual festival. He's out there helping with the doin's."

"I'll get him on his cell, then."

Rowan hung up the phone and stared at it as if that would give him answers. Nowhere was only a couple of hours south. He could be there to help if they needed it. It was his day off and this wasn't official business.

He knew that Stewart Pennington was already there by now, skulking around, laying in wait. He reached for the phone again, punched in the number and waited.

ℵ

The Nowhere Annual Festival was in full swing. The turnout phenomenal. Everybody in Nowhere seemed to be there, having the time of their life.

Plates heaping with food were distributed. Folks sat at picnic tables munching down or seated on blankets under the trees. Around mouth-fulls of food, there was talking and laughter.

And Harleigh loved it. She'd never been able to attend functions like this where everything was so open. The Rose House in the distance seemed to reign over it all.

Ten contestants had entered the Prince and Princess contest. She looked on, smiling, her teeth clamped on her lower lip as the children went through their spiel. She laughed as a little girl stepped up to the microphone and sang Animal Crackers.

Caleb rested his arm around her shoulders and pulled her close. He bent to whisper in her ear that one day it may be their daughter up there. That remark had her heart tripping so fast it made her insides ache.

She laughed up at him only to have it catch in her throat. Fine lines etched the corner of his eyes as he smiled down at her. The scent that was essentially Caleb drifted to her nostrils and she breathed him in. Her pulse tap-danced as those long fingers of his walked up and down her arm to some unknown tune.

This isn't a dream, she reminded herself. This is real. She felt like pinching herself just to make sure.

In the background, she could hear the music of the talent contest going full blast. A rowdy country song merged into a soft ballad. The clink of horseshoes, the swish of arrows in the warm afternoon sunshine created an illusion that nothing could go wrong with this day.

Something crawled along the nape of her neck causing her to whip her head around. She glanced over at the tree line, gasped loud enough to turn heads as her knees wobbled and nearly gave way. Caleb held on to her as he turned to see what had caught her attention.

Her image was walking toward her, a determined set to her chin. She was trailed by the same male companion she'd seen in her visions.

Harleigh was frozen to the spot, barely able to breath. Nothing was between them now. The abyss had closed.

Caleb was in front of her in a flash. "What the hell?"

The sisterhood fronted by Caleb and Grady, backed up by the Prophett brothers, surrounded Harleigh. The good citizens of Nowhere hovered nearby.

The girl closed the distance with long, ground eating strides. She stopped in front of the crowd, surveyed them and grinned. "What's with the posse?"

Harleigh pushed herself between protecting bodies to encounter the young woman who had haunted her and helped her through the worst of times. Helped her by somehow taking her to a safe haven in her mind when reality came crashing down around her shoulders.

"I'm Harleigh Bleu. I think I know you. Somehow."

"I should say so. I'm Caileigh Bleu, your twin sister. Glad to see you kept our name."

She was in shock, Harleigh knew. Her body felt the brunt of it as the girl with her smile stepped forward to envelop her in her arms.

Home. That was the word that entered her head as

she returned the embrace. She'd come home. She was complete.

Grady stepped forward, tapping on Caileigh's arm. "I don't mean to interrupt this sisterly reunion of yours but we're kinda protective of our own here. You look like our Harleigh but where's your proof."

"Grady, it's okay. It's true."

He knew it was true, too, but with what Rowan had told him, all stops were out. He was taking no chances. "Okay, then who's that crazy you brought with you that's running around with that gadget in his hand like a hound dog on the scent of a coon?"

Caileigh glanced over her shoulder, groaned when she caught sight of Aidan Cain with his transceiver in hand, using it as a metal detector. How could she ever explain about him? They'd run screaming if she told them he was from the future come back to right a wrong. They'd probably call in the little men in white coats to haul her, and him, off to the looney bin.

"He's harmless, looking for Shera. Something about auras and karma. Besides, you wouldn't believe me if I told you."

He and Caleb exchanged knowing glances. Caleb turned to the Prophett brothers, whispered something to them and they smiled. All except Judah. His face was grim and shadowed. But he turned with his brothers and walked away.

They sat in a circle under an enormous live oak tree, the sisterhood and the newly acquired twin. They couldn't help but stare, their heads swiveling back and forth like a tennis ball across a net. They could find no flaws between the two. The girls were alike in every way. From the little dimple by the corner of their mouth to the color of their eyes. The only difference was the way they talked. Each had the expressions and dialect of the portion of the country they were raised in.

Not far from the circle stood Caleb in a long legged defensive stance, arms crossed over his chest. Once in a while, he would bounce forward on his toes. Grady, close by, leaned a shoulder against the tree, his right hand resting near the weapon on his hip. Butch took up space on the opposite side of the tree, thumbs slipped inside his belt, fingers hanging loose over the front of his jeans.

"How were you able to find Harleigh?" Phoebe asked. "It must have been a miracle."

"Or a helluva stroke of luck," Sunny added.

"I found out I was adopted, I guess I wasn't ten yet, and had a twin. My adoptive parents were wonderful people. They didn't have any information about my real parents, only that my name couldn't be changed. I began a frantic search, became an internet junkie. I finally came across this article about a family by the name of Bleu, tons of money, who had their three children, all girls, kidnapped. The kidnappers demanded a ransom, it was paid but the children were never seen again."

The image Harleigh had been shown in the clearing flitted across her mind. And her heart stepped up its beating. Was it possible she had a family after all? She turned her attention back to what Caileigh was saying.

"That was strange in itself, almost as if the kidnapper knew the family and that the day would come when all this would be exposed. Then suddenly there was an investigator knocking on my door. He'd been hired by the Bleu family several years ago, looking for leads on the girls. My mother," Caileigh reached out for Harleigh's hand and squeezed, "*our* mother, never gave up hope. She said her heart would know if her children were dead. Thank goodness, our father …"

Harleigh's heart leaped into her throat. "You mean, I have a mother and father? A real mother and father?" Her voice trailed off. "A … real …"

"Yes, my dear sister," Caileigh told her and hugged her tight. "They're very real."

Harleigh's right hand flew to her chest, her breathing strained with excitement. "My dear, God! Real parents." There was so much to take in, she felt the burn of tears behind her eyes.

"So that was it then?" Delilah wanted to know.

"No, we went through the whole DNA thing. They needed proof positive since the daughters are heirs to such a massive fortune. Our family has more money than God! Anyway, I didn't care about the money, still don't. But my mother and I started searching for my sisters." She held Harleigh's face between her hands. "Oh, Harleigh, I've been searching for you for such a long time. Sometimes I would see a light in the distance. I guess that started in my teens."

"Yes," Harleigh replied, "I saw a light, too."

"Then when I met that nutcase running around back there," she joked, motioning with her thumb over her shoulder, "he has this marvelous little gadget that finds things, finds people, zooms in on, heck I don't know. He's a wizard with that thing. He needed help to find what he was looking for and I needed help to find you. So we joined forces and here you are."

"What's he looking for?" Sophy asked. This was getting stranger by the minute, she thought.

"Somebody named Shera. Something to do with auras and mystical entities. He's about as eccentric as you can get."

The sisterhood glanced around at each other, a strange expression on their features. The question was there, eyebrows raised then they all turned to Harleigh for the answer.

She smiled knowingly over at Caileigh. For once she'd be able to help someone.

"This entity, does she look like an angel? And this aura you speak of, does it glow around her?"

"You're asking the wrong person there, sister," she chuckled. "Have you seen someone like that?"

She nodded enthusiastically. "Yes, I have. She showed me those images of us as children being kidnapped. I didn't know what it meant at the time but I think she was trying to show me how it happened, to show me I was part of that."

"This is great," stated Caileigh emphatically. "Maybe with the help of this glowing angel of yours, we can find our sister!"

א

Stewart watched the picnic crowd through the trees. He didn't like it here. There was a sense of doom in this place that made his skin prickle and crawl as if bugs crept along his flesh.

Still, it all would be worth it when he got his hands on that bitch. He saw her there in the distance. She was laughing up at a handsome man who bent and whispered something in her ear. Saw her allow that man put his hands on her. For that, he was going to have to devise a punishment worth the crime.

He felt a tingle of a beginning erection as his mind wandered through his stash of films. Oh, yes, she would definitely be punished. And tonight, it being a full moon, tonight would be the perfect night.

That man would have to pay as well. No man laid a hand on Stewart Pennington's property and got away with it.

To punish him would be tricky. But he would handle it. Nothing would stop him now.

א

The women scooped up the food left from the picnic dinner into small containers to fit into the boxes for the social. Dusk was falling and they hurried, anxious to involve themselves with the ball. Lanterns and lights had been lit, casting a mystical glow over the area near the forest where the platform had been placed for dancing. Smaller lanterns had been strung around the dance floor in strings like Christmas lights.

Attendees of the festival had disbursed to dress and were slowly returning wearing their costume of choice. Soon the music was playing and as promised Judah had agreed to call the dances when it came time. Couples, young and old, were on the dance floor as the band played a slow song.

Under protest, Caleb tugged Harleigh onto the floor. She kept pulling at him, saying something that he couldn't understand. Without warning, an iron hand clamped on his arm.

He looked up into eyes the color of frost and just as cold. He saw Aidan's mouth moving and some kind of strange language he didn't understand coming out of it. Then the man touched something in his ear and just as smooth as glass the words spurted out in English.

"I would advise you, mister, to take your hands off the female."

Caleb looked down at the steeled fingers wrapped around his arm and back up at the giant standing over him. There were few men that had that privilege but this one didn't impress nor intimidate him. As a matter of fact, it rubbed him the wrong way.

"If I were you, mister," he said in a cold voice of his own, "if I were you, I'd take *your* hand off me or you just might lose it."

Aidan growled deep in his throat as a warning but the Earth male paid no attention. Was he not showing that it was he that was the possessor of the female earthling?

It was a face-off as far as Caleb was concerned. He could take the man, he knew a few back alley tricks. The Prophett boys had nothing on him.

"Back off, buster," Caileigh told Aidan. "You're being a horses' ass."

Aidan tapped his transor, trying to make sense of the phrase Caileigh used. The frown brought his brows together like furry little creatures across his brow.

While Aidan was in a state of translation, Caleb became aware right away that he had grabbed the wrong twin. He released Caileigh like he'd been burned.

Caileigh laughed, a tinkling kind of sound reminiscent of the woman he loved. The redness crept up the back of his neck, extending forward to blush his cheeks. He was ever so thankful that the dance floor was dimly lit. No telling what ribbing he'd have to take from the rest of the gang.

Harleigh tapped him on the shoulder. "You looking for me, Doc?"

He turned quickly, saw a young woman with a kissable mouth, tapping her toe. Her arms were crossed over her chest, her head tilted at an impish angle.

Now that he was thinking, he should have known this was Harleigh. When he touched Caileigh, there had been no instant tingling of his fingertips, no zap of hot desire that rushed blindly through his body as if he'd just stuck his finger in a light socket.

"Yes." He wanted to tell her he'd been looking for her all his life. "Now that I've found you, would you give me the honor of this dance?"

Her answer surprised him, especially with everyone looking on. She slid her hands up his chest, over his shoulders and encircled his neck with her arms. She ran one hand up his nape, stood up on her toes and dragged his mouth down to hers.

She'd never done this type of thing in public before, wasn't even sure she should be doing it but with the encouragement of the crowd, she didn't care. She was doing what she wanted to do. She kissed him with everything she felt. It came straight from her heart.

She felt his strength pour into her, felt the heat of his body melt her bones. There was so much to take in, his taste, his scent, the wonderful sensation of his body leaning into hers. This was what she wanted, she thought as the soft sigh of pleasure escaped her lips. This was what she needed.

They were in a world all their own. She could hear the murmur of the crowd in the background, could hear the soft strains of violins, the faint rustle of leaves in the cool evening breeze. But all her other senses were so absorbed and so attuned to Caleb that nothing else existed.

She pulled back, saw the desire she felt staring back at her through his eyes and smiled. The world flickered back on and they began to sway to the music.

She'd never felt such happiness. It washed over her and into her heart, warming her from head to toe.

Caleb looked deep into her eyes, noticed there was a difference in the way she looked now than when he'd first met her. Gone was the tortured spirit, the bruising that was soul-deep. And, he hoped he'd had something to do with it.

The slow dance ended, Judah calling a square dance. Caleb and Harleigh stepped out of the ring of dancers aware of only each other. Hand in hand, they walked into the shadows, lingered, kissed and stepped into the gazebo.

He drew her down beside him, tugged her into his side, and looked up into the full moon, thought he'd never felt so content, so complete.

"Doc! Where are you?"

Caleb stood up at the first call, Harleigh's hand clasped tightly in his. "What is it?"

"Old Binder got tangled up in his own feet and fell. We just want to make sure he didn't break anything."

"Be right there."

Caleb turned back to Harleigh, wrapped her up in an embrace and kissed her hard on the mouth, a deep kiss that zipped down her thighs and right on down to curl her toes. He bounced his fingertip off her nose. "You stay right here. I'll be right back and we'll start where we left off."

When the darkness enveloped his shape, she leaned back, crossed her arms and let Caleb sink into her body. She sighed with contentment, settled in to wait for him to return.

Just as her head reached the back of the bench, a wave of nausea collided with an upsurge of bile bringing her into an upright position. She gagged, gasping for breath as the nausea poured over her in such strength she dropped her head to her knees, and prayed it would go away.

After several deep breaths, her stomach stopped rolling, leaving her to wonder what had happened. It had come on her so fast, it had taken her by surprise. She remembered these feelings would sometimes come over her when she'd realize the dark mood he was in.

Stewart. Was he here?

She knew he was coming. The girls had held a meeting on that, too. They'd gone over what weapons were at their disposal. Who was adept at using what. Each member of the sisterhood had been assigned their weapon of choice. They'd also chosen a site for each one to be hidden around the grounds, easily accessible if Stewart happened to show up and the boys were otherwise engaged, well, the sisterhood would step in and give him what he deserved.

But she, Harleigh, knew they'd never be able to get to them in time.

None of the weapons had been hidden in or near the gazebo. Harleigh had been so drenched with happiness that it never entered her mind that she would be isolated from the crowd. She rubbed her hands up and down her arms as an icy chill danced down her spine. She hoped whatever was wrong with Binder wasn't serious and Caleb would hurry back to her, erasing this ghastly dread that had seeped into her body that she couldn't seem to shake.

She decided to think on something pleasant and maybe that would take it away. She'd think of Caleb, their life together, sure now more than ever that there would be one. She'd have a good man to wake up to, to drink a steaming cup of coffee with while watching the morning sun kiss the horizon, and best of all, the best thing of all, she'd have her dream.

She would have that little yellow house with the white picket fence, with flowers growing ever which way. The daisy petals had told her so and she believed them.

Her future was so bright. Not only did she have Caleb and her dream, she had true sisters and parents. A family she had never known. And friends. And she needed to give thanks to the powers that be that brought her to this place. To this little piece of heaven in Nowhere.

She heard him whistling in the distance. He was coming back to her.

א

Stewart stood just behind the gazebo. What a stroke of luck that that silly old man had been kicking up his heels like a fool! He had to fight the urge to wrap his hands around the throat of that devious false-hearted whoring wife of his and squeeze until the last drop of air was pushed out of her lungs.

He warred with making that a phase of his plan but feared there were still too many people about. He'd go with his plan of dragging her deep into the woods and tying her to a tree, no, he decided, he'd seen a log in that little clearing. That would be perfect. He'd tie her there, he loved tying the bitch up, and while the moon rested its light on her body, he do all the things he'd dreamed of doing these past months.

Then he'd make her pay.

First, though, he had to take care of that sono-fabitch that dared put his hands on a Pennington pos-session. That sent such a renewed sense of power through him that his body tingled from the sensation.

Just as the force of his strength over Harleigh dipped and swayed, he felt something cold and repul-sive brush against the back of his neck. He reached up a hand to slap it away but found nothing. He should just get it done, he decided, and to hell with the man. He'd come for Harleigh. And was close to realizing his ob-jective. She was within a hair's breadth. He could al-most reach out and touch her.

Just as he decided he'd do just that, he heard whis-tling in the distance. It was just as well, he decided, he needed to bide his time. Getting itchy about it would ruin it all.

The taking of Harleigh had to be perfect.

CHAPTER SEVENTEEN

ℵ

She heard the thud, felt Caleb fall forward across her. Before she could catch him to keep him from falling, Stewart's hand was full of her hair. His hand was clamped tightly over her mouth that it was such an effort to breath, dark edges appeared in her vision.

He yanked her hard against him, her back fitting into his body and she gagged, the bile rising swift and hard.

"Hello, my sweet and lovely wife. It's been a long time. Did you miss my loving?"

He inched her backward out of the gazebo, keeping to the shadows. The sounds she made strangled helplessly in her throat. It only seemed to urge him on.

She tried to gain a sense of balance. Knew if she could catch a toehold, she may be able to come out of this alive. Just the thought of what he would do flipped the bile back up her throat. When he groped her breast, she prayed that she'd pass out. She couldn't let this happen again.

"Make one sound, Harleigh baby, just one sound and I'll go back and finish your lover off. It would feel so good to feel the knife slice into his throat. I'll even let you watch. And if you're a good girl, I just might let you live."

She fought back the tears, the memory sliding into her that he liked her tears when they were alone. She bit the inside of her mouth, clamped down hard when he slammed her front up against a tree and ground himself into her backside.

"Oh, baby," he growled through his teeth. "God, how I've missed you. Missed this."

For a moment she was transported back into the past and she started that long slow slide into that secret place because this reality was just too much. She saw the light, yet it was different, closer, warmer, comforting. Then it exploded and was gone.

"Not here," he babbled, nearly out of control, "not here."

Cruelly, he snatched her head back, twisted his fingers through the hair on the top of her head and bent it forward, exposing the softness of her shoulders. "So white, so soft, like silk."

He sank his teeth deep into her flesh. The shriek of pain gurgled in her throat as she tried to swallow it back. "Ah, that's more like it, baby."

He didn't know what was happening to him. Stewart felt like he was going to come apart if he didn't get her clothes off where he could get at her. It had never been like this. This all-consuming fire that was burning his brain. He'd always had to have help to sustain an erection but this, this was what he'd been searching for. And he couldn't wait another minute.

He pushed her forward, she fell to her knees, didn't have the strength or the willpower to get to her feet. She knew if she tried to run, he'd fulfill his promise to go back and hurt Caleb. She couldn't let that happen.

She'd do whatever she had to do to protect him. Even if it meant, obeying Stewart's every command.

But could she do it? Would she be able to have his slimy hands on her after the love she'd found with Caleb? What would he want her to do? No, she determined, Caleb wouldn't want her to be his victim again. And that thought gave her the strength she needed.

From somewhere in the back of her mind sprang images, the sisterhood, the citizens of Nowhere, the Rose House, the angel, Caleb. How the town and these people enveloped her. How the angel had shown her, her family.

She knew she had to do something to distract him, keep his mind focused on her. There's no way anyone would know where she was. So she had to devise a plan to get herself out of this by herself. Too many people were counting on it. She prayed that Caleb was okay but he'd probably be out for a while as hard as Stewart had struck him so she had time to lure him away.

He reached out his foot and kicked, sending her forward on her cheek. The forest floor abraded her skin as she slid along its path.

"Get up, baby, and let's get this thing going. I always thought you were a frigid piece of meat." He was breathing so heavily he was panting. "But you've got me so hot tonight I'm about to pop."

He snatched her up off the ground as if she weighed nothing. Just as she was airborne, her hand slipped over a smooth rock that fit into her palm as if it had been molded to it. She folded her fingers around it and held it like a lifeline. She slid it into the pocket of her denim skirt.

Stewart tried to gain control but he was beyond

caring about those people back at the grounds. They were such hicks anyway. Couldn't have a brain as big as a pea to actually think that living here in this back-woods was some kind of a life.

He felt the cold on his neck again. The kiss of death, he thought and shivered. The cold seemed to wrap itself around him and squeezed. His vision went black from the outside in and he pitched forward in an unflattering heap.

Harleigh heard Stewart stumble, took a quick look over her shoulder in time to see him fall.

He grunted, glanced up at Harleigh through glazed eyes, snarled and leaped unsteadily to his feet. "Don't even think about running, Harleigh."

Without thinking, she flung back her arm and let the rock fly, hitting him directly between the eyes. He went down without a sound.

א

The dance was in full swing as the full moon rose higher in the sky. Judah, for once, was on a roll. He wasn't quite so uptight tonight, still unsure why. He watched with a rare smile as the couples twirled, stomped and laughed, enjoying the moon-illuminated night. Then the slow rotation of his insides felt like he'd been slammed in the gut with a concrete block.

The new owner of the Hometown juke joint his brothers had torn apart stepped up on the stage with Rowan Colby. Something twisted and curled, hot and heavy inside him as he inhaled. He stepped away from the post he'd been leaning against to see if that would ease the clawing of desire that had seized him. He did his best to ignore her ... and it, but his gaze was locked on every move she made. Try as he might, he couldn't look away. Then by sheer force of will, he turned and stepped into the shadows. He didn't want or need that kind of misery.

Caileigh watched from the sidelines, trying without progress to explain to Aidan the concept of dancing. Suddenly, without warning, she was slammed back against a tree, the blinding pain in her head shooting down her spine.

The light sprinted bright and white through her brain. She gasped for breath. Aidan clutched her arm to steady her when he saw her sway. He slapped at his ear, hitting his transor. The loud crashes of the music squealed the frequency. He toned it down to its lowest level.

"Caileigh. What is it? What's happening."

"I don't know. The light. The pain." She inhaled deeply. "Where's Harleigh?"

"She and the doctor paired off toward that structure that sits behind the yellow cube."

"Dammit, Aidan, just for once could you speak English!"

He closed his eyes, pressed a button on his transceiver and let the glossary run. "Gazebo behind the yellow house."

He opened his eyes, ready for his reward in the way of a great compliment. All he saw was her retreating back.

She ran like the wind, crashing into Grady. "Harleigh's in danger," she screamed, pushing him away from her.

Aidan came to his side, pointing as Caileigh ran. "The gazebo structure."

Grady placed two fingers in the corner of his mouth and gave a shrill high-pitched whistle. The music died away and the Prophetts, Rowan Colby and Butch Cassidy immediately surrounded him.

"Fan out, boys. Caileigh says Harleigh's missing. Let's head toward the back of the house."

They formed a line, heading in the direction that Caileigh ran. Phoebe caught sight of the men spread out, walking forward with purpose and her blood chilled in her veins. She went on a search of her own, found the sisterhood and followed.

א

Her side was splitting. Her breath ragged in her throat. But she kept running. She could hear the rustling of the forest floor and knew he was closing the distance. She was in the clearing now where she'd first picked the flowers. She'd never been farther than this but hoped on the other side of that meadow the forest would be denser and would hide her safely.

The light of the moon lead the way. But the closer she came to the line of trees, the more alarmed she became. She could hear the crunch of twigs under his feet, the swish of the shrubbery against his clothing. He was faster and ran more rapidly than she would have thought after she knocked him out.

Just as she neared her destination, he snatched her by the hair and dragged her to the ground. They were both panting. He flipped her over onto her stomach and sat in the small of her back, increasing her need to force air into her lungs.

"I think we need to have a little talk, Harleigh baby." He wiped the spittle off his chin. "You're making this difficult for me. And you know how I hate that sort of thing."

She drew in a breath or tried to. The little trickle of air she managed to get inside her left her struggling for more. Her strength was nearly gone. Her escape had drained her. But somehow she had to find more. He was not going to beat her down again, she vowed.

She tried bucking him off but he rapped her on the back of the head. She vaguely wondered what it was until she felt the cold steel of the gun barrel against her cheek.

He leaned close to her ear, whispering, "This is going to be so much fun, my lovely one. This," he tapped the gun against her cheek, "this may be my pastime device tonight."

Harleigh shuddered as he raised, placed a knee in the middle of her back and ran the barrel of the gun over her shoulder, down her spine and across the curve of her bottom.

"Please, Stewart. Please don't do this."

The laugh that rented the air was maniacal. She wasn't sure he even heard her plea.

He leaned forward, ran his tongue along her ear lobe and up her cheek. "Mmm, good. This is going to be the best ever."

He yanked up her skirt, the barrel cold against the skin on the back of her knee. He traced the contour of her thigh upward until he encountered pale violet lace.

Disgusted, he rose to his feet, lashed out with the

toe of his shoe and connected with her ribs. She
groaned in pain, curling her body into a ball, the sting
of the attack bringing tears to her eyes.

"You almost ruined it for me, you bitch. You know
I don't like you wearing underwear around me. Get up
off your ass. I've got a place all picked out for you to
be taught why you should never run from me."

א

Grady found Caleb trying to sit up on the floor of the
gazebo. He was groggy, his head splitting with a blinding pain. They helped him to his feet, nudged him down
on the bench until he could catch his breath. The girls
crowded around the front entrance.

"What happened, Callie?" Phoebe didn't want to
know. Deep in her heart, she knew.

He shot upward, realizing Stewart had Harleigh.
The pain momentarily blinded him but he waved it off.

Without a word, he turned, stumbled and grabbed
onto a post for support until the dizziness and nausea
passed. His brain diagnosed his condition as a slight
concussion. But he waved that off, too. He didn't have
time for injuries.

He stepped off the back of the gazebo, hoping he
could get to Harleigh before Stewart could hurt her.
They followed. The boys, the sisterhood. Caileigh, with
Aidan, punching buttons.

"Here," he said suddenly, pointing off to the right
of the direction Caleb was heading. "He took her this
way."

The bent grasses showed recent passage. Encouraged, they followed the man with the gadget, putting their trust in him that he could find Harleigh.

Caileigh trembled with fear for her twin. She'd never encountered someone so evil. Couldn't comprehend that a human being would go to these lengths to hurt another and prayed they would find her sister before it was too late.

Aidan glanced back at her as if he read her mind, saw the anxiety in her eyes and her face. His own turned to ice and he stepped forward with more determination.

He was a stranger in an even stranger land. This place called Earth. He didn't understand the way of these earthlings and their penchant for destruction. If destroying the world they lived in wasn't enough, they tried to destroy each other.

But one thing he did understand, and that was the pain in the woman companion he wanted to make his. His soul could not bear it.

He'd find this one she searched for. This one she called twin that made her eyes light up like the stars at night. He would find her and he would wreak destruction of his own on the man who dared take her away.

א

Harleigh didn't know where Stewart was taking her. They didn't step back into the meadow and cross to where they had been. Instead, they circled around it, keeping to just outside the tree line. Through blurred vision, she thought she saw movement near the center. But she was prodded forward with the gun in her back.

"You make a sound and I'll send a spray of bullets in that direction. It'll hit someone, maybe even that lover of yours we left behind. I should have cracked his skull, made sure he was dead. I bet you wouldn't have hesitated then, would you?"

She kept silent, staring ahead. She'd do everything she could to lead him away from the people she cared about.

He had to change his plans, Stewart realized, that little clearing he'd had in mind to punish his wayward wife was no longer an option. He'd take her back to that house, it was deserted now due to the carryings on at that infernal shindig of theirs and would serve his purpose. He needed to take her now before he lost his edge.

He kept pushing at her until she wanted to scream. The bright light of the moon shone down on the Rose House as they stepped through the trees. The celebration was still going strong, a ways down the stretch of lawn from the direction they were headed.

She wanted to scream to get their attention but knew they couldn't hear. The music was a din in the night. Nothing could be heard over that.

He took her around the front of the house, eased open the front door and shoved her in. Closing the door behind him, he shifted his eyes left and right to get the lay of the room. He advanced farther, took Harleigh by the wrist and hauled her after him. She went along, her mind working furiously for an out.

"Where's your room, you nasty little bitch. You've made me wait long enough. What a payback to take you in your own room!" He dragged her up into his face, their noses nearly touching, snarling, spittle flying. "And for that, dear girl, you are going to pay and pay!"

She directed him to her room where he thrust her inside. She went sprawling, her knees burning as she skidded on the carpet. She blinked as her eyes focused. Behind Stewart, a soft glow had formed.

She nearly cried out in relief. She was safe. Now all she had to do was stay calm and let her guardian angel handle things. The glow moved forward, circling to position herself between Harleigh and Stewart.

Startled by the sudden appearance of the ethereal being, he backed up. "What the hell is this? What kind of trick are you trying to pull? I'm not going for that, you bitch?"

He raised the gun, pointed it at the glowing form. "I'll fire straight through this ... this thing and straight into you so don't try anything."

Harleigh raised herself off the floor into a sitting position, scooting backward until she hit the bed, eyes wide at the crazed expression on his face.

The entity circled more, nudging him toward her private patio. He kept waving the gun but inch-by-inch she prodded him to the doorway.

As Stewart stepped out into the night, he realized he'd been maneuvered successfully away from Harleigh. Whoever this was in this costume had done a brilliant job of it, he concluded. He had to applaud him for that.

Now he had nowhere to go but over the railing. He looked down, gauged the distanced and threw a leg over the top. He levered himself over the side until he could easily drop to the ground below.

His only alternative was to return to the forest. But

that route was cut off. That idiot of a law enforcement officer had sniffed him out. Stewart hid behind a tree and waited, watching as several people emerged behind the sheriff. That little affair upstairs with that costumed freak had rattled him a little, he presumed, as he was seeing Harleigh take a step forward out of the tree line, followed by a big, well-muscled man.

He'd never seen this man before. The fury that ran through him was a rage so hot it choked him. How many men had she spread her legs for? Was there no end to the humiliation she bestowed on him?

Well, he seethed in the dark, we'll see about that!

Stewart was on Aidan before he could react. He whacked him at the base of his skull and he went down easily. He seized Caileigh's wrist in steeled fingers and shoved the gun into her mouth.

"One word, Harleigh, and I'll blow you away. You and your friends have done enough to me for one night. Now, be a good girl before I lose my temper and get your ass back into those trees. Don't stop until I tell you to."

Caileigh did as she was told after looking into those eyes that teetered on the edge of insanity. She didn't dare tell him she wasn't Harleigh. She'd keep quiet, do what he said, and give the team enough time to find her sister and then come after her. She was no pushover, after all she was a Bleu.

א

Harleigh was rising from the floor when Caleb reached her. He pulled her into his arms, holding on to her so tight she couldn't breathe. The girls surrounded them, waiting for their turn, their hands touching her back and shoulders. The rest of the troop stood at the doorway.

Harleigh wiggled, managing to loosen Caleb's hold on her somewhat. When he realized he was crushing her against him, he pushed her back so he could check her over.

"Are you hurt? Did that bastard hurt you, Harleigh?" Caleb didn't want to think about what loathsome thing he'd done.

"Just my pride, darling. Maybe a few bruises here and there but for the most part, I'm okay."

Relief surged through him like a tidal wave. "I'll run you down to the clinic and check you out."

Grady stepped forward. "Wait. Where is he, Harleigh?"

She stepped away from everyone, moved over to the doorway, sliding her palm down the frame. "She steered him out here. I think he must have jumped. I lost sight of him when she blinked out." She spun around, realizing Caileigh wasn't among the crowd in her room. "Where's my sister?"

When Grady realized Caileigh was missing now, he knew that somehow Stewart had gotten his hands on her, mistaking her for Harleigh. He made a mad dash for the door, bodies parting to let him through.

"You girls stay here," Caleb ordered.

The boys were barely out the door when the unspoken consensus of the sisterhood followed. They rounded the house, watched them help Aidan to his feet. When they moved into the forest, so did they.

They saw the light ahead, a soft glow that had stopped everyone in their tracks. Aidan had stepped forward, talking in that strange language of his. Stewart had Caileigh down on her knees, the gun pressed tightly against her temple. They were in the clearing where the hewn-out log sat waiting.

Harleigh moved forward into the light so Stewart could see her. She spoke softly, knowing he was slipping over the edge. "Stewart, you have the wrong person."

"Get back, you're only trying to distract me. You're just someone dressed up like my wife."

She took another step, saw Grady pull his weapon out of his holster. She put her hand on his arm as he started to aim. She'd never been so calm in her life.

"Let me handle this, Grady. Let's not shed any more blood than necessary. He's mad and you raising a weapon against him isn't going to help the situation."

Caleb entered the circle of light behind Harleigh and took her hand in his. Reassurance ran the length of her arm and she smiled.

"No, Stewart, look at me. Listen to my voice. You know it's me. Now let Caileigh go and I'll go with you anywhere you want me to go. I'll be whatever you want me to be."

She could see the confusion in his eyes. She could see his brain trying to separate fact from trickery. She waited a couple of heartbeats and took another step. She brought Caleb's hand to her lips and brushed a soft kiss across his knuckles then released her fingers from his.

She inched closer, stopping within a few feet of where he had her sister. "Let her go and take me. You know she's not me. You've known all along. Just think about it, Stewart. How did I get out of the house? How did I get passed you? You jumped from the balcony. There's no way I could have gotten in front of you. Isn't that right?"

His eyes twitched, going back and forth between Harleigh and Caileigh, trying to find the logic in what she said. Then with a growl he placed his foot against Caileigh's back and sent her sprawling forward, seizing Harleigh's wrist, hauling her against him.

Frantically, Caleb ran forward to protect Harleigh.

"Another step, mister and she dies."

He halted his progress immediately, his heart in his throat. He gave a silent prayer that this madman not hurt her.

Aidan dragged Caileigh backward, dropped to the ground beside her and held her in his arms where he could protect her. Where she was safe. He thought he was immune to terror but with that weapon compressed against the side of her head, he had failed to act. All he could think of was that the Earth female that he coveted was in danger and there wasn't a frishkin' thing he could do about it.

"Can't you do something, Aidan?" She whispered the anxious appeal against his neck. "Don't you aliens have some kind of phaser thing you can take him out with?"

Aidan stared at the man with the gun against the Earth female's head. This female twin of the earthling he held in his arms. Yes, he thought. He could, and would, do as she asked.

This he would do for the woman who had some-how entwined herself in his life. A woman he intended to keep. He'd overlook the fact that she was an Earth female. He wanted her just the same.

Harleigh felt it before she recognized what it was, glanced down at her hands and saw the transparent glow around the fingers. The ground beneath her knees vibrated and trembled. She glanced ahead of her and no one moved.

Everyone felt the earth move underneath their feet, wondered about it and passed it off as a minor occurrence. There were other issues that needed to be solved here and the earth moving was at the bottom of the list.

They saw a light, slowly growing bigger until it enveloped Harleigh and Stewart. They were getting use to this so it was another minor occurrence to wonder about.

The sisterhood hovered in the background protected by the men. They wanted to be in the forefront where they could help but arms were stretched out in front of them preventing them from moving forward. Grady had already warned them about staying put. All they wanted was for Harleigh to get out of this unscathed.

They saw Grady step forward to where Caleb stood legs spread, ready to spring. Saw Stewart raise a shaky hand and take aim. They reached out to each other and held hands.

"Please, Stewart," Harleigh whispered up at him, her eyes on Caleb's. He saw her eyes brim with tears, heard her voice so soft it was like a caress. "I don't care about these people. They mean nothing to me. No one does, except you, of course. It's always been you."

Caleb understood what she was trying to do, gave her the encouragement she needed in his gaze that reached out and touched her with all the love he felt for her in his heart. He nodded, stepped back and closed his eyes. Sometimes you just had to let fate run its course.

Aidan edged closer to where Harleigh knelt, to where Stewart frowned, deeply absorbed in the light surrounding his victim and himself. There was a loud hum, a warming surge of light and the gun in Stewart's hand disappeared. The light winked out as if someone had turned off the switch.

Harleigh scrambled forward on her knees, Caleb reaching out to snatch her up and draw her to safety. She was in the circle of his arms, a place she meant to stay.

Illuminated now by only the silver light of the moon, Grady started forward to cuff Stewart and haul him in. The cold metal of a knife glowed in the night. Stewart turned the knife, handle forward as if to throw it at a target. That target was Caleb Forrester, the man whose hands were all over his wife.

He just wouldn't tolerate that for another minute. The snarl was wiped from his face as he was shoved to the ground from behind. A double barrel shotgun glinted in the hands of Wilbur Nexley against the back of Stewart's head.

He stood there bathed in moonlight with a tooth-less grin on his face. "Got him for ya', Sheriff. Want me to blast his head off?"

Grady's chest rumbled in delight and relief. "Nah, Wilbur, you done enough for one night. What you do-ing out this way?"

As Grady twisted Stewart's hands behind him to cuff him, Wilbur explained. "Well, see, bein' a full moon and all, my girls usually are out and running hard and fast on a night like this. Don't know what hap-pened. Didn't want to run. Didn't want to bark. So's I was takin' myself off to that dance of yours, seein' if Miz Justine wanted me to twirl her around the floor and all. I came upon you guys and this creep hurting my Harleigh girl and I had to take him down."

"Well, Wilbur," Caleb said, shaking his head. "I think that's the most I ever heard you say at one sitting."

Wilbur ambled over to where Harleigh stood in the circle of Caleb's arms. "I couldn't let him hurt my Harleigh girl, now could I?"

Harleigh released Caleb and slipped her arms around Wilbur Nexley. His wiry frame seemed a bit frail in her arms. "You're my hero, Wilbur. What would we do without you?" She kissed his weathered cheek and placed her hand in his. "Come on back to the dance. We'll make Miz Justine jealous."

His bent shoulders straightened as much as he could get them to. He winked up at Caleb, Harleigh standing inches over him. "You just lost your girl, Doc."

Caleb put his hand over his heart in mocking anguish. "You're killing me. You're killing me!"

He looked on as the sisterhood walked back to the festivities following close in the footsteps of Harleigh and Wilbur. The men lingered behind. They had more important things to do, like take care of this pervert that had come into their town and tried to hurt one of their own.

Butch, Rowan and the Prophett boys formed a wall, shoulder to shoulder behind Grady Sackett, Gentry Beckett and Caleb Forrester. Aidan Cain was out in front alone.

Stewart took in the united front and his heart

ripped in fear. He'd never been afraid but the danger he encountered in those eyes and faces, terrified him. Ten angry men stood behind the giant. The sharp daggers they were throwing at him were nothing compared to the frosty glare of the figure that stood there looking down at him with revulsion in every part of his body.

He could feel his own fear now, it was a vile taste in his mouth. He felt the liquid spill down his pants as he lost a bodily function. The man who seemed to have grown in the last few minutes halted his forward motion just inches from where he sat on the leaf-strewn forest floor.

Aidan looked into the eyes of the man he stood before. Looked deep into his soul and what he found there soured his stomach. He knew it was time that he alone took care of this being that was the most evil thing he'd ever come across in all his travels.

Aidan raised his right hand and the glow appeared. A being was centered inside. She surrounded Stewart in her light, it swirling upward from the Earth like a swirling dervish. When Stewart tried to move, it was as if he were caught in some web and couldn't get loose. He was thrashing on the ground trying to get free.

Aidan swiveled his body to face the man who had held on to the Earth woman who looked like his own. Yes, he decided, that female earthling would be his. He was the prevailer of ownership so she had no cause to object.

"I shall take care of this performer of acts of cruelty and mistreatment. You shall return to the festivities and take care of the Earth women."

The Prophett brothers raised their eyebrows, gave the impression that they thought he was a looney tune and stepped forward to take care of the little weasel on their own. Caleb reached out as Judah passed him by and put his fingertips on his forearm.

"Judah, the man might be right. Strange things have occurred here tonight. It's only right that we leave this scum to someone who has no conscience."

They stopped in full stride, considered what Caleb said, nodded and traipsed back to the dance.

Butch and Gentry waited for instructions from Grady whose eyes were on the stranger. What Grady perceived in the way of things was that this weirdo, whoever he was and wherever he came from, might be more of a solution to this problem than the law could provide.

It went against the grain, though. Everything Grady had been taught in life and everything he'd been trained as an officer of the law told him that he should haul his ass to jail. But he also knew that this man, Stewart Pennington III, had the money to buy himself out of any situation. He wouldn't be behind bars for long nor would he be punished for the pain and suffering he'd caused.

Before he had the chance to choose the path he wanted to walk, the choice was taken from him. Aidan raised his right hand again, the light went out and with it went Stewart Pennington.

The spot where Stewart had been was empty. Not a trace left behind to show he was even there.

It was on the tip of his tongue to ask but Grady decided he didn't want to know. Neither did the others.

At once, as if they were one unit, they turned from Aidan and walked away.

א

Dawn was breaking. It was one of those beginnings of a new day that had the morning sun welcoming the pinks and blues with a sweet dewy kiss.

Harleigh rested her body back against Caleb's as they stood in the coolness, sipping their morning coffee from steamy mugs. Every now and then, his lips would rest against her shoulder.

"Beautiful, isn't it?"

"More beautiful with you here," he claimed.

"I'm here and I'm not ever going away, Caleb."

He murmured something unintelligible, breathed in her scent and was content. He nipped at her skin. "Here's where you belong. Always."

"You lost me to Wilbur, though, you know."

"Did you see the way pride had his shoulders riding high? He and Miz Justine were kicking up their heels."

"Miz Justine is a lovely woman. Lonely. But Wilbur doesn't have a chance against a ghost."

"Yeah, but they make good companions." Caleb thought on that for a moment, his chin resting gently against the top of her head. "Looked good out their on that dance floor, those lights flickering."

"Caleb?" She shouldn't ask but she had to know.

"Mmm?"

"What happened to Stewart? Everyone seems to be so tight-lipped all of a sudden."

"Your friends are suffering from short-term memory loss." He joked, though he knew it was no joking matter.

"It's more than that."

"Yes, it is," he admitted. "One minute he was there and the next he wasn't."

Harleigh stiffened, not wanting to think that Stewart was on the loose. "He's still out there then?"

Caleb set his cup down on the porch rail, removed Harleigh's and did the same. He turned her in his arms to face him. He caressed her cheek. "He'll never hurt you again, babe."

"He'll be back."

Caleb smiled at her and brushed her lips with his. "No, he won't. Aidan. Whatever he and that ethereal glow did, it took care of him. Aidan raised a hand, the entity appeared on cue, wrapped Stewart up in that light of hers and took him with her. It was all very bizarre. You'll never have to worry about him ever again."

He ran a hand down the back of her head, loving the feel of her hair on his palm. He kissed her gently, then kissed her again, deepening the kiss, wanting more.

"Mmm. Sweet," she murmured.

"And, good," he agreed.

Yes, she agreed in her mind. Everything about her life was good and sweet.

She walked him backward through the open door, through the living room, into his bedroom. When the back of his knees hit the bed, she pressed him down and slid in beside him.

A deep sigh of contentment slipped through her lips as he slid the gown off her shoulder. As the golden orb rose higher, the steam evaporating from coffee turning cold in the rays of the sun, Harleigh took the man she loved to bed.

EPILOGUE

א

In the sleepy little town of Nowhere, the Rose House stood warm and welcoming in the early morning of dawn. A soft ethereal being floated on the patio that had been Harleigh's temporary home. Now she was ensconced in the safety of Caleb Forrester's embrace in the house of her dreams. Shera looked down on the yellow house with the white picket fence, a soft smile gracing her lips.

She turned, curved her head to the side, gave that same smile to Aidan Cain and faded from view, leaving the great searcher to stand-alone in the cool shadows of the new day.

He'd found what he came for. Shera, the caretaker. The golden light. The one that had been left behind all those years ago. His plans were made, his job done.

The transporter sat in the circle of light in the glade that had been created by Quentin Demascus, waiting for him. It would be so simple. All he had to do was wait for the dawn and he'd be home.

He knew she was there. All he had to do was turn and the Earth woman would be within his grasp. Her scent filled his nostrils. She was like a drug and he was becoming more addicted with each passing of the orbs they called the sun and moon.

It had been like this since that first day he'd turned that corner and she'd taken his breath away. He hadn't known what happened, he'd seen her and the very sight of her had blown him away. Everything else was insignificant. Only the Earth female with that cool light hair and silver eyes existed for him.

When the earth righted itself and he was able to focus again, all that filled his nostrils was her scent. It was a struggle, a battle hard won to walk on by. Then just as he thought he was going to make it, she glanced up at him. He looked into her eyes and drowned.

That one look was all it took. He was caught, floating out in space on a string.

Then if that wasn't enough, she smiled. And it devastated. He was engulfed in a blaze so volatile he was burning from the inside out and gasping for his next breath.

He'd always thought he was strong. But she brought him down. She had the power. He tried to pull back but it was like swimming against the tide.

When she spoke to him, the silken currents of her voice washed over him in shades of color. An uncontrollable desire shot through him like a current of electric energy and all he could think of was taking her with such a savage craving that he was consumed by it.

And when he'd first touched her, well, he was lost in the softness of her skin. And her response to him was just as volatile. He could hear the snap and crackle of the currents between them. And at that moment in time, nothing else mattered.

He was the searcher. With Caileigh's help, he

found what he was searching for. And now, it was time to go home. He'd been given the instructions how to return if he ever found the open space that had been created for that very reason. It was so easy. Wait for the dawn. Walk into the glade. Sit. Close your eyes and let your auditory senses kick in. When you heard the signal, breathe deep, and you'd be home.

The timing had to be right, of course. The window of opportunity had to be perfect or it would take the revolutions of many trips around the sun for a blue moon to come again.

But, now, there was a decision to be made.

How could he leave this Earth female who bore into his senses, carving out a place in his heart?

He heard the faint slip of her feet on the carpet, heard the faint rustle of clothing being discarded, the whisper of his name on her lips.

He turned and she was there, waiting, a smile on her lips, arms open to take him in.

א

FOR A FREE PREVIEW
TURN THE PAGE

THE BRINGER OF RAPTURE

COMING SOON FROM
Rose♥Heart

THE BRINGER OF RAPTURE

Her father was dead. And, he was responsible. But now, she was obligated to the man. Grateful she may but that was not going to stop her from doling out her own form of punishment for his crime against her family. Amid a constant struggle against an unwanted desire for her nemesis and an ever-increasing promise of what could be, she must stay focused on the path she set for herself. Will she remain true to herself or will her heart be his next victim?

Suddenly, with a swiftness that nearly took her breath from her, Damien pulled her roughly against him. She felt the strength in the long lines of his trim body pressing into her own, each and every sinewy muscle of him. A strange euphoria overtook Sara, one she neither recognized nor could control. Her mind told her to pull away but her body pressed closer instead. Just as suddenly as he had pulled her to him, he roughly shoved her away again, she, nearly losing her balance from the thrust. His features closed, holding only a deep frown on his handsome face.

Sara gazed into those eyes with wonder, which now were projecting a darker blue to match those of her own. She waited, bewildered, knowing it was inevitable that he would kiss her yet again, and yes, she wanted him to. But she was frightened just the same.

In unison, as if it were scripted, Damien lowered his head as Sara raised hers to meet his descending mouth. Neither was prepared for the fire that flowed between them. Slow, sensuous at first, it exploded into a searing, demanding, heated duel of two passions vying for control, one over the other. A feeling of tenderness surged through him as she melted against his, words welling up inside him that was foreign to his lips, tender whisperings of love and longing.

Damien raised his head, his expression befuddled as if he had lost his sense of direction. Slowly again, his mouth claimed hers, a deep growl that he tried to hold back escaped on its own now that he was more conscious of what her inexperience was doing to him, yet the very taste of her clouded his reasoning. He wanted her with an intenseness he had not felt since he was a very young man. He wanted to ravish her, make her his, give her pleasure. No woman had ever done that to this degree before. He clamped his hands gently on her shoulders, setting her away from him with a determination he certainly did not feel.

Sara felt the trembling of his controlled emotions. Confusion was heavy on her face as he stepped away, turning his back, striding toward his waiting mount.

Sara observed him walking away, cat-like, graceful, dangerous. The muscular strength in his back rippling as he rearranged his shirt and stuffed it into his trousers. He swung one long powerful leg over the stallion, saluted and rode away, master of himself, slave to none.

Finally realizing he was really gone while she remained rooted to the very spot he left her, Sara vainly attempted donning her garments with all the dignity she could muster, failing in the end, draping them around her in a haphazard fashion.

Her eyes lifted to the granite cliffs overhanging the green valley. Atop, in the distance, she spied a black stallion and a lone rider. She was flooded with remembrance, warm, pleasurable and annoying.

Loud noises erupted in the stillness and filled the air, awakening her finally to the world around her. Terror engulfed her as she viewed the horrific scene that lay before her. The few animals her family owned were bellowing, running in confused circles. Everything was in a state of disorder. The pounding hooves tore up the earth. The drying shed lay wrecked, demolished, one wall left standing. Her roses she so faithfully tended, lay trampled, beaten down by those same hooves. The stoop half-stood, the door hanging by one leather hinge. She ran toward it.

Shouts from behind compelled her to reel around. Sara shrank inwardly, repulsed by the men and what they were doing. A scream escaped her throat as they dragged her father behind them, tied by his wrists with ropes connected to their mounts.

"No!" she screamed in torment, "you must stop this!"

They did stop when they spied her running toward them, dropping their ropes and heading in her direction. A shot rang out, heads jerking in the direction of the resounding report. Sara rapidly dashed to her father's side, his injured body, still and lifeless against the beaten earth. Through her tears running unchecked down her checks, she tore frantically at the ropes on his bleeding wrists.

She continued her struggle with the ropes restraining her father. A tanned hand reached down to still her wildly pulling fingers. Damien undid the roped wrists, turning the limp form face up.

"Papa," she cried in horror, her shoulders heaving convulsively. "What have they done to you?"

Damien extended his hand, brushing her cheek lightly, gently wiping the wetness away with his thumb. Sara slowly brought her tear-filled eyes to the hand that stroked her softly and stiffened in recognition.

She rose, as did he. Uncontrollable rage welled up inside her and she gathered spittle in her mouth and spat all the venom she felt toward him onto his face. His jaw clenched in anger as he wiped the spittle away, anger that darkened his rugged features then just as swiftly died away, understanding her pain.

Damien pivoted quickly, mounting his steed in one smooth liquid motion, the prancing stallion so close Sara felt its hot breath blowing the fine blond hair on her arms. Still, she did not move.

Damien stared down at her from atop Lucifer then spun away. His last glance saw a deep shining hatred staring at him through icy, crystal blue eyes. He galloped away without looking back.

Through body-wracking sobs, Sara screamed at the diminishing figure. "You vile heathen! I'll kill you for this, you murdering savage!"

She dropped heavily to her knees, lowering herself protectively over her father's battered body. "I'll get him, Papa," she whispered her vow of revenge, it not occurring to her that Damien had naught to do with this atrocity, that she had occupied his time while these men rained destruction upon those she loved.

"I will see him dead! I promise you! Murderer!" Sara screamed again, her piercing cries penetrating the hushed silence of her surroundings, she, unaware none could hear her outburst of agony.

The stillness of the bruised and battered body that lay before her sent wave after wave of shock through Sara. She had never seen her father anything but healthy and this mangled body with its misshapen features, shredded skin hanging from bloodied wrists, turned her insides cold while fingers of ice ripped her to pieces. A raging hatred consumed her until nothing was left of her emotions but a hollow space deep inside her soul. Her eyes narrowed, her lips drawn into a thin line, teeth clenched as thoughts returned to moments before when she basked in new emotions from the attentions of the man she now vowed vengeance upon.

Tears brimmed anew in her crystal blue eyes as guilt overrode her hatred. How could I have allowed such liberties? she asked herself as she raised her head skyward. She spread her arms wide and cried out to the heavens, "Is this my punishment for it?"

WATCH FOR THE SEQUEL
TO NOWHERE

KISS OF THE MYSTIC NIGHT WIND

COMING THIS FALL FROM
Rose♥Heart

Printed in the United States
50556LVS00001B/3